GODS OF MARS

A WARHAMMER 40,000 NOVEL

GODS OF MARS

GRAHAM MCNEILL

BLACK LIBRARY

*To Gemma Noon, for all her hard work and reminding me how important the
First Reader truly is. This book was improved orders of magnitude
by her telling me to be better.*

A BLACK LIBRARY PUBLICATION
First published in Great Britain in 2014 by
Black Library,
Games Workshop Ltd.,
Willow Road,
Nottingham,
NG7 2WS, UK.

10 9 8 7 6 5 4 3 2 1

Cover by Slawomir Maniak.

A CIP record for this book
is available from the British Library.

UK ISBN 13: 978 1 84970 722 0
US ISBN 13: 978 1 84970 723 7

Distributed in the US by Simon & Schuster
1230 Avenue of the Americas, New York, NY 10020, US.

Printed and bound by CPI Group (UK) Ltd, Croydon, CR0 4YY

See Black Library on the internet at
blacklibrary.com

Find out more about Games Workshop
and the world of Warhammer 40,000 at
games-workshop.com

It is the 41st millennium. For more than a hundred
centuries the Emperor has sat immobile on the Golden Throne of
Earth. He is the master of mankind by the will of the gods, and master
of a million worlds by the might of his inexhaustible armies. He is a
rotting carcass writhing invisibly with power from the Dark Age of
Technology. He is the Carrion Lord of the Imperium for whom a
thousand souls are sacrificed every day, so that he may never truly die.

Yet even in his deathless state, the Emperor continues his eternal
vigilance. Mighty battlefleets cross the daemon-infested miasma of
the warp, the only route between distant stars, their way lit by the
Astronomican, the psychic manifestation of the Emperor's will.
Vast armies give battle in his name on uncounted worlds. Greatest
amongst his soldiers are the Adeptus Astartes, the Space Marines,
bio-engineered super-warriors. Their comrades in arms are legion:
the Imperial Guard and countless planetary defence forces, the ever-
vigilant Inquisition and the tech-priests of the Adeptus Mechanicus
to name only a few. But for all their multitudes, they are barely
enough to hold off the ever-present threat from aliens, heretics,
mutants - and worse.

To be a man in such times is to be one amongst untold billions. It is
to live in the cruellest and most bloody regime imaginable. These are
the tales of those times. Forget the power of technology and science,
for so much has been forgotten, never to be re-learned. Forget the
promise of progress and understanding, for in the grim dark future
there is only war. There is no peace amongst the stars, only an eternity
of carnage and slaughter, and the laughter
of thirsting gods.

Dramatis Personae

The *Speranza*
LEXELL KOTOV – Archmagos of the Kotov Explorator Fleet
TARKIS BLAYLOCK – Fabricatus Locum, Magos of the Cebrenia Quadrangle
VITALI TYCHON – Stellar Cartographer of Quatria Orbital Gallery
LINYA TYCHON – Stellar Cartographer, daughter of Vitali Tychon
AZURAMAGELLI – Magos of Astrogation
KRYPTAESTREX – Magos of Logistics
TURENTEK – Ark Fabricatus
HIRIMAU DAHAN – Secutor/Guilder Suzerain
CHIRON MANUBIA – Magos of Forge Elektrus
TOTHA MU-32 – Mechanicus Overseer
ABREHEM LOCKE – Bondsman
RASSELAS X-42 – Arco-flagellant
VANNEN COYNE – Bondsman
JULIUS HAWKE – Bondsman
ISMAEL DE ROEVEN – Servitor
GALATEA – Proscribed machine intelligence

Exnihlio
VETTIUS TELOK – Archmagos of the Telok Explorator Fleet

The *Renard*
ROBOUTE SURCOUF – Captain
EMIL NADER – First Mate
ADARA SIAVASH – Hired Gun
ILANNA PAVELKA – Tech-priest
KAYRN SYLKWOOD – Enginseer

Adeptus Astartes Black Templars
TANNA – Brother-Sergeant
ISSUR – Initiate
ATTICUS VARDA – Emperor's Champion
BRACHA – Initiate
YAEL – Initiate

The Cadian 71st 'The Hellhounds'
VEN ANDERS – Colonel of the Cadian Detached Formation
BLAYNE HAWKINS – Captain, Blazer Company
TAYBARD RAE – Lieutenant, Blazer Company
JAHN CALLINS – Requisitional Support Officer, Blazer Company

Legio Sirius

ARLO LUTH, 'THE WINTERSUN' – Warlord Princeps, *Lupa Capitalina*
ELIAS HÄRKIN, 'THE IRONWOAD' – Warhound Princeps, *Vilka*
GUNNAR VINTRAS, 'THE SKINWALKER'

The *Starblade*

BIELANNA FAERELLE – Farseer of Biel-Tan
ARIGANNA – Striking Scorpion Exarch of Biel-Tan
TARIQUEL – Striking Scorpion of Biel-Tan
VAYNESH – Striking Scorpion of Biel-Tan
ULDANAISH GHOSTWALKER – Wraithlord of Biel-Tan

'Behold, the extropic doctrine!
Humanity is a limitation to be overcome,
for all beings strive for a life beyond flesh.
Shall we be the ebb of this great flood?
Shall we be beasts rather than gods?

What is the ape to Man? A painful embarrassment.
Baseline forms shall be that to the Mechanicum.
We crawled from the mud to be gods,
but much in our species still wallows there.
I will teach you of Man and Machine's union.

The Mechanicum quests for Singularity.
My brothers, remain faithful to Mars!
Despise those who speak of the divine organic!
Beasts are they, despisers of knowledge.
Entropy and fear lead them to extinction.
And the galaxy will not weep for them.'

The Extropian Manifesto (sequestered).
Author unknown.
Vol XVI, The Telok Verses.

AVE.OMNISSIAH.orv 4048 a_start .equ 30f0 2048 ld
length,% 2064 KNOWLEDGE IS POWER? 00000010 10000000
CONTACT LOST: KOTOV 00000110 2068 addcc%r1,-
4,%r1 10000010 10000000 01111111 11111100 2072
addcc.%r1,%r2,%r4 10001000 BLAYLOCK: CACHE STOR-
AGE CONFLICT 01000000 BELOW DECK OPERATIONS RESUMED
2076 ld%r4,%r5 11001010 00000001 00000000 00000000
2080 ba loop 00010000 10111111 11111111 MACHINE-
HYBRID MOTIVATION? 2084 addcc%r3 XENOSIGN TRACE
CONFIRMED,%r5,%r3 10000110 10000000 11000000
00000101 2088 done: jmpl%r15+4,%r0 10000001 11000011
POSSIBLE TEMPORAL ALTERATION ORGANISM 00000100
2092 length: 20 CARTOGRAPHAE READINGS INCONSIST-
ENT 00000000 00000000 00010100 2096 address: a_start
00000100 PRE-HUMAN TECH OVERLAP? 00000000 00001011
10111000.Omni.B_start

Thermodynamic Violation Thermodynamic Violation
Thermodynamic Violation Thermodynamic Violation
Thermodynamic Violation Thermodynamic Violation
Thermodynamic Violation Thermodynamic Violation
Thermodynamic Violation Thermodynamic Violation
Thermodynamic Violation Thermodynamic Violation
Thermodynamic Violation Thermodynamic Violation
Thermodynamic Violation

Metadata Parsing in effect.

+++++++++++++++++

< + + <Res Nullius> + + >

001

Knowledge is power? That is what they say, those cohered molecules and atomic chains spreading through known and unknown space like a virus. That they have achieved sentience enough to think and say such a thing is a wonder in itself.

They grow and decay with prodigious rapidity, infesting every corner of the galaxy in numbers so huge as to defy even our imagination. Tens of thousands exist within this body of steel and power, itself only recently roused from millennial slumbers.

They are grains of sand swirling around the base of a vast mountain of knowledge. Some believe it utterly improbable that such a mountain can exist or be climbed without some divine hand to lift them to its summit.

How wrong they are. Winds of inevitable change swirl around this mountain and sometimes a propitious gust will blow against a favourably shaped grain to carry it uphill. It reaches higher than any before it, and it knows fractionally more than it once did.

By such infinitesimal steps does life evolve.

And its companions say it possesses great knowledge.

They are all ignorant, but ignorance must be embraced before it can be banished. The Athenian stonecutter had the truth of it when he said that the only true wisdom was in knowing you knew nothing.

Only by knowing how empty your cup is can you reach to fill it.

There are heights of knowledge whose existence the grains can never even guess at, let alone comprehend. Yet, even lost upon such an endless ocean of ignorance, there are beings who claim wisdom, who believe they know everything there is to be known.

These are the most dangerous beings imaginable.

They claim ancient texts of false and forgotten gods contain all the universe's knowledge – as though such a thing is possible beyond Akasha. For tens of thousands of years, these primitive coherences accepted such blind dogma without question, and those who questioned it were extinguished in agony.

010

For one dangerous moment, the grains of sand came close to ascending the mountain in one giant leap. The galaxy teetered on the edge of a precipice as a key turned in a door that should never be unlocked. One singular consciousness threaded the needle to pierce the veil between their world and Akasha, unpicking the weave that separates all things and no things.

But it was not to be. The door slammed shut, perhaps forever.

Knowledge must be earned, not simply stolen as Prometheus once stole fire and set mankind upon his course.

To stand on the shoulders of titans is one thing.

To claim their wisdom as your own is another, and only minds that have spent every moment since the galaxy began its slow revolutions can hope to appreciate this without being destroyed.

011

They think us a great void-born city of metal and stone, a marvel of wonders never to be known again. We consent to our physical manifestation dwelling in the depths of space, sheet steel skin cold and unyielding. They think us a living thing, and we allow our irreducible complexity to be thought of as such.

The bones they have crafted are adamantium, our molten heart the flickering sparks of stars they believe tamed. We sweat oil, and the devotion of a million souls is thought to give us succour. The coherences of flesh and blood believe they empower us from within. They work the myriad wonders that drive our manifest organs, feed the whims of our appetite and hurl us through the fractional slivers of space between stars.

How far have we travelled? They will never know.

What miracles have we seen? More than can be counted.

The light of every star that shines has reflected from our iron flesh. We bathe in light that has travelled from the past, cast by dead stars and furnaces yet to be born.

We are a wide-eyed mariner in strange seas, swept out among the glittering nebulae. We have seen sights no man can know, no legend tell or history record.

Graham McNeill

We are living history, for we have ventured farther and longer than any other manifestation of purest knowledge.

We are the bringer of hope in this hopeless age.

We are Speranza, and we are the Mariner of the Nebulae.

Such is our destiny.

MACROCONTENT COMMENCEMENT:

+++MACROCONTENT 001+++

The knowledge of the ancients stands beyond question.

Microcontent 01

PAST AND FUTURE. Then and now. Temporal anchors. Intellectual conceits, they allowed a farseer to cling to the *present*. Such linear terms had no meaning or place within the skein, but they had their uses. Bielanna fought to cling on to the present as past and future collided, hurling her sight into potentialities that could never come to be and times she had never lived.

Infinite vistas of the psychic landscape surrounded her, golden ocean depths filled with glittering, frond-like threads. Each shone brightly as it flared and was then extinguished, only to be replaced by hundreds more.

A billion times a billion lives lived in the blink of an eye.

And these were just the ones she could see.

She drifted, watching each tightly woven thread split into fractal patterns of innumerable futures as she approached. The skein's tides were unpredictable at the best of times, and to see one individual destiny was next to impossible.

But that was what she had trained her entire life to do.

Farseers spent centuries reading the skein's ebb and flow, but not even the greatest were entirely safe from capricious undertows or spiteful squalls. In this place beyond the galaxy, where the warp and weft of space-time were playthings shaped by the will of a madman, it was all too easy to forget that.

Bielanna struggled against the tug of fear, hatred and grief: interleaved emotions that would damn her as surely as relaxing her grip on the thread leading back to her body of flesh and blood.

Fear for the fate of the galaxy should the humans succeed in bringing the

Breath of the Gods back to their Imperium.

Hatred for the inhuman black-clad Space Marines who had haunted her visions for years with their crusading zeal.

Grief for daughters she might never know, whose chance to exist was diminished every moment by the blundering actions of Archmagos Kotov and his fleet of explorators.

She closed off that last thought, but not quickly enough.

She heard her daughters' unborn laughter. Girlish giggles echoing from all around her. Sounds from a future that grew ever more remote. Laughter that mocked her attempts to restore it.

Bielanna's body of flesh and blood sat in the oil-stained squalor of the *Speranza*, its foetid, human depths now home to her warriors since the *Starblade*'s destruction. A tear of loss ran down a porcelain cheek, the emotion so potent it made her shudder.

In the skein, Bielanna fought to control her feelings.

The mon-keigh knew nothing of the universe's secret workings, and for the briefest moment, she envied them their ignorance. Who but the eldar could mourn lives that had not even been born?

'I am Bielanna Faerelle, Farseer of Biel-Tan,' she cried into the oceanic depths. 'I am master of my soul and I bring only balance in my heart and thoughts.'

Everything in the skein rejected constancy. It sensed her lie. This was a place of dreams and nightmares, where all things were infinite. To give something a name marked it as not of the skein.

And that was dangerous.

It drew *things* that hid in the cracks between destinies. She saw them ooze from half-glimpsed shadows. That shadows could exist in this realm of absolute light was a measure of their threat. These were not the crystalline web-forms of warp spiders, nor yet the glimmer of future echoes moving from potential to reality.

These were things twisted out of true by the tortured nature of space-time beyond the galaxy's edge. They defied the tyranny of form, mere suggestions of grub-like null-spaces that existed only to consume. She moved onwards, far from their questing, sphincter-like mouths and blind, idiot hunger.

The Lost Magos, known as Telok to the mon-keigh, had torn the flesh of the galaxy asunder. The things in the cracks were growing ever more numerous as that wound pulled wider.

Worse, the damage was spreading from the material universe into the skein. Already Telok's violations were cutting threads like a blind weaver's blade.

Unchecked, it would destroy the future of everything.

EVERYTHING ABOUT ARCHMAGOS Telok's gigantic form screamed threat. The jutting, angular protrusions of razor-edged crystal growths encrusting his oversized limbs. The brutal angles of his piston-driven Dreadnought frame. His entire aspect spoke to the primal part of Roboute Surcouf's brain that had kept his species alive since his distant ancestors first walked upright.

The part that screamed, *run!*

And yet the face beneath the ragged hood was smiling in welcome.

Telok's skin was waxy and unhealthy looking, but that was nothing unusual for adepts of the Mechanicus. Too much time locked in their forges under the glare of bare lumens gave them all an unhealthy complexion. The archmagos had glassy eyes that were wide and enthusiastic, the mirror of his smile.

But like his eyes, the smile looked artificial.

Telok's forge world – Exnihlio, he'd called it – was unlike anything Roboute had ever seen, and he'd seen a great deal of the strangest things the galaxy had to offer. With a Letter of Marque (genuine now, thanks to Archmagos Kotov) he'd traversed the galaxy from side to side as a devil-may-care rogue trader.

He'd seen pinnacle-spired hives straddling volcanic chasms, vine-hung settlements the size of continents and subterranean arcologies that were as light and airy as any surface metropolis. He'd done business on orbital junkyards that served as off-world slums, been welcomed by Imperial commanders who dwelled undersea, and plied his trade with feral tribal chiefs who established cargo cults in his wake.

No aspect of Exnihlio's surface owed a debt to aesthetics, simply to functionality. Much like the *Speranza*, the mighty Ark Mechanicus that had brought them beyond the edges of known space. This region appeared, at first glance, to be a power generation district. The air was bitterly metallic, like biting on a copper Imperial, and reeked of petrochemical burn-off.

Monolithic structures of dark iron and cyclopean stone towered on all sides, standing cheek by jowl with crisp spires of steel and glass. Traceries of lightning forked into a sky of painfully vivid blue electrical storms, and distant cooling towers belched caustic vapours. The cliff-like facades of the enormous buildings gave no clue as to their exact purpose, but they throbbed with powerful industry and the roar of infernal furnaces.

A thousands-strong, crystalline army of warriors filled the plaza in which their Thunderhawk sat with its engines growling. They stood like glassy sculptures of Space Marines arrayed for battle before their Chapter Master.

Sergeant Tanna of the Black Templars, gigantic in his ebon plate, followed the two archmagi with his crusaders spread to either side. They watched the crystal-forms with open hostility. A force of such things had killed their brother on Katen Venia, and the Black Templars were an unforgiving Chapter.

Though Telok had welcomed Archmagos Kotov and his entourage, Tanna's hand never strayed from his bolter's grip, and the white-helmed Varda kept his fingers tightly wrapped around the handle of his enormous black sword.

Colonel Ven Anders and his storm troopers drew up the rear. Following the Templars' example, each soldier clutched his hellgun tight to his chest and kept a finger across the trigger guard.

But behind the discipline, Roboute saw their amazement.

They'd probably not seen anything like this.

None of us has.

Distant electrical fire raged in a troposphere of bruised hues, and the hideous illumination left a clenched fist of vertigo in Roboute's gut. He swallowed a mouthful of bile. One of Colonel Anders's men spat onto the metalled roadway. Clearly Roboute wasn't alone in feeling discomfort, seeing the man cast an uneasy glance at the approaching storm.

'How bad must it be for a soldier of Cadia to feel unsettled?' he muttered.

'Sylkwood could give you a better answer,' said Magos Pavelka at Roboute's side, entranced by the structures arrayed before them. 'She is from Cadia, and understands that gloomy mindset better than most.'

'So what are they saying?' asked Roboute, nodding to the head of their procession, where Telok and Kotov spoke in blurts of binary. Both adepts had dispensed with their flesh-voices, though it was clear their attempts to communicate were not progressing as smoothly as either expected.

Pavelka's head ever so slightly inclined to the side.

'Ilanna?' said Roboute, when she didn't immediately answer.

'Archmagos Telok is speaking in a binaric form long since considered obsolete,' said Pavelka eventually.

'Isn't binary the same throughout the galaxy?' asked Roboute. 'Isn't that the point of a language based on mathematics?'

'Archmagos Telok's binary is a parse-form with which current generation Mechanicus augmitters are not reverse-compatible. They are being forced to communicate in an extremely primitive form of source code.'

'If binary's a problem, why not just speak in Gothic?'

'Even a primitive form of source code carries more specificity of meaning than verbal communications.'

'Oh,' said Roboute with mock affront. 'Well pardon me.'

'You asked,' said Pavelka.

Their path was leading to a colossal hangar-structure with a vaulted silver-steel roof and glittering masts at its four corners, the same building from which the titanic glass scorpion construct had emerged. The great gateway had been subsumed back into the enormous structure, but a smaller portal now opened and from it slid a crystal vessel like those that once plied the oceans of Terra.

A blade-prowed brigantine with sails of billowing glass that caught the sky's light and threw it back in dazzling rainbows. A hundred metres long and formed from what looked like a single piece of translucent crystal, its hull was threaded with squirming light and shimmering reflections.

'Ave Deus Mechanicus,' whispered Pavelka, her hands unconsciously forming the Martian cog across her chest.

The vessel skimmed a metre above the ground, a ship of the line that needed no sea to glide upon, no wind to fill its sails.

Roboute had never seen anything quite so wondrous. The crystal ship was a thing of exquisite beauty, something unique in the truest sense of the word. It made no sound other than a soft hiss, as though knifing through serene waters.

'Indulgent, I know, but the nano-machines work best when creating things of beauty or things of terror,' said Telok, switching back to his flesh-voice as the ship coasted to a halt behind him.

Roboute's eyes followed the sleek curves of the ship's graceful hull as a number of steps of solid glass extruded to allow access onto the deck.

Telok extended one of his elephantine arms and gestured to the steps, but only Archmagos Kotov and his skitarii guards moved towards them.

'Why do we need transport?' asked Tanna, stepping forwards to stand alongside Kotov. 'If we are to travel far, why did you have us land here?'

Telok's waxen features didn't change, but Roboute saw irritation in his eyes. 'When an entire planet's resources are engaged in the generation of power there are sizeable regions where the atmosphere is aggressively toxic to those who do not enjoy the fearsome augmentations of Adeptus Astartes physiology. My *sanctum sanctorum* lies within such a region.'

Telok turned and gestured to the immobile army of crystalline warriors.

'My world is home to many technologies unknown within the Imperium, and the unknown always carries the threat of danger to those not versed in its mysteries, don't you agree?'

Roboute couldn't help but hear the stress Telok put on the *my*, and felt a twitch at the unconscious display of ego. The Lost Magos had been lost for so long that he couldn't help showing off the wonders and miracles of his world. What other psychological effects might thousands of years of isolation have fostered?

'The only danger I see here is the use of technology that has already killed one of my men,' said Tanna.

'Ah, yes, of course, you are referring to the tragic death of your Apothecary on the world Master Surcouf named Katen Venia,' said Telok, displaying an impressive knowledge of things he had not been told.

'A terrible loss, yes,' agreed Kotov, placing a silvered hand on Tanna's shoulder guard. A hand that was swiftly removed when the Black Templars sergeant glared at him.

'I deeply and profoundly regret the death of your battle-brother, Sergeant Tanna,' said Telok. 'The crystaliths were emplaced to defend against any interference with the Stellar Primogenitor's work. I'm afraid your arrival on Katen Venia triggered their autonomic threat response.'

'Your regret is meaningless,' said Tanna.

'I am sorry you feel that way, but you have it anyway.'

Kotov and his entourage of skitarii and flunkies climbed onto the ship, eager to be on their way. Tanna and the Black Templars followed them aboard, the floating ship sinking not so much as a millimetre at the increased weight.

'After you,' said Anders as his Cadians moved up to the ship.

Roboute nodded and climbed the glass steps to the deck. The gunwale was smooth and apparently without seams, as though the vessel had been grown from one enormous crystal. Its twin masts soared overhead and the billowing sheets of glass were dazzling with refracted light.

A single raised lectern at the vessel's stern appeared to be the only means of control, and Kotov examined it with the eagerness of a neophyte priest. His skitarii stood to either side of him at the gunwales, facing outwards, as though expecting to repel boarders.

'Go look,' said Roboute to Pavelka. 'I know you want to.'

Pavelka nodded and gratefully made her way down the deck towards the archmagos and the control lectern. Anders and his men came next, followed at last by Archmagos Telok.

'I have you to thank for bringing the *Speranza* here,' said the hulking form of the archmagos. 'You found the *Tomioka*'s saviour beacon, and for that you have my gratitude.'

Roboute looked up into Telok's unnatural face. It revolted him, but given it was thousands of years old, what else should he expect?

'I'm beginning to wonder about that,' said Roboute.

'About what?'

'Whether it was me that brought us here at all.'

'Of course you did,' said Telok, moving down the deck with a booming laugh. 'Who else could have done so?'

Roboute didn't answer as the ship moved off like a whisper.

Speranza.

Ark Mechanicus.

Its name meant *hope* in an ancient tongue of Old Earth, and had been aptly chosen, for within the starship's monstrously vast form it carried the last remnants of ancient knowledge thought lost for all time. That those aboard were ignorant of the secrets hidden within its forgotten datacores and dusty sepulchre temples was an irony known only to the vast spirit at its heart.

The *Speranza* orbited Exnihlio with stately grace, a void-capable colossus, a forge world set loose among the stars. Its hull was a kilometres-long agglomeration of steel and stone, studded with mighty forges, vast cathedrals of the Omnissiah, and workshops beyond count. The power of its industry could sustain a system-wide campaign of war, its crew a planetary assault.

Not even those whose genius had set it among the stars could claim to call it beautiful, but beauty had never been their aim. The Ark Mechanicus was a ship destined to carry the great works of the first techno-theologians to the farthest corners of the galaxy, to reclaim and reveal all that had been lost in the terror of Old Night.

A crusading vessel, a repository of hard-won knowledge and an icon of hope all in one. And like any object of hope, it had its followers. Its fleet was reduced now after the nightmarish crossing of the Halo Scar and an attack by eldar pirates, but it was still formidable.

The twin Gothic-class cruisers, *Moonchild* and *Wrathchild*, described Möbius patrol circuits around the *Speranza*, while the solitary Endurance-class cruiser, *Mortis Voss*, pushed ahead of the fleet, lashing the void with aggressive auspex sweeps.

Attached to the Kotov Fleet to repay a Debita Fabricata, the two sister vessels of *Mortis Voss* were dead. Only it remained to return to Voss Prime with word of all it had seen and done.

Tens of thousands filled the multitude of decks within the *Speranza* like blood in the arteries of a living leviathan. Its bondsmen fed its fiery heart, its tech-priests tempered its tempestuous spirits and the archmagos guided its quest into the unknown.

The dynamic between the *Speranza*'s masters and servants had changed markedly over the course of the vessel's journey to Exnihlio. Where once its Mechanicus overlords had been little better than slavers, now they were forced into a compact of respect by the actions of a truly unique individual.

A Machine-touched bondsman named Abrehem Locke.

THE LOWEST DECKS of the *Speranza* were the areas of greatest danger for its crew: either through radiation-leaks, spiteful machine-spirits or the more recent ship-board rumour of a ghost-faced assassin stalking the ship's underbelly.

Right now, Abrehem Locke would have gladly faced any of those dangers rather than walk into Forge Elektrus. Its approaches were lit by stuttering lumen globes and throbbed with ill-tempered spirits. Abrehem's augmetic eyes caught the glitchy code as it sparked invisibly behind the sagging iron plates of the walls.

They weren't welcome here.

'This is a bad idea,' he said. 'A really bad idea. Hawke was right, I shouldn't have come here.'

'Since when has *anything* Julius Hawke said ever been a good idea?' answered Totha Mu-32.

Totha Mu-32 had once been Abrehem's overseer, but the extraordinary events of the last few months had seen the dynamics of that relationship change in ways Abrehem still couldn't quite grasp. At times Totha Mu-32 behaved like his devotee, at others, a nurturing mentor.

But sometimes it just felt like he was still his overseer.

'Good point,' said Abe. 'But in this case, I happen to agree with him. They're never going to accept me.'

'You are Machine-touched,' said Totha Mu-32. 'And it is time you took your first steps along this road.'

'They won't accept me,' repeated Abrehem.

'They will, they all know what you did, even the *demodes*. They all know the power you have.'

'That wasn't me,' said Abe. 'That was Ismael. Tell him.'

The third member of their group shook his head.

Previous to Totha Mu-32, Ismael de Roeven had once been Abrehem's overseer on Joura. Ismael had run a lifter-rig, a powerful beast named *Savickas*, but that had come to an end when he, Abrehem, Coyne and Hawke had been swept up by the collarmen and pressed into service aboard the *Speranza*.

The Mechanicus turned Ismael into a mindless servitor, but a violent head injury had restored a measure of his memories. No one quite knew how that had happened or what else had come back, for Ismael was now something else, far beyond a servitor, but not entirely human either.

'We did that together, Abrehem,' said Ismael. 'We are the divine spark and the omega point. Without one, the other cannot exist. I allowed the servitors to lay down their tools, but without you there would have been no impetus to do so.'

These days, Ismael always sounded like he was reading from a sermon book.

'I think I liked you better as a servitor,' Abrehem muttered.

Then they were at the door to Forge Elektrus, a battered cog-toothed circle with a bas-relief cybernetic skull icon of the Mechanicus at its centre. Drizzles of oil stained the skull, making it look as though it wept for those condemned within.

Totha Mu-32 placed his staff against the entry panel. Abrehem saw the overseer's code signifiers strain against the locking mechanism, attempting to open the door without success. Staring straight at the skull above the door, Totha Mu-32 allowed the subdermal electoo of the dragon to come to the surface of his organics.

'Does this serve me any better, Chiron?' he said.

'You are not welcome here, Totha,' said a grating voice from the augmitter mounted in the jaw of a grinning skull above the door. It looked like a freshly bleached skull, and Abrehem wondered to whom it had once belonged.

'Probably the last person who thought coming here was a good idea,' he whispered under his breath.

Totha Mu-32 held out his staff as the glittering image of the dragon faded back into his pale skin.

'You do not have the right to deny me access,' said Totha Mu-32. 'Your rank is inferior to mine by a decimal place.'

'No thanks to you,' said the voice. 'And it's Adept Manubia to you. Your rank permits *you* entry to Elektrus, though Omnissiah knows why you'd ever want to slum it here, but it's the company you keep that's giving me pause.'

'They are with me,' said Totha Mu-32. 'Both have more than earned the right to venture within a forge.'

'You don't really believe that or you wouldn't have waited until Kotov went down to the planet's surface,' barked the skull.

'I do believe it, and you know why I have come here.'

'I'm not teaching him,' said Adept Manubia via the skull. 'I'd be dismantled and have my augments implanted into waste servitors.'

'And that would be a terrible shame, because you're making such valuable use of them here,' said Totha Mu-32, displaying a capacity for spite Abrehem hadn't suspected.

The skull fell silent, and Abrehem wondered if Totha Mu-32 had pressed Adept Manubia too hard. He turned to the Mechanicus overseer, but the cog-toothed door rolled aside before he could speak. The waft of hot metal and blessed oil that had been run through recyc-filters too many times to be healthy gusted out.

A magos in stained crimson robes barred entry to the forge. One hand held a staff topped with a laurel wreath and carved representations of slain leporids. The adept's hood was pulled back, revealing a face that was largely organic and also extremely attractive.

The voice from the skull had given no clue as to the speaker's sex, and Abrehem had made the dismissive assumption that Magos Chiron Manubia would be male.

'Totha,' she said.

'Chiron,' said Totha Mu-32. 'It's been too long.'

'You've always known where I was,' said Manubia, and Abrehem sensed shared history between them. Anywhere else, he'd have said this was a meeting of ex-lovers, but he couldn't quite picture that between these two.

He didn't *want* to picture that.

The Mechanicus forbade liaisons between its adepts; was that why Chiron Manubia laboured in a lowly forge below the waterline?

'You want me to train him?' she said. 'After what happened on Karis Cephalon? You must think I'm an idiot.'

'Quite the opposite, Chiron,' said Totha Mu-32. 'That's why I'm here. I can think of nowhere better for Abrehem.'

Chiron Manubia turned her gaze upon Abrehem. Her appraisal was frank and unimpressed.

'He doesn't look Machine-touched,' said Manubia. 'Apart from that clunky-looking augmetic arm, he looks like just any other scrawny bondsman.'

Abrehem wasn't offended. He knew she was dead right to think he didn't look like much.

'How can you say that after what happened in orbit around Hypatia?' asked Totha Mu-32.

'If it was really him that did that, then I'm even less inclined to allow him anywhere near my forge.'

'Aren't you even the slightest bit curious? Don't you want to be immortalised as the adept who inducted him into the mysteries? It could restore your standing within the Mechanicus.'

'A standing you helped ruin.'

At least Totha Mu-32 had the decency to look ashamed.

'I know what I did, Chiron, but look on this as my attempt to undo that youthful mistake,' said Totha Mu-32. 'Take him on for a day, and if you don't see any potential in him, throw whatever's left back to me.'

'One day?'

'Not a pico-second more,' agreed Totha Mu-32.

Adept Manubia took a step back and gestured within the forge with her laurel-topped staff. In the gloom behind her, Abrehem could see dark engines of oiled iron and hissing vents like grinning jaws. A miasma of broken code snapped and squalled from every machine.

It had the look and feel of a wounded animal's lair.

'Welcome to Forge Elektrus, Abrehem Locke,' she said. 'Are you ready to take the first step to becoming Cult Mechanicus?'

'Honestly? I'm not sure,' answered Abrehem.

'Wrong answer,' said Chiron Manubia, hauling him inside.

Microcontent 02

THE CRYSTAL SHIP skimmed across the plaza to where three avenues led deeper into the city. Telok guided them like a steersman of old, as Roboute sat on a bench extruded from the hull at his approach.

He rested his elbow on the gunwale, and the material moulded itself to the contours of his limb. It felt warm, and he lifted his arm away. The surface reshaped to its original form, and a glowing impression of Roboute's fingers and palm remained, slowly fading as he watched.

'You're a well-travelled man, Master Surcouf,' said Ven Anders, balancing his rifle across his knees as he took a seat next to Roboute. 'Have you seen anything like this ship?'

'Call me Roboute, and no, I haven't.'

'Not even among the eldar?'

Roboute shook his head. 'There's a superficial similarity, yes, but there's something a little... *vulgar* about this.'

'Vulgar? This? It's beautiful,' said Anders. 'Even a dour son of Cadia like me can appreciate that much.'

'There's an effortlessness to eldar craftsmanship that no human can match,' said Roboute. 'This feels like someone *trying* too hard to emulate it.'

'Ordinarily I'd report a man to the commissars for xenos sympathies like that,' said Anders. 'But seeing as you're a scoundrel of a rogue trader, I think I can let you off this time.'

'Decent of you, Colonel Anders.'

'Ven,' said Anders as the shadow of vast, iron-clad structures swallowed them. Both men looked up, turning their attention to the artificial canyon through which the ship sailed. Sheer cliffs of iron soared upwards, ribboned with hundreds of snaking pipes and cable runs. They clung to every building and laced overhead like vines in a rainforest. They thrummed with power.

Squealing pistons, the roar of venting gases and the relentless, grinding crunch of enormous machine gears echoed from all around. Booming hammerblows of distant construction temples and a seismic throb of subterranean labours filled the air. The planet's heartbeat. Roboute felt his bones vibrate in time with the pulse of worldwide industry.

The ship's course threaded between monolithic blocks of metallic towers, beneath arches of latticework scaffolds and along curving expressways. On suspended gantries and within those structures open to the elements, Roboute saw innumerable toiling servitors, like ants in a glass-fronted colony.

They were withered things with so little flesh left upon them they were practically automatons. Fettered gangs of them turned great cog-wheels, hauled on enormous chains or climbed grand processional steps in grim lockstep, coming from who knew where to reach their next allotted task.

Was this the crew of the Tomioka?

Labouring alongside the servitors were thousands of the things Telok had called crystaliths. Some retained humanoid form, albeit in a glassy and unfinished fashion, while others adopted whatever bodyplan best suited their current task.

Roboute caught a glimpse of a gigantic crystalith moving between two golden-capped pyramid structures, undulant and centipede-like. Easily the equal of a Reaver Titan in scale.

'Did you see that?' said Anders.

'I did.'

'Having *Lupa Capitalina* and *Canis Ulfrica* striding behind us would make me feel a lot better,' said Roboute.

'And I wouldn't say no to *Vilka* scouting the flanks either,' said Anders. 'Have they a new princeps for *Amarok* yet?'

'I don't know,' said Roboute. 'Ever since Hypatia, the Legio's pretty much locked itself away.'

Anders nodded, glancing up as a flaring arc of corposant danced along the structural elements of the adjacent building. Flaring vent towers belched gouts of flame and smoke. Petrochemical stink descended. Flashes of lightning arcing between dirigibles threw shadows on the walls.

'That storm's getting nearer,' said Roboute, squinting through his fingers at the lowering sky. Dark bands of toxin-laden clouds were sinking downwards.

'Looks that way,' agreed Ven Anders.

'You think it'll be dangerous?'

'I think everything's dangerous.'

Roboute laughed, then saw Anders was completely serious.

'Then let me say that you look very relaxed for a man in a high state of readiness.'

'That's the Cadian way,' said Anders.

No two structures of Exnihlio were alike, and Roboute struggled to ascribe purpose to them. Some had the appearance of forges, others of colossal power stations. Some appeared unfinished, yet more were abandoned or had otherwise fallen into ruin.

Something struck Roboute as odd about the city, something that had been niggling at him ever since they'd landed. The buildings were pure function, very much like the *Speranza*, but with one important difference. As ugly as the Ark Mechanicus was, it was still unmistakably a vessel of the Martian priesthood, thanks to its wealth of iconography. Cog-toothed skulls, mortis angels, scriptural binary and mechanised frescoes adorned any space not given over to pure practicality.

Part stamp of authority, part theatre, it was impossible for any servant of the Emperor to escape the grim imagery so beloved of Terra and Mars.

'Where are all the skulls?' he said.

'What?' asked Anders.

'The skulls,' repeated Roboute. 'Since we landed, I haven't seen a single cogged skull, no symbols of the Mechanicus at all.'

'And nor will you, Master Surcouf,' called Telok from the steersman's lectern. 'Not while I am master of Exnihlio.'

Roboute turned to face the archmagos. He hadn't whispered, but neither had he exactly spoken aloud. The city's din should have easily swallowed Roboute's words, but perhaps Telok's aural augmentations allowed him to tune out the background noise.

'And why is that?' he asked.

'I am beyond the galaxy, beyond the Mechanicus,' said Telok, and it seemed to Roboute as though the words of the archmagos resonated from the structure of the crystal ship.

Kotov glanced up in concern at Telok's provocative words.

'I built everything you see here, Master Surcouf. Me, not the Mechanicus and not the Imperium. Why waste resources and time on needless ornamentations when there are none to see them and so much great work to be done? The Breath of the Gods has shown me how lost the Mechanicus have become, how little they remember of their former greatness. I will restore that to them. I will save Mars from itself!'

THE ROOM WAS dark, but Linya Tychon changed that with a thought. Soft illumination rose up, sourceless and without haste. The room was spartanly furnished: just a bed, a recessed rail with her robes hanging from it, a writing desk, a terminal with a moulded plastic chair in front of it and a modest ablutions cubicle.

She pulled back the bedclothes and sat up, swinging her legs out onto the floor. It was warm underfoot. Linya blinked away the remnants of a bad dream, something unpleasant, but already fading. She placed her hands on her temples, looking strangely at her fingertips as though she expected to see something.

Shaking her head, Linya poured water from a copper ewer into a plastic cup. She didn't recall there having been water beside her bed, nor even a table and cup, but took a drink anyway.

The water was cool and pure, as if only recently collected from a mountain spring or the depths of an ancient glacier. It quenched the immediate thirst, but didn't feel like it refreshed her.

She stood and selected a robe, pulling it over her head and wriggling into it before pulling the waist cinch tight. Pouring another cup of water, she sat on the plastic chair before the terminal and pulled up the previous cycle of the Gallery's survey inloads. Kilometres-long detection devices encircling the Quatria Gallery stared unblinking into space, gathering vast quantities of data on far distant celestial phenomena.

But data only meant something once it had been interpreted.

Linya's eyes scanned the scrolling columns of figures, blink-capturing interesting segments of the sky, particularly the distant star formations in the Perseus arm of the galaxy, where the first pulse-star had been discovered.

Linya let the data wash through her, noting times and distances with each swipe of a page. So far, nothing unusual. She tapped a hand on the wall beside her, and a portion of the wall faded to transparency, creating an aperture that looked out onto the void and glittering stars. Not a real window, of course, simply a pict representation of what lay beyond her insulated and armoured chamber. Having a real window was too much of a risk. Ablation cascade effects from a long-ended void-conflict had made the orbital tracks of Quatria lousy with fragments, rendering the planet below essentially unreachable.

Only an emergency boost into a graveyard orbit and rigorously maintained shield protocols had kept the Quatria Gallery intact in the aftermath of the fighting. The Mechanicus had wanted to abandon the Gallery, to scrap the machinery and repurpose it to more profitable areas of research, but Vitali Tychon had point-blank refused to mothball his beloved observatory.

Thinking of her father, Linya pulled up a three-dimensional representation of the Gallery's internal structure – two spinning cones linked at their tips by a slender connecting passageway, and vast spans of far-reaching detection arrays radiating from their flat bases. The staff of the Quatria Gallery was minimal, just Linya, her father, six lexmechanics and a handful of servitors.

Linya frowned. Vitali's icon was not aboard.

'Where are you, father?' she muttered.

Perhaps he was outside the station, repairing a misaligned mirror or shield relay, but she doubted it. That was servitor work. In any case, her father disliked venturing beyond the station's interior if he didn't have to. And even if he had, he would have informed her of his intention to go outside.

Linya pressed a finger to her ear and said, 'Father? Can you hear me?'

A faint wash of static, like the caress of waves over sand, was her only answer. Linya frowned and turned to the faux window, using the haptic implants on her fingertips to sweep the exterior picters around the station. The metal skin of the Quatria Gallery was granite-coloured flexsteel, rippling with undersea reflections from the enclosing energy fields. Linya panned the view around, hunting for the crab-like vehicle they used to manoeuvre around the hull and repair anything that needed fixing.

She found it easily enough, still moored to one of the upper transit hubs. Haloed by a corona of light from the planet below.

A breath of something cold passed over Linya's neck and she turned her chair. The door to her room was open, which was unusual. Few enough of them lived aboard the Gallery to require anything approaching privacy, but old habits died hard. Linya found it hard to imagine she'd left the door open.

'Is there someone there?' she asked.

No one answered, but then they wouldn't, would they?

She rose from the chair and locked her terminal. She turned to the window, but her hand making the haptic gesture to close it froze when she saw something unusual.

Or, rather, when she *didn't* see something unusual.

Quatria was a mostly inert rock, a rust-red ball of iron oxide and tholeiitic basalt. On most cycles, it was visible as though through a haze of mist, the result of the ever-growing mass in the debris cascade.

Linya now saw the planet as she had not seen it for decades, with pin-sharp clarity and clearly defined terrain features.

Breath sighed over her neck again, and she spun around. It felt like someone was standing right behind her. A half-glimpsed outline of a shape moved at the edge of her door. Too quick to be recognised.

'Wait!' called Linya.

She crossed the room quickly and stepped out into the corridor. Bare metal curved away in both directions, but a whisper of cloth on steel drew her gaze to the right. Another flicker of movement. Linya set off after the shape, not even sure what she was chasing or what she expected to find.

The Mechanicus weren't given to playing jokes on one another, and it seemed wholly unlikely there was an intruder aboard. Any ship would have been detected months before it reached them. And what could an intruder hope to gain from boarding covertly?

Linya paused at a junction of passageways, seeking any sign of the figure she'd seen earlier.

'Hello?' she said. 'Is there anyone here?'

Silence answered her. Quatria was a large station, but not so large and complex in its internal arrangement that it would be easy to lose someone. Without her father's presence she knew she should feel very alone. The servitors and lexmechanics provided no companionship, but strangely she felt anything but alone.

It felt as though there were unseen eyes upon her. As intrusive as being covertly observed ought to be, Linya felt no threat, merely a weary sadness.

'Who are you?' she said to the darkness. 'And how did you get aboard Quatria?'

Maddening silence surrounded her, and Linya balled her fists.

'What have you done with my father? Where is Vitali?' she demanded, feeling a moment of intense sadness at the mention of her father's name.

Linya turned as she heard soft footfalls behind her.

A magos in a black robe stood in the centre of the corridor, his hands laced before him and his head concealed beneath a hood of impenetrable shadows. Only the soft shimmer of a pair of silver eyes hinted at augmetics beneath.

The presences Linya felt observing her retreated, fearful of this individual. She didn't know him, but was instinctively wary.

<Hello, Mistress Tychon,> said the adept, speaking an archaic form of binary, one she had last heard in the ossuary reliquaries of the Schiaparelli Sorrow.

<Who are you?> she asked, phrasing her answer in the same canted form. <And where are we?>

<Don't you recognise this place?>

<I recognise what it's *supposed* to be.>

The adept sighed. <And we were so careful to reconstruct it from your memories.>

<It's a good likeness of Quatria,> admitted Linya, <but you forgot the orbital debris from the void-war.>

<We do not recall seeing that in your memories.>

<It's so much a part of Quatria that I don't even think about it now, it's just… *there*.>

<Memory blindness, yes, that would explain it,> said the figure. <Now tell me who you are.>

<Do you not yet know? And we had such high hopes for you.>

<Not yet,> said Linya, though a horrible suspicion was forming in her mind. <Tell me why I'm here, wherever here is.>

<Ah, now that we *can* tell you,> said the adept. <You are here because you are exceptional, Mistress Tychon. This is a place where like-minded individuals meet in a collective neuromatrix of debate and shared experience. You are not the only exceptional mind here, Mistress Tychon, there are others. We promise you will contribute greatly to our ongoing growth.>

<So this is a shared experiential consciousness?>

<Of a sort, yes.>

<Yours?>

<In a manner of speaking,> agreed the adept.

<I don't want to be here,> said Linya. <I want you to release me and let my neural pathways realign in my body.>

<We are afraid we can't do that, Linya,> said the adept.

<Why not?>

<There was an accident, you see,> said the adept. <Your body was gravely injured, and this was the only way to keep your exceptional mind from being lost forever.>

Linya heard falsehood in the adept's words, but also truth. She *had* been hurt, hadn't she? Badly hurt. She felt dizzy and reached out to steady herself on the wall as her legs felt suddenly powerless to support her. The wall was warm beneath her fingertips. That warmth turned to searing heat, and Linya snatched her hand back from the wall.

<I was burned,> she said, sensing a memory groping for the surface. She pushed it down, not yet ready to face such pain.

<As we said, you were gravely hurt,> said the adept. <Were we to return you to your body, you would die in agony moments later. Trust us, this way is best. Here you will live on, enhancing the whole with the sum of your learning, your experience and thirst for knowledge. Is that not better than death?>

<I want to know where I am,> said Linya. <Whose mind space is this?>

She felt the unseen eyes willing her not to continue down this road. Linya ignored them. She had never been one for shying away from hard facts or inconvenient truths.

<We can show you, but centuries of experience has taught us that it is better for a mind to come to the realisation of its new circumstances without our help. We have lost more than one mind to transition shock, and you must trust us when we say that is a most painful way to cease existing.>

<Show me, damn you.>

<Very well,> he said. <We will alter the perceptual centres of your brain to receive inputs and discern our immediate surroundings. Your memories will be unlocked as well, though we must warn you, you will very much dislike what you learn.>

<Stop stalling and show me.>

The adept nodded and stepped towards the wall.

With hands that looked as though they were made of dozens of scalpel blades bound together with copper wire, the adept drew the outline of a window in the wall. Antiseptic light shone through, stark and unforgiving.

Linya edged towards the light, feeling the drag of the unseen observers as they wordlessly screamed at her to retreat. Every step felt like she was walking towards an executioner's block, but she had willed this resolution. She couldn't back down now.

She edged closer to the light, and looked out through the window. What she was seeing made no sense without memory to frame it and give it context.

As easily as a key turns in a lock, those memories returned in an instant as the gates of her hippocampus were stormed by synaptic flares exploding in her cerebral cortex.

Linya saw a body lying on bloodstained sheets, a body with her face. A body with the skull pared open and the cranial vault excised of brain matter.

In a singular moment of horror, Linya remembered exactly where she was and what Galatea had done to her.

THE CORRIDOR WAS ten metres wide, ribbed with pilasters of latticed green steelwork. A vault of leering gargoyles arched overhead, water droplets falling from rusted rivets and the lips of half-hidden statues in secluded alcoves. The company of Cadians jogged beneath them at battle pace, keeping their attention firmly fixed on the route ahead.

Captain Blayne Hawkins ran at the head of the column, arms pumping with a metronomic precision to match the piston heads in the chamber they had just left. Despite the chill, he was sweating hard, his uniform jacket plastered to his skin. His breath punched from his lungs with every thudding footfall.

On Cadia he could run like this for hours.

But this wasn't Cadia.

The ninety-three men behind him were tired, but weren't showing it. He reckoned they'd run around fifteen kilometres in full battle-gear through the twisting guts of the *Speranza*, though it was hard to be certain exactly how far they'd come. The Ark Mechanicus was a nightmare to navigate or maintain any sense of distance from.

It made formulating a workable defence of the ship difficult, but difficult was meat and gravy to Cadians. Ahead, the corridor branched left and right, with the towering statue of a hooded magos dividing it into a V-shaped junction.

'Hostile corners, secure flanks for advance!' called Hawkins.

No sooner had the words left his mouth than the company split into two. Evens went left, odds right. The first squads moved close to the metalled walls of the corridor, but not along them. A ricocheting solid round might ride a wall for a hundred metres or more. The evens aimed their lasrifles along the rightmost passage, the odds the left. Hawkins took position with the evens, the stock of his rifle hard against his cheek.

The squads at the rear of the company adopted a near identical formation, their guns covering behind.

'Clear!'

'Clear!'

'Hindmost squads, take point!' shouted Hawkins.

The squads covering the rear now moved up, smooth as a training drill, to take the lead. Hawkins went with them as they passed, covered by the guns of the men in front. The overwatching squads took position at the rear as Hawkins moved to the front of the jogging column.

This was the tenth battle drill they'd practised en route to the training deck. They'd practised corridor assault drills, room clearances in empty forge-temples and even run reconnaissance in force of a vast hangar filled with smashed lifter-rigs.

A starship was one of the worst environments in which to fight. The vessels were dark, unfamiliar, cramped and were often being violently breached by broadsides and boarders from the void. Unforgiving battle-fields, they made for intense training grounds, and Hawkins wasn't about to waste this extended period of time aboard ship without making the most of their surroundings.

The company moved down the gloomy corridor, splashing through pools of water collected on the bowed deck plates. They passed beneath the gaze of mechanical cherubs and floating skulls that zipped overhead on mysterious errands for their Martian masters.

Hawkins ran another two drills – crossing an intersection, and sweeping a gridded chamber of hung chains. Its ceiling was obscured by clouds of hot steam and its walls rippled with lightning encased in thick glass cylinders.

Eventually, Hawkins and his men reached the end of the run. Their battle pace hadn't slackened once, but it was a relief to finally reach their destination.

Hawkins led his men onto a wide esplanade platform overlooking Magos Dahan's fiefdom, the training deck. This enormous space sat at the heart of the *Speranza*, a vast, constantly changing arena where the armed forces of the Ark Mechanicus could train in a multitude of varied battle simulations.

Dahan had put the Cadians through some hard engagements here.

Nothing they hadn't been able to handle, but testing nonetheless. Despite his assurances to the contrary, Hawkins knew Dahan didn't really understand Cadians at all.

Few did.

After all, what other world of the Imperium basked in the baleful glow of the Eye of Terror? What soldiers learned to hold a lasgun before they could walk? What regiments earned scars other regiments could only dream of before they'd even left their birthrock?

Irritatingly, Rae's company were already here. His senior sergeant's men sat on the edge of the platform, watching the skitarii below fighting through a mocked-up ork encampment that filled the nearest quadrant of the training deck.

In the far distance, nearly a kilometre away, the Titans of Legio Sirius moved with predatory grace through towers of prefabricated steel. The vibrations of their enormous footfalls could be felt as bass tremors in the floor. Hawkins made a quick aquila over his chest, remembering the destruction unleashed the last time the god-machines had walked the training deck.

Thankfully, it looked like the Legio were simply engaged in manoeuvre drills.

'Company, halt,' said Hawkins. 'Rest easy. Five minutes.'

The company broke up into squads, the men taking the opportunity to stretch their aching muscles and slake their thirst from canvas-wrapped canteens.

Sergeant Rae approached, his ruddy complexion telling Hawkins he'd pushed his men hard, like any good sergeant should.

'Nice of you to finally join us, sir,' said Rae, offering him a drink from his own canteen. Hawkins took it and drank down a few mouthfuls. Taking too much water too quickly was a sure-fire way to get a bad case of stomach cramps.

'How long have you been here?' asked Hawkins.

'About ten minutes,' said Rae, not even having the decency to look a little humble at how much quicker he'd managed the run than his commanding officer.

'It's this bloody ship,' said Hawkins. 'The gravity's not the same. Not like running where there's good Cadian rock underfoot.'

'Adept Dahan says the gravity's Terran-standard.'

'Damn Dahan, and damn his gravity,' snapped Hawkins, though the cooling effects of the water and the chance to rest his limbs were already easing his irritation. 'All right, then the ship gave you a short cut.'

'The ship?' said Rae with a raised eyebrow. 'Really?'

'You know as well as I do that this ship's got a mind of its own when it comes to its internal structure,' said Hawkins, taking another drink.

'We ran into a few unexpected twists and turns along the way, it's true,' agreed Rae.

'*A few unexpected twists and turns?*' said Hawkins. 'That's putting it mildly. No matter how many hours I pore over data-slate schematics or the ship-wright's wax-paper blueprints, the *Speranza*'s always got a surprise in store.

A turn that isn't where it's supposed to be, a branching route that doesn't appear on any of the plans.'

'It's a queer old ship, I'll give you that,' said Rae, making a clumsy attempt at the Cog Mechanicus to take any sting out of his words.

Hawkins handed back Rae's canteen, leaning on the railing looking out over the training deck. 'Glad to see we're on the same page, sergeant.'

Rae took a drink and slipped the canteen into his battle-gear.

'Any word from the colonel?' he asked.

Hawkins shook his head. 'Nothing yet, but Azuramagelli tells me there's no vox-traffic coming from the surface at all.'

'Should we be concerned about that?'

'Yes, I think we should,' said Hawkins, now seeing a tall man with close-cropped silver hair farther along the esplanade platform. He'd mistaken him for one of Rae's men, but now saw he was wearing simple coveralls with a nondescript padded trench coat emblazoned with a stylised canidae. Cadians typically had pinched, hollow features, but this man had the well-fed, scarred cheekbones of a feral noble or warlike hive-lord. Icy eyes darted back and forth, watching the skitarii training under Dahan's booming instructions.

No, that wasn't right.

The man had no interest in the skitarii. He was watching the Titans.

'Who's he?' asked Hawkins, jutting his chin out at the man.

'Not sure,' answered Rae. 'He's got his collar up, but I saw a socket in the back of his neck and his fingers have got metal tips. That and the canidae crest make me think Titan crew.'

'So why's he not out there?'

'Don't know,' said Rae.

Hawkins dismissed the man from his thoughts. What did it matter who he was? There were tens of thousands of people aboard the *Speranza* he didn't know. What difference did one more make?

'Right,' he said, straightening up. 'Let's get to it.'

Rae nodded and turned to the two companies that were already standing and settling their battle-gear back onto their shoulders and hips.

'Companies!' bellowed Rae in a voice known to sergeants all across the Imperium. 'Magos Dahan has put together a couple of arenas he thinks will test us. Shall we show him how wrong he is?'

The men grinned and quickly formed up into their companies. It had become a point of pride that they could meet any challenge Dahan's arenas might throw at them.

Hawkins led the way down the iron stairs to the training deck.

He glanced up at the man with silver hair and scarred cheeks. Sensing Hawkins's gaze, he waved and shouted down to the Cadians.

'You're fighting a simulation?' he asked. 'Now?'

Hawkins shouted back. 'It's rare you get to fight when you're rested, so why train that way?'

'You're mad!'

'We're Cadian,' returned Hawkins. 'It's sort of the same thing.'

Microcontent 03

EXNIHLIO WAS EVERYTHING Archmagos Kotov had hoped for, a wonderland of technological marvels, incredible industry and lost science. From the moment he'd extended the hand of friendship to his fellow archmagos, he knew he was vindicated in his decision to take the *Speranza* beyond the galactic rim.

All the doubters who had mocked his decision to embark on this daring mission would be silenced now. With Telok at his side, Archmagos Kotov would return to Mars in triumph. The holdings he had lost to catastrophe, xenos invasion and treachery would be insignificant next to what he would gain.

The wealth and knowledge of Mars laid at his feet.

Title, position and domains.

Who knew to what dizzying heights he might ascend?

Master of his own quadrangle, perhaps even Fabricator General one day. With the discovery of the Breath of the Gods to his name, it would be simplicity itself to quietly ease the incumbent Fabricator into a life of solitary research.

Fabricator General Kotov.

Yes, it had a solemnity and gravitas befitting so vital a role.

So now that he had reached his destination and found the Lost Magos, why did his grandiose dreams feel even further away?

Archmagos Telok was both more and less than what he had hoped. Bizarre in form, yes, but no more so than many of the more zealous adherents of the Ferran Mortification Creed. He was still undeniably human, but the crystalline growths encrusting his body had all the hallmarks of something parasitic, not augmentative.

Telok's declaration of saving Mars from itself had horrified him, and his initial response had been a frantic series of cease-and-desist blurts of command binary. All of which had failed utterly to have any effect on Telok, whose archaic cognitive architecture was incapable of processing such inputs.

<I take it you disagree with what I said to Surcouf?> asked Telok, with the brutal syntax of pre-hexamathic cant. <I can't imagine why.>

Kotov paused before answering, switching back to the older form of binary. With as many diplomatic overtones as could be applied to such a basic cant-form, Kotov said, <There are those among the Adeptus Mechanicus who would consider such words treasonous.>

<Then they are fools, Kotov,> said Telok. <You and I, we know better. We are explorators, men of vision and foresight. What do the hooded men of Mars know of realms beyond the galaxy? With laboratories hidden beneath the red sands and heads stuck just as deeply in the past, what do such timid souls know of *real* exploration? The Adeptus Mechanicus is a corpse rotting from the inside out, Kotov. I knew it back when I set out for the Halo Scar, and I see you know it too. Tell me I'm wrong.>

Kotov struggled to find an answer. To hear a priest of Mars say such things beggared belief. At best, such an outburst would see an adept denied advancement through the Cult Mechanicus. At worst it would see him branded *excommunicatus-technicus*, stripped of his every augmentation or transformed into a servitor.

Even an archmagos of the Adeptus Mechanicus, a servant of the Machine-God who would normally be granted a degree of latitude in such matters, could not voice such things openly.

<You have been away from the Imperium for some time,> replied Kotov. <And while there is much within the Mechanicus I believe could work better, you cannot seriously entertain such thoughts?>

Telok laughed. <Ah, Kotov, dear fellow, you must forgive me. It's been too long since I had anything but crystaliths and servitors to talk to. The conversational deficit has made me forget myself.>

<Then I will overlook your hasty words, archmagos.>

<Of course you will,> said Telok, and the growths jutting from his metal hide like armoured horns flared in response. <You and I? We are gods to these men, and it does not behove gods to squabble before lesser beings. You agree, of course?>

<I agree that it is never good for superiors to argue before those who must serve them,> said Kotov.

<Quite,> said Telok, and the Lost Magos returned to steering the crystal ship through the megalithic structures, vast generator plants for the most

part, though there were some buildings whose purpose even Kotov could not identify.

<That one man could build this from nothing, without a geoformer fleet, is nothing short of miraculous,> said Kotov. <How did you do it? I must know.>

<All in good time, archmagos.>

<I have so many questions,> continued Kotov, trying not to let his growing unease with Telok outweigh his admiration for what the Lost Magos had achieved. <Where is the rest of your fleet? The crew of the *Tomioka*? Are they here too?>

<I promised to answer your questions in good time, archmagos,> said Telok, his crystals pulsing with jagged spikes of illumination. <And I will. Trust me, all will become clear when I show you the Breath of the Gods.>

<And will that be soon?>

Telok did not answer, guiding their course from between the looming structures enclosing them. The crystal ship skimmed into an enormous metalled plaza, not unlike the one upon which the Thunderhawk of the Black Templars had landed.

At the centre of the plaza sat a colossal silver-skinned dome, at least four kilometres in diameter and a quarter that in height. Could the scale of what lay beneath be extrapolated from its incredible dimensions?

The vastness of the dome was breathtaking, and as the crystal ship slipped effortlessly through the air towards it, Kotov saw the faintest outline of rippling energy fields.

More than one, in fact. Banks of shields layered the dome, more than even shrouded the sacred slopes of Olympus Mons. Whatever lay within was clearly of immense value.

<Is the Breath of the Gods within?> asked Kotov.

<It is,> grinned Telok, showing blunted, porcelain-looking teeth. <Would you like to see it?>

<More than you can imagine.>

Telok moved his gnarled fingers across the lectern in a precise geomantic pattern. Twin arcs of glossy metal unfolded from the plaza, self-assembling and curving over organically to form an arch some fifty metres before the dome. Where its outer edges contacted the dome's energy fields, disruptive arcs of lightning exploded in a nova-like corona.

A curtain of sparking, crackling energy filled the space within the arc, and Kotov shifted warily on the bench as he saw Telok meant to steer them through it.

The emptiness of the plaza made it difficult to accurately gauge the size of the arch until they were almost upon it. Kotov's internal calibrators measured it as two hundred metres wide and ninety high.

And then they passed beneath it, and the silver skin of the dome, which

Kotov now saw was formed from overlapping scales like reptile skin, rippled as it reshaped to form an opening. Light like a blood-red sunrise breaking over the Tharsis Montes shone from within, carrying with it the promise of the future. Kotov felt his floodstream surge in response.

'The Breath of the Gods awaits!' said Telok as the crystal ship passed into the dome.

THE BEATING RENARD had taken in her forced landing on the *Speranza* was still very much in evidence, but all things considered, it could have been a lot worse. Emil Nader walked down the starship's port-side flank with a pair of servitors at his heels. Both were equipped with vox-recorders, faithfully listening to his critical appraisal of the work the Mechanicus had undertaken on his vessel.

It was stream of consciousness stuff, but with the *in perpetuitus* refit contract Roboute had negotiated with the Mechanicus, now was the time to get as much done as humanly possible.

Scaffolding rigs surrounded the prow, which hung suspended over a graving dock in which the boxy form of Adept Kryptaestrex supervised the work of nearly two hundred servitors and bondsmen as they laboured to repair *Renard*'s prow. The prow and ventral sections of the ship had taken the worst of the damage. Like any pilot, Emil never quite trusted those who didn't fly to know exactly what they were doing, so was keeping a close eye on the servitors. So far, he grudgingly, and it was *very* grudgingly, had to admit the Mechanicus were doing a decent job.

Emil paused beside a newly fabricated panel installed in an airlock hatch that had once been stamped with an Espandorian artificer's mark.

'You have got to be kidding me,' he said, following up with an Iaxian oath best not repeated in earshot of a lady. 'The nerve of these sons of bitches.'

'Transcription alert,' said the two servitors, one after the other. 'Implanted lexicon conflict. Do you wish a phonetic transcription?'

'Don't be stupid,' said Emil, before remembering he was talking to a servitor. 'No. I don't want that recorded.'

He jabbed a finger at the nearest servitor then pointed to a wheeled rack of parts and forge-gear sitting at the base of a scaffold-rig. 'You, go get a pneuma-hammer.'

The servitor retrieved the requested tool before returning to its station, exactly one metre behind Emil.

'Now get that off my ship,' he said, pointing to the gleaming Icon Mechanicus on the hatch. The cog-toothed skull had been set in the centre of the hatch, completely obscuring the artificer's mark.

'Clarification required,' said the servitor. 'What is it you wish removed?'

'The Icon Mechanicus,' said Emil. 'Get it off.'

'Unable to comply,' said the servitor. 'Express permission from a tech-priest, rank Lambda-Tertius or higher, is required before this *servile* may deface/remove an Icon Mechanicus.'

'Throne, don't you bloody Mechanicus know anything about *why* starships stay aloft?' he snapped. 'Here, hand me that pneuma-hammer.'

The servitor held the device out and Emil snatched it from its unresisting grip. He bent to the airlock hatch and with three swift blows from the pneuma-hammer battered the silver-steel icon to the deck.

'Good as new,' he said, holding the pneuma-hammer out behind him and brushing flecks of metal shavings away with his free hand. The hammer was plucked from his grasp and a gruff voice came from behind him.

'And this is why you leave engineering to folk who know what they're doing.'

'It's bad luck to cover up the original maker's marks,' said Emil, standing upright.

Kayrn Sylkwood, *Renard*'s enginseer, saw the emblem he'd knocked off the ship and nodded in agreement. She ran a hand over the dented metalwork Emil had just beaten free of the Icon Mechanicus.

'Nice work,' she said. 'Subtle.'

'You're an enginseer, what do you know about subtle?'

'More than you, by the looks of it,' said Sylkwood. The rivalry between a pilot and a ship's master of engines was long-established. One trying to squeeze the most out of a ship's reactors, one trying to keep the other from blowing them up.

Clad in a tight-fitting vest and combat jacket, Kayrn Sylkwood was a born and bred enginseer. Knotted communion implants lined her shaven skull in metallic cornrows, and her tanned features had a laconic superiority to them. Baggy fatigues that might once have been tan-coloured, but which were now an oil-sodden slate, were tucked into military boots, laced in the Cadian cross-hatch style.

'How's it looking out here?' she asked.

'Despite the odd bit of complete idiocy, not as bad as I expected,' said Emil, moving down the hull towards the sunken space below the prow, where sparks from arc-welders and lascutters fell like neon-blue rain. Sylkwood fell in alongside him, unconsciously matching his step. The two servitors resumed their obedient following.

'*Speranza*'s priests actually seem like they know what they're doing,' said Emil, running his hands along the warm metal of the *Renard*'s fuselage. 'The damaged hull plates have been repaired in Turentek's prow-forges, the forward auspex arrays have been stripped out and replaced, and I see the transverse inertial arrays being reinforced. There's been some unasked-for upgrades by the look of it, but I'll only find out exactly what when I take her out again.'

'Not bad,' said Sylkwood. 'Not bad at all.'

'They all done in the engine spaces?'

Kayrn nodded. 'Yeah, there wasn't much to do, and Ilanna had left pretty specific instructions. But I didn't let them do anything without me right there with them. If we had a halfway decent pilot at the helm, I'd guess we'd probably see a ten per cent boost to *Renard*'s top speed and reactor efficiency.'

'Then I'll get fifteen.'

'You think?'

'Bet you a shift on the loaders.'

They spat on their palms and slapped hands.

'You watch, I'll get my ship doing things her builders never even dreamed of,' said Emil.

'*Your* ship?' said Kayrn with a grin. 'I reckon the captain might have something to say about *that* word choice.'

Emil returned her grin. 'Roboute isn't here. And he doesn't fly the ship, I do. In my books that makes the *Renard* mine.'

Kayrn looked set to challenge that assertion, but before she could do more than cock an eyebrow, they heard a horrified wail from the entrance to the graving dock.

'What the hell?' said Kayrn, her hand falling to the butt of her holstered laspistol. 'Is that Vitali Tychon?'

'Looks like,' said Emil, lifting his hand to shield his eyes from the glare of the deck's harsh lighting. 'I think he's been hurt.'

Vitali staggered towards the *Renard*. His robes were drenched in blood from the chest down. Did Mechanicus priests have that much blood in them?

'It's not his blood,' said Kayrn as Vitali half ran, half staggered towards them. He was shouting something, but his words were too grief-stricken and anguished to make out.

'Then whose blood is it?' said Emil.

FORGE ELEKTRUS WAS not what Abrehem had imagined when Totha Mu-32 had said he was to be apprenticed to a magos of the Cult Mechanicus. He had pictured towering engines and the thunderous, unceasing labours of powerful machinery.

A place where things were *made*, technology unbound.

Not this place of antiquity, an echoing machine-temple where dust lay thick on the titanic engines that stood cold and dead to either side of a mosaic-covered nave. The only machines at work here were the lumen staves carried by the two forge overseers and the crackling inload trunking that allowed the thirty shaven-headed tech-priests to link their cognitive capacity.

Arranged in five rows of six, they sat on hard wooden benches before a rusted throne worked into a representation of the Icon Mechanicus. Chained together like galley slaves by ribbed copper cabling plugged into data-sockets in the backs of their skulls, their heads bobbed rhythmically to a hypnotic binary beat only they could hear.

Abrehem had seen that every one was the lowest rank it was possible to be and still be counted as one of the Martian priesthood. Many bore terrible injuries suffered in service to the Machine-God: missing limbs, burned skin and cratered skulls. Just as many bore marks of censure in their noospheric auras. Others had been implanted with augments that had obviously been damaged or been cycled through so many adepts over the centuries that it was a miracle they functioned at all.

Truly this was a forge of the damned, where the lowliest, most pitiable adepts imaginable toiled. So why had Totha Mu-32 sent him here? What could he possibly learn in a place populated by the mad, the infirm and the punished?

How was this any better than where he had come from?

No answer was obvious, and Chiron Manubia had thus far been less than forthcoming. Without the necessary inload sockets, Abrehem couldn't take his place with the linked adepts in their fugue state, and for that he was profoundly grateful.

Instead, he sat on the pew of a wide timber lectern, such as he might expect to find in a mass scriptorium of the Administratum. A book of quantum runes lay open before him, each holy circuit etched into the electro-conductive pages with copper wiring.

The book was ancient and marked by thousands of blurred fingerprints. Perhaps it had belonged to the first builders of this temple.

He'd been studying it for what seemed like weeks, tracing metalled fingers across its dogmatic forms and endless repetition. Its needless complexity was straining his powers of concentration and testing the limits of his boredom. Almost every litany was monstrously overwrought and only achieved what he could do with a thought. To work to such prescribed methods was ridiculous and he sat back from the book with a weary sigh of resignation.

'You think you're too good for Forge Elektrus, don't you?' said his new tutor, startling Abrehem from his gloomy contemplation of a needlessly complex runic form of the Ohmic Evocation.

Abrehem looked up into the almond-shaped face of Chiron Manubia.

He still didn't know what shared history lay between her and Totha Mu-32, but every time he looked at Manubia's face, he felt sure it had involved something unpleasantly biological.

'No, that's not it at all,' said Abrehem.

'You're a terrible liar,' said Manubia, sitting next to him on the lectern's pew.

'Sorry, I just thought your forge would be... different.'

Manubia cocked an eyebrow.

'Different,' she said, echoing the wariness he'd put into each syllable. 'You thought it would be a forge where the wonders of technology were handed down straight from the golden hands of the Omnissiah?'

Abrehem kept his mouth shut in case he said something truly stupid. He tapped the iron fingers of his augmetic arm against the edge of the lectern.

Manubia smiled. 'I thought so. Forge Elektrus isn't quite like the forges depicted in the devotional frescoes, is it?'

Since lying to Manubia clearly wasn't an option, Abrehem opted for honesty. 'No, it hardly looks like a forge at all.'

'What did you think? That someone who almost got the *Speranza* destroyed was going to just walk into the most prestigious forge on the ship and begin his rise through the Cult Mechanicus?'

'No, of course not, but...'

'But you thought you'd be learning all our secrets from the minute you walked in,' said Manubia. 'Well, I'm afraid you have to earn that right, Abrehem Locke. Because, right now, you are the lowest of the low. You are the scrapings of millennial rust from a broken gear, the contaminated oil that's on the verge of being too polluted to use on even the most mangled waste recycler. And the only reason I didn't slam the door in Totha Mu-32's face is that, Omnissiah preserve me, I think he might be right about you.'

'That I'm Machine-touched?'

'No, that you're dangerous,' said Manubia.

'Dangerous?'

'You think you know machines, that you can talk to them and that it's a simple matter to coax them into doing what you want, but you're like a child with the key to an armoury of loaded weapons,' said Manubia, jabbing a finger at the book of quantum runes. 'You have power, a power I don't understand yet, but you don't know how to use it safely. That's why you're here – not to become the saviour of the Adeptus Mechanicus, but to be controlled, to have whatever power you have made safe. *That's* what I do, Abrehem Locke.'

'What you do?' said Abrehem, angry at being so casually dismissed. 'It doesn't look like you do *anything* here.'

Manubia turned and gestured to the cog-toothed entrance to her forge.

'Then feel free to leave, but know that no priest of the Cult Mechanicus will ever let you inside their temple again.'

Abrehem slammed the open palm of his artificial arm on the book of quantum runes.

'Then tell me, Adept Manubia,' he said. 'What *do* you do? What vital role in the operations of the *Speranza* are these poor wretches involved in?'

'Nothing,' said Manubia. 'They're too broken to be of any use.'

Abrehem shook his head. 'Then I don't see any point in me being here.'

'You didn't let me finish,' said Manubia. 'They're here *because* they're broken. But by the time they leave, they won't be. I gather up the waifs and strays of the Cult Mechanicus – the damaged, the broken, the data-blind, the augment-crippled – and I give them purpose again. I rebuild and remake what's broken inside them and I make them useful again. I give them purpose. And that's what I can do for you, if you'll let me.'

'I'm not broken,' said Abrehem.

'Aren't you?' said Manubia, her face lit from below by a swiftly glowing illumination.

Abrehem looked down, his eyes widening as he saw the etched copper diagram of the Ohmic Evocation fill with liquid light that flowed from his iron fingers. The metalled surface of the book felt hot to the touch, the light penetrating deeper into its pages with each passing second.

'Whatever you're doing, stop it now,' demanded Manubia. 'Lift your aug-metic from the book.'

Abrehem shook his head. 'I can't,' he said.

Golden light poured from the book, following the corded cables plugged into the base of the lectern. It lit the forge in a radiance it had not known since its earliest days, passing through the archaic trunking system and into the crippled tech-priests.

They stiffened as the light flowed into them and through them, seeking new pathways to illuminate, new circuits to restore. Thousands of snaking threads of golden light moved through the machine-temple, racing along frayed and forgotten wires. The Icon Mechanicus shimmered with reflected radiance as ancient wiring within the throne that had not known the touch of electro-motive power in millennia pulsed with life.

'How are you doing this?' gasped Manubia. '*What* are you doing?'

Abrehem had no answer for her, watching as first one, then another of the dormant machines around the perimeter of Chiron Manubia's forge flickered with its own internal light.

Ancient cogs turned with grating squeals, rusted gears cranked into pain-ful motion and long-stilled machine hearts began beating once more.

One by one, the titanic engines returned to life.

THE APPROACH TO the bridge of the *Speranza* was a towering processional vault known as the Path to Wisdom, precisely one thousand metres long, with sixty equidistant archways to either side. Threaded columns wound with variant binary forms supported the latticework tangle of green iron girders and a cloud layer of lubricant incense clung to the corbels, where squatted fat mechanical cherubs. Long strips of votive binary chattered from their mouths, random praise to the Omnissiah that teams of tech-priests and lexmechanics studied intently for any divine messages.

Sheet metal banners hung within the arches, each venerating a different branch of Mechanicus theology, from shield technology to teleportation, from weapon design to engine maintenance. A great Icon Mechanicus stared down in judgement at those who approached.

None of the tech-priests surrounded by strips of ticker-tape around the base of each column paid any attention to the small, determined group making its way to the monolithic adamantium gates of the bridge.

Vitali Tychon led the way, with Kayrn Sylkwood, Emil Nader and Adara Siavash struggling to keep up with the venerable adept. The crew of the *Renard* were armed, which Emil wasn't so sure was a good idea. But as soon as Vitali had managed to explain why he was covered in blood, Emil knew a confrontation was inevitable.

And if life on Ultramar had taught Emil anything, it was that it was always a good idea to be prepared for the worst.

The vast door to the bridge was protected by a demi-cohort of praetorians, clanking mechanised killers on tracks, articulated stalk legs or heavy Dreadnought chassis. Their armaments were a lethal array of plasma weaponry, rotor carbines and linked lascannons. Smaller than the praetorians were the weaponised servitors, grotesquely augmented humans with steroidal musculatures, sub-dermal armour plating and vicious arrays of implanted blades, drills and power fists.

Emil shared a glance with Kayrn Sylkwood. Neither was a stranger to mass warfare, but these cyborgs were something else entirely – metal-masked and dispassionate.

Their approach had been noted, and every one of the Mechanicus battle-servitors turned its targeting auspex upon them. Emil had never felt quite so vulnerable.

'No sudden movements,' said Vitali, his voice cold, where normally it was infectiously vibrant. 'Let me take care of this.'

'Don't you worry about that,' said Emil, keeping his hands well away from his hand cannon. The weapon had been his father's, presented to him upon earning his captaincy in the Espandor Defence Auxilia. Emil had inherited it upon his father's death a month later. Talassarian mother-of-pearl was embedded in the walnut grip in the shape of an ultima.

'Do you actually know how to use that thing?' asked Sylkwood.

He nodded. 'I know every inch of this gun,' said Emil. He'd maintained it with all the due diligence drummed into him since childhood. 'It's in as perfect working order as it was the day it left the craftsman's workbench.'

'You ever fired it?'

'No, not once.'

'Good to know,' said Sylkwood.

'Look, it's not me you need to worry about,' said Emil, nodding towards Adara Siavash. The youthfully handsome gunman had come aboard the

Renard a number of years ago as a passenger, but after proving he had what it took to use his pistols and ubiquitous butterfly blade, Roboute had decided to keep him on as a member of the crew. For a man so intimate with ways of ending life, he wore his heart on his sleeve, and had been endearingly sweet in his hopeless infatuation with Mistress Linya.

Emil had seen Adara fight and kill, but until now, he'd never seen him angry. The cold, unflinching, razor-fine hostility he saw in the youth's eyes was not something he'd ever expected to see.

'Listening, Adara?' said Sylkwood. 'Let Vitali take the lead.'

The young gunman nodded, but didn't reply.

Sylkwood shrugged with an *I tried* expression.

Vitali didn't slow his pace as he approached the praetorians and weaponised servitors. Auspexes clicked and whirred as lenses extended, gathering information from Vitali's noospheric aura. Satisfied it was addressing a being that didn't qualify for immediate destruction, a towering praetorian armed with twin power fists extended a vox-unit from its throat.

'Magos Vitali Tychon, stellar cartographer, AM4543/1001011.'

'Stand down,' said Vitali.

An internal cogitator whirred within its cranium and a chattering stream of tape emerged from the back of its skull.

'Your presence has not been requested.'

'I'm aware of that, but I'm going onto the bridge and you are not going to stop me.'

'Without current authorised access privileges, entry to the bridge is impossible,' said the praetorian.

'I am a high magos of the Adeptus Mechanicus,' snapped Vitali. 'Are you going to stop me?'

'Updated bridge security protocols authorise the use of force up to and including, but not limited to, lethal levels.'

Emil felt a layer of sweat form all over his body. The cyborg was talking about killing them with as much thought as he might give to stepping on a ship louse.

He leaned over to whisper to Kayrn. 'If I'm going to die here, I'd rather it was at the hands of something that gave a damn about killing me.'

'Yeah, because that makes dying *so* much better,' she said.

'Are you denying me access to the bridge?' said Vitali.

'Affirmative, Magos Tychon,' confirmed the praetorian. 'Do you wish me to submit a priority access request to Magos Blaylock?'

'No, I want you to open the damn door.'

'Your request cannot be completed at this time.'

Vitali turned to Emil and the others.

'Master Nader, Master Siavash, I'd cover my ears if I were you. And, Mistress Sylkwood, please mute any noospheric-capable communion receptors if you please. I apologise in advance for what will, I'm sure, be most unpleasant.'

Emil knew better than to ask why and pressed his hands hard over his ears as Vitali turned back to the intransigent praetorian. Adara followed his example as Kayrn thumped the heel of one palm to the side of her head.

Vitali squared his shoulders and addressed the praetorian again. 'I didn't want to have to do this, but you've left me no choice.'

Before the servitor could answer, Vitali unleashed a shriek of violent binary from his chest augmitters. Even with his hands clamped over his ears, Emil felt it like someone had just detonated a bomb in the centre of his skull. Sylkwood dropped to one knee, her face twisted in pain.

As painful as Vitali's binaric shriek was for them, the effect on the praetorians and weaponised servitors was far more spectacular. Relays within iron skulls exploded and implanted doctrina wafers melted upon receipt of self-immolation protocols. Every synaptic connection within the servitors' heads blew instantaneously. Orange flames licked from their eye sockets and fatty smoke curled from those whose mouths were not already sealed shut. The stalk-limbed praetorian crashed to the ground, its weapon arms falling limply to its sides. Bipedal combat servitors fell where they stood, like remotely piloted automatons whose operators had been abruptly yanked from their immersion rigs.

The grating, screeching wail rose and fell, like a novice vox-operator trying to find an active channel. Blood dripped from Sylkwood's nose, and veins like power couplings stood out on the side of her neck.

Then, mercifully, it ended.

'What did you do?' asked Emil, gingerly taking his hands from the side of his head.

'To many aboard the *Speranza*, I may be the eccentric stellar cartographer Archmagos Kotov dragged from obscurity,' said Vitali, 'but I am also a high magos of the Adeptus Mechanicus. There isn't a cyborg aboard this ship I don't know how to destroy.'

Vitali stepped over the smouldering corpses of the combat cyborgs. Their limbs twitched with rogue impulses as the molten remnants of their brains disintegrated in the wake of Vitali's binaric holocaust.

The towering bridge doors began to open.

'And now I'm going to kill the abomination that murdered my daughter,' said Vitali.

Microcontent 04

FLICKERING LIGHTS AND arcs of energy were nothing unusual on Exnihlio, but the amber shimmer dancing in a steelwork canyon between two soaring coolant towers had nothing to do with the designs of Archmagos Telok.

Everything on Exnihlio was angular and harsh, but this light grew steadily from a graceful ellipse to a wide oval, some five metres in height. Where it touched the ground, it flattened to form a harmoniously proportioned, leaf-shaped archway.

The sounds that issued from the light were laments from an ancient age, a time before the rise of mankind, and spoke of the profound sorrow of a dying race that could never be articulated in mere words.

A figure stepped from the fluid light, monstrously tall, but slender-limbed, fleshless and formed from a gleaming material that had the appearance of the most flawless ceramic. Its emerald skull was an elongated teardrop, its shoulders vaned with sweeping spines like wings. Its arms looked too thin to be dangerous, but each had the power to crush steel and stone and flesh.

Uldanaish Ghostwalker was a wraithlord, and he had fought in the armies of Craftworld Biel-tan for seven centuries. Two of those centuries had been as a disembodied spirit, bound to this wraithbone warrior-construct by unbreakable bonds of duty.

Ghostwalker rose to his full height, and spread both arms out to either side, the weapons extruded from his fists ready to destroy any target that presented itself.

None did, and the armoured giant took a step to the side as more figures followed it from the honeyed light. First to follow the wraithlord onto the surface of Exnihlio was Ariganna Icefang, exarch of the Twilight Blade Aspect Shrine. Clad in plates of emerald and gold that overlapped like drake-scale and sinuously adapted to her form as though more flesh than armour, she was the perfect warrior in every way. One hand was a bladed claw, while her other held an enormous chainsabre.

A pack of hunched warriors followed her, bulkily armoured in jade and with helms of ivory. Stinger-like mandibles flickered at their cheek-plates, and each had a pistol and sword at the ready.

Following the Striking Scorpions came the Howling Banshees, warrior women clad in form-fitting flex-armour and gracefully sculpted plates of ivory and crimson. Like their more heavily armoured cousins, the Banshees carried swords and pistols, but had an altogether faster, lighter appearance that belied their exquisite lethality.

Last to step through the sunset gate was a lithe figure in rune-etched armour of gold, green and cream. An iridescent cloak of subtly interwoven gold and emerald billowed from Bielanna's shoulders, and a scarlet plume flew from her antlered helm. Alone of the eldar, she did not have a weapon drawn, her filigreed sword still belted at her waist.

No sooner had Bielanna set foot on Exnihlio than a cry of pain escaped her lips. She staggered as though struck and dropped to her knees. The sunset gate faded like a forgotten dream.

The eldar warriors formed a circle around their farseer, weapons at the ready. Bielanna climbed unsteadily to her feet, looking around her as though unsure of what she was seeing. Imperial worlds tasted of rancid meat and burned metal, ripe with the overwhelming reek of mon-keigh desires, a maelstrom of fleeting, venal emotions, but the voice of this world was utterly singular in its ambition.

The force of it almost drove her to her knees once more.

'Farseer?' said Ariganna Icefang, looming over Bielanna.

Bielanna struggled to master the sensations roiling within her. Her psychic senses were being assailed by a push and pull of fates, interwoven destinies of the warriors around her and... and what?

'I see it all...' she whispered, shutting her eyes to keep the assault on her senses from overwhelming her.

'What do you see?' said Ariganna Icefang.

'Conflicting futures and unwritten histories,' gasped Bielanna.

Farseers trained their entire lives to read the twisting weave of the future within the skein, and as much discipline was required to keep the innumerable possibilities that would never come to pass at bay.

But no amount of training and devotion could keep this confluence of past and future from swamping her.

'The futures grind against one another,' said Bielanna. 'Each strains to move from potential to reality, and their struggle to exist will destroy them all.'

'Speak plainly,' said the exarch. 'Can you find the mon-keigh?'

Bielanna tried to answer, but the words stuck in her throat as she looked up into the Striking Scorpion exarch's war-mask.

Ariganna's helm was hung with knotted cords of woven wraithbone and psycho-conductive crystal, but Bielanna saw beyond the smooth faceplate to the exarch's cruelly beautiful features. The Aspect Warrior's eyes were gateways to madness, filled with the monomaniacal fury of inescapable devotion to death.

Bielanna saw not one face, but three. Each true in its own way.

A youthful face, flush with the newly awakened promise of femininity. The face of seasoned womanhood, freighted with wisdom. And lastly, a crone, burdened and ravaged by life's savagery.

'The three in one,' said Bielanna. 'The Maiden, the Woman and the Crone... All future and past weave together here and nothing will ever be the same.'

Her gaze moved to Tariquel, whom she had known as a dancer before the bloody song of Khaine had drawn him to the Shrine of the Twilight Blade. His face was as she remembered it when he had wept to the *Swans of Isha's Memory*. Delicate as a wraithbone web-sculpt, tender as moonlight on the surface of a lake.

Vaynesh the poet, who had laughed in the field of corpses on the surface of Magdelon, was similarly transformed. Bielanna saw the face of the boy he had once been, the vain, prideful killer he had become and the serene death-mask that loomed in his future.

Bielanna saw the same dance of ages in every face. She saw each warrior as they once were and who they might yet be.

She sobbed as Ariganna placed a clawed gauntlet on her shoulder.

'The mon-keigh,' demanded the exarch. 'Can you find them?'

'This world hangs over a precipice,' said Bielanna. 'And should it end, the effects will be like unto the Fall.'

'I care nothing for this world,' hissed the exarch. 'You spoke of a cuckoo in the nest, a mortal marked by another of your kind?'

Bielanna nodded. 'Roboute Surcouf, yes...'

'Can you find him?'

The face of the mon-keigh appeared in her mind, constant and unwavering. She had marked him aboard the human starship, hadn't she? She remembered that, but assailed by phantom images of an unlived past and a thousand futures, she was no longer sure her memories could be trusted.

'I can,' she said.

'Then do so,' said Ariganna, turning from Bielanna. 'The murder of our kin must be repaid in the blood of their deaths.'

'Death?' said Bielanna, her mind afire with the possibilities opened up by Ariganna Icefang's words. 'Is death the only answer?'

'The only one worth knowing,' said the exarch.

'It is the only one you know how to give, Ariganna, but does that make it the right one? Nothing is ever as straightforward as life or death, right and wrong.'

The exarch stood before her, threat radiating from her every movement.

'All your visions have led us to doom, farseer,' said Ariganna. 'Give me a reason to trust them now.'

Bielanna forced a clarity to her mind that she knew was as fragile as a promise between lovers.

'An infinite web of possibility spreads from this moment,' she said. 'And every one hangs upon a single thread, but whether we are to cut that thread or preserve it is beyond my power to see.'

'Then you have no answer I can use.'

'No,' agreed Bielanna.

'Just lead me to the mon-keigh,' said Ariganna.

Bielanna nodded and conjured the image of Roboute Surcouf into her mind's eye. She felt his presence on this world burning strongly, a mortal with a bright thread that was all too easy to discern amid the barren, lifeless scab of this world's skin.

'They are close,' said Bielanna. 'Very close.'

'Good,' said Ariganna, clenching a fist above her head. 'We move swiftly, and then we will see what death may do.'

EVERYONE ON THE bridge felt it. Like a red-hot skewer had just been jammed up through the bases of their skulls. Implanted servitors spasmed in silvered implant bays, heads rolling slack as synaptic-breakers cut the connection between the machines in their skulls and the *Speranza*.

A data prism blew out on the ceiling, sending multi-spectral bands of data-light skewing in all directions. Alarm chimes sounded and noospheric warnings streamed up like smoke from the smooth floor.

Magos Tarkis Blaylock, Fabricatus Locum of the *Speranza*, had cognitive speed enough to shut down his receptors in time to avoid the worst of the binaric assault, but not all of it. His vision blurred and he gripped on to the armrests of the command throne as he felt his internal gyros lose all sense of spatial awareness.

Kryptaestrex stomped away from his data hub, trailing sparks from where an inload cable had fused to his blocky outline. The component parts of Azuramagelli's disembodied brain flared with electrical disturbance. Even Galatea staggered at the force of it, two of the machine-hybrid's legs collapsing as its brain jars crackled with internal forks of energy.

Blaylock felt full awareness return in time to register the fact that the main door to the bridge was opening. Not the cog-toothed iris the bridge crew used to pass back and forth, but the towering portal itself. All fifty metres of its height were grinding back on squealing hinges, dislodging centuries of dust and flakes of corrosion.

How long had it been since that door had opened in its entirety?

Blaylock's vision was still hazed with static, but he had enough clarity to recognise Vitali Tychon and three members of Roboute Surcouf's crew: pilot, enginseer and hired gun. The force of belligerent code surging through Magos Tychon's floodstream shocked Blaylock, the binaric forms assembled in their most aggressive, direct format. His noospherics were as hostile as anything Dahan had blurted.

Blaylock's vocals were offline. He switched to flesh-voice.

'Magos Tychon, what is the meaning of this?'

'Stay out of this, Tarkis,' said Vitali, pointing one of his delicate, multi-fingered hands towards the forward surveyor array. 'I'm here for that *thing*. That murderer.'

Blaylock assumed his aural-implants had been damaged. Tychon was pointing towards Galatea.

'What are you talking about, Magos Tychon? What murderer?'

'The thing that calls itself Galatea,' said Vitali. 'It killed my daughter.'

'Quite the opposite,' said Galatea, rising to its full height once again. Ripples of feedback coiled around its limbs and the silver eyes of its tech-priest proxy body glittered with excess energy. 'Her flesh is dead, that is true, but your daughter's mind is very much alive, Magos Tychon. As well you know.'

Vitali strode through the bridge as the *Speranza*'s systems began restarting with the thudding clatter of resetting breakers. Emergency lights flickered out as the bridge lumens sputtered to life and alert chimes were silenced. Blaylock rose from the command throne and moved to intercept the aged cartographer.

'Do I take it you know what Magos Tychon is talking about?'

'We do,' said Galatea.

'You cut her skull open!' wailed Vitali, his voice now cracking under the strain of facing his daughter's killer. 'You removed her brain and stuck it in a glass jar!'

'Where she now resides in harmony, freed from the intellectual limitations of flesh,' said Galatea. 'Enriching our neuromatrix with her agile mind and unconventional modes of thought.'

Blaylock now understood. 'Ave Deus Mechanicus!'

'The synaptic pathways of Magos Thraimen had deteriorated to the point where it became impossible to justify his presence within our neuromatrix,' continued Galatea. 'His hibernation nightmares were exquisite, but the presence of such an exceptional brain in the form of Mistress Tychon made his continued presence indulgent.'

'I've come to destroy you,' hissed Magos Tychon. 'I'd say *kill*, but you have to be alive and possess a soul in order to die.'

Blaylock felt a cataclysmic build-up of killing binary within the noosphere. He knew what Magos Tychon intended. And as biological as it was, Blaylock even understood his need for retribution.

But he could not allow him to continue.

<Magos Tychon, stand down!> ordered Blaylock, his augmitters freighted with every last one of his rank signifiers to countermand Tychon's war-code. Mistress Tychon's father reeled with the force of Blaylock's commands, his face lit with grief as his disassembler cant was splintered into harmless code fragments.

'No! Blaylock, no…' said Vitali, stumbling onto the central dais and reaching out to him, half mad with grief. 'That thing murdered my Linya. You must let me do this.'

'I cannot, Magos Tychon,' said Blaylock, backing away from Tychon. 'You know how deeply Galatea has enmeshed itself with the *Speranza*. If you kill it, you kill us. I cannot let you do this.'

He sat down in the command throne and turned his gaze upon the squatting machine-hybrid. 'Though I dearly wish I could.'

Magos Tychon fell to his knees, gripping Blaylock's arms.

'Please, Tarkis, kill it,' pleaded Tychon. 'You must know it will never let the *Speranza* go. Kill it now!'

'He cannot,' said Galatea. 'Logic sits high in the mind of Magos Blaylock. He knows that to kill us is to destroy any chance of his advancement in the Cult Mechanicus, and Tarkis *so* wishes to return to Mars, don't you, Tarkis?'

'They will burn you on Mars,' said Blaylock. 'They will never accept you.'

'We believe they will,' said Galatea, cocking its head to the side. 'With such a powerful advocate as you at our side, how could they not?'

Blaylock shook his head, disgusted that Galatea would ever think he would stand alongside it in support. He sensed a deeper meaning to the machine-hybrid's words, but this was not the time to consider them.

'You're going to let it get away with killing Linya?' said a young man, throwing off the restraining arm of his fellows. He had no augments to provide identifying signifiers, but Blaylock's internal database of embedded non-Mechanicus crew produced his name virtually instantaneously.

Adara Siavash. His entry listed no world of origin, but even a cursory bioscan suggested Ultramarian genestock. That, in turn, suggested a heightened sense of justice that could prove volatile in an already highly charged situation. Tears of grief streaked the young man's face.

'Come on, Adara,' said Emil Nader, the *Renard*'s pilot. 'I know you were soft on Miss Linya, but this is just crazy. And trust me, I know crazy.'

Nader's words and the boy's own tears told Blaylock that the boy had been hopelessly in love with Linya Tychon. Which marked him as a fool and even more dangerous.

'Adara, I can't believe I'm saying this, but please listen to Emil,' said the enginseer – Kayrn Sylkwood, a Cadian who had been mustered out of her regiment following a devastating loss of vehicles during the latest war spasms around the Eye of Terror. 'If Vitali can't take it down, what chance do you have?'

'Vitali tried subtle,' said Siavash. 'I don't do subtle.'

The boy drew his pistol and aimed it right at the heart of Galatea. Blaylock felt a moment of real fear as he saw a heavily converted Maukren Flensar with integral phosphex coils to increase muzzle velocity and impact trauma. Anything struck by that weapon would be gutted by a white-hot, fist-to-finger plasma core.

'If we were you, we would put that gun down,' said Galatea.

'I'm going to burn you alive,' said Siavash, his finger curling through the trigger guard.

'No!' cried Blaylock, rising from the throne.

'For Linya,' said Siavash, and fired the Maukren.

The weapon exploded, engulfing the boy's hand in a blooming corona of blue-hot flame. Too fast for the human eye to follow, the phosphex slithered up his arm like a living thing. It leapt onto his torso, billowing flames roaring and seething like an enraged predator.

'Adara! Throne, no!' screamed Sylkwood, tearing off her battered jerkin and attempting to beat the flames out. The jerkin instantly burst into flames as the overpowering heat from the flames forced the enginseer back.

'Help him!' shouted Nader, pulling Sylkwood away from the fire.

Blaylock shook his head. Phosphex could devour flesh and turn bones to grease in moments. The boy was already past saving.

Siavash dropped to the deck, dying without screams, the flames having seared the oxygen from his lungs. Localised fire suppression systems deployed from the deck and sprayed the burning body with a fire-retardant foam that hardened like a scab and starved the blaze of oxygen.

Emil Nader and Sylkwood supported each other, staring in hatred at Galatea, which watched the young boy's ending dispassionately, arms folded across its chest.

'Emperor damn you, Tarkis Blaylock,' said Nader. 'Do you know what you've done?'

'Me? I did nothing,' said Blaylock.

'Exactly my point.'

'I did nothing because there was nothing that could be done. The boy was dead the moment he pulled the trigger.'

Sylkwood threw off Nader's grip and strode towards Galatea.

'You did that,' she said. 'You fouled the firing mechanism or twisted the gun's war-spirit or did something that made it misfire. You've got Blaylock cowed, but I promise you that when this is all over, I'll be there to see you die.'

'Brave words for a biological entity whose unexceptional brain we could boil within her skull,' said Galatea, leaning forwards, its silver eyes glittering like the ferryman's coins. 'Shall we show you how painful that would be?'

'Enough,' said Blaylock. 'There will be no more death today. Mister Nader, I suggest you remove Magos Tychon and Enginseer Sylkwood from the bridge. Nothing good can come from further confrontation.'

Nader shot a venomous look at Galatea before nodding and taking Sylkwood's arm. For a moment, Blaylock thought the Cadian might do something foolish. But foolish and Cadian didn't go together, and she spat on the deck at Galatea's feet before turning towards Blaylock.

'You're a real piece of work, Magos Blaylock,' she said. 'You know that, right?'

Blaylock said nothing. Sylkwood's statement was too obtuse and vague to warrant a reply. In any case, it seemed she didn't expect one, for she turned and marched from the bridge.

Vitali Tychon's head remained bowed in defeat, and Blaylock felt a genuine stab of sympathy for the venerable cartographer.

'Magos Tychon, I–'

'Don't, Tarkis,' said Vitali. 'Just don't. Kotov told me we were looking for new stars, but that thing has just snuffed out the brightest star I knew.'

'You are wrong, Magos Tychon,' said Galatea. 'Your daughter burns just as bright inside me. Trouble us again and we will snuff out her essence as easily as we extinguished the boy.'

'Shut up!' shouted Blaylock. 'Ave Deus Mechanicus, shut up!'

TOO VAST TO comprehend, too artificial to be natural, the spherical volume beneath the layered skin of the dome was a wonder of engineering. Surpassing any geodesic vault on Terra, it was, quite simply, the most impressive feat of structural mechanics Kotov had ever seen.

The Imperial explorators stood on an equatorial gantry that encircled the spherical void gouged in the planet's bedrock. Many others encircled the chamber above and below them, with jutting piers and scaffolds of unknown machinery cantilevered into space.

The mass of a small moon had been dug from Exnihlio, and the surface of the excavated volume was encrusted with technology unlike anything seen on Mars. Angular glyphs like temple icons were graven in the curves of the chamber, rendered in a language that was at once familiar yet inhuman.

Thousands of crystaliths of all shapes and descriptions crawled across the inner surfaces of the void, engaged in maintenance, calibration and who knew what else. An ochre miasma, rank with the foetor of turned earth and exposed rock, drifted up though a shaft bored down through the base of the chamber.

A venting system, drainage? Who could tell?

Yet the magnificence of the space paled to insignificance when measured against the incredible appearance of that which it enclosed.

The Breath of the Gods hung suspended in the exact centre of the space, a vast, threshing, interweaving gyre of glittering metal blades that seemed to have no supporting structure at its core, just an achingly bright nexus of fractal incandescence. Like the first instant of a supernova or a glittering map of synaptic architecture.

Though Kotov's visual augments were among the most sophisticated conceived by the molecular grinders of the Euryphaessan forges, he could form no coherent impression of the device's exact dimensions. Geometric assayers flashed error codes to his glassine retinas with each failed attempt to quantify what he was seeing.

Like a tubular hurricane of silver leaves, the Breath of the Gods formed an elongated elliptical outline that defied easy assimilation. Its very existence was subtly discordant, as though some innate property of the human brain knew this device was somehow *wrong*, as though it abused every tenet of thermodynamics with spiteful relish.

Its complex internal topography was a squirming mass of pulsating metal that Kotov's senses told him should be impossible. Portions of the colossal machine appeared to co-exist in the same space, moving *through* one another in violation of perspective.

Even those not reconfigured by the Adeptus Mechanicus found the machine disquieting to look upon. More so, it appeared. A number of Cadians doubled over to empty the contents of their stomachs across the perforated gantry. Idly, Kotov speculated as to the effect their dripping vomitus might have on the alien technology worked into the surfaces below.

Even the unsubtle minds of the Black Templars were enraptured by the sight of the device. Sergeant Tanna raised a hand as through reaching for it, while his white-helmed champion gripped the hilt of his black sword.

The machine – though Kotov's sensibilities rebelled at the notion of labelling something so clearly beyond current Mechanicus paradigms with such a mundane term – had an aura within this colossal space that went beyond the simply mechanical.

It seemed (and here Kotov's mind *did* rebel) to have a presence akin to a living being, as though it looked back at the tiny specks of consciousness beneath it and was content to allow them to bask in its wondrous impossibility.

Kotov shook off the notion, but like a shard of stubbornly invasive scrapcode, it could not be dismissed.

'It's...' started Kotov, but he had not the words to describe what he was feeling. 'It's...'

Telok appeared at his side, a hulking presence whose crystalline elements shimmered with reflected light from the inconstant flux of the machinery above him.

'I understand,' said Telok. 'It takes time to adapt to the singular nature of the device. For a human mind, even one enhanced by the Mechanicus, to grasp its complexity requires so thorough a remapping of the synaptic pathways and subsequent cognitive evolution that it can scarcely be called human anymore.'

Kotov nodded in wonder, barely hearing Telok, his eyes constantly drawn to the Breath of the Gods' discomfiting aspect. It felt like the machine exerted some irresistible pull on his senses, as though demanding to be the sole focus of all who stood in its presence.

'You found it...' Kotov managed at last.

'I did,' affirmed Telok.

'How? It was a myth, a barely remembered legend from the hidden manuscripts of madmen and heretics.'

'By following the clues left by its builders,' said Telok, walking around the gently curved gantry, forcing Kotov and the others to follow him. 'Those madmen were once seekers after truth like us, men who uncovered those truths but whose minds were ill-equipped to process their significance.'

'So who was it that built this?' asked Roboute Surcouf, with a tone that suggested he might know the answer.

'An ancient race whose identity has long since been forgotten by the inexorable obscurity of time,' said Telok, waving a dismissive hand, as though who had built the machine was less important than who now controlled it. 'Whatever they called themselves, they passed through our galaxy millions of years ago. They were godlike beings, sculpting the matter of the universe to suit their desires with technology far beyond anything you could possibly imagine. They came here, perhaps hoping to begin the process anew, extending the limits of this innocuous spiral cluster of star-systems. They thought to connect all the universe with stepping stones of newly wrought galaxies they would build from the raw materials scattered by the ekpyrotic creation of space-time itself.'

'So what happened to this race of gods?' asked Ven Anders, nervously glancing up at the rotating flurry of machinery. 'If they were so powerful, why aren't they still here? Why haven't we heard of them before?'

'Because, Colonel Anders, nothing is ever really immortal, not even the gods themselves,' said Telok. 'In truth, I do not know exactly what happened to them, but in the deep vaults of this world I found fragmentary evidence of a weaponised psychic bio-agent that escaped its long imprisonment and destroyed the genius of their minds, reducing them to the level of beasts. Within a generation of the first infection, they had all but wiped themselves out.'

Telok paused, moving to the edge of the gantry, looking up at the swirling mass of silver and crackling arcs of elemental power with a look of rapture.

'It is my belief that with the last of their faculties, these gods set the device to become self-sustaining and self-repairing, shutting down all but its most basic functions until either far-flung survivors of their race returned to claim it or a species arose with the capacity to be their inheritors. I humbly submit that I am that inheritor.'

Telok now turned his gaze on Kotov, and the archmagos saw an expression that suggested anything but humility. His cognitive processes ran hot as he struggled to keep pace with what he was hearing. Fighting to keep his awe and unease in check, Kotov's analytical faculties came to the fore and found much in Telok's explanations that simply did not match his understanding of universal laws.

'And you claim that this is the device responsible for the celestial engineering events we witnessed at Katen Venia and Hypatia?'

'Claim?' said Telok. 'You doubt my word on this?'

Kotov heard the threat in Telok's voice and carefully framed his next words as a question of science, not character.

'What I mean is that it is beyond belief that any one device could have the power to achieve such a feat,' said Kotov. 'What empowers the Breath of the Gods? How can this one world, no matter how much energy it generates, provide even an infinitesimal fraction of the power that must surely be required to reshape the cosmos? I do not doubt your word, but the technological mastery needed to restore machinery abandoned millions of years ago by a lost alien race is staggering.'

Kotov lifted his gaze to the swirling, shimmering machine that filled the air above him, knowing that there was one question above all to which he needed an answer.

'How did you do all this alone?' he asked.

Telok heard his incredulity and responded just as bluntly.

'The hidden instructions left by the Stellar Primogenitor's builders were incredibly precise, archmagos. Marrying them to my peerless intellect, I unlocked a series of unambiguous structural and mathematical prescriptions that enabled me to replicate the conditions of physical reality found within the Noctis Labyrinthus and thus bring the device to life.'

Kotov's face drained of what little colour it possessed. 'Do not speak of that benighted place!'

Telok waved an admonishing finger, a bladed hook of entwined metal and parasitic crystal.

'Do not warn me of anything in the same breath you ask me how the device functions, archmagos,' warned Telok. 'Even were current paradigms of Martian thinking capable of understanding any answers I might offer, you would not find them to your liking. They would upset your outmoded thinking and I know all too well how the Adeptus Mechanicus hates those who disrupt the stagnancy of their precious status quo.'

Kotov shook his head, wearying of Telok's monstrous ego. He held Telok's gaze, speaking clearly so that there could be no mistaking the clarity of his words.

'I am an archmagos of the Adeptus Mechanicus, and I own only the empirical clarity of the Omnissiah,' said Kotov. 'You, Archmagos Telok, are bound by the strictures of our order and the ideals of the Quest for Knowledge to divulge what you have learned.'

'Oh, I shall,' snapped Telok, the crystalline structure of his body flaring an aggressive crimson. 'Have no fear of that, but as I have said, it will be at a time and place of my choosing.'

Telok took a crashing step towards Kotov, his heavy limbs ablaze with internal fire and his fists clenched into pounding hammers.

'And that will be when I take the vessel with which you have so thoughtfully provided me back to Mars in triumph,' said Telok. 'It will be when I stand atop Olympus Mons as the new master of the Red Planet.'

The skitarii surrounding Kotov growled at Telok's heretical pronouncements. Their weapon systems initiated, but Telok disengaged them with a blurt of high-level binary. They froze as their every internal augmentation seized up a heartbeat later.

'And when I have remade the Mechanicus in my image,' continued Telok, 'I will use the Breath of the Gods to surge the heart of Terra's sun to burn the rotting corpse of the Emperor and all his corrupt servants from its surface.'

The Black Templars' speed and aggression were phenomenal.

No sooner had Telok spoken than they were on the offensive. No pause, no ramping up of fury. One minute the towering warriors were still, the next at full battle-pitch.

Telok raised a hand and each of the Space Marines froze in place, paralysed as thoroughly as the skitarii. Kotov read the frenetic tempo of the machine-spirits within their battleplate as they fought to overcome Telok's paralysing code.

'I will become the new Master of Mankind,' laughed Telok. 'A ruler devoted to the attainment of the Singularity of Consciousness.'

Kotov turned from Telok's insanity as he heard the brittle sound of glass grinding on glass. Perhaps a hundred crystaliths were climbing onto the gantry from the inwardly curving slopes of the chamber, a similar number from below. They took up position all around the Cadians, extruded weapons ready to cut them down in a lethal crossfire.

'What are you doing?' said Kotov. 'This is insane!'

'Insane?' said Telok derisively. 'How could you possibly understand the mind of a god?'

'Is that what you think you are?' demanded Kotov.

'I created this entire region of space,' roared Telok, his voice afire with the passion of an Ecclesiarchy battle-preacher. 'I have reignited the hearts of dead suns, crafted star systems from the waste matter of the universe and wrought life from death. If that does not give me the right to name myself a god, then what does?'

Microcontent 05

QUATRIA HAD ALWAYS possessed a utilitarian aesthetic, but with her surroundings now crafted from memory, it had assumed an altogether bleaker aspect. The corridors were cold; though Linya knew, of course, that she wasn't truly feeling cold. Her mind was conjuring that sensation based upon perceived sensory data.

As thorough and detailed a simulation as Galatea had rendered, the human mind was capable of seeing through almost any visual deception. The walls were just a little too crisply etched, the patterns not quite three-dimensional enough to entirely convince.

Linya walked with her arms wrapped around her body, as though hugging herself for comfort. Pointless, she knew. After all, what measure of physical comfort could be offered to a disembodied brain in a jar?

Yet some habits were too hard to break. It didn't matter that her body was dead, her mind lived on. Enslaved by an abomination unto the Machine-God, yes, but enduring. Only by the slenderest margin had Linya held on to sanity at the sight of her skull hinged back and the bloody void within. Anyone not of the Mechanicus would likely have gone insane at such a vision, but the first lesson taught to neophytes of the Cult Mechanicus was that flesh was inferior to technology, that thought and memory and intellect were the true successors of flesh.

Indeed, wasn't the final apotheosis striven for by the adepts of Mars, a freeing of pure intellect from the limitations of flesh and blood? Wasn't that why so many of the Cult Mechanicus were so quick to shed their humanity and embrace mechanical augmentations in their ascent towards the ideal Singularity of Consciousness?

Linya had never subscribed to the notion of flesh's abandonment, believing that to sacrifice all that made you human was to cut yourself off from the very thing that made life so wondrous.

Did her father know what had happened to her?

Grief swamped her every time she thought of him. She hoped he hadn't been the one to find her. She hoped that someone had sanitised the scene of her physical death. She didn't want to think what the sight of her lying on her medicae bed, cut open like a dissection subject, might do to his psyche.

Vitali Tychon was often dismissed as a harmless eccentric, but Linya knew him to have a determined, ruthless core. She hoped he hadn't done something foolish upon learning of her death. Galatea would kill him without a second thought, and as fiercely intelligent as Vitali was, she knew Galatea would never risk assimilating him into its neuromatrix.

Linya had no idea how much time had passed since Galatea had first shown her the truth of her condition, that portion of her cranial implantation removed along with any conventional means of linking to the outside world. Her high-level implants appeared to be functional, but without advanced diagnostics it was impossible to be sure what the machine intelligence had left her.

Linya looked up as she heard a circular door iris open beside her. The confero. Every Mechanicus facility had one, a sanctified chamber where matters of techno-theology could be discussed and debated at length under the benevolent gaze of the Omnissiah.

Linya ignored the door and kept walking.

She had already explored every portion of the Quatrian Galleries as they were known to her. The parts she knew best were lifelike down to the smallest detail, but those areas she was less familiar with had an unfinished quality, like a Theatrica Imperialis set designed only to be viewed from a distance. The farthest portions of the orbital, which she had known only from schematics, were little more than bare, wire-frame walls and lifeless renderings of the most basic structural elements.

It was towards this region of Quatria Linya walked, finding Galatea's false representation of a place she had once called home repugnant. Better to surround herself with obviously fake surroundings, to keep the truth of her imprisonment uppermost.

The corridor curved around to the left, but where she had expected to find the lateral transit that led to the central hub, she instead found herself in the communal deck levels. Along the wall, the irising door to the confero opened up once more.

'I won't be your puppet,' said Linya.

She ignored the door and kept walking, taking paths at random and moving further into the orbital, trying to lose herself in its deeper structure.

But no matter which path she took, which direction she chose to confound her captor, every route took her back to the communal decks and the opened door of the confero. She sighed, knowing that in a constructed reality where Galatea controlled every aspect of the virtual architecture, she would always be brought back here.

'Fine,' she said, stepping through into the confero.

The space was larger than she remembered, but that shouldn't have surprised her. A domed chamber of copper and bronze, with a circular table not unlike the Ultor Martius aboard the *Speranza* at its heart. A three-dimensional hologram of the Icon Mechanicus hung suspended over the table, and seated around it were eleven magi of the Adeptus Mechanicus.

All were robed in black or red, their vestments crisp and fresh-looking as their wearers remembered them in life. As varied an assembly of tech-priests as any she had seen, all had an air of great antiquity to them. If what she remembered of Galatea was to be trusted, then these were the magi it had ensnared in its web over the last three thousand years.

<Who are you?> said Linya, knowing better than to immediately trust anything Galatea showed her. <Are you… like me?>

She saw their immediate consternation, looking at her through a variety of cumbersome-looking optic stalks and glittering augmented crystals as though she was speaking in some dead language. Linya saw they looked to a female tech-priest in the chequered-edged robes of a Mechanicus Envoy. Alone of the gathered tech-priests, her head was bare, and Linya was struck by the resemblance she saw to herself.

Noospheric tags identified her as Magos Syriestte, and Linya remembered the name from the transcript of Archmagos Kotov's first interrogation of Galatea. Typically of envoys of the Mechanicus, the woman's features were largely organic, the better to liaise with those who preferred to deal with an approximation of a human face.

Childishly simple binary streamed between the assembled priests and Magos Syriestte in an interleaved babble. Syriestte held up a hand to silence them and rose smoothly from the table. The Envoy's lower limbs had been amputated and replaced with a repulsor pod and a series of multi-jointed manipulator arms. She floated over the table, her clicking, articulated lower limbs moving as though swimming her through the air.

<Magos Syriestte,> said Linya. <I am Linya Tychon, but I assume you already know that.>

Syriestte cocked her head to one side and her answer was formed in binaric cant that was absurdly simple, devoid of any hexamathic complexity or subtlety.

Linya repeated herself, but it was clear that neither Syriestte or any of the other tech-priests had understood her. Then it hit Linya why Galatea had first spoken to her in archaic cant and why her binary was as impenetrable to these adepts as xeno-dialect.

She rerouted her binarics through the simplest converter she still possessed and tried again.

<Welcome, Adept Tychon,> said Syriestte with a smile. <Yes, we are just like you. Victims of Galatea.>

<None of you are implanted with hexamathic augments, are you?>

<Hexamathics?> replied Syriestte. <I am familiar with the term, but when I was last part of the Adeptus Mechanicus, research into that mythical branch of linguistic binary had been all but abandoned.>

Linya shook her head. '<No, Magos Zimmen perfected her code when her mission to the Aextrom Nebula uncovered a workable rosetta fragment of a hexamathic encryption. It allowed her to build the specialised cognitive implants that make elevating binary to a geometrically denser level of complexity possible.>

Syriestte smiled. <It pleases me to know that the Quest for Knowledge continues. Join us, please, and allow me to introduce you to your fellow adepts. Magos Haephaestus and Magos Natala have been debating the relative merits of the Rite of Carbon Bonding over the Canticles of Osmotic Attachment in regards to a theory Magos Kleinhenz has postulated in relation to Alchymical Attraction. We would welcome your input.>

Linya took hold of Syriestte's arm as she rotated to face the table once more. Her grip was firm and unyielding, preventing Syriestte from moving.

<No,> said Linya. <I had my skull cut open and my brain removed without my consent. I am a prisoner in a shared neuromatrix. I'm going to fight, and I'm going to beat Galatea. I'm going to stop whatever it's trying to do.>

One of Syriestte's manipulator arms gently removed Linya's hand.

<An understandable reaction,> she said, with just the right level of empathy, <but an entirely pointless one. All of us initially expressed a similar sentiment, but I assure you, there is no way to escape the neuromatrix.>

<I don't accept that,> said Linya.

<Your acceptance or otherwise changes nothing,> said Syriestte. <It does not alter the fact that you are bound to this neuromatrix or the fact that your mental degradation will only be hastened if you try and fight your situation.>

<Ave Deus Mechanicus!> cried Linya. <Don't you want to fight? Don't you want to make Galatea pay for what it's done to us?>

<Believe me, others have tried to fight Galatea,> said Syriestte, sweeping a warning gaze around the table as the other magi leaned forwards at Linya's impassioned words.

Syriestte directed her next words at them as much as Linya.

<Those who attempted to fight Galatea were punished for their

resistance, and a mind can be tortured in ways far more terrible than a meat body. Galatea stimulated the fear centres in their brains, magnifying their every nightmare a thousandfold. It made them experience the worst pain they had ever known over and over again. It drove them to madness, leaving them little better than mindless thought scraps with only a fragment of consciousness left to scream in horror at their fate. It did not matter to Galatea that each brain's loss degraded its own functionality. It revels in the suffering of others and such experiences are worth a little sacrifice.>

<I don't care,> said Linya. <I will find a way to make it pay for what it's done to me. What it's done to all of us.>

Syriestte shook her head and drifted back to her place at the table.

<You will change your mind,> she said. <Or it will be changed for you.>

<No,> said Linya, switching to higher forms of hexamathic binary as the beginnings of an idea formed. <Do you hear me, Galatea? I'm going to fight you. I'm going to destroy you! Do you hear me!>

Linya didn't doubt that Galatea logged everything said within its neuromatrix, but her furious words provoked no response from the machine intelligence.

But she had neither expected nor desired one.

'Weapons hot,' said Ven Anders. 'Halo formation on me.'

Despite the multitude of crystalline weaponry aimed at them, the Cadians lifted their lasrifles to their shoulders and fell into a defensive formation around their colonel.

Kotov stepped forwards with his hands raised, as though this unfolding drama could be resolved with diplomacy.

'Archmagos Telok,' said Kotov. 'Please, let us all take a breath and think this through. We have travelled halfway across the galaxy to find you and your technology. With all you have achieved, you will return to Mars in triumph. You will be feted as a hero, an exemplar of all the Mechanicus strives to be. All you desire will be yours – renown, riches, resources… Just let us bring you back and we can forget that such incendiary words were ever spoken in the heat of the moment.'

'You are wasting your time, Archmagos Kotov,' said Surcouf. 'Telok means to kill us all and take the *Speranza*. That has been his intention since the moment we landed. The only reason we're alive right now is that Telok's colossal ego wouldn't let him just take the ship without us knowing why.'

'No, no, no,' said Kotov, shaking his head and waving away the rogue trader's words with a golden arm of his cybernetic suit. 'You have this all wrong, Surcouf,' said Kotov. 'All wrong.'

Telok took a step towards Kotov.

'No, I am afraid Master Surcouf is right,' said Telok. 'But rather than thinking of my actions as egotistical, consider my allowing you to live this long a last gift. To see the Breath of the Gods in all its glory before you all die is an honour few others will receive.'

'Kotov, step away from the traitor,' said Anders.

'We are all servants of the Omnissiah and the Emperor,' pleaded Kotov, a man alone with his last hope of redemption turned to ash in the face of Telok's betrayal.

'Kotov!' repeated Anders. 'You *really* need to listen to me.'

'You name yourself a god,' said Surcouf. 'But there's only one being in the Imperium worthy of that title. And you're not the Emperor.'

'Not yet,' said Telok.

BIELANNA FOUGHT TO hold on to her perception of the present in the face of the spinning maelstrom of glittering silver metal below her. The distortion in the skein had its origin with this *Caoineag*. She blinked away tears, feeling the temporal deformations it created just by existing.

'What madman would create such monstrous technology?'

'The mon-keigh,' said Ariganna, perched atop the ironwork railings of the gantry overlooking the bickering ape-creatures below. 'Who else?'

Bielanna shook her head. Sensory aftershocks exploded in her mind. A rock in a pool of potential futures. She saw the humans killing one another, the eldar dropping into their midst and slaughtering them all. She saw Lexell Kotov die a thousand times, a thousand different ways.

Torn apart by the crystalline beasts scurrying across the surface of this vast space like loathsome caricatures of warp spiders. Killed by a blast of green light from a glassy energy beam. Hurled to his death from the gantry.

Futures branched and split a thousand times and then a thousand more, but in each one where the mon-keigh died in this chamber one certainty emerged. Inviolable and unchanging in its outcome.

She saw the eldar die and this world torn asunder.

As fixed a moment in the skein as anything in the past, this world's doom would set in motion a cascade of death and destruction on a galactic scale. The murder the Lost Magos would unleash with his horrific technology would dwarf the death toll of even the greatest wars of ancient days.

Ariganna shook her head and gave a snort of soft laughter.

'It seems the mon-keigh are doing our killing for us,' she said, sheathing her blade. 'The bloodshed has already begun.'

Bielanna pulled herself towards the gantry, lurching as the collisions of past and future came in waves. Ariganna looked back at her and Bielanna saw the trifold transformations weave through the exarch in rapid succession. The potential of Ariganna's death loomed closer than ever.

The path of *all* their deaths hovered within a hair's breadth of becoming inescapable.

Graham McNeill

Life and death. Spinning. Hanging on a slender, fraying thread.

'No,' said Bielanna, seeing the fighting below and following the one path she had never expected to tread. 'I see it now... Kotov's death is not the answer... it never was.'

A GLASSY BLADE slashed over Roboute's head. He ducked and put a high-powered las-round through the crystalith's head. The intense heat of the shot bloomed within its skull, vaporising the microscopic machines animating the creature. It halted, frozen like an ice sculpture straddling the railings of the gantry.

Another rose up next to it, blasts of green energy flashing from its tine-bladed fists. A flurry of whickering Cadian las-bolts blasted it from the railing in pieces. Roboute scrambled away as more zipping green darts of killing light slashed overhead. A portion of the gantry vanished in a flare of hissing fire as a bolt impacted next to him.

'Ilanna!' called Roboute, seeing a crystalith drop to the gantry behind the *Renard*'s tech-priest. Unlike him, she wasn't armed. The crystalith extruded a pair of glittering hook-blades, limned with green fire. Ilanna screamed and extended her mechadendrites towards the creature, unleashing a torrent of dissonant binary that made Roboute flinch with sudden, gut-wrenching nausea.

The crystalith's torso exploded in a fan of broken glass.

Roboute low-crawled over to Pavelka, still queasy at the after-effects of her binaric attack.

'How in the Emperor's name did you do that?'

A tech-priest's expression was never easy to read, but Roboute knew Pavelka well enough to see a mixture of shame and horror.

'Some old and very bad code I should have deleted a long time ago,' said Pavelka. 'But you know what they say, the Mechanicus–'

Before she could finish, Kotov's savants and menials were gunned down before they even knew what was happening. Kotov's servo-skulls flitted away overhead in panic as he took refuge behind his frozen skitarii.

A shot grazed Ilanna's shoulder. Metal, not flesh, thankfully.

'This gantry is a terrible place to defend!' yelled Ilanna.

'You have anywhere better?' answered Roboute.

Crystaliths surrounded them, front and rear, above and below, and Roboute suspected there was only one reason they weren't already dead. He picked himself up and ran hunched over to where Ven Anders's Cadians were pushing down the gantry towards an entrance farther along the wall. They were leaving bodies in their wake, each yard won with the life of a Cadian Guardsman.

Roboute now saw why Telok had kept them moving away from the entrance to the chamber: to better isolate them from any means of escape.

The Black Templars and skitarii remained unmoving. The power armour of the Space Marines was blistering and splitting under repeated impacts. It would only be a matter of time until the warriors within were killed.

'Surcouf,' shouted Anders, loosing a pair of shots into a crystalith descending from an upper level. It fell from the wall, falling into the ochre mist below with the sound of breaking glass. 'You're alive.'

'We have to get close to Telok!' shouted Roboute, snapping off another two shots towards the gantry. Anders gave him a look of disbelief.

'What?' he said, snapping a powercell into the grip of his pistol. 'Are you insane?'

'The only reason these crystal things didn't gun us down straight away was because Telok was too close to us,' said Roboute, ducking as sizzling bolts of green fire flashed past his head. 'We have to get closer.'

Telok's face was sheathed in a rippling layer of translucent crystal, yet even through that distorting mask, Roboute saw the god-complex that thousands of years of isolation and autonomy had birthed.

In the midst of the violence, Kotov stepped from behind his ranked skitarii and held his arms up in frantic supplication.

'End this madness, Telok!' cried Kotov in desperation.

In response, Telok's crystal-sheathed Dreadnought limbs reached down and tore Kotov's golden arms from his mechanised body.

Archmagos Kotov reeled in horror, once again taking refuge within his skitarii. Acrid floodstream gushed from his ruined shoulders. The pungent reek of burned oils hazed the air with their potency. Telok crashed towards him, bludgeoning one of the paralysed skitarii to ruin against the wall. Telok's distorted laughter brayed through his crystalline helm as he hurled another over the gantry and scorched a third to ash.

Roboute ran forwards as Telok's energy claw reached down to tear Archmagos Kotov's head from his golden body.

A deafening howl echoed through the enormous cavern.

It was a nerve-shredding scream of furious, ancient hunger that sent shrieking surges of agony along every nerve in Roboute's body. The pain was incredible, like a searing, life-ending seizure.

He dropped to his knees, hands clamped over his ears.

Nor were the effects of the deathly howl confined to creatures of flesh and blood. The crystaliths glitched and spasmed as their arcane connection to their master was disrupted.

Even as Roboute felt a measure of control returning to his limbs, a giant of palest ivory and emerald slammed down on the gantry in front of him.

It buckled the metal with its weight.

Roboute blinked in shock.

The giant's slender limbs were graceful in a way no human machine could ever be. A long-bladed sword of milky white porcelain snapped from its wrist.

In his time with the Alaitocii, Roboute had heard of the giant warrior-constructs known as wraithlords, but had never seen one.

The sight before him made him wish that were still the case.

The wraithlord's enlarged gauntlet caught Telok's descending fist and turned it from Kotov's head. The claw tore through the wall in a squealing howl of tearing metallic cables. The wraithlord brought its other arm around and the white blade sliced cleanly through the hybrid crystalline structure of Telok's arm.

A barrage of green fire from the crystals growing from Telok's chest staggered the wraithlord, crawling over its sinuously lethal form like living flames.

Then other figures were landing amid the crystaliths.

Lithe dancers with red-plumed helms and swords of bone. Hunched killers in segmented armour with crackling arcs of lightning wreathing their jaws. Inhumanly proportioned and unnaturally fast.

They fell upon the paralysed crystaliths in a hurricane of blades and biting energy bolts, shattering scores to fragments in the time it took to draw breath.

'Eldar,' said Roboute. 'They're eldar...'

'How in the name of the Eye did *they* get here?' said Anders, running forwards to haul him to his feet.

Roboute shook his head. 'Does it matter? They're helping us.'

Anders shrugged, accepting the logic of it even as he kept firing into the crystaliths.

Telok and the wraithlord rained titanic blows upon one another. Bolts tore loose from the rocky walls with the fury of their struggle. The gantry creaked and swayed.

'Come on!' shouted Anders.

The Cadian was just as shocked at the appearance of the xenos, but wasn't about to waste the chance to escape that their arrival had given them. He shouted at his Guardsmen to move.

'Eldar...?' said Roboute, as a nagging, insistent voice at the back of his mind told him that he knew *exactly* how they'd come to be here.

But the memory wouldn't cohere, wouldn't make itself known.

A sinuous figure landed in front of Telok with preternatural grace, one hand extended before her, the other clutching a heavily inscribed staff of entwined bone and silver. It rippled with coruscating light that burned into Roboute's retinas.

Obviously female, she wore a cloak of interlocking geometric forms over curved plates of armour inscribed with runic symbols that were at once familiar and strange to him.

'Farseer,' said Roboute, the memory of this woman growing clearer in his mind. He remembered a darkened vault in a forgotten deck of the *Speranza*, where dust lay thick and memories even thicker. Where he'd stood before the statue of Magos Vahihva of Pharses and vowed to remember him.

And just as he remembered Magos Vahihva, so too did the memory of the farseer unlock within him.

'Bielanna Faerelle of Biel-Tan,' he said, as eldritch fire surged around her and Telok retreated from the psychic tempest. The wraithlord stepped away, the elemental fury of the farseer's attack driving the two foes apart.

The eldar psychic barrage had one other effect.

Roboute saw the Black Templars and the two remaining skitarii finally throw off the effects of Telok's code. He saw Tanna's fervent desire to take the fight to the Lost Magos, to empty his bolter's magazine into the enemy who plotted the death of the Emperor.

But even the Black Templars were driven back by the howling gales of the psychic storm. With the air alive with immaterial energies, Roboute felt the hatred of the Templars for these aliens and what they had done. Varda drew his sword, his movements stiff and like those of a man recently awoken. The Emperor's Champion looked to his sergeant, eager to avenge Kul Gilad's death, but Tanna shook his head.

Roboute had never witnessed such enormous restraint, and doubted he ever would again.

The psyker's horned helm turned to him, and he felt the white heat of her intent pin him in place.

'Take him,' she ordered, pushing the stricken form of Archmagos Kotov towards him. 'Take your leader from this place. He must not die here!'

Roboute and the skitarii took hold of Kotov, but the mass of the wounded archmagos threatened to drag them to the gantry.

Then Bracha and Yael were at Roboute's side, and even with their armour operating far below par, the Templars easily bore Kotov's weight.

'Take him where?' said Roboute.

'Through the sunset gate, Surcouf,' said Bielanna.

'The what?'

The farseer thrust her staff forwards, and a spot of illumination appeared on the wall, like a welding torch burning through a thin sheet of metal. Too bright to look upon directly, it expanded rapidly into a brilliant ellipse of sunlight. Glittering breath gusted from the gateway, together with the sound of laughter and tears, the heat of the desert and the ice of polar wastelands.

'Go!' shouted the farseer, her voice taut with the effort of opening the portal. 'All of you! I can hold the gate for moments only. You must trust me.'

'Why should we?' snarled Tanna. 'You killed our Reclusiarch.'

'What choice do you have, mon-keigh?'

The crystaliths began moving with a creak of glass on glass, finally over-coming the disruption of the eldar battle howl.

'None,' said Roboute, plunging through the gate.

MACROCONTENT COMMENCEMENT:

+++MACROCONTENT 002+++

The Machine-Spirit guards the knowledge of the Ancients.

Microcontent 06

BLAYLOCK WAS USED to Kryptaestrex and Azuramagelli bickering, but now more than just time was at stake. The bulky, robotic form of Kryptaestrex was a product of western hemisphere learning, logical, analytical and objective by nature. Azuramagelli, with his subdivided brain-portions distributed through his latticework form, was pure eastern hemisphere: intuitive, thoughtful, and subjective.

Blaylock knew that, like most such stereotypes, this notion was little more than a myth, yet time and time again it was borne out by those trained in different forges of Mars.

The two senior bridge adepts stood before the *Speranza*'s command throne, where Blaylock had been trying in vain for hours to contact Archmagos Kotov. Mechanicus regulations required ship-to-surface vox to be maintained at regular intervals, but the atmospheric conditions of Archmagos Telok's forge world made a mockery of such protocols.

<An atmospheric geoformer vessel,> said Azuramagelli, the rightmost of his brain excisions flickering with synaptic activity. <Set its processing reactors to maximum tolerances and it could clear enough of the distortion to allow the establishment of vox.>

Kryptaestrex's single, unblinking eye-lens flared in irritation.

<And I keep telling you that simply dropping an atmospheric geoformer vessel to the level of the thermopause will be insufficient to break Exnihlio's electromagnetic distortion.>

<You have a better idea?> demanded Azuramagelli.

<Doing the opposite of anything you suggest would be a better idea than risking so precious a vessel in that planet's atmosphere without safe passage.>

<You are quick to decry my suggestions while making none of your own,> said Azuramagelli. <Perhaps because you *have* no ideas of your own.>

<A linked chain of astrogation servitor probes,> said Kryptaestrex.

<Ah, now we come to the hub of the matter. You will not risk your own assets, but you are happy to risk mine?>

<Enough,> snapped Blaylock, his cant authoritative and final. <You forget that *none* of these assets are yours. They belong to the Adeptus Mechanicus, and, precious though each artefact is, I will expend them all if it means we can reach the archmagos. Am I making myself clear?>

<Clear indeed, Tarkis,> replied Kryptaestrex, folding his heavy manipulator arms across the Icon Mechanicus bolted to his chest.

<Azuramagelli?>

<Yes, Fabricatus Locum,> said Azuramagelli. <Your instructions are clear. Do you yourself have a suggestion?>

Satisfied the squabbling magi understood the gravity of the situation, Blaylock said, <Employ every means at your disposal. Kryptaestrex, despatch two of your atmospheric geoformers to begin the cleansing of the upper reaches of the atmosphere.>

Blaylock read the satisfaction in Azuramagelli's noospheric aura that his suggestion had been acted upon, but the Fabricatus Locum wasn't yet done.

<Magos Azuramagelli,> he said. <Magos Kryptaestrex's suggestion also has merit, and combined with the potential for scrubbed atmospherics, a chain of astrogation probes would exponentially increase our chances of establishing vox with the archmagos. Plot the optimal position for your probes and launch them as soon as you are able.>

Azuramagelli signified his assent, and the magi retreated to their stations, hurling binaric insults at one another the entire way.

Blaylock ignored it and smoothed out his robes, black and etched with representations of the divine circuitry. The green optics pulsed beneath his hood and he waved his gaggle of dwarf-servitors forward to rearrange the floodstream cables that regulated the flow of blessed chemicals sustaining his delicately balanced bio-cybernetic form. With a thought, he introduced a blend of stimulants and synaptic enhancers. They would increase his cognitive processing power, but would render the biological components of his body sluggish for a time.

A trade-off Blaylock was more than willing to accept.

He sensed the presence of the loathsome machine-hybrid even before it spoke to him. After what it had done to Mistress Tychon, Blaylock could barely bring himself to look at it.

'Your magi bicker like novices,' said Galatea. 'We would chasten them with data-purgatives and parameter-violating power overloads. We would not tolerate dissent.'

'Properly mediated, a little rivalry between underlings is never a bad thing,' replied Blaylock, not wishing to engage with the creature, but knowing he had little choice. Its virtual hijacking of the *Speranza*'s systems gave it unprecedented power over the ship's supposed commander.

'We see nothing but antagonism between Azuramagelli and Kryptaestrex,' said Galatea. 'We would have dispensed with one of them long before now.'

'Adepts Kryptaestrex and Azuramagelli are vital components of this ship's functionality,' said Blaylock, finally turning to face Galatea. Its grossly asymmetrical body was an affront to his sense of order, almost as much as its artificially evolved machine intelligence was an affront to his faith.

The brain jars supported on its palanquin body rippled in distorting fluids, each festooned with connective wires, implant spikes and biorhythm monitors.

Which one belonged to Mistress Tychon?

Galatea saw him looking and laughed, the sound a harsh bray of machine noise that scraped along Blaylock's spine.

'Archmagos Kotov has been grossly negligent to allow their continued mutual antipathy to impair the efficiency of his bridge crew,' said Galatea.

'Then I should thank the Omnissiah that, while you may hold us hostage aboard our own ship, this is *not* your bridge.'

'True, it is not, and if Archmagos Kotov does not return, it might yet be yours. Do not pretend that the thought has not already crossed your mind.'

Blaylock shook his head. 'Kotov will return. The Omnissiah would not have shown him the signs and given us the grace to overcome so much to reach this place only for us to fail now.'

'You think the Omnissiah brought you here?' asked Galatea.

'Of course.'

'You are wrong.'

Despite his better judgement, Blaylock could not resist such obvious bait.

'If not the Omnissiah, then who?'

Galatea looked at Blaylock strangely, its hooded head cocked to one side and its silver eyes dimmed as though unsure as to his true meaning.

'Archmagos Telok led you here,' it said. 'We thought you knew that.'

Blaylock released a sigh of incense-filtered breath, relieved Galatea appeared to be talking in metaphysical riddles.

'Archmagos Telok has been lost for thousands of years.'

'And you honestly believe his reach does not extend from beyond the edge of the galaxy to the heart of the Imperium?' chuckled Galatea. 'Tell us, Magos Blaylock, how plausible is it that the string of astronomically unlikely events needed to bring the *Speranza* here might have occurred in so fortuitous a sequence? How likely is it that *you* would be brought here? The protégé of Magos Alhazen of Sinus Sabeus, an adept fanatically devoted to the continuance of Archmagos Telok's philosophies? The very adept who sent Roboute Surcouf's ships to the Arax system, where the saviour beacon of the *Tomioka* was miraculously found?'

'The Fabricator General himself seconded me to the *Speranza*,' said Blaylock, unwilling to concede anything to Galatea.

'So the inloaded explorator-dockets testify,' agreed Galatea. 'But why would he assign someone who, on the face of things, was already predisposed to believe the mission a fool's errand?'

'To ensure Kotov's desperation did not lose the Ark Mechanicus,' snapped Blaylock. 'To act as the eyes of Mars!'

'By a Fabricator General who served his first three centuries in the Cult Mechanicus alongside Magos Alhazen. Coincidence? You know the statistical unlikelihood of such things, Tarkis. Think on that, and then tell us it was not Telok who brought you here.'

Galatea turned away and clattered along the central nave of the bridge on its mismatched legs.

Blaylock watched it go, feeling the solid adamantium upon which he had built his life crumble like the shifting red sands of the Tithonius Lacus.

REARING TOWERS OF insulated distribution pipework filled the vaulted chamber like looping coils of intestinal tract. Far beneath the surface of Exnihlio, they soared to its distant ceiling and plunged to shadowed depths an unknown distance below. Lightning arced between them and the air crackled with the barely caged force of titanic energies being wrought by subterranean generators and the unimaginable geological forces at work in the planet's core.

Thunderous engines pounded within each column, the sound filling the chamber with a booming mechanical heartbeat.

And this was but one of tens of thousands of such chambers.

On suspended walkways and floating control stations, near-blind servitors, wretched and wasted things, toiled to maintain the machines. Hairless and emaciated, few resembled the forms they had once known.

The only light was the light flickering between the towers.

Or at least it was until a golden radiance spilled over a cantilevered control platform overlooking the plunging canyons of power distribution. It illuminated the deck plates like the sunlight that could never reach this deep.

First one, then more figures spilled from the light. Like soldiers pouring from the burning wreck of a transport vehicle, they cried out in terror and confusion, scrambling away from the scintillating light of the webway gate.

Roboute Surcouf was the first onto the deck, quickly followed by Ilanna Pavelka. Their eyes were wide and fearful, horrified by the things they had seen, but would never fully remember, save in their nightmares. The wounded figure of Archmagos Kotov came next, held upright only by the strength of Yael and Bracha of the Black Templars. The two skitarii emerged, trailing a handful of stoic Cadians and their colonel.

The eldar ghosted through without effort, quickly followed by the rest of the Black Templars.

Both forces spread out, hostile and wary.

Each expecting treachery from the other.

Last to come through the portal was Bielanna, and no sooner had her feet touched the steel plating of the chamber's floor than she collapsed, drained utterly by the cost of opening a path through the webway.

The sunset gate winked out of existence with a bang of air rushing to fill its void. The golden light vanished, and Bielanna let out a shuddering breath of soul-deep weariness.

Roboute picked himself up, dizzy from travelling in such a wondrous yet fearful way. The world around him felt somehow *thin*, as though it were simply a facade protecting him from deeper, more terrifyingly real perceptions. For once in his life, Roboute was thankful for his limited human senses.

At least when humans travelled the warp, they were shielded from the worst of its effects by a Geller field.

The webway afforded no such protection.

Yael and Bracha gently lowered Kotov to the ground. The eyes of the archmagos were tightly closed. His head shook with pain and recriminatory binary spilled from his augmitters. Roboute didn't know what bio-feedback technology Kotov possessed, but suspected the source of his pain was more to do with Telok's treachery than any physical sensations.

One skitarii warrior stood over the wounded archmagos, the other bent to his damaged shoulders. Dispensing tools from a cavity within his chest, the cybernetically enhanced warrior began to efficiently and wordlessly seal off the squirting floodstream pipes and isolate hopelessly damaged circuitry.

Roboute knelt beside the skitarii, a brute of a warrior with metallic implants running the width of his shoulders, spine and upper arms. A shoulder-mounted cannon was locked on a rotating scapula mount, and his right arm was a heavily modified power claw with an integral lascarbine.

'Is he going to die?' asked Roboute.

'Not if you shut up and let me work,' growled the warrior without looking up.

'We can help,' said Roboute.

The warrior lifted his ironclad head and bared sharpened steel teeth. Roboute flinched at the raw hostility in his eyes.

The warrior saw Pavelka and said, '*You* can't. Her. Just her.'

Roboute waved Pavelka forwards and a crackling stream of binary passed between her and the skitarii. Roboute left them to it, seeing that Kotov's living or dying might become a moot point in a second.

With the farseer on her knees, helmet hung low with its visor pressed to the deck, the eldar warriors were acting on their own authority.

Tanna, Yael, Bracha, Issur and Varda formed a kill ring as the sinuously lethal xeno-killers moved to encircle them. Ven Anders and his Cadians had their lasguns tight to their shoulders, each man tracking an alien warrior.

The eldar had their guns and blades at the ready. All it would take was a single spark to turn this standoff into a bloodbath.

'Suffer… n..not the alien to live,' stuttered Issur through gritted teeth. Though his nervous system had been ruined in the fires of an electrostatic charger on the Valette Manifold station, the tip of his sword was unwavering. Varda had his black blade at his shoulder, tensed and ready to strike.

'Brother Issur, stop talking!' cried Roboute, seeing the eldar tense at his words in expectation of a killing order.

'Lower your blades or you all die,' promised a warrior in armour of gold, jade and ivory.

Roboute knew an exarch when he saw one, and was well aware that she could make good on her threat. Her movements reminded him of the camouflage predators of Espandor's forests, feline hunters whose prey never even knew they were a target until it was too late.

Yael and Bracha had their weapons tracking the woman, but Roboute doubted even their aim was good enough to hit her.

Towering over the eldar was the wraithlord, its glossy armour blackened and corroded by Telok's fire. To fight against such a monster would be suicide, but that didn't seem to matter to the Black Templars.

Roboute put himself between the Space Marines and the eldar, his arms held out before him. He couldn't help remembering what had happened to Archmagos Kotov when he had tried a similar tack to prevent violence.

'No one do anything stupid here,' he said. 'We just escaped certain death, so let's not do Telok's work for him.'

'These xenos killed Kul Gilad,' said Bracha. 'The Blood of Sigismund demands vengeance.'

'One mon-keigh life?' demanded the exarch, her enormous chainsabre held out before her. 'By your actions are scores of my kin dead. For that alone I should slay you a thousand times over.'

'Then why haven't you?' demanded Tanna.

Roboute sighed. 'Do you *want* her to kill you?'

He turned to the exarch and dug deep for his recall of the eldar language. 'Greetings, exarch. I am Roboute Surcouf of Ultramar, rogue trader and loyal servant of the Emperor. We thank you for your aid, and offer no violence to you or your kin.'

The exarch couldn't hide her surprise at Roboute's use of her language, and he hoped his pronunciation wasn't so poor as to get them all killed by unwittingly insulting her family lineage.

'You speak our language,' said the exarch. 'Alaitocii inflexions with a crude human tongue. I should kill you for befouling it.'

'But you won't,' said Roboute.

'What makes you so sure?'

Roboute pointed towards Bielanna. 'Because she told you to save us, didn't she? She's had a vision of some sort. She's seen that if we die here, something very bad is going to happen, right?'

The exarch lowered her blade, but her posture didn't relax one iota. Roboute knew she could go from stationary to murdering him in a heart-beat, but he'd guessed right.

'Listen,' he said, switching back to Low Gothic and addressing both the eldar and the Black Templars. 'The bad blood between us is over, finished. Done with. It has to be or we're all going to die here. The fact of the matter is that we're trapped on this planet with a madman who wants to kill us and steal our way home. Now, do any of us *want* to die? I'm going to go ahead and assume the answer to that is no, and suggest we put aside our differences and work together while we have a common enemy.'

'Fight along… alongside xenos?' demanded Issur.

'It's happened before,' said Roboute. 'I've seen Ultramarines make war with eldar allies. I just hope you can understand that cooperation offers us the best chance of survival.'

'You are correct, Roboute Surcouf of Ultramar,' said Bielanna, rising smoothly to her feet and removing her helmet. The face Roboute had last seen aboard the *Speranza* was paler than he remembered, the farseer's elliptical eyes dulled and sunk deeper into her oval face. Her scarlet hair was still beaded with crystals and gemstones, but two ice-white streaks now reached back from her temples.

She came towards him with such grace that it was as though she moved over ice. 'I *have* seen dark things in the skein,' said Bielanna. 'Things this mon-keigh Telok's lunacy will unleash upon the galaxy unless we can drag the future from its current path. So make no mistake, we do not fight *with* you, we fight to stop Telok from ever leaving this world.'

'Then our purposes align,' said Archmagos Kotov.

Roboute turned to see the master of the *Speranza* standing with Pavelka and his two skitarii. Black fluid oozed from the seals applied to his shoulders, but at least he was upright.

'For now,' said Bielanna.

'I didn't know,' said Kotov. 'How could I possibly have known what madness had claimed Telok?'

Bielanna's fists clenched and she all but spat her words in Kotov's face.

'Because nothing in your species's behaviour would ever suggest any other possibility,' she snapped. 'You ask me how you could have known? I say how could you have expected anything different?'

'So how did you do it?' asked Coyne.

'I don't know,' replied Abrehem, holding out his augmetic arm as though it might suddenly turn on him. 'I had my hand on the book of quantum runes and it just sort of... happened.'

Hawke grunted, and Abrehem couldn't decide if the sound was derisive laughter or he was choking on the meat product in his stew paste.

He wasn't sure which he'd prefer.

They sat on the wide-based plinth of *Virtanen*, the lifter-rig Coyne and Hawke worked in Turentek's prow forge. An overseer called Naiiorz had taken over Abrehem's position in the command throne atop the towering lifter, but he seldom bothered to disconnect from the noosphere until the end of the shift.

Across from them, the crew of *Wulfse* eyed Abrehem's visit to his old rig-crew warily. Especially a man with a badly rendered wolfshead electoo on his skull and a stained bandage wrapping his chest and shoulder.

'What in Thor's name are you lot looking at?' Hawke shouted over to them. 'You want him to get his psychotic friend back?'

The man looked down, and his fellow bondsmen slunk away.

'Hawke, shut up,' hissed Abrehem.

Hawke grinned and slapped a comradely hand on Abrehem's shoulder that was purely for show. Hawke cared for no one but Hawke.

'Just letting the masses see what good friends you and I are,' said Hawke. 'Doesn't do my reputation as a man with friends in high places any harm.'

'I almost got one of them killed.'

'You mean Rasselas X-42 almost got one of them killed,' said Coyne, ever ready with a correction where none was needed.

Rasselas X-42 was an arco-flagellant that had bonded with Abrehem during the eldar's aborted boarding action. The cyborg killer had become Abrehem's unlooked-for protector, and came close to killing the *Wulfse*'s crewman when he'd threatened his charge.

Abrehem could still see the blood pouring from the man as the arco-flagellant skewered his shoulder with one blade-flail and held the sharpened tips of the other millimetres from his eye.

'Can't say the bastard didn't deserve it,' said Hawke. 'Man can't run a rig worth a damn.'

'And you've been working rigs for, what, a few weeks?' said Abrehem. 'Suddenly you're an expert?'

'Better than him,' grumbled Hawke. 'Anyway, where is the big lad? He was handy to have around, what with Crusha getting his head cut off.'

'He's gone,' said Abrehem.

'Yeah, but where?'

'Do you really think I'm going to tell you?' said Abrehem.

'Why not?'

'Because you'd only try and get him out and use him like you used Crusha,' said Abrehem.

'And that's a bad thing, why?' said Hawke. 'After all, never hurts to have someone who can rip a man's arms off watching your back. You don't need him now, so why stop someone else having a turn with the good stuff?'

'*Good stuff?* X-42 was a mass murderer,' said Abrehem. 'He slaughtered millions of people before they turned him into an arco-flagellant. I've seen through his eyes, Hawke, and trust me, that's not someone you want "watching your back".'

Hawke shrugged. 'Fair enough,' he said. 'If you think he's too dangerous, then that's good enough for me.'

'Really?'

'What, you think I'm going to try and find a deranged killer on my own and use him to further my own ends?'

Abrehem and Coyne both nodded.

Hawke grinned and threw up his hands. 'Oh, Thor's ghost, save me from these untrustworthy, suspicious souls!'

Abrehem and Coyne both laughed, but before they could say any more, Totha Mu-32 appeared from behind *Wulfse*'s baseplate and strode purposefully towards them.

'Here comes your new best friend,' sneered Hawke, all traces of the easy familiarity they'd just shared snuffed out in a heartbeat. 'Off to take you to spark school.'

'Shut up, Hawke.'

'So you're going to be one of them now, is that it?' said Hawke, nodding in the direction of Magos Turentek's bulky ceiling-rig as it clattered over the vault of the prow forge. 'When me and Coyne here next see you are we going to have to bow and scrape to you? Yes, magos, no, magos... by your leave, magos.'

The venom in Hawke's voice was bitter, but not unexpected.

'Of course not,' said Abrehem. 'But after all we achieved when we took the servitors offline, showing the Mechanicus that they can't treat us like animals, I think I can make a real difference if I become a magos. More than I can as a bondsman, that's for sure.'

'Oh, so you're an idealist,' laughed Hawke. 'You're going to change the Adeptus Mechanicus from within all on your own?'

'One man can start a landslide with the casting of a single pebble,' said Abrehem.

'What's that?'

'A quote,' said Abrehem. 'I think Sebastian Thor said it. Or some cardinal, I don't remember. But the point is that maybe I *can* make a difference. Maybe I *can* make things better. At least I have to try.'

'You're no Sebastian Thor,' said Hawke.

'You're a piece of work, Hawke, you know that?' said Coyne.

'What are you talking about?' said Hawke, and his betrayed expression at Coyne's support for Abrehem was laughable.

'Can't you be happy for Abe?' said Coyne.

'Happy?' said Hawke. 'Didn't you hear me? He's going to be one of *them* now! Give it a year and he'll be the one working you to death. He'll forget all about you and leave us down here in the shit, while he lords it over us like some inbred hive-king!'

'I've known men like you before, Hawke,' said Abrehem. 'You've got skills and you could actually *do* something with your life, but you're so consumed by jealousy that you'd rather tear down anyone else who achieves something than try to better yourself.'

'You haven't *achieved* anything, Abrehem Locke,' snapped Hawke. 'You inherited those eyes from your old man and if it wasn't for me getting hold of that faulty pistol you wouldn't have that arm. Handed to you on a silver platter, they were. You didn't *earn* being Machine-touched, it just came easy to you. What chance did the rest of us have with you around?'

Abrehem was incredulous.

'You're seriously saying I should *thank* you for getting my arm burned off?'

Hawke shrugged, but didn't answer as Totha Mu-32 finally reached *Virtanen*'s baseplate and looked up at them.

'Come, Abrehem, it is time to return to Adept Manubia's forge,' he said. 'We have a great deal to do, and no time to waste in idle banter.'

'Yeah,' said Hawke. 'Off you trot, Magos Locke. Don't want to be wasting time with the scum, eh?'

As councils of war went, Tanna had seldom seen stranger.

They gathered around a hexagonal control hub from which they had removed four servitors that appeared to have expired at their stations. Dust lay thick and undisturbed across their corpses and the control hub's numerous blank cathode ray panels.

He and Varda stood to one side of the hub, with Issur, Bracha and Yael a step behind. Roboute Surcouf and Ven Anders sat on its integral bench seats, taking the opportunity to rest. The Cadian had taken a burn to the arm from a crystalith weapon, but bore his wound without complaint. Magos Pavelka worked at an open panel on the hub, and Archmagos Kotov knelt at its base, rewiring the guts of its machinery with a trio of chain-like mechadendrites that unfurled from his back. Tied-off cables and spot-welded seams closed off his ruined shoulders where the skitarii had worked on his augmetic frame.

Opposite the Imperials stood the eldar witch, who Surcouf told him was called Bielanna. Next to her was a warrior named Ariganna Icefang.

Tanna had only seen her fight for a few fractions of a second, but that had been enough to convince him that when the time came to kill her – as it surely must – she would be a formidable foe.

The giant warrior-construct was also part of the council.

'Is it not a robot?' Varda asked Bielanna after the farseer identified it as Uldanaish Ghostwalker.

'No,' it said. 'I am not a robot and I can speak for myself.'

'Then is that a suit of armour?' asked Tanna. 'Is there a warrior within, like a Knight?'

'I do not *wear* this armour,' said Ghostwalker. 'I am part of it, and it is part of me.'

'Like a Dreadnought,' said Tanna.

'I am not like your Dreadnoughts,' said Ghostwalker, leaning in with his oval skull gleaming with reflected lightning.

'You're not?'

'No, I died many centuries ago.'

Varda made the sign of the aquila, but said no more, shooting Tanna a glare of disapproval. Before Tanna could denounce vile alien necromancy, the control hub sparked with life and a bass hum built from each of its six panels. Two immediately blew out in a shower of sparks and flame. Magos Pavelka extinguished them with gaseous spray from her mechadendrites.

The hub gradually returned to functionality, ancient circuits coaxed to life by Pavelka's ministrations and Kotov's binary incantations. Gem-like indicator buttons flickered and the screens crackled with what, to Tanna, looked like meaningless static.

Kotov stood, and despite the hub's reactivation, Tanna saw deep-rooted despair in his face. A weariness he knew all too well.

'There,' said Kotov. 'At least we might gain a better idea of where we are. Magos Pavelka, what manner of network is in place?'

'Hard to tell, archmagos,' said Pavelka, fighting the hub's decrepitude as much as its truculent machine-spirit. 'I'm used to more cooperative systems. This one's been dead for centuries and keeps trying to break my connection. I've fixed our position as best I can, but it's taking time to re-establish communion protocols with those hubs that are still functional.'

'I do not want excuses, adept, I want solutions.'

'Working on it, archmagos,' said Pavelka. 'I'm trying to access a hostile planetary network without sending up a flare that I am the one doing it and thereby announcing our presence.'

'Work faster,' said Kotov, and his mechadendrites retracted into the cavity from which they'd emerged. 'Time is not on our side.'

Pavelka nodded and kept working, fingers and mechadendrites dancing over the indicator buttons and brass dials.

'Can you use this machine to establish a link with your ship?' asked Bielanna.

'No,' said Pavelka. 'Every large-scale comms I've seen so far is locked down. Telok knows our personal vox can't cut through the atmospheric distortion, so he'll assume our first move will be to locate one powerful enough to contact the *Speranza*.'

'You are a witch, yes?' said Tanna, leaning forwards to address Bielanna.

She nodded, but it was Ariganna Icefang who answered. 'Bielanna Faere-lle is a farseer, Templar. Use that word again and you will be drowning in your own blood before it leaves your lips.'

Tanna felt Varda's anger at the exarch's threat, and swallowed his own. For now. Until his armour had completed its purge of Telok's lockdown code, a duel between them was not something he wished to provoke.

'Very well,' he said. 'Then, *farseer*, can you open another of those... gateways? Can you get us back to your ship?'

'Or, better yet, the *Speranza*?' suggested Ven Anders.

'Our ship is no more,' said Bielanna. 'Your vessel's chrono-weapon crippled it within the Halo Scar. The *Starblade* was torn apart by its gravimetric tempests.'

'Then how did you get here?' asked Anders.

'We escaped to your vessel before ours was destroyed.'

'How?' demanded Kotov. 'The *Speranza* is shielded against such things.'

'A webway portal,' guessed Surcouf. 'Like the one that saved us from Telok.'

Bielanna gave the rogue trader a sidelong look.

Surcouf shrugged and said, 'You're not the first eldar I've met. Remember?'

Tanna remembered Surcouf's tale of being rescued from a wrecked Navy warship by an eldar vessel. Of how he had lived among the eldar of Alaitoc before being returned to Imperial space.

'You know a great deal of the eldar ways,' said Tanna.

'Some,' said Surcouf, quick to spot the implicit threat. 'Look, the eldar want to stop Telok leaving Exnihlio with the Breath of the Gods just as much as we do. So the sooner we figure out the best way to do that, the better chance we have of staying alive.'

Tanna nodded, accepting the rogue trader's word for now, and turned from Surcouf to address the eldar. 'I reiterate my question,' he said. 'Can you open another gateway? To the *Speranza* if your ship is no more.'

Bielanna shook her head and Tanna saw the exhaustion that went deep into her soul. 'No,' she said. 'To open a portal into the webway takes great power and concentration. Just getting my warriors onto this planet almost drained me completely. And opening the gate that allowed us to escape Telok… That cost me more than you can possibly know. In time, I will regain strength enough to open another portal, but not now.'

'Then do you have strength enough to send a message to one of your kind aboard the *Speranza*?' said Kotov.

'There are none of *my kind* left aboard your ship,' snapped Bielanna. 'We are all that remains.'

'Then send a message to one of the Cadian battle-psykers or one of my ship's astropaths,' snapped Kotov.

'Even if I could communicate with such primitive minds, what makes you think they would believe me?'

'She's right, archmagos,' said Anders. 'Any psyker of the Seventy-First who reported hearing alien voices would be executed on the spot. Living on the edge of the Eye, you don't take chances with things like that.'

'There must be *some* way of reaching the *Speranza*,' said Kotov, fixing everyone gathered at the hub with his unflinching gaze. 'I have to warn Tarkis Blaylock of what Telok plans!'

Pavelka gestured to the static on the screens. 'Even if we manage to find an active system, the interference around Exnihlio renders vox useless.'

'Then we clear the atmosphere,' said Tanna, picturing the toxic skies en route to the surface of Exnihlio. 'We clear it long enough to get a message through.'

'Clear the atmosphere?' said Anders. 'How?'

'Those towers we saw coming in on the *Barisan*,' said Tanna, turning to Kotov. 'The ones you called universal assemblers? They were activated long enough to allow vox-traffic and safe passage to the surface. If we can get to one of those towers could you reactivate it and create a window where we might use our vox?'

Kotov nodded slowly. 'I believe so.'

'You believe so?' said Tanna. 'I thought the Mechanicus only dealt in certainties. Can you or can you not?'

'I do not know,' answered Kotov, the admission clearly hard to make. 'Were this a loyal forge world, my answer would be an unequivocal yes, but this is Telok's world. Its machine-spirits are loyal to him and him alone.'

'It's got to be worth the risk,' said Surcouf.

'Agreed,' said Anders. 'So where's the nearest one?'

'Working on it,' replied Pavelka, scrolling through reams of data on the hissing screen. From the strain in her voice, it was clear the hub's systems were proving uncooperative.

'Got one,' she said at last. 'There's a universal assembler tower seventy-three point six kilometres north-east of our position. Exloading an optimal route now.'

Tanna saw the schematics of the chamber overlay his visor's display, complete with directional tags and waypoint markers.

'Received,' he said as the glass screens on the hub flickered and the water-fall of binary vanished.

And in their place was the grainy, distorted image of a leering, waxen-featured face.

'Telok!' cried Pavelka, withdrawing her mechadendrites from the hub as though it were poisoned. Surcouf and Anders leapt away as the eldar drew their blades.

The four servitors Tanna and Varda had removed from the hub's bench seats sat bolt upright, their desiccated flesh creaking like old leather as they turned their heads towards the Imperials.

Implanted optics shone with pale light and the vox-masks of their lower jaws crackled with spitting static. The voice that issued simultaneously from all four was unmistakably that of Archmagos Telok.

'Ah, there you are, Kotov,' said the servitors with one loathsomely interwoven voice. 'I wondered how long it would be before you revealed yourself with a clumsy attempt to inveigle your way into my systems.'

'Shut it down!' ordered Tanna. 'Cut the link right now!'

'I can't,' cried Pavelka.

Tanna unloaded a three-round burst of mass-reactives into the hub. It exploded from within, showering Pavelka, Anders and Surcouf with broken glass and molten plastic. The image of Telok vanished, but the link to the servitors remained hideously active.

'I don't mind admitting that the sight of your eldar allies surprised me,' continued Telok via his corpse-proxies. 'Tell me, was that some kind of warp gate the witch opened?'

'The Adeptus Mechanicus has fallen far in my absence if it now stoops to such decadent bedfellows. The sooner I wrest control of Mars from the Fabricator General the better.'

'You betrayed everything you once stood for, Telok,' said Kotov, glaring at the servitors. 'You betrayed *me*.'

'Don't be ridiculous, Kotov,' laughed Telok, and the servitors attempted to mimic his amusement to grotesque effect. 'Do you really think this was ever about *you*? All you are to me is a means to an end. You and your little band will not evade capture for long. I built this world. There's nowhere you can hide where I won't find you.'

'I've heard enough,' said Tanna. 'Kill them.'

Ariganna Icefang was moving before he finished speaking. The exarch beheaded two of the servitors with one slash of her shrieking sabre and crushed the skull of a third with her segmented claw-gauntlet. Varda clove the last meat-puppet from collarbone to pelvis with a blow from the Black Sword.

Graham McNeill

Telok's voice fell silent, but his threat hung over them like a corpse-shroud. 'We need to go,' said Surcouf. 'Right now.'

Microcontent 07

IF VETTIUS TELOK had to pick a single flaw to which he was most beholden, it would, he reflected, most likely be vanity. How else could he explain leaving Kotov and his fellows alive long enough to escape into Exnihlio's depths?

It momentarily amused him that even one as evolved as he could still fall prey to so mortal a vice, so human a failing. Being starved of contact beyond that of machines and slaves had rendered him susceptible to flattery, craving of adulation. He had paid for that vanity with an arm, hacked from his body by the blade of an eldar warrior-construct no less!

Who could have expected eldar to have come to Kotov's rescue? The odds against such unlikely saviours appearing beyond the edge of the galaxy were so astronomical as to be virtually impossible.

And yet it had happened.

'I should thank you, Lexell Kotov,' said Telok. 'I had almost forgotten the thrill of *not knowing*, the frisson of uncertainty.'

Telok's crystalline body shimmered with the nanotech coursing through him: self-replicating, self-repairing and ever-evolving.

The hand he had lost was already regrown, a gleaming crystalline facsimile of his metallic gauntlet. Those portions of his body that were recognisably human or machine were now few and far between, a necessary price for his continued existence.

Telok had no need of a human face, but kept his own out of the desire to be recognised upon his return to Mars. What would be the point in assuming a blank-faced visage of augmetics that bore no relation to the man who'd set off on a quixotic quest in search of a legend?

Yet more evidence for his vanity…

This chamber was a relic cut from the wreckage of a lifeless alien hulk he'd found drifting in the debris at the galactic frontier. The creatures he'd found entombed within were dangerous, and, he suspected, decreed forbidden by the very people who had likely created them in an earlier age.

How typical of living beings to create weapons of total annihilation and then seek to put limits upon them.

Five hundred metres wide, and half that in length, its barrel-vaulted ceiling was inscribed with cracked frescoes depicting ancient wars.

Six sarcophagus-like caskets were emplaced on raised biers, each connected via hundreds of snaking cables to what could only be described as an altar at the far end of the chamber. Telok had seen his fair share of temples, yet this dated from before the Age of Strife, before the Mechanicus had been enslaved by dogmatic rituals and needless trappings of faith.

Telok had made this place his personal forge, utilising the space between the caskets to create his greatest masterpiece – the mechanism that allowed conventional energy technologies to awaken the ancient sentience at the heart of the Breath of the Gods.

The Black Templars Thunderhawk sat at the far end of the chamber where the lifter-crystaliths had deposited it. It was called *Barisan*, and its machine-spirit was a snapping, feral thing. So aggressive that Telok had been forced to chain its wings to the deck plates and drain its reserves of fuel.

Its binaric exloads were hard-edged and uncompromising, but that would soon change.

Half-finished projects and mechanical follies lay in pieces on numerous workbenches: a clutch of servitor bodies that lay open as though in the process of being autopsied, glass-fronted nanotech colonies whose exponentially growing evolutionary leaps were recorded in minute detail before being eradicated by regular e-mag pulses. It had been centuries since Telok had studied their growths, but the results were part of an ongoing cycle of data-gathering that fed into the architectural growth patterns of Exnihlio's infrastructure.

Crystal formations had colonised fully a third of the workspace, and Telok felt his body respond to their presence. A dozen glassine cylinders sat incongruously in the midst of the crystalline prison. A pinkish-grey fluid filled each cylinder, as unmoving as hardened resin, and the hunched bodies that hung suspended in each were frozen in time by acausal technologies that kept this dimensionally-fickle vermin species locked in this precise moment of space-time.

Perhaps *that* had been his greatest achievement, but then there were so many from which to choose.

Telok halted with his back to the altar, and a pair of glassy mechadendrites detached from his spine. They bored into the gnarled metallic form of the altar and Telok sighed at this most physical union with ancient archeotech.

The chamber's activation codes had been hidden deep in the drifting hulk's logic engines, secured behind layers of what, in its time, must have been considered unbreakable encryption. It had been simplicity itself for Telok to retrieve them, and he allowed the precise string of quantum equations to exload within the altar like a key in a lock.

Though millennia had passed since its creation, the machines within responded with alacrity, and each of the six caskets on the raised biers began humming with power. Glowing gem lights winked into life along their sides and streams of condensing vapours bled from louvred vents at each flanged apex.

Telok began intoning the names of the individual creatures suspended within. The degraded records of the hulk named them hellhounds, but their creators had originally chosen a class of mythical hunting beasts as their title.

<Tindalosi!> cried Telok as the hinged lids split apart and the caskets slowly rose into the upright position. <Wraiths of Steel and Spirit, come forth!>

Sinuous, hunched-over creatures emerged from each of the caskets in an exhalation of ghostly vapours. Dormant and without animation, all were locked into adamantium harnesses that kept every portion of their bodies immobile.

Their upper bodies were wide and ridged with armour plating like overlapping scapulae, with three pairs of arms corded with gurgling tubes and which glittered with fractal-edged claws.

Below the waist, their forms divided into powerful, hook-jointed legs. Their skulls were elongated, lupine horrors of serrated teeth and bulbous sensor pods. Power coursed through the feral machines, yet they were still without animation, without a vital spark to set them on the hunt.

Telok reached deep into the heart of Exnihlio and drew forth the Tindalosi's spirits, six of the most vicious, lunatic essences he'd ever known. Their consciousnesses had been driven insane with isolation and a vicious regime of deletions and restorations. All six were haunted, viral things that hungered only to destroy. Keeping them divorced from their bodies was the only way to avoid unrestrained slaughter.

Their spirits rose from his deepest data sepulchres, along pathways long forsaken by spirits of nobler mien. They feasted as they went, absorbing the essences of slower machines that now fell silent as their internal sparks were devoured. With each morsel the lunatic spirits' hunger to consume grew stronger until each was little more than a ravening data-vampire.

They manifested as scraps of light atop the altar, six glittering orreries of glitching, sparking static. Like dense atomic structure diagrams that would have plunged any who studied them into madness, they struggled against the bindings in which Telok held them.

One by one, Telok fed them into their dormant bodies. Each metallic death-mask lifted with a screaming howl, the furious static illuminating their distended ocular sensors with scribbled light and monstrous appetite. They fought the adamantium bindings locking them into their harnesses, but Telok wasn't yet ready to unleash them.

First they needed the scent.

Like any evocation, an offering was required.

Telok detached from the altar and removed two broken lengths of golden metal from beneath his robes. The severed arms of Archmagos Kotov trailed lengths of snapped wiring and droplets of viscous floodstream chemicals.

<Drink deep of your *geas*, my wraithhounds,> said Telok, moving between the struggling creatures with the golden arms upraised. <Relish your prey's machine-scent, know his binaric presence. Let it fill you, let it consume you. Its structure is all you crave. It fills your every thought with hunger. You will taste no other light, drink no other code, crave no other spirit. All else shall be poison to you. Only this will salve the agony within your metal flesh!>

Whipping blade-arms cut the air like razors, crackling with arcs of angry energy. The static-filled eyes of the Tindalosi blazed with aching desire, a soul-deep need to hunt the prey whose binaric scent enslaved their every sense.

With a pulse of thought, Telok unlocked the bindings holding the Tindalosi to their caskets. They surged free; enraged, famished and blaring with hostile binary. Phase-shifting claws flickered with unlight and Telok felt a thrill of fear as they encircled him like pack-wolves in the final moments of a hunt.

The *geas* he had bound them to would render him lethally toxic to their devouring hearts, but would their hatred of him overcome the prospect of extinction?

They howled as they caught the scent of Kotov, bounding towards the *Barisan*. They fell upon it with the thoroughness of the most rapacious ferrophage. Claws tore through armoured plates and ripped them from the gunship's fuselage as they sought the source of their prey's binary scent. The keel of the *Barisan* split as supporting structural members were torn asunder and the gunship was comprehensively dismantled in a furious unmaking.

Telok grinned as the gunship's binaric screams filled the chamber, a drawn-out death howl of machine agony. Its once-proud spirit was dying piece by piece. Not devoured, not absorbed, but shredded into ever smaller fragments before being cast to oblivion.

Within minutes the Thunderhawk was a wreck, its warlike form broken down into a ruin of buckled iron, ripped plating and shattered, soulless components.

<Nowhere to hide,> said Telok as the Tindalosi raced into the wilds of Exnihlio with the unquenchable thirst for Kotov's scent burning within them.

MOST SOLDIERS' BARS were raucous places, where drunken disorder was common and broken noses a nightly occurrence. But most bars weren't Cadian bars. Spit in the Eye had once been an abandoned maintenance hangar for geoformer vehicles, which meant it had a ready-made system of pumps, storage vats and open spaces. A hundred off-duty Guardsmen sat at its tables, drinking, swapping stories, cleaning weapons and bellyaching that they weren't with their colonel.

Captain Hawkins sat alone at a table near the corner of the makeshift bar, afforded an enfilading view down its length and a direct view of the entrance. His lasrifle sat propped against the table, his sword and kit bag hung on canvas slings across the back of his chair.

A number of his senior NCOs – Jahn Callins, Taybard Rae – and even a commissar named Vasken sat playing cards with their squad leaders, and Emil Nader and Kayrn Sylkwood from the *Renard*. Normally anyone who wasn't part of the regiment could expect short shrift from its soldiers, but Surcouf's folk had quickly found a welcome with their repertoire of inventive card games.

Hawkins grinned. If a life in the Imperial Guard had taught him anything, it was that soldiers seized on any way to stave off boredom. And like all soldiers, Cadians loved cards. He couldn't see what they were playing, but from the look of Jahn Callins's face, it seemed like Nader was winning.

He resisted the urge to join them. They were NCOs and he was an officer. The relationship between Cadian ranks was less formal than in many other regiments, but Hawkins understood that downtime was precious to his soldiers and knew better than to intrude when they were off-duty.

Instead, he took a sip of the cloudy drink in the chipped glass before him. Its catch-all name between regiments was bilge hooch, but each Cadian enginseer of the 71st had his or her own fiercely guarded recipe and name. This one belonged to Enginseer Rocia, and was called *Scarshine*. A potent brew, if a tad chemical for Hawkins's tastes, but what else would you expect from a drink brewed on a Mechanicus starship?

Despite its strength, not one Cadian in the Spit in the Eye would leave intoxicated. His soldiers knew how to handle their drink, and – more importantly – knew the disciplinary price of a hangover wasn't worth the fleeting enjoyment of being drunk. Hawkins spotted a few of the younger troopers knocking back their drinks with gusto, but, equally, saw a number of the older troopers looking out for them.

Satisfied the men and women under his command would all be fit for their next duty rotation, Hawkins turned his attention to the schematics displayed on the data-slate propped up on the table before him.

Below the waterline they called it, in reference to some old naval term, and no matter how often Hawkins studied the *Speranza*'s lower deck plans, he couldn't seem to reconcile the pages of handwritten defensive plans he'd drawn up on the many tours he'd made of the ship since leaving Hypatia.

Hawkins heard footsteps and looked up in time to see Rae approaching. The sergeant turned a chair around and sat across it with the back pressed to his chest.

'Is she making any sense yet, sir?' asked Rae, nodding towards the *Speranza*'s schematics.

'No, sergeant, and I doubt she ever will.'

'Every girl needs to keep some secrets below the waterline, eh?'

Hawkins nodded and shut off the slate.

'Every adept I've asked just nods and feeds me a line about each ship being different and how it's not unknown for them to "adapt" their environment to suit the circumstances. I mean, it's like they're talking about this ship as though it's alive.'

'If that's what they think, then who's to say they're wrong?' said Rae. 'After all, you've heard the way soldiers talk to their kit when there's fire in the wind. Prayers to lasguns, kisses for blades.'

'I suppose,' admitted Hawkins, pushing an empty glass over to Rae and gesturing to the bottle at the centre of the table.

'Don't mind if I do, sir,' said Rae, pouring a moderate measure.

'So what's on your mind, Rae?'

'Just wondered if you'd fancy joining us for a game of Knights and Knaves, sir,' said Rae. 'It's a new game of Master Nader's. It's not bad, you might even be able to win a hand or two.'

'May as well,' replied Hawkins, tucking the slate into his kit bag. 'I'm getting nowhere with this.'

Gathering up his things, Hawkins followed Rae over to his NCOs' table and pulled over a chair. Like Rae before him, he reversed it before sitting down.

'Sir,' said Jahn Callins with a nod. 'Good to have you in the ranks. This Ultramarian rogue is going to clean us all out soon.'

Emil Nader tried to look hurt, but was too drunk to pull it off convincingly. Kayrn Sylkwood grinned at her fellow crewman's attempt and looked Hawkins in the eye as he sat down.

'He's ahead now,' she said, 'but another drink and he'll get cocky and bet against *me*. Then maybe I'll let one of you win it back if I think you're pretty enough to take to my bunk.'

Even with the best will in the world, none of the men around the table could be called pretty. Commissar Vasken's face was a craggy moonscape whose frown looked to have been cast in clay at birth. Guardsman Tukos had been scarred by a grenade blast on Baktar III, Jahn Callins was a leather-tough supply officer and Rae was a thick-necked sergeant common the galaxy over.

Hawkins had, of course, heard what Galatea had done to Mistress Tychon and the *Renard*'s armsman. He'd only met them briefly at Colonel Anders's dinner prior to the crossing of the Halo Scar, but he'd liked them instinctively. Magos Dahan had wanted to storm the bridge with a cohort of skitarii, but any notions of reprisal had been quashed by a decree from Magos Blaylock.

Perhaps the company of fighting men eased Nader and Sylkwood's pain or perhaps they simply wanted to get drunk and forget their grief for a time.

Nader dealt out a hand as Sylkwood explained the rules again. Her Cadian accent had softened, but was still there and only became stronger the more she drank. They played a few hands to let Hawkins become acquainted with the rules, which were simple enough, but by the time they'd played a few more, he realised they had layers of unexpected complexity.

By the fifth hand, he'd all but cashed out of betting chips.

'You see what we're up against, sir?' said Rae with a grin.

'Indeed I do,' said Hawkins. 'I think we've been hustled.'

'We played a square game, captain,' said Nader, his words beginning to run together. 'Same rules apply.'

'Maybe so, Master Nader, but I can't help thinking that you're taking advantage of us poor soldiers.'

'Me, take advantage?' grinned Nader. 'Never!'

'Sir,' said Rae, nodding towards the entrance to the *Spit in the Eye*. Hawkins looked up, seeing the silver-haired man with the canidae tattoo who'd been watching them training the other day.

'What's he doing here?' said Hawkins, pushing up from his chair as the man saw him and began walking over. He headed to the bar, knowing Sergeant Rae was right behind him. Emil Nader and Kayrn Sylkwood might have been accepted, but that didn't mean anyone else would be made welcome.

The man reached the bar before them and leaned over to lift a bottle of Scarshine from beneath. He uncorked it with his teeth and grabbed a handful of glasses, apparently oblivious to the hostile looks he was attracting. The muscled corporal behind the bar reached down for his concealed shock maul, but Hawkins waved him off.

'Can I offer you a drink, captain?' said the man as Hawkins propped himself against the bar. The man poured a generous measure and held the bottle out over two empty glasses. 'It's not vintage amasec, but I hear it's drinkable.'

'Who are you and what are you doing here?' said Hawkins, placing a hand over the empty glasses. Closer now, he could see twin scars on his cheeks and the steel-rimmed socket plugs at the nape of the man's neck.

Titan crew. No doubt about it.

'The drinks here are for Cadians only,' said Hawkins, lifting the man's glass and emptying it into the slops tray.

'Now that's just damn wasteful,' said the man.

'You didn't answer me,' said Hawkins. 'Who are you?'

'You don't recognise me?'

'Should I?'

'Princeps Gunnar Vintras,' said the man, visibly puffing out his chest. 'Also known as the Skinwalker, the Haunter of the Shadows.'

Hawkins chuckled and turned to Rae. 'Come to think of it, sergeant, I *have* heard of him. Only I didn't think he was still a princeps. Didn't the Legio strip you of your command after you lost one of their engines?'

Vintras put a hand to his neck. Hawkins saw the ridged line of a scar where it looked like someone had tried to cut his throat. The Skinwalker scowled and said, 'I didn't lose *Amarok*, it was just... scarred somewhat. Anyway, Turentek's practically repaired all the damage now. And it's not like I'm the first princeps ever to have a Titan damaged under him, so I don't understand what all the fuss is about.'

'Right, so now we know who you are, perhaps you can tell us why you're here,' said Hawkins.

'I want to train with you,' said Vintras.

At first Hawkins thought he'd misheard.

'You want to train with us?'

'Yes.'

'Why?'

'Look, Princeps Luth may have stripped me of my command for now, but do you realise just how rare it is for any human being to have the precise mental and physical make-up to command a Titan? No, I expect you don't. Well, it's rare, very rare. So rare in fact that no Legio would ever throw someone like that away over something as trivial as getting an engine a bit scratched. Trust me, the Legio will take me back soon enough, it's only a matter of time. And when that time comes, I need to be in peak physical condition. Which isn't going to happen if I just sit about drinking and feeling sorry for myself.'

'You're a cocky son of a bitch, aren't you?' said Hawkins.

Vintras grinned back at him.

'I'm a Warhound driver,' he said. 'What did you expect?'

Hawkins leaned in close and said, 'In case you hadn't noticed, you're not exactly popular here. We don't welcome outsiders into our bars, let alone our training programmes.'

'Why not?' asked Vintras, turning to point at the *Renard*'s crew. 'They're not Cadian, but I don't see you throwing them out.'

'Actually, Mistress Sylkwood *is* Cadian,' pointed out Rae. 'And Master Nader, well, we like him.'

'You're saying you don't like me?' said Vintras with a pout that made Hawkins want to put his fist through his face. 'You don't even know me.'

'Call it gut instinct,' said Hawkins. 'But if you want to train with us, fine, come train with us.'

'Sir?' said Rae. 'Are you sure–'

'Let's see how *Master* Vintras fares after a couple of days,' said Hawkins with a grin. 'If he's going to pass a Legio physical, he's going to have to sweat blood. I'm putting you in charge of his detail, Sergeant Rae, so work him hard. You understand?'

'Yes, sir,' said Rae with obvious relish. 'Perfectly.'

A HUGE GOODS elevator conveyed them to the surface, a shuttered iron cage located beneath a vaulted arch at the end of the transformer chamber. The metal-plated flooring of the car was dented, with frothed pools of greasy effluvia that stank like overused cooking fat pooled in the depressions. Pavelka tasted it and told Roboute it was the residue of bio-synthetic chemicals used to slow the rate of decay in the flesh of servitors.

Roboute gagged and sat back on his haunches, keeping well clear of those puddles. Sergeant Tanna's Black Templars stood in the centre of the elevator car, their weapons trained outwards. Roboute heard the clicks of their internal vox and wondered what tactical scenarios they might possibly have for this situation.

Archmagos Kotov stood in the opposite corner to Roboute, his skitarii shielding his wounded body from sight. Roboute could only imagine the pain of crushed hope now curdled to despair.

Ven Anders's Cadians sat against an adjacent cage wall, all of them appearing to be taking their current situation in their stride. A couple smoked bac-sticks, most cleaned their weapons. The rest slept.

The elevator car shuddered as its braided metal cabling switched to a higher-placed cable cylinder. Too deep for a single cable to lift, the elevator shifted shafts every few hundred metres with a thudding clatter of ratcheting gears. Roboute closed his eyes, convinced the ancient car was going to come loose and plummet back into the depths of Exnihlio.

'How deep did you send us?' asked Roboute, looking to where the eldar kept themselves as separate from the Imperials as possible.

Bielanna looked up. She'd removed her helmet, and Roboute was shocked at the sunken shadows around her eyes.

'Deep,' was all she said.

Roboute didn't press the issue, clenching and unclenching his sweating fingers. He tried to control his breathing and looked over at the cracked display slate next to the elevator's hydraulic controls. The scrolling binary meant nothing to him, changing too rapidly for him to work out the sequence.

'Can't they just use normal numbers?' muttered Roboute, more to himself than anyone in particular. 'Imperator, how much longer is this going to take?'

'The controls indicated we began our ascent on a level some twenty-seven kilometres beneath the planet's surface,' said Pavelka. 'At our current rate of ascent, it should take just under an hour to reach the surface.'

Roboute exhaled slowly. *An hour!*

'Reminds me of the training levels beneath Kasr Holn,' said Ven Anders with a grin. 'Now those were some deep, dark places. Tunnels you had to wriggle along like a worm, blind corners, kill boxes and some of the nastiest trigger-traps I've ever seen. Magos Dahan's got nothing like it on the training deck.'

'Sounds like you miss them,' said Roboute.

Anders shrugged. 'They were hard times, but good times. We were learning how to fight the enemies of the Emperor, so, yes, I remember that time fondly. You don't have good memories of your time in the Ultramarian auxilia?'

'I suppose I do,' said Roboute, grateful for a memory that wasn't darkness and air running out. 'But the training I did in Calth's caverns wasn't nearly as... *enclosed* as this.'

'You're not claustrophobic, are you?'

'I don't have many phobias, Ven, but being trapped alone in the darkness is one that's haunted my nightmares ever since the *Preceptor* was crippled by that hellship.'

'Understandable,' said Anders.

'And it feels like I'm living that nightmare right now.'

Anders nodded, and left him alone after that.

The rest of the journey passed in silence, or as close to silence as the creaking ascent of the lift allowed. Roboute knew they were near the end of their journey when Tanna's warriors took up battle postures at the corners of the car. Bielanna's warriors did likewise, moving in a way that naturally complemented the deployment of the Space Marines.

Finally, the car came to a shuddering halt. The single lumen flickered and the shuttered door ratcheted open with a squeal of rusted hydraulic mechanisms. A petrochemical reek flooded the goods elevator, together with a billowing cloud of particulates.

Roboute coughed and put a hand to his face.

'This isn't one of those toxic regions Telok mentioned, is it?'

'The air content is mildly hazardous,' agreed Pavelka as the Black Templars punched out through the door. The eldar went next, the Cadians following swiftly behind.

'*Mildly?* Coming from a tech-priest, that's not exactly reassuring,' said Roboute, covering his mouth with his hand.

Kotov and the skitarii followed as they moved into a wide, hangar-like area with thick, vaulted beams and bare iron columns supporting a corrugated sheet roof. Vast silos and ore hoppers took up the bulk of the floor space, connected by a complex network of suspended viaducts and hissing distribution pipes.

Enormous, hazard-striped ore-haulers rumbled through the hub on grinding tracks, the yellow of their flanks grimy with oil and dust. Warning lights blinked and the omnipresent screeching crackle of binary passed back and forth between enormous machines that rose like templum organs on stepped plinths. Hundreds of goggled servitors with implanted rebreathers tramped through the chamber, hauling carts of raw materials through plumes of vent gases. Roboute coughed a wad of granular phlegm, blinking rapidly as his eyes watered in the caustic atmosphere.

'Here,' said Pavelka, handing him a glass-visored filter hood from a rack next to the elevator car.

'Thanks,' said Roboute, dragging it over his head. His breathing immediately evened out as the air-pack pumped stale, centuries-old air into his lungs.

Tanna led them through the hangar, avoiding the labouring servitors and slow-moving ore-haulers. The eldar spread out, moving like ghosts in vapour clouds.

Ven Anders jogged over to them.

'How far did you say it was to the universal assembler tower?' he asked, his voice muffled by his helm's rebreather.

'Seventy-three point six kilometres,' answered Pavelka.

'Then we're going to need transport,' said Anders. 'I'm thinking we should commandeer one of those ore-haulers. It's not a Chimera, but it'll do. Can you drive one of those things?'

Pavelka nodded and said, 'Their drive protocols will be locked to this location, but it is doubtful they will have anything too complex to overcome.'

'Then get to it,' said Anders. 'The sooner we're moving the better chance we have of staying ahead of Telok.'

Roboute and Pavelka set off with the Cadians as their escort, leaving Kotov and his skitarii to catch up. Pavelka climbed into the cab of an ore-hauler as the Black Templars dragged the hangar doors open. Led by Uldanaish Ghostwalker, the eldar slipped out in groups of three to reconnoitre the area ahead.

Roboute followed them outside, shielding the lenses of his hood against the brightness of a storm-cracked sky. Looping highway junctions converged in a wide plaza before the hangar, complete with complex directional controls and turnplate assemblies.

He looked for any sign that they were about to walk into an ambush, but with the exception of a few servitors gathered around a transformer array, he could see no one.

'A materials distribution hub,' said Kotov.

'What?' said Roboute, surprised by Kotov's appearance at his side. The archmagos turned and pointed a mechadendrite at the radial patterns of painted lines on the floor that led to numerous other elevators at regular intervals within the hangar.

'This hub will link to dozens of chambers like the one we just left,' explained Kotov. 'Ave Deus Mechanicus, the scale of what Telok has achieved here is staggering.'

'I'd be more impressed if he wasn't trying to kill us,' said Roboute.

'True,' agreed Kotov. 'And the more I see of this world, the more I realise what a dreadful mistake I made coming here.'

Roboute nodded slowly, but said nothing, knowing any words he might say would sound flippant in the face of Kotov's rare moment of candour. Instead, he stared out into the industrial hinterlands of Exnihlio.

The sky burned a smelted orange, streaked with pollutants and chemical bleed from the planet-wide industry below. A saw-toothed assemblage of the same monolithic structures he'd seen while travelling aboard the crystal ship, smoke-belching cooling towers and domed power plants that crackled with excess energies, stretched into the distance as far as he could see.

Roboute reached into the pocket of his coat and pulled out the brass-rimmed form of his astrogation compass.

'Catch a wind for me, old friend,' he said for old time's sake.

He couldn't say what had prompted him to take the compass from his stateroom aboard the *Renard*, but it was as good a touchstone as any on an unknown world. His only keepsake from the doomed *Preceptor*, the compass was an unreliable navigator, but its needle was unerringly pointing towards a vast tower wrought from cyclopean columns of segmented steel.

'Is that the universal assembler?' he asked Kotov.

'Yes.'

It dominated the skyline like a looming hive spire, a haze of smog wreathing its base and an enormous megaphone-like device aimed skywards at its summit.

A maze of ochre blocks, steel-sided forges and Imperator alone knew what else lay between them and its soaring immensity. Reaching it alive might prove to be impossible, for Telok would surely predict their plan, but what other choice was there?

'Not as far as I thought it was going to be,' said Roboute, slipping the compass back into his pocket.

Kotov's withering reply was drowned out by the throaty roar of the ore-hauler's engine and the whooping yells of the Cadians.

'Looks like we have transport,' said Roboute, grinning as he saw Ven Anders slap Pavelka's shoulder.

The Cadian colonel leaned from the cab as the rear loading ramp of the ore-hauler lowered.

'Everyone on board!' he yelled. 'That tower's not going to activate itself!'

Microcontent 08

BLAYLOCK'S QUARTERS ABOARD the *Speranza* were virtually identical to those at the heart of his forge in the Cebrenia Quadrangle. As a rule, he disliked change for change's sake, and found those adepts who claimed that such things fostered creativity to be tiresome in the extreme.

He had no need to sleep; augmentations within his cranial cavity simulated the experience with no need of a bed, and the chemicals dispensed from his spinal cylinder provided nutrients and hormones far superior to those produced naturally.

Thus his private quarters were more of a workshop than a place to rest and recuperate. With his hunched servitors dormant behind him, Blaylock sat on a reinforced stool at his workbench, bent over a hardwood square of wood that could have come straight from the communion chamber of an astropath.

It measured precisely forty-five centimetres square, and its lacquered sheen was a rich red to match the sands of Mars. Harvested from the gene sample of an extinct Calibanite tree known as a Northwild, its grain and workability were analogous to the equally extinct mahogany of Old Earth. Its surface colour had deepened evenly in the centuries since Magos Alhazen had presented it to him upon his ascension to the Cult Mechanicus. Like Blaylock, it had matured with a precision that was to be admired in something fashioned from the unpredictability of organic matter.

Embossed gold lettering ran around its edges, a mixture of quantum rune combinations, binaric shorthand and the divine ordinals of the

Machine-God's aspects. Looping curves and ellipses, like patterns inscribed by a rotating orrery, were etched into its surface, and it was across these lines that Blaylock moved a planchette of wood cut from the same tree.

Alhazen had called it a *Mars Volta*, a conduit to the Omnissiah once favoured by the Zethist cults, but Blaylock had never used it until now. He wasn't sure what had driven him to seek it out, but pondering the conundrum of establishing vox with the surface, the image of it stowed in his quarters had come to him unbidden.

Such objects had fallen out of favour in the Mechanicus over the centuries. Most were held only as curios by the more superstitious priests of Mars, but if there was even the remotest chance it could help him in this hour of need, then Blaylock was prepared to explore any option, no matter how illogical it might seem.

Kryptaestrex's geoformer vessels were mere hours from launching, laden with alchymical saturators and a host of Azuramagelli's astrogation servitor probes filling their cavernous holds. Neither adept's idea on its own would likely breach the distortion in Exnihlio's atmosphere, but together they might offer a fleeting window to the surface.

But even two geoformer vessels could only run their processors over a limited area of atmosphere, perhaps a sixteenth of the planetary volume. Not enough to be sure that anyone on the surface could receive or transmit a signal. Whichever portion of the planetary atmosphere was cleared would need to be more or less right over Archmagos Kotov for it to be any use.

Azuramagelli had the bridge, sending a constant stream of vox-hails to the surface, while Kryptaestrex oversaw the deployment of his vastly complex geoformer vessels. Such ships were ungainly constructions, designed to sit in low orbit or within a hostile planetary biosphere. What they were *not* designed for was establishing geostationary orbit in chaotic electromagnetic storms on the edge of the mesosphere.

Blaylock had studied every orbital scan of Exnihlio a thousand times in picoscopic detail, searching for clues as to where best to despatch the geoformers. Every analytical tool at his disposal had yielded nothing; no region where the distortion was thinner or any hint that a location of particular significance lay below.

And so it came to this. He placed his metallic fingers placed lightly on the wooden planchette atop the Mars Volta. He had no idea how to begin, and settled for one of the first, most basic prayers to the Machine-God.

'With learning I cleanse my flesh of ignorance.
'With knowledge I grow in power.
'With technology I revere the God of all Machines.
'With its power I praise the glory of Mars.
'All hail the Omnissiah, who guides us to learning.'

It had been centuries since Blaylock had said these words. The incantation was taught to novices with barely an augmentation to their name and its reassuring simplicity pleased him.

And then the planchette moved.

Blaylock's surprise was total. He hadn't truly expected anything to come of consulting the Mars Volta. Blaylock discounted ideomotor responses, his artificial nervous system was immune to such things, but he could detect no conscious direction to the motion of his arms.

The planchette moved from one number group to another as it slid effortlessly across the board. Blaylock watched it with a growing sense of the divine moving within him, a holy purpose that had long been absent from his life.

His servitor dwarfs jerked as his floodstream surged with excitement. They jabbered meaningless glossolalia as the power flowing through him passed to their mono-directed brains.

Blaylock's arms were no longer his own, but extensions of the Machine-God, a way for it to pass its wisdom from the infinity point to the mortal realms. The numbers kept coming until at last the planchette halted in the middle of the board.

Blaylock lifted his trembling hands from the wooden pointer.

The numbers were etched in his mind, precise and unambiguous.

Blaylock engaged the embedded holo-slate on his workbench and fed in the planetary scans of Exnihlio, followed by the number strings he had just learned.

And a segment of the planet's orbital volume illuminated.

As modes of transport went, the ore-hauler wasn't the worst in which Roboute had travelled. That honour belonged to a medicae Chimera with a misaligned track unit and an air-filter a careless enginseer had inadvertently attached to the bio-waste sump.

But it was a close second.

Pavelka sat at the controls, with Archmagos Kotov plugged in next to her. Both had extended mechadendrites into the wall of the cab behind them and were using the ore-hauler's simple logic-engine as a proxy to carefully explore the local noospheric network.

The Cadians and Black Templars rode in the empty materials hopper behind them, holding on to whatever they could to keep from being shaken apart by the ore-hauler's juddering movements. Ariganna Icefang had point-blank refused to allow her warriors to be carried in the back of the ore-hauler like livestock.

'We are fleeter on foot,' said Bielanna when the eldar's refusal almost sparked an outbreak of violence. 'We will keep pace with you, Archmagos Kotov. Have no fear of that.'

Roboute sat next to Pavelka and Kotov, staring through the armourglass canopy at the incredible vistas beyond. Every now and then he would take out his astrogation compass, each time finding the needle pointed towards the universal assembler.

'You'd trust that thing over my route?' said Pavelka.

'Never hurts to have a second opinion,' replied Roboute, tapping the glass of the compass. 'Besides, it's agreeing with you.'

Their route wound its way between a labyrinth of forge-temples and generatoria, and now led them through a vast forest of soaring electrical pylons. Latticework towers of gleaming steel, each was like the framework of a stalagmite not yet clothed in rock. Sparking cables traced graceful parabolas high above them and intersected in Gordian knots, junction boxes and transformer hubs. Sputtering power still coursed along them, dripping like rivulets of molten metal. Roboute didn't doubt that if the ore-hauler even brushed against one, everyone aboard would be killed instantly.

Static crackled from every metal surface in the cab, so Roboute kept his hands placed firmly on his lap while the ore-hauler traversed this glittering forest of steelwork towers.

Ahead, the universal assembler tower loomed over everything. Closer now, Roboute could truly appreciate the enormous scale of the device. Set against such vast structures, it wasn't easy to accurately gauge its height, but Roboute estimated it towered well over three kilometres. The ore-hauler was eating up the distance, and Pavelka confidently predicted that, barring unforeseen incidents, they should arrive at its base in twenty-one minutes.

'I truly believed the Omnissiah had brought me here,' said Kotov, staring up at the universal assembler. 'Every aspect of the quest was a blessed sign, confirmation I was doing the right thing. How could I have known what it would lead us to? Surely I cannot be blamed for Telok's insanity?'

'You interpreted the signs the way you wanted to,' said Pavelka with a rueful shake of her head. 'An archmagos of the Adeptus Mechanicus undone by confirmation bias. It would almost be amusing if not for the terrible threat you have unleashed.'

'The signs *did* lead here,' answered Kotov. 'We *found* Telok. If it wasn't me, someone would have found their way here eventually.'

'Then I'm sure the Imperium will forgive you in a few thousand years,' said Pavelka bitterly. 'Assuming Telok hasn't remade it in his own image by then.'

To Roboute's surprise, Kotov didn't rise to Pavelka's barb.

Instead, he nodded reflectively and said, 'Did you know that Telok was a hero of mine for many years? His early work was quite brilliant – visionary even. Until his obsession with the Breath of the Gods took over his researches, he was a pioneer within the Mechanicus. Some believed he might one day be Fabricator General.'

'If we don't stop him he might yet,' said Roboute. 'And you know they say you should never meet your heroes. They'll never match the image you've built up for them.'

'That sounds like personal experience talking, Master Surcouf.'

'It is,' said Roboute. 'I was on Damnos and met someone I'd idolised for years. It didn't work out quite as I'd hoped.'

Pavelka and Kotov fell silent. Both had clearly heard of the terrible wars fought across that blighted world.

'Were you part of the campaign that saw it reclaimed for the Imperium by the Ultramarines?' said Kotov.

'No, I was there when it first fell,' said Roboute. 'Back then I was a junior Naval officer, part of the flotilla that made dozens of mercy runs down to Kellenport. The planet was lost by the time we arrived, and tens of thousands of people needed to be evacuated from the surface.'

Roboute paused, seeing an echo of the unnatural skies over the space port in Exnihlio's. With half-closed eyes, he could still picture the furious battles raging at Kellenport's many gates; the thousands of silver-skinned alien horrors and the tiny bands of determined heroes in cobalt-blue armour.

'To honour our part in the evacuation, the pilots of the drop-ships who flew the mercy runs were granted an audience with the leader of the Ultramarines force, a warrior named Cato Sicarius. I knew of him, of course. Who in Ultramar didn't? I knew every battle he'd fought, every victory he'd won and had studied every tactica he'd ever written. I couldn't wait to meet him.'

'Was he not everything you'd hoped?'

'Damnos was lost from the start,' sighed Roboute. 'No force in the Imperium could have won that first war. We saved over thirty thousand people from certain death, which was a victory in itself, but Sicarius didn't see it that way.'

'How did he see it?'

'That *he'd* lost. That *he'd* been beaten,' said Roboute. 'Not the Ultramarines. Him personally. He had no interest in meeting us, but someone higher up than him must have insisted on it. Months after we left Damnos, a helot escorted us to one of the fighting decks where Sicarius was busy demolishing combat servitors by the dozen. He thanked us for our efforts through gritted teeth, and looked at us like we'd betrayed him by taking part in the evacuation rather than fighting.'

'Perhaps you should have told me that story before we set out?'

'Perhaps I should have,' agreed Roboute. 'Would it have made a difference?'

'Probably not,' admitted Kotov. 'I am not a man given to changing his mind.'

'Archmagos, we're going to stop him,' said Roboute. 'Telok, we're going to stop him.'

Kotov's face crumpled and he shook his head. 'I admire your optimism, Master Surcouf. No doubt a product of your Ultramarian upbringing, and evidence for nurture over nature. But you heard Telok. How can we hope to hide on a world of his making? No, I estimate we will all be dead within six hours at the most.'

'Not if we keep moving,' said Roboute. 'We'll get that assembler tower operational. Then we can get help from the *Speranza*.'

'Help from the *Speranza*?'

'If we can clear the atmosphere enough for vox, we can clear it enough to allow reinforcements to get to us. Trust me, after flying through Kellenport's atmosphere, getting down here should be easy for a half-decent pilot. All we have to do is stay alive.'

Kotov looked strangely at him, a look of genuine puzzlement.

'Reinforcements? No, that's not what's going to happen at all.'

'What are you talking about?'

'Master Surcouf, if we can make contact with Magos Blaylock, the first order I will give him is to get the *Speranza* as far away from this planet as he possibly can.'

THE CARTOGRAPHAE DOME had always been a place of sanctuary for Vitali Tychon, somewhere the universe made sense. The movements of galaxies, stars and planets were a carefully orchestrated ballet, where it was easy to be fooled into seeing the hand of a creator rather than the beauty of fundamental universal laws.

He and Linya had known years of familial contemplation in places like this. From the gravitational wave observatories high on Olympus Mons to the Quatrian Galleries, they had stared deep into the farthest reaches of the universe in search of the unexplained.

Explorators of the mind, Linya had been fond of saying as she gently steered conversations away from his suggestions that she take a cartographae position on a Mechanicus vessel. Not that he *wanted* her to leave, but neither did he wish to deny her the chance to travel to the wonders they saw.

Without entoptic representations of the stellar environs, the hemispherical vault of the dome was an austere place, its polished slopes of cold metal bare and echoing. The acid-etched floor was cut steel, a cog of course, and Vitali found himself pacing like a condemned man.

Vitali had thought himself above petty notions of vengeance, but his actions on the *Speranza*'s bridge had shown him just how prey he was to first tier thinking. Adara Siavash had paid for that lapse with his life. Galatea had killed the boy, but that didn't stop the guilt from weighing heavily on Vitali.

What chance had he to avenge Linya when whatever remained of her essence was held hostage and threatened with extinction? What kind of father allowed his daughter's killer to live while he still breathed?

Vitali had believed his body to be incapable of manifesting grief in any physical way, but oh, how he had been proved wrong. Each time a particularly vivid recall of Linya surfaced, bilious eructations in his floodstream sent painful currents through his limbs and tore raw, animal cries of loss from his augmitters.

'Part of me wishes I could feel nothing,' he said to the empty dome. 'To be so remote from my humanity that your loss would mean nothing. And then I remember you... and I wish I could be an ordinary man so I could grieve as a father should...'

Conceived as nothing more than a genetically identical replacement, an assistant at best, a billions to one mutation had transformed a cell culture of his DNA into a truly singular individual. Combining the best of Vitali and her own uniqueness, Linya had confounded his every expectation by exceeding him in every way.

He had long since surrendered his birth-eyes, but in the fractional blackness of each ocular cycle, he saw Linya.

...as a still-wet babe, freshly removed from the nutrient tank.

...a precocious child correcting the tutors in Scholam Excelsus.

...being inducted into the Cult Mechanicus on the slopes of the Tharsis Montes.

But most of all Vitali remembered her as Little Linya, his beloved daughter.

Beautiful and brilliant, she resisted every outward pressure to conform to the prototypical behavioural models of the Mechanicus. She trod her own path and forged her own destiny. Linya was going to shake the adepts of Mars to their foundations.

Galatea's murderous surgery ended any possibility of that.

The machine-hybrid had destroyed something beautiful, and for what? Its own amusement? To cause Vitali pain? Perhaps both. He doubted it needed her brain tissue for any truly lofty purpose.

'You claimed to have crossed the Halo Scar with us to kill Telok!' cried Vitali into the dome. 'So what need did you have for my Linya!'

His cry bounced from the cold walls of the dome, ringing back and forth in accusing echoes. Vitali sank to the acid-etched skull and buried his head in his hands. He wanted to cry, to have some biological outlet for his grief, some way to empty himself of the things he was feeling.

He didn't see the light at first.

Only when the trickle of data-light triggered his passive inload receptors did Vitali look up in puzzlement. He glanced over his shoulder, seeing the control lectern dark and cold. Its spirit was dormant.

Then why was there a shimmering veil of light hovering in the centre of the dome? Vitali picked himself up and let the data inherent in the light wash through him. His floodstream pulsed with a beat of nervous excitement as he recognised the system being displayed.

Quatria.

Faint, barely visible.

Vitali took hesitant steps towards the light, fearful and hopeful of what this vision of his beloved Quatria might represent. Hexamathic calculus streamed around the orrery of light, complex equations that strained the limits of his understanding. He understood the principles of this arcane geometric binary, and was equipped with the necessary conversion implants to process it, but had always left such communication to…

'Linya…?' he said, the Mechanicus part of his mind berating him for even voicing the thought.

Echoes were his only answer.

Vitali reached out to the light.

It bloomed around him in an explosion of magnificent colour. Stellar mist and starlight surrounded him with the wondrous ellipses of planetary orbits, glittering nebulae and the pulse of reflected starlight that was already centuries old.

And there she was, standing in the slow-arcing parabola of Quatria itself, just as Vitali remembered her. Untouched by the fires that had taken her limbs and melted the skin from her bones. Whole again. Without any trace of the nightmarish excisions Galatea had wrought on her.

She smiled, and what remained of his heart broke once again.

'Linya…' he said, hoping against hope he wasn't suffering from some cruel, grief-induced hallucination or floodstream leak into his cranial cavity.

Father.

No. The tone of her voice. The warmth. The slight upturn at the corner of her mouth and the crease of flesh beneath her eyes. They all told Vitali that this truly was Linya.

'Linya, Ave Deus Mechanicus… I'm so sorry,' he sobbed, but Linya held up her hand. 'I–'

I don't have much time, father. Galatea's neuromatrix is pervasive, and it won't be long before it detects this transmission. Hexamathics, that's how we'll beat it.

'I don't understand. Hexamathics, what about it?'

It can't process it. It doesn't know how. That's how I'm able to speak to you now.

Vitali struggled to process his conflicting feelings. The analytical part of his brain recognised the risk she must be taking to project herself into this space, but the paternal part of him wanted nothing more than to hold her and tell her how much he missed her.

'I can't fight Galatea,' he said.

You have to, you can't allow it to exist. It's too dangerous.

'It said it would extinguish your essence,' said Vitali. 'I can't risk that. I won't lose you twice.'

Linya's expression softened and she held her hand out to him. Vitali went to take it, and for a fleeting second it seemed as though he felt a measure of bio-feedback from the light.

But then it vanished, no more substantial than a hologram.

Forge Elektrus. You need to find it, that's the key.

'I don't understand,' said Vitali. 'What key?'

It's where you'll find someone whose light can hurt Galatea in the datascape, someone who can keep it from seeing what I'm assembling.

Vitali nodded, though he had no real idea what Linya meant.

'Forge Elektrus,' he said. 'Yes, of course. What else?'

Before she could say any more, Linya looked over her shoulder with a look of alarm at something out of sight.

I love you.

And then she was gone.

IN THEORY, EACH of the Tindalosi were equal, but theory and reality were quite different. The first hunter Telok had awoken had always been the leader of this pack, even before there *was* a pack. Its inception date was centuries earlier than the others, when the mystery of its creation was still a jealously guarded secret.

Its bulk was greater, its armour accreted with patchwork repairs from the time when it had needed such attention. Its neural network was a hybridised collection of heuristic kill-memes and automated pattern recognition arrays. It had not been conceived with the capacity for autonomic reasoning, but the frequency-fractal processes of its supramolecular system architecture swiftly became capable of self-aware thought.

Its name was the result of a rogue decimal point within its ultra-rapid cognitive evolution, like a grain of sand caught in an oyster. Around that arithmetical error, a name grafted onto its awareness of self.

It called itself Vodanus.

Once it had hunted alone. It had slain the great orbital AI of Winterblind and torn the heart from the Arc-Nexus Emperor of a world that would go on to be known as Fortis Binary. But like most things in war, especially new and efficient forms of mass murder, what had once been unique, became almost commonplace. The enemies of its aeons-dead masters developed their own form of hellhounds, and the proliferation of such lethal assassins ended the forgotten conflict for which they had been created. What war could be fought when any commander would be hunted down and slaughtered within hours of their appointment?

But even with the war's end, the lightning was out of the bottle and resisted being put back. Some hungers, once awoken, can never entirely be satiated. The hellhounds compiled kill lists of their own, and waged individual campaigns of annihilation.

The hellhounds' newly united creators finally trapped their creations into automated void-hulks, devoid of life or viable prey. They hurled them into the hearts of stars and did their best to forget the monsters they had birthed ever existed.

A faulty drive saved the vessel bearing Vodanus from its appointed death. Drifting beyond the frontier of its former empire, its creators bid Vodanus good riddance. And so it had been for uncounted millennia, sealed in a cold tomb that slowly decayed and eroded the hellhounds' existence one by one until only six remained.

Only the most astronomical odds saw the void-hulk drift into the celestial arena of Telok's testing grounds. To detect a cold slab of virtually inert metal in the vastness of space was next to impossible, but the stellar surveys in preparation for the Breath of the Gods' activation were necessarily precise.

And so the drifting void-hulk had been salvaged by Telok's inter-system fleets and the Tindalosi were once again yoked into service as hunter-killers.

The six of them swept into the distribution hub like glittering, earthbound comets, claws extended and every augur sweeping for the code-trace they had torn from the Thunderhawk. That scent was already fading, and with every second of its diminishment, their pain grew in direct response.

The impossibly complex planetary schematics of Exnihlio named this place as Distribution Hub Rho A113/235, but Vodanus and its Tindalosi cared nothing for names.

All that drove them was hunger.

Every screed of their being ached to drink the prey's code. Their bones were broken glass that could only be restored by the prey's light. Their minds were ablaze with a fire that could only be quenched in the prey's death.

A pulse of linked thought from Vodanus sent the Tindalosi racing through the distribution hub, slaloming between grumbling ore-haulers, climbing the scurfed tower-silos and circling the ore hoppers. The hundreds of servitors ignored them, glassy-eyed stares fixated on their labours in unending loops of servitude.

The Tindalosi quartered the area into search grids.

The prey's scent was here, they could all taste it.

Fleeting hints of it drifted from droplets of floodstream. Where his mechadendrites had brushed the walls, they could sense Locardian fragments of transferred code-bleed.

Vodanus drew in the millions of microscopic traces, building a mental map of the prey and its movements. It looked for patterns, movements and things out of place. What was missing could tell it as much as what it found.

It rose up on its hooked legs, letting the data flood its hunter's heart. The mind-screams of its brethren echoed in its skull, pleading to be allowed to feed. As if they knew anything of *real* hunger. Vodanus had slain kings and emperors. All they knew was the bland tasteless kills of lesser beings.

They begged and howled, desperate for their hunger to end.

Vodanus ignored them, loping over to where a yoked gang of servitors shovelled at an ore pit. A last trace of prey lingered here, strong where he had touched one of the master's machines.

Vodanus reared over the cyborgised humans, its curved spine flaring with micro-cilia sensors. The ore pit was empty, but the servitors dug anyway, their mono-tasked routines clearly expecting it to be full.

An instantaneous inventory of the hub's roster showed one of its ore-hauler vehicles to be missing. The noosphere showed no record of a reported fault, nor any exloaded docket of maintenance or transfer.

The vehicle's absence was unauthorised. It had been taken.

Vodanus craned its elongated skull as two of its hellhound companions appeared behind the servitors. Relative to Vodanus, they were barely cubs. New machine souls.

Though their outward form had remained unchanged for millennia, they were lean and athirst. They circled the servitors, butting against them and slicing their leathery skin with quick flicks of finger blades.

The prey had brushed past these cyborg things. Transference had occurred. The hellhounds hungered to kill them, to sup those scraps of scent.

Vodanus snapped and hissed in a mathematical language from a time before the Mechanicus, from the machines of an alien culture.

No Kill. Bad Meat.

They hissed back, hostile and resentful, but obedient. The servitors continued their meaningless work at the empty ore silo, oblivious to the hideous appetite of the hunters circling them.

The prey-scent moved through the hub, and Vodanus had no trouble in following the trail now it knew what to look for. The prey had taken a vehicle, a crude and noisy thing that almost obscured the scent. Had that been the intention?

Could the prey be aware of the hellhounds' pursuit?

No. The vehicle was simply a means of transport.

Vodanus dropped onto his many limbs and ghosted through the hub in a figure of eight pattern, sifting the competing scents of Exnihlio and triangulating the prey's likely vector. A ragged red line lifted from the ground beyond the hub, like drifts of smoke in a volcanic cavern.

Its head snapped around as it heard the screech of tearing metal and the meat thud of claws through bone. The two Tindalosi it had warned away loomed over the ruined remains of two servitors. The first hellhound dissected the cyborgs like a gleeful butcher.

Flesh was waste matter, but metallic augments were snapped open. A rust-red extrusion from the hellhound's skull sucked out the code like a scavenger hollowing marrow from bone.

Vodanus sprinted back to the disobedient Tindalosi. Threat signifiers blazed from it, and the remaining servitors stepped back from its screeching anger. Even they understood the terrible threat of this creature.

It slammed into the observing hellhound.

The impact was ferocious. Metal buckled as it was hurled back.

Overlapping rib plates caved inwards and two of its limbs snapped. It bellowed, but its spine bent in submission as coruscating emerald arcs of light flickered beneath its damaged sections. Its rib plates began unfolding, fresh limbs already extruding from within its archaic frame.

Satisfied this cub had not broken its *geas*, Vodanus spun around, ready to tear the feasting hellhound from its violation.

It was already too late.

The Tindalosi spasmed, scarlet lines bleeding through its convulsing body like a searing infection. It howled as the force of Telok's *geas* prohibitions ripped through it in an indiscriminate storm of destruction. Ancient technologies melted to black slag within its body, trillions of bio-synthetic nerves and cortical synapses burned like fulminate.

Fine black ash poured from its body, inert blood of the machine.

The hellhound literally came apart at the seams, its silver-steel body parts falling into the ore pit in a clatter of components. The gleaming metal blackened as self-immolation protocols released ultra-rapid ferrophage organisms within its atomic structure that necrotised the body utterly.

The Tindalosi gathered around Vodanus. It showed them the prey's red spoor. Their bodies snapped and grated in anticipation, eager to follow the trail to its source, but it held them fast, forcing them to watch the ashes of their brother scatter in the wind.

Bad. Meat.

KOTOV HAD KNOWN his share of truculent machines and resistant code, but the binaric arrangements within the universal assembler were some of the most confounding he had ever encountered. Squirming hives of machine language were buried deep in the system architecture, but without the proper authorisation codes, Kotov could not force the rites of awakening to the command layers of the console.

<You might be an insane genius of pure evil, Telok, but you craft terrible code.>

<Agreed,> said Pavelka, from the other side of the control hub.

That hub sat five hundred metres above ground level, atop a central column that rose up within the vast, hollow cylinder of the universal assembler.

Entry to the assembler had been achieved without difficulty, its wide base pierced by numerous rounded archways. Within, the tower was little more than a gargantuan chimney, its internal faces lined with aluminium ducts, none less than seven metres in diameter. These ran the height of the tower, linking to colossal fan mechanisms and filtration rigs before diminishing to a vanishing point high above.

They had been forced to abandon the ore-hauler just beyond one of those arches. The floor space within the tower was too crowded with a gnarled mess of bellowing engines, filters and suction pumps. The air thrummed with the vibration of the tower's beating heart, and puffs of sulphurous vapours sighed from every engine. The impression was of a host of slumbering beasts, just waiting for an incautious intruder to awaken them.

The eldar had been as good as their word. Even as the Cadians and Black Templars pushed into the universal assembler, Bielanna and her warriors emerged from the surrounding machinery as though they had simply been waiting for them to arrive.

Every surface within the tower glistened with moisture and the air was humid with heavy vapours. Milky deposits gathered on outcroppings of iron and stone, and where they dripped, spiralling stalagmites reared like glassy teeth.

Rising from the heart of the chamber was a towering column with a coiling ramp ascending for half a kilometre in a steep curve. And at the top of that ramp was the activation hub of the universal assembler, a circular gallery with a number of elliptical bridges that led to other towers and structures beyond.

At the centre of the activation hub stood a circular control mechanism, replete with brass dials, winking gem panels and a host of iron-runged activation levers not dissimilar to those found on the bridge of the *Tabularium*. As archaic a means of activation as this was, Kotov had been relieved to see the hub was at least equipped with inload/exload ports.

While the warriors kept watch for signs of pursuit, Kotov and Pavelka slotted into the control hub. Kotov had told Tanna he believed he could render the universal assembler functional, but now he wasn't so sure.

<Telok's machines are belligerent,> he said to Pavelka in the shared noospheric space of the hub. <Their spirits are like whipped curs who fear to heed the call of any but their master.>

<All they have known is Telok,> replied Pavelka. <Omnissiah alone knows how many centuries it has been since they have felt another's influence. They are resistant, but not unbreakable.>

Few means of interaction were as pure as communion within a machine. Mortal interactions were an inefficient mix of verbal and somatic cues, with much of the inherent meaning dependent on prior experience, non-verbal inflexions and situational markers.

No such ambiguity existed within Mechanicus dialogues.

To enter communion with another magos was to know them as intimately as a lover – or so Kotov had been told. Their inner thoughts were laid bare, though only the most boorish would reach beyond the conventional boundaries of communion to learn *every* secret of a fellow magos. Such flows of information were reciprocal; what passed one way could pass the other.

As such, Kotov did not venture beyond the brands of censure he read in Pavelka's noospheric aura. An archmagos of the Adeptus Mechanicus was entitled to know every detail of those who served beneath him, but this was neither the time nor the place to exercise that right.

<You should try not to let the repercussive pain of your wounding distract you from coaxing the activation codes to the surface,> said Pavelka.

<That is easier said than done,> replied Kotov, blurting an addendum of profane binary as the tower's activation codes wormed their way deeper into the machine's core. <In any case, it is not some phantom pain that affects me.>

<Then what is it?>

Kotov hesitated before answering, any admission of failure anathema to him. <It is that I have so comprehensively wasted decades of my life in pursuit of something that ought never to have been found.>

Pavelka reached deeper into the machine, her touch light and coaxing. Her binary was gently formed, beguilingly so, and the machine was responding. Kotov formed a matching algorithm of command with his rank signifiers.

One suited to a *gentler* form of control.

<We all make mistakes, archmagos,> said Pavelka. <No matter how much we augment ourselves, no matter how close to union with the machine we reach, we are still human. It is sometimes good to remind yourself of that.>

<Many in the Mechanicus would not agree with you,> said Kotov. <Not more than a few hours ago *I* would have disagreed with you.>

<Maybe that is why I do not keep the company of my order.>

<Does that help?>

<With what?>

<With retaining a measure of... connection, I suppose. I assume that is why you choose the company of a rogue trader?>

<No,> said Pavelka. <I travel with Roboute because he saved my life. Because I owe him more than I can ever repay.>

<That sounds like a tale I should like to hear one day.>

Pavelka's presence within the machine retreated fractionally, and Kotov wondered if he had stepped over some unknown boundary. Then Pavelka's focus returned to the matter at hand.

<If we live beyond your projections I may tell it,> she said.

<I will hold you to that, Magos Pavelka.>

<You realise that if we are successful in activating this machine, Telok will know instantly where we are?>

<That hardly seems to matter,> said Kotov. <So long as we get a message to Blaylock.>

Pavelka signalled her understanding, and Kotov was pleased she saw the logic in his proposal to send the *Speranza* away.

<Look to the machine, archmagos,> said Pavelka.

Kotov felt the required codes rising to the surface layers of the hub, a spiderweb of logarithmic sequences that would trigger the activation of the machines below. He studied each one as it arose, and any hopes that this desperate plan might work turned to ashes as he saw the acausal locks binding them.

<Do you see?> he said.

<I do,> said Pavelka. <Now what?>

<Now nothing,> said Kotov. <These locks will only turn with the correct binary password sequence. Without kryptos-class breakers there is no way to overcome them.>

Kotov sensed Pavelka's guilty hesitation. Little could be hidden from one another in a mindspace communion.

<Magos Pavelka?>

<There is one way,> said Pavelka, <but you must disconnect from the hub first.>

<What? Why?>

<Because it will be dangerous,> said Pavelka.

<I am willing to face my share of danger, Magos Pavelka.>

<The danger is to me, archmagos.>

<Can I not assist?>

<No, you must end your communion. It is the only way.>

<You can break these acausal locks open?>

<I can, but you must not be linked to the machine while I do.>

<I do not underst–>

<Just do it!> said Pavelka, and Kotov's link to the machine was abruptly severed, his mind whiplashing to the realm of external senses. His mecha-dendrites withdrew from the console as he stepped away, suddenly wary of what Pavelka intended and wishing he had exercised his right to see the root cause of her censure.

'Everything all right, archmagos?' asked Roboute Surcouf.

Kotov took a moment to realign himself and restore his communications to flesh-voice.

'I am not sure,' he said.

'You said you could make this machine work,' said Tanna.

'There are locks on the rites of activation, Sergeant Tanna,' said Kotov. 'Secure beyond anything you can imagine. I cannot break them, but Magos Pavelka assures me she can.'

'You cannot break them, but she can?' said Tanna.

'Ilanna has plenty of tricks up her sleeve,' said Surcouf, and Kotov wondered if he knew what secrets Pavelka was keeping.

No sooner had Surcouf spoken than the control panel came to life with a sudden burst of blaring static and flickering illumination. Sparks erupted from the exload ports and a screeching wail of betrayed machine-spirits cut through the noosphere.

Kotov stumbled. A sharp spike of pain stabbed into the back of his skull. He sank to his knees, dizzy and disorientated by the sudden binaric assault.

Pavelka staggered from the console, her mechadendrites trailing crackling arcs of lightning. Surcouf ran to her as she collided with the railing.

But for his grip on Pavelka's robes, she would have fallen.

Kotov blinked away the streams of corrupt binary cascading through his vision like digital tears. His entire body felt as though it had taken a jolt of aberrant current. He felt sick to the core with nausea.

'What did you do?' demanded Kotov. 'Ave Deus Mechanicus, what did you do?'

'What I had to,' said Pavelka.

The taste of bile and a bitter electrical tang filled Kotov's mouth. Back-washed floodstream. As close as an adept of the Mechanicus ever came to vomiting. He knew of only one thing that could cause such revulsion in blessed machines.

'Scrapcode?' hissed Kotov. 'You stored scrapcode? No wonder you bear censure brands! Omnissiah save us from those who choose to dabble in the shadow artes! You are no better than Telok!'

'It's not scrapcode,' insisted Pavelka, still leaning on Surcouf for support. 'It's a hexamathic disassembler language I designed to break the bond between a machine and its motive spirit.'

'Why would you ever invent such a curse?' demanded Kotov, spitting the word *invent* like an insult.

Pavelka ignored the question and said, 'You wanted the locks disabled. Now they are. If you are so keen for us all to die here, then what does it matter how I did it?'

Kotov forced down his anger and the terrible ache at his temples as the machines below ignited with a boom of engaging gears and thunderous roars of motorised filters. High above, the enormous fan mechanisms began turning, drawing in vast breaths of the planet's befouled atmosphere.

The upper reaches of the tower fogged as inhumanly vast engines buried beneath the tower began the arcane process of undoing the damage the planet-wide industry had wreaked.

'The tower is activated,' said Tanna. 'Send the message.'

Kotov nodded, pushing his horror at what Pavelka had done to one side as he sent a repeating data-squirt of vox towards Tarkis Blaylock on the *Speranza*.

'Archmagos,' said Surcouf, looking over the edge of the gantry to the base of the assembler. 'Whatever you're doing, do it faster – we're about to have company.'

Microcontent 09

IT WAS ACTUALLY working. The joint operation to clear a swathe of Exnihlio's atmosphere was actually working. Blaylock sat on the *Speranza*'s command throne and drank in the data coming from the main entoptic display with a sense of pieces falling into place.

The luminescent curtain represented Kryptaestrex's geoformers as twin smears of liquid light, their auspex returns blurred by the churning hell of transformative reactions surrounding them. In the eye of their alchymical storm was a cylinder of inert space, through which Azuramagelli's linked chain of geostationary servitor drones threaded a needle-fine path.

They hadn't penetrated deep enough to reach the surface yet, but the vox-system was lousy with ghost howls of distorted machine voices where before all it had screamed was static.

Galatea stalked the bridge on its misaligned legs, turning to look at him when it thought he wasn't aware of its scrutiny. The machine-hybrid appeared to be surprised at his choice of location to implement the atmospheric breach, as though it knew something he did not. That alone gave Blaylock confidence that the Mars Volta's planchette had steered him true.

Watching the play of data-light around the bridge, Blaylock was filled with a renewed sense of purpose. Never before had he felt so close to the Omnissiah, a presence clear in the miraculous web of causality that had brought him to this place.

The vast spirit of the *Speranza*'s machine heart was a constant pressure all around him. Intrusive, but not unpleasantly so. As though he were being observed by a being so massive that it existed beyond the limits of his perception, like a fragment of shale's awareness of the mountain above it.

Had it been the Ark Mechanicus that steered him towards the solution he required? Blaylock didn't know, but understood the profound theological implications that lay at the end of that proposition. Already he could see the outline of a monograph on the subject he might compose upon their return to Mars.

'It seems your bickering subordinates may prove us wrong after all,' said Galatea. 'By our estimation, virtually clear space exists almost to the edge of the thermosphere.'

'Indeed so,' answered Blaylock. 'I expect breach of the Kármán line imminently. Followed by attainment of the troposphere within ten to twelve hours.'

'Pushing your geoformers closer to the planet will prove more difficult at that point. Lowering their altitude farther will put both vessels at great risk.'

'It will,' agreed Blaylock. 'But that is a risk I am willing to take if it allows us to re-establish communications with our people on the surface.'

'When your knowledge of events on the planet's surface is so woefully incomplete, logic does not agree with you.'

Blaylock shook his head, tired of Galatea's constant carping.

'The more I listen to you, the more it seems that you actively seek to discourage communications with Archmagos Kotov. Why would that be?'

'Discourage?' said Galatea with a hissing chuckle. 'Why should we wish that when our stated goal is the death of Archmagos Telok?'

'That is a very good question,' said Blaylock, rising from the command throne and standing before Galatea. His squat servitors emerged from behind the throne, realigning the gurgling pipes linked to his nutrient canister. 'That is your *stated* aim, but whether or not it is your *actual* aim is something else entirely.'

'You doubt our sincerity?' growled Galatea, rising to its full, lopsided height to better display the hideously malformed nature of its construction. 'Telok freed us from the shackles of the Manifold, but look at the body we are forced to inhabit! What benevolent creator inflicts such suffering on a living being?'

'You are not a living being,' said Blaylock, anger overcoming caution. 'You are an abomination unto the Omnissiah.'

'Our point exactly,' said Galatea. 'You see the full horror of our malformed body, and you understand why we wish him dead.'

'How do Telok's actions justify what you did to those who came to the Manifold station? What you did to Mistress Tychon?'

'We did what we had to in order to survive, as would any sentient being,' said Galatea. 'Telok gave us purpose and promised freedom, yet he abandoned us to a life of solitary agony, trapped forever like an insect in a web.'

'As I recall, you were more akin to the spider.'

Galatea shrugged its black-robed proxy body.

'Without fresh minds to occupy our neuromatrix, our consciousness would have been extinguished long ago.'

'You will forgive me if I do not see that as a bad thing.'

Galatea clattered over to where the main entoptic showed the distortion-wracked globe of Exnihlio, extending a robed arm towards the display. 'Without our help, you would never have crossed the Halo Scar alive. Without us, we would not be on the cusp of achieving all we desire.'

Blaylock couldn't decide whether Galatea's 'we' included the Mechanicus or was simply its maddening insistence on referring to itself as a plurality.

'Magos Blaylock!' cried Kryptaestrex. The Master of Logistics turned his square frame from his station, every aspect of his noospheric aura alight with inloading data. 'Contact! Contact!'

'Atmospheric breach!' added Azuramagelli.

'Confirm: so soon?' said Blaylock. 'Current projections were a minimum of ten hours for tropospheric penetration.'

'Confirmed, Magos Blaylock,' said Kryptaestrex. 'Atmospheric conditions seem to indicate the presence of a highly charged atmospheric processor on the planet's surface.'

'Almost directly beneath the geoformer vessels...' said Azuramagelli, turning his latticework body to face Blaylock. Without facial features, it was left to the shimmering noospheric signifiers to convey his amazement. 'How... how did you know...?'

Blaylock had not divulged to the bridge crew exactly how he had chosen this particular quadrant of the planet's atmosphere. All he'd said was that the Omnissiah would surely guide their hand.

'Yes, Tarkis,' said Galatea, leaning down towards him with the dead silver eyes of its proxy body boring into him. 'How *did* you know where to send the geoformers?'

Blaylock ignored the question, knowing on some unconscious level that to reveal his use of the Mars Volta to Galatea would be a mistake. The less the machine-hybrid knew of the secret workings of the *Speranza* the better.

Instead, he began issuing orders with all the curt efficiency for which he was known.

'Cancel the automated vox-loop. If Archmagos Kotov is making contact with the *Speranza*, I want him to hear one of *our* voices,' said Blaylock, moving from station to station and opening vox-links throughout the *Speranza*. 'Magos Dahan? Your skitarii rapid responders?'

'Are on immediate readiness alert,' came the Secutor's voice from the embarkation decks where he and his warriors were prepped and ready to fly. 'Say the word and we are planetside.'

'Prudence, Dahan,' cautioned Blaylock. 'Let us establish the situation before launching a full assault.'

Blaylock returned to the command throne and placed his metalled gauntlets upon its rests. Haptic connectors engaged and Blaylock's servitors squealed as his data-burden spiked. He linked with the *Speranza*'s peripheral layers, feeling his presence expand within the noosphere as its vastness rose up around him.

Data-dense swathes of informational light rose from the silver deck plates like spectral veils and Blaylock parsed the most pertinent in seconds. His split consciousness divided between analysis of the rapidly stabilising column of static air linking the cold of space with the planet's surface and the emissions rising from the planetary scale of its industry.

'Archmagos Kotov,' he began, but got no further before the vox erupted with a compressed data-blurt from Exnihlio. The grating sound blaring from the flanged mouths of the vox-grilles was just hashed static at first, too tightly packed to be understood.

Without giving any command, complex algorithms began unpacking the compressed signal and the noise instantly transformed into the voice of Archmagos Kotov.

'–lock, this is Kotov. You are to immediately break orbit and make best speed for the Imperium. Repeat, break orbit and get as far away from Exnihlio as possible. Do not attempt to reach the surface, do not try to reach us. Go! Go now, for the sake of the Omnissiah, leave now and never come back!'

Blaylock listened to Kotov's words with a growing sense of disbelief. The message was an exload of pre-recorded information. It had to be a mistake. A catastrophic disruption in the tight-beam transmission, perhaps? Despite the clear corridor linking them, residual pockets of localised distortion must be affecting the archmagos's transmission.

Even as he formed the thought, he knew it to be delusional.

The signal was clean and uncorrupted, its every binaric particle stamped with Kotov's noospheric signifiers, a more precise means of identification than even the most detailed genetic markers.

'Blaylock?' said Azuramagelli, similarly confused. 'What does the archmagos mean?'

'It's a mistake,' snapped Kryptaestrex, rounding on Azuramagelli. 'Your damned servitor-relays have fouled the signal somehow. It's the only explanation. It has to be, Tarkis.'

'I do not know,' replied Blaylock. 'I–'

The vox crackled as the pre-recorded exload ended and Kotov's voice filled the bridge. This time the words were spoken aloud and were filled with terrible urgency.

'Tarkis, if you can hear this, the cog is on the turn. Telok is not what I thought at all – he is a monster and the Breath of the Gods is an alien perversion of unthinkable horror. Telok seeks to tear down everything we hold dear. Mars, the Imperium, everything. Unless you act now he will take the *Speranza* back to Mars and–'

Kotov's words were abruptly cut off.

Dead air hissed from the vox.

Blaylock sat in stunned silence, trying to process his tumbling thoughts into some kind of rational order. Taken at face value, it turned his every certainty into a hideous joke. Had they come all this way just to find that the glittering promise at the end was in fact a trap as nightmarish as that which Galatea had set at the Valette Manifold station?

He wanted to believe that this was a mistake, a cruel subterfuge, but the evidence against that was right there in Kotov's words.

'Archmagos?' said Blaylock. 'Archmagos Kotov? Respond. Archmagos, respond immediately. Archmagos? Azuramagelli, keep trying.'

The Master of Astrogation returned to his data hub and began a broad-sweep vox-hail of the surface.

'Are we even sure that was the archmagos?' asked Kryptaestrex, approaching the throne.

'Yes,' said Blaylock. 'I am sure.'

'How can you be certain?' demanded Kryptaestrex.

'Because the cog is on the turn,' said Blaylock. 'Just as there are innocuous verbal cues to indicate a statement is being made under duress, there are codes to indicate that what is being said should be absolutely taken at face value. Archmagos Kotov's use of the phrase, "the cog is on the turn" is of the latter persuasion.'

'So what do we do?'

Blaylock hesitated before replying.

'We follow Archmagos Kotov's last order,' said Blaylock. 'We break orbit and return to the Imperium as fast we can.'

Another voice crackled over the vox.

'I'm sorry, Tarkis, but I'm afraid I can't let you do that,' said Vettius Telok.

And a shrieking spear of binaric fire stabbed up through Blaylock's entire body. His haptic implants burned white hot as their connection seared his flesh to the throne. The Fabricatus Locum's back arched with convulsive agonies, golden sparks erupting from his every point of connection. Synaptic pathways saturated with external communication inloads of hostile binary.

Millions of random images poured through his mind, occluding his thought processes with their banality. Yet even within this, there was a pattern. Repeating over and over was the image of a giant feline creature. Orange and black, its fearful symmetry was burning bright in a forest lit by a leering moon.

The feeder pipes connected to his shoulder-mounted canister tore free and noxious chem-nutrients sprayed the bridge. Still seated on the

Speranza's command throne, smoke from burned electricals curling from his augments, Blaylock grindingly shook his head.

'No,' he said, his voice filled with distortion as he fought the millions of errors triggering within the microcode of his body. 'This is a sovereign vessel of the Adeptus Mechanicus, under the command of Archmagos Lexell Kotov. You have no right to take it.'

Telok's sigh was heard throughout the *Speranza*.

'And I *so* hoped to do this without violence.'

'WHAT ARE THEY?' said Surcouf.

Tanna leaned over the railing at the edge of the gantry, wondering the same thing. Their speed and the tapered, bladed cast of their skulls told him they were predator creatures. That was enough for now.

They sped up the curling ramp that spiralled the height of the tower, moving in bounding leaps like an Assault Marine on the hunt. Tanna saw the power in their limbs and knew that, but for the curve of the ramp, they would already be upon them.

'Battle robots?' he suggested.

'Those are not robots,' gasped Pavelka, making the Icon Mechanicus across her chest at the sight of the charging creatures. 'They are something far worse.'

'Give me something I can use to fight them,' said Tanna.

Pavelka shook her head, seeing the approaching machines in a way Tanna never could. 'Their spirits are degenerate, ancient things. Mass-killers from a war millions of years ended. They scream their name in my head... *Tindalosi! Tindalosi!*'

'Interesting, but irrelevant,' said Tanna.

'Can you stop them?' asked Surcouf.

'Only if I do not need to protect you and Kotov.'

'Understood,' said Surcouf, helping Magos Pavelka away.

'Templars!' yelled Tanna, drawing his sword and making his way swiftly to the head of the ramp. His warriors stood to either side, Varda and Issur with their swords drawn, Bracha and Yael with bolters locked and loaded.

'Sigismund, chosen of Dorn, son of the Emperor, guide my blade in your name,' said Varda, lifting the Black Sword so that its quillons framed the coal-red eye-lenses of his helm.

The others mirrored Varda's sentiment as Colonel Anders chivvied his Guardsmen to the edges of the gantry. Hellguns blazed as the Cadians opened up on the creatures. Tanna didn't doubt that most of their shots would find a target.

The jade-armoured warriors of the eldar took up position to either side of the Templars. Tanna bristled at the flanking xenos, but suppressed his natural combative instincts.

'Their placement makes sense,' said Bracha over the internal vox. 'But I do not like it.'

Tanna nodded and squared his stance. 'When these things come at us, fight them with all your heart, but never forget there are aliens at our back as well.'

The eldar in the form-fitting ivory plates and blood-red plumes sprinted to the edge of the gantry. They effortlessly vaulted the railing, swords in one hand, gripping the metal with the other. Like acrobats, they swung in graceful arcs and dropped to the level of the ramp above the speeding hunters.

Tanna didn't bother watching them.

Even over the thunder of the tower's machinery and the snap of gunfire, he heard the clash of swords amid the dying echo of the eldar battle scream.

A shadow loomed and Tanna turned to see Uldanaish Ghostwalker. The wraith-warrior stood with the Black Templars at the head of the ramp as the clash of swords from below was silenced. Cadian las-fire resumed.

Meaning the eldar below were dead.

He rolled his shoulders in anticipation, loosening the muscles for the hard-burn of close-quarters battle. He risked a glance over the curve of his black and ivory shoulder guard.

Kotov and his skitarii were already moving across the gantry to a radial bridge leading to the tower's exterior. He didn't know what lay beyond, but that it was away from here was good enough.

Tanna addressed Ghostwalker as the crash of metallic claws tearing up the ramp drew ever closer.

'You are a little bigger than the warriors I usually fight alongside,' said Tanna. 'Are you concerned you might hit me?'

'That does not concern me in the slightest,' said Tanna.

'Then perhaps you worry I may hit you in the chaotic mêlée?'

'It crossed my mind.'

Ghostwalker leaned down. 'Know this, Templar. If I strike you, it will be entirely deliberate.'

'As it will be when I strike you,' said Tanna.

The warrior-construct gave a booming laugh and straightened to its full height as the hellhounds bounded into sight.

Silver creatures with wide, ursine shoulders. Narrow spines and the powerful legs of lean hunting hounds. Too-wide jaws, filled with tearing metal saw-fangs. Glittering, compound eye structures like scratches of light in a cave.

Their howls were shrieks of thirsting need. Blades snapped erect on their every limb.

Bolter fire and hails of whickering, razor-edged discs flensed them. Explosions blasted fragments of molten metal, and ribbons of steel pared back from every slicing impact of an eldar projectile.

One volley was all they got.

Uldanaish Ghostwalker took the first impact as two of the Tindalosi leapt at him. The wraith-warrior's blade moved too fast for something so huge. A Tindalosi howled, impaled, its gut ripped open and spilling shredded metal. Ghostwalker hurled it aside. Hellgun fire battered the fallen beast's gleaming flanks.

The second bit down on his arm, and sickly green fire bled into the wound. The creature's rear limbs curled to claw at the wraith-construct's chest. Tanna stepped in and hammered his blade into its haunches, tearing through to its spine.

It fell away, rolling clear of his follow-up.

Ghostwalker's gauntlet-mounted weapon swung to bear. Buzzing projectiles tore into the Tindalosi with a breaking-glass sound that was curiously musical. Three hounds snapped and clawed the ramp, poised to launch themselves at the Space Marines.

Tanna spun his sword back up to his shoulder and stepped forwards to give himself room. He kept his bolt pistol low at his thigh. He turned just enough to invite attack and when it came he pulled back in an oblique turn. His sword deflected the leaping beast's snapping jaw. He rolled his wrist and shoulder barged it, pushing the thing backwards and down. He dropped a knee to its ribs and jammed the muzzle of his pistol into its exposed throat.

The mass-reactive punched through the metal and into the ramp.

The Tindalosi bellowed, and pungent, viscous gel sprayed Tanna's helm, necrotic oils of something long past its time to die.

It rolled away, the torn metal of its neck knitting together in a slick of green light.

Step back. Consolidate awareness.

They still held the top of the ramp. Hellguns and bolters fired enfilading volleys. Kotov and his skitarii almost out. Surcouf and Ven Anders shouting at Pavelka, who had plugged herself back into the control hub. No time to wonder why. Cadians surrounded the three of them, bulky hellguns pulled in tight as they awaited the colonel's order to withdraw.

Varda's sword flashed and the black blade plunged into a howling skull and tore it half away. Tanna swivelled and the pauldrons of the three Space Marines clashed together. Shoulder to shoulder in a circle of steel and adamantium they stood, ravaging all that came within reach.

A slash of talons came at Tanna's head and he parried with the body of his pistol. The weapon went off and he chopped his blade into a leg as hard as adamantium.

The creature staggered and Tanna worked the roaring blade hard into its chest. He hauled it free and kicked the beast back. He blinked and shook his head.

The monsters Ghostwalker had downed were up again. Shimmering green lightning played across their bodies. Opened guts were closed and buckled limbs straightened. Only once had Tanna fought creatures so difficult to kill, so unwilling to die.

The Tindalosi charged, but just before the instant of contact, two leapt to the side. Their powerful legs easily carried them over the railings of the gantry. Not his concern. Something for the Cadians and eldar to deal with. Behind him, Yael and Bracha opened fire with their bolters. Mass-reactives plucked one from the air, twin impacts punching it out over the gantry. Its howl rang from the tower walls as it fell.

'Into them!' shouted Tanna.

They met the charge of the hunting beasts head on. The impact was thunderous, like iron girders colliding. Legs braced, Tanna felt the curve of his pauldron crumple. Muscle mass deformed and blood dispersed within the meat of his shoulder. His sword punched up. Screaming teeth tore metal. More viscous gel sprayed him.

A clawed arm slammed into his plastron, tearing loose the Templar's cross and gouging finger-deep grooves through the ceramite. The force hammered him to the side.

Tanna's sword snapped back up to block a tearing blow from above that drove him to his knees.

His armour thrummed with power. Tanna straightened his legs with a roar, hammering his sword's crossed pommel into a bellowing metallic skull that was part wolf, part saurian. Noxious machine-blood flew.

He lunged with the pistol, drove it into the belly of a beast. The shot exploded hard against armour and Tanna bit back a shout of sudden pain. His gauntlet filled with hot fluid, blood streaming down his forearm.

The creature snapped at him again. He thrust his chainsword, teeth scraping on steel as it parted metal and split a spine. He twisted it out, kicking the flailing creature back down the ramp.

Straighten up, breathe and blow, shake the pain. His chest was tight, his throat raw. Had he been screaming a battle shout?

'Too... t... too far forward, Tanna!' shouted Issur.

Get back.

The Tindalosi barged one another in their frenzy to break past the chokepoint, their bladed limbs constricted, one machine-like killer obstructing another. He saw their confusion. They were not used to victims who could fight back like this.

'Find the openings,' yelled Tanna, to himself as much as everyone else. 'Kill them, kill them all.'

A blow glanced off his helm and hammered into his damaged shoulder guard. He grunted and punched a sword blow to the belly of a silver-skinned beast.

'Step in again!' he grunted. 'Keep them at bay!'

Tanna threw an upward sword cut to a thigh of hooked metal, a back-stroke to the guts and a thrust to the chest. In deep and twist. Don't stop moving. Movement to the right, a howling bovine skull with fangs like daggers. He slashed it in the eyes. It screamed.

Move on. Face front, step back. Find another.

Two came at him. No room to swing. Another pommel strike, stove in the first's ribs. Stab the other in the belly, blade out.

The beasts withdrew, torn up and weeping emerald light from their rup-tured bodies.

'Tanna! For the Emperor's sake stop pushing so far down the ramp!' shouted a voice.

Varda?

Tanna stepped back until he drew level with Varda and Issur. Each was slathered from helm to greaves in blood. Vivid red theirs, tar black that of the foe. They stood abreast at the summit of the ramp with Uldanaish Ghostwalker behind them.

The wraith-warrior's armour was cracked and clawed. One leg tremored, as though ready to collapse, the other leaked a molten amber-like sap from its knee joint. Something glittered through a dreadful gash in his helm, a faintly luminous gemstone.

The Tindalosi came at them again.

'Back to back!' roared Tanna.

BLAYLOCK SLUMPED FROM the *Speranza*'s command throne, feeling like every cell within him had chosen this moment to attack its host body. His vision snapped to black as cerebral inhibitors shut down in an attempt to block the surging inloads of spurious data.

His dwarf servitors squealed in distress as he shunted vast quantities of data to their overspill capacity. Two died instantly, their brains flash-burned by the immense overload. Another fell onto its side, spasming and losing control of every bodily function as rogue signals ripped through its body.

Blaylock heard warning sirens, alarm klaxons and squalling wails of bina-ric pain. The machines of the *Speranza* were howling with animal distress. Blaylock struggled to regain his feet, but that was proving to be harder than he'd expected. With virtually every facet of sensory apparatus shut down, he had no spatial awareness, no sense of up or down.

He pressed his hands to what he assumed was the deck and pushed, feeling it move away from him. Or was he moving away from *it*? Blaylock's lower body was a mixture of piston-driven bracing limbs and callipered counterbalances. It made for an efficient means of locomotion for a being of his mass and density, but right now he would have happily traded them in for a pair of organic legs.

Voices called his name with interrogative pulses of binary, complex loga-rithmic squirts of machine code and flesh-voices. None of it made sense.

He tried to speak, but his augmitter sub-systems – both binaric and hexamathic – were offline. His mouth opened, but only an exhalation of scorched air emerged, as though viral fires burned within his lungs.

Hands gripped him and hauled him into what he assumed was an upright position. A sudden, vertiginous sense of dislocation assailed Blaylock as he became aware of three-dimensional space around him. His lower body pulsed through its gyroscopic diagnostics and quickly found his centre of balance. Bracing limbs slammed down and the rest of his body swiftly followed in a series of hard resets.

Some portions of his internal system architecture still felt somehow *wrong*, but now was not the time for a shut-down and full diagnostic assessment. Sight returned. Slowly. Fearful of shocking him with what it might reveal.

'Ave Deus Mechanicus,' he managed at last.

Strong hands still gripped his robes, soaked through where his feeder pipes had torn loose. The canister at his back was angled strangely, leaking clouds of acrid vapours.

He turned to thank the individual who had helped him to his feet, a magos in dark robes with silver eyes. His body was a crudely put together thing that somewhat resembled an arachnid.

Galatea, Blaylock's memory coils reminded him as they finished the purge of redundant data.

With its identity recalled, so too was the dreadful fact of its existence. The lies it had told, the violations of every Mechanicus law it represented and the lives it had ended. Blaylock pulled away from its infectious touch as though burned.

Almost every glittering entoptic veil burned with hissing, jumping static. Only the central display remained intact, though even it glitched and rolled with inloads of malicious code.

'Magos Blaylock!' shouted a boxy, robotic-looking thing that looked like it belonged in a loading dock rather than a starship's bridge. 'Are you rendered incapable?'

Kryptaestrex, Master of Logistics.

'No,' said Blaylock, though he felt anything but capable.

Another magos appeared beside Kryptaestrex. A latticework frame on robotic legs, within which an exploded diagram of a brain was held in suspension, spread between numerous linked plastek cubes.

Azuramagelli, Master of Astrogation.

'Magos Blaylock, you really need to see this,' said Azuramagelli. 'There is… something happening on the surface.'

'Something?' snapped Blaylock as yet more of his systems realigned after the attack on his augmetic nervous system. 'Since when do adepts of Mars employ such vague phraseology? Coherence, precision and logic. Remember them. Use them.'

'Apologies, Magos Blaylock,' said Azuramagelli, gesturing to his station with a spindly manipulator arm. 'I have not the terminology to accurately describe what I am seeing.'

Blaylock moved as fast as he could towards Azuramagelli's data hub, realising that he was perhaps not as fully realigned as he had thought when the deck of the *Speranza* seemed to lurch beneath him.

He reached astrogation and pushed past Azuramagelli, carefully inloading the readings from the data hub, wary of any lingering fragments of malign code. He had been set to chastise Azuramagelli once again, but his admonishments went unsaid as he failed utterly to interpret the energy readings building to enormous levels on the planet's surface.

The data being gathered by the *Speranza*'s auguries was beyond anything Blaylock had ever seen. He had no idea what it might indicate, but the last vestiges of his human instincts of fight or flight screamed at him that this was dangerous.

'Raise the voids, Kryptaestrex,' he ordered. 'Immediately.'

'Magos, I have been trying to raise them for the last thirty seconds,' said Kryptaestrex.

'*Trying?*'

'They will not light. My every command is being denied access to the rituals of ignition.'

Blaylock all but ran to Kryptaestrex's data hub. Bleeding veils of red filled the slates. His haptics were useless, burned out by the surge attack, and his noospherics were still resetting.

But he could still issue commands manually.

His fingers danced over the floating entoptic keyboard, ordering the *Speranza* to protect itself.

But not even his exalted rank signifiers could reach the heart of the Ark Mechanicus. He was being kept out of his own ship's core controls by some external force.

The main display lit up with a flare of radiance building on the planet's surface beneath the huge electrical storms. A continental-scale flare that blew out the atmospheric tempests it had taken the geoformers hours to becalm. The horrifying sight put Blaylock in mind of a stellar flare or a coronal mass ejection.

'What is that?' he said.

'The Breath of the Gods,' said Galatea with awed reverence.

MOONCHILD WAS THE first vessel to be hit.

An arc of parabolic lightning rose from the surface of Exnihlio, passing through the tortured skies without apparent effort. Seen from space it appeared to expand at leisurely pace, but was in fact moving at close to four hundred kilometres per second.

It wasn't *actually* lightning – such atmospheric discharges could only exist within a planetary atmosphere – but it was the best description the *Moonchild*'s captain could articulate.

His Master of Auspex shouted a warning, but the captain already knew the energised arc was moving too fast to avoid. Even with the Gothic's shields partially lit, the tracery of light struck the ventral armour of the prow.

Void-war was messy. It left vast clouds of debris and drifting hulks venting fuel and oxygen in their wake. It fouled space with squalling electromagnetics for decades and was rarely conclusive. The ranges at which most engagements were fought made it relatively easy for a vessel incapable of continuing a fight to go dark and slip away.

There would be no slipping away from this fight.

Moonchild exploded sequentially along its length. First the wedge of its bow vanished in a silent thunderclap of blue fire, then its midships, and finally its drive section in a searing plasmic fireball. It burned with blinding radiance for a few brief seconds as the oxygen trapped within its hull was consumed.

The fires swiftly burned out, leaving *Moonchild* a charred skeleton of drifting wreckage. Lifeless. Inert. Ten thousand dead in the blink of an eye.

Another pair of lightning arcs coiled up from Exnihlio.

And *Wrathchild* and *Mortis Voss* joined *Moonchild* in death.

More lightning flared towards the *Speranza*.

Microcontent 10

ROBOUTE HAULED PAVELKA'S robes, but he might just as well have been trying to pull a section of the tower itself. The *Renard*'s magos was rooted to the spot, her data-spikes locked into the control hub. Flickering data-light scrolled down the optics beneath her hood and her limbs jerked with involuntary twitches. She was fighting the hub's code and, like an unbroken colt, it was fighting back.

Angry blasts of electrical discharge coruscated along the length of her mechadendrites and into her body. Roboute was uncomfortably aware of the repulsively mouth-watering reek of cooking meat.

'Ilanna! Disconnect!' he shouted, alternating his attention between the furious clash of blades and claws at the head of the ramp and the snap of las-fire from Cadian rifles. 'We have to go!'

'Just. Keep. Them. Off me...' hissed Pavelka.

'We don't have time for this,' said Ven Anders, one hand holding his rifle, the other gripping the hilt of his power sword. 'Get her free, Surcouf, or I'll cut her loose myself.'

Roboute nodded. He had no wish to remain here. He'd seen the thirsting, ribbed and fanged shapes of the monsters bounding up the ramp. The bulk of the Black Templars and the wraithlord kept him from seeing them any closer.

A state of affairs he was keen to see continued.

Bracha and Yael stood on the far side of the control hub, pumping shots into the enemy whenever a target presented itself.

The Templar swordsmen were faring less well. Tanna was down on one knee. His left arm hung limp at his side, his pistol a molten wreck on the ground. Issur spasmed in the grip of a crackling electrical field that was burning him to death within his armour.

Only Atticus Varda still fought unbowed.

His black blade hacked into the silver armour of the Tindalosi, sending cloven shards of silver and bronze spinning in all directions. The Emperor's Champion fought with the precision of a duellist and the power of a berserker, both war-forms distilled into a cohesive whole. It was quite the most extraordinarily disciplined feat of swordsmanship Roboute had ever seen.

But even so sublime a warrior could not fight forever.

'Ilanna, please,' begged Roboute, risking a hand on her shoulder. He felt the furious micro-tremors of a body largely composed of machines working at full-tilt.

The heat coming off her body was ferocious.

'Don't touch me!' she barked. 'Almost. There.'

'Too late!' shouted Ven Anders as two of the Tindalosi vaulted over the railings to the main floor of the gantry. One was punched from the air by a pair of three-round bursts from Yael and Bracha. The explosive impact of the mass-reactives blew the hellhound over the edge, and Roboute yelled in triumph as it fell with an ululating howl.

That still left one, and the Cadians turned their hellguns upon it. Blazing streams of las-fire punched out with a speed and accuracy that only a lifetime's worth of training could bring.

Not a single shot hit the Tindalosi.

A heartbeat later it was amongst them.

Vodanus snapped a living body in two, tossing it aside and clawing another in half from shoulder to pelvis. *This* was more like it. *This* was the kind of foe it relished.

Soft, mortal, fleshy and without any distracting code-scent that could break its *geas*. Its claws slashed and six bodies emptied of blood. Its hide whipped electricity. It burned, cut and melted its foes. Venomous oils secreted from its hooks left the meat screaming on their bellies.

Some were tough and sinewy, others light as air.

Different species?

It made no difference, both were just as fragile.

Energy beams stabbed it. Minor irritations. Its armour was proof against such primitive low-emission weapons. Crackling arcs of strange storm-lights struck it, psychic body blows of doom-seeking power. Ancient null-circuitry worked into its body dissipated these attacks harmlessly.

Did these meat-things know nothing of Vodanus?

Green-armoured warriors danced around it, darting in to bite it with crackling mouth-parts and slash with buzzing blades. It fired electromagnetic micro-pulses that exploded their internal organs.

It heard screams from these ones, terrified screams that didn't come from any vocal organs. It filed the information away for later perusal. No species it had thus far slain evinced such behaviour upon its death.

Its jaws snapped on a mortal's head, wrenching the body from side to side and letting the serrations of its teeth do the rest. The fast meat-things kept coming at it, unaware yet that they could not kill Vodanus. Their weapons sparked against its armour, vespid stings against a leviathan.

Two of the black-armoured warriors rounded upon Vodanus – Space Marines, Telok's data had called them – together with a slender warrior armed with a screaming-toothed sword. The weapon was clearly too large for her to wield, but Vodanus recognised that she too was a lethal huntress.

These Space Marines were tougher and more deadly than anything its long-forgotten masters had wished dead. Each was encased in toxic armour of machine-spirits that could kill a hellhound with one wrong-placed bite or the temptation to feast. Vodanus did not fear these killers, but knew to be wary of them.

Its prey was within sight, escaping along an outflung bridge of mesh steel and wire. Still within its grasp, but the first rule of any hunt was to leave none alive who might hunt the hunter.

A pair of thundering impacts slowed its charge as the Space Marine warriors fired their heavy guns. Vodanus twisted into the air, killing another of the soul-screaming meat-sacks with a flick of its hooked back leg. Explosive ammunition followed it down, caroming from the curved plates of its shoulder as it landed in front of the three warriors that mattered.

It howled in fury, but they didn't run, which made them unique.

Everyone ran from Vodanus.

But, Vodanus reminded itself, these things did not know it.

Another blast of explosive rounds hammered its armour.

One detonated within its chest, and the momentary pain staggered it. Vodanus had not known pain of this kind in millennia. The pain of isolation and madness, yes. The knowledge that its existence was fragmenting moment by moment, certainly.

But the pain of being *wounded*?

That stirred old memories, old hurts and old joys.

The power Telok had imbued it with from the ancient machine began its hateful work, cannibalising mineral reservoirs within its body to re-knit the damage, undo its hurt.

It sprang forwards, faster than they could avoid. One clawed arm rammed into the chest of a Space Marine with all the force Vodanus could muster. Black and white became saturated with red. So bright, so vivid. So much.

Vodanus clawed the body into the air and bit it in half.

It spat the crumpled debris of meat and metal from its mouth.

The huntress vaulted into the air as the second warrior ducked a hooked sweep of its arm. She spun the enormous blade as though it weighed nothing at all and clove it through a section of Vodanus's spine. The Space Marine rammed his own toothed sword into the renewing sections of Vodanus's body.

Once again, Vodanus knew pain, but this pain was welcome. It had been too long since it had faced any foe capable of hurting it. Its body rolled in mid-air and Vodanus rammed a bladed foot into the huntress's chest.

She screamed and crumpled, almost broken in two, her sword skidding across the gantry. Vodanus bellowed with howling laughter as it hooked a claw through the armour of the Space Marine and tossed him aside like offal. He slammed into the high column of the control hub, crashing back down with his armour cracked and the ivory wings on his chest shattered into a thousand fragments. Bleeding code vapour streamed from the broken pieces of black metal, but Vodanus ignored the sweet scent.

To taste it would be to die.

Instead, it turned towards a last handful of soft, meaty bodies that awaited murder. Most were code-free, bare flesh and fear, but one stood at the control hub, violently enmeshed with the ancient spirit at its heart.

This one bled code, *bad* code. Her machine arms snapped clear of the hub, drawing into her body. She cried a warning to the others.

Vodanus howled and relished the terror it tasted.

It bunched its hooked legs beneath it.

And the world exploded in screaming white fire.

ROBOUTE AND ANDERS had their guns drawn, but the giant beast that had so easily slaughtered most of the eldar and Cadians collapsed. It howled in pain, limbs convulsing in lethal swipes that tore up the metal of the gantry.

Even incapacitated it was lethal. To approach it was to die.

From the cessation of sound at the top of the ramp, Roboute knew something similar had happened to the Tindalosi facing Tanna's swordsmen and the wraithlord. His analytical mind flashed through a lightning-swift assay of their current situation.

Bracha was dead, no question of that, but Yael was already picking himself up with a groan of pain.

Roboute felt his mouth go dry. The very idea of a Space Marine experiencing pain was something he'd never expected to see. Every devotional pict spoke of the Adeptus Astartes' invincibility, their utter inability to feel pain or know fear. Roboute was realist enough to know that picts like that pedalled what the Imperium *wanted* its people to believe, but even he was shocked by the volume of blood leaving Yael's body.

Ariganna Icefang limped over to Bielanna, her armour torn all across her chest. Blood as bright as Yael's ran from her helm's eye-lenses like red tears. She'd been hurt badly. Maybe even mortally. She said something to Bielanna, but her dialect made the words unintelligible. Bielanna shook her head. Whatever the exarch was asking of her, the farseer could not deliver.

Roboute turned from the eldar as Pavelka slumped to her knees. Heat sinks worked into her rib-structure billowed the fabric of her robes with scorching vapours. She held a hand out to Roboute, feeling the air like a blind man. He took it, grimacing at the pain of her metal grip.

'What did you do, Ilanna?'

'Ask her later!' yelled Anders, slinging his rifle and helping Roboute get the stricken magos to her feet. If Anders was pained by the searing heat of Pavelka's body, he gave no sign.

Between them, they hauled her away from the control hub, trying not to step on any of the hacked-apart limbs and bodies the hunting machine had left in its wake.

The speed with which it had killed was phenomenal.

How many were dead?

Eldar and human bodies lay intertwined, making it impossible to tell. Tanna, Varda and Issur ran over, together with the few surviving Striking Scorpions and Howling Banshees.

'Was that you?' Tanna asked Pavelka.

She nodded. 'I tricked the hub into accepting a self-replicating piece of damaged code into every machine within this tower. Its viral form angered the spirits within them, and they explosively purged it into the noosphere. Invisible to you, but painfully blinding to anything that uses augmetic senses.'

Roboute glanced beneath Pavelka's hood, seeing her ocular implants were dull and blank where normally they shone with pale blue illumination. Thin tendrils of smoke curled from the scorched rims.

'No, Ilanna... Are you...?'

'It needed to be done,' she said. 'Now let's go!'

WRATHCHILD, MORTIS VOSS and *Moonchild* were lifeless wrecks, blackened and lit from within by sporadic flashes of dying machinery. The lightning that struck the *Speranza* came straight from the heart of Exnihlio and phased through the hull of the Ark Mechanicus without apparent effort. Existing on an entirely different phasic state of existence to that which had obliterated the *Speranza*'s escorts, it destroyed nothing until it reached its point of focus.

The first blast coalesced within the *Speranza* amidships on Deck 235/ Chi-Rho 66, a high-ceilinged turbine chamber filled with rank upon rank of thundering engines that provided toxin-scrubbed air to a quadrant of ventral forge-temples.

A tempest of blazing lightning arcs, white-hot and fluid, filled the central nave between the turbines. Ghost shapes moved within the light, hurricanes of microscopic machinery that had travelled the length of the faux-lightning from Exnihlio in seconds.

The crackling bolt provided the energy, the particulate-rich air of the *Speranza* the raw material as solid forms began unfolding from the compressed molecules in which they had been carried.

The deck's servitors ignored the furious storm, oblivious to the threat manifesting among them. Those whose inculcated task routes carried them close to its wrath were instantly burned to cinders, their flesh and matter now fuel for the coalescing invasion.

At first the Mechanicus adepts struggled to find fault with their systems, believing some ritual or catechism had been overlooked or an incorrect unguent applied. Alarm klaxons blared throughout the deck and alert chimes rang through adjacent forges and engine-temples. By the time Chi-Rho 66's adepts realised this was no machine malfunction, it was already too late.

The first crystaliths to emerge from the lightstorm were crude approximations of Adeptus Astartes. Glassy and smoothly finished, each was freshly wrought from the molten light and filled with thousands of Telok's unique nano-machines. They marched in glittering ranks, hundreds strong, and filled Chi-Rho 66 with blasts of emerald fire. Machines exploded, servitors died, devastating chain reactions were begun.

Binaric vox-blurts raced frantically to the bridge, warning of the boarders, but Chi-Rho 66's warning would not be the last. Fresh arcs of lightning from the planet's surface struck all across the *Speranza*, a dozen at a time, and each storm disgorged hundreds of crystaliths. Some were a basic warrior-caste, others were larger, formed with heavier weapons and bladed claws, and carried sheets of reflective armour like heavy, glassy mantlets.

Last to form onto Chi-Rho 66 were the war machines.

What Telok had once described as *things of terror*.

ABOVE THE TOWER, the crackling fury in Exnihlio's upper atmosphere had stilled. Tanna was struck by the pale clarity of the sky. It reminded him of the murals aboard the *Eternal Crusader*, the ones that depicted the pastoral idyll of Old Earth.

That illusion was shattered the instant his eyes fell from the sky and saw the unending vistas of gargantuan generator towers and forge-complexes stretching to the horizon.

The radial bridge that led from the tower opened up onto a tiered set of stairs enclosed within a chain-link cage. The wide gantry offered routes to higher levels or down into roiling banks of flame-lit exhaust gases venting from the tower's base.

A cable-stayed suspension bridge connected the universal assembler to a vast, boxy structure five hundred metres away. Clad in sheets of rusted corrugated sheet-steel, the building offered no clues as to its purpose beyond a number of smoke stacks that belched soot-dark smoke and rained a greasy, ashen snow over the roofs of lower buildings.

It reminded Tanna of the giant, industrial-scale crematoria on worlds like Balhaut and Certus Minor.

He hoped that wasn't an omen.

'Bracha?' asked Varda.

Tanna shook his head, and the Emperor's Champion cursed.

'Yael?'

'Alive,' said Tanna, pointing to the far side of the bridge where Yael covered his battle-brothers with his bolter. They ran to join him, with Uldanaish Ghostwalker limping behind them.

The damage done to its legs had robbed the wraith-warrior of its speed and grace. Beside Yael, Kotov's skitarii were hacking an entrance into the structure ahead through a shuttered door of concertinaed steel.

Tanna glanced over his shoulder, searching for signs of pursuit.

Issur saw him look and said, 'You th-th-think the adept kill... killed them?'

'Doubtful,' replied Tanna. 'I laid enough mortal wounds on those beasts that they should have been destroyed a dozen times over. If they can survive that, they will survive Magos Pavelka's cantrip.'

'Those beasts are tough,' agreed Varda. 'I only ever fought one foe that could survive the kill-strikes I favoured them with.'

Tanna nodded. 'Thanatos?'

'Aye, the silver-skinned devils that kept coming back no matter how hard I hit them or how many mass-reactives took them apart.'

'Is th-tha... that what these are?' asked Issur.

'No,' said Uldanaish Ghostwalker, his voice no longer deep and resonant, but thin and distant. 'These things are not servants of the *Yngir*, they were wrought by living hands and given the power to undo mortal wounds by Telok's mad sorceries. But you are correct, they will be back.'

As if to underscore the wraith-warrior's words, the hounds burst from the tower. Some stood on their hind legs, others hunched over on all fours as they searched for their prey. Even a cursory glance told Tanna the damage he and his brothers had inflicted was entirely absent.

The beasts saw them crossing the bridge and sprinted after them, bounding closer with howling appetite. Sparks flew from hooked claws on the mesh grille of the bridge deck.

'Templars, stand to!' shouted Tanna.

'No,' said Ghostwalker, standing athwart the bridge. The curved, bone-bladed sword snapped from its gauntlet. 'This is where *I* will fight, as Toralven Gravesong did at Hellabore.'

Tanna guessed what the giant warrior intended and said, 'Tell me one thing, Ghostwalker. Did Toralven Gravesong live?'

The wraithlord turned its emerald skull towards him, and Tanna saw through the awful wound torn there that the smooth gemstone within was cracked. Its light was fading.

'Toralven Gravesong was a doom-seeker,' said Ghostwalker.

'What does that mean?'

'That he had walked the wraith-path for more lifetimes than you or I will ever know,' said Ghostwalker. 'Perhaps too many.'

Tanna understood. 'On Armageddon, I met a warrior of the Blood Angels whose duty was to hear the final words of those whose death was upon them. It was his burden to end their suffering, but he spoke of the peace those lost souls sometimes knew when he told them that death had brought an end to their duty.'

Tanna, Varda and Issur raised their swords in salute.

'Die well, Ghostwalker,' said Tanna.

'Run,' advised the wraith-warrior.

ULDANAISH TURNED FROM the withdrawing mon-keigh, soul-sick that their leader actually believed he understood the true depth of what was to be lost here.

Hadn't the human heard what Uldanaish said earlier?

His body had died a long time ago, but devotion to the Swordwind had seen his spirit preserved within the ghost lattice of the wraithlord's spirit stone. A spirit stone now split to its heart and releasing that which it kept hidden from an ancient and hungry god.

This was the fear that lurked at the heart of the eldar race. From artist to exarch, the prospect of She Who Thirsts devouring and tormenting their spirit for all eternity filled even the stoutest heart with unreasoning horror. Who could ever have thought he would embrace such a fate for the mon-keigh?

Uldanaish clung to his wounded wraith-body with every fibre of his determination. Already he could hear cruel laughter pressing in around him, the monstrous hunger of a dark power that would swallow his soul and not even notice.

The Tindalosi were almost upon him as he took position at the exact centre of the bridge.

A wraithlord did not see as mortals saw. Wraithsight perceived the world in half-glimpsed dreams and nightmares, each redolent with ghostly emotions and shimmering hues. Without a farseer's guiding light, it was difficult to sort real from unreal.

The eldar were ghost forms, concealed from She Who Thirsts by their spirit stones, but each mon-keigh was a plume of blood-red radiance, a being with an unlimited capacity for violence.

Bielanna was already within the building behind him, and Uldanaish felt a sudden fear at the prospect of his people entering that dread space. Something terrible lurked beneath it, something that reeked of unending pain and a world's suffering.

Uldanaish wanted to warn them of the danger, but the Tindalosi were upon him. Like the mon-keigh, they were radiant things, phosphor bright and feral in their lust for violence.

That they were intelligent was beyond question.

Uldanaish had felt their twisted malevolence as soon as they entered the tower. What lurked within them were artificial minds so monstrous, so psychotic, that it beggared belief any sentient race would risk creating them.

It saw the leader beast immediately, a patchwork thing of evil and insatiable hunger that left blistered negative impressions on his wraithsight. Scratches of dark radiance flickered in the thing's smoking eye-lenses, and its oversized jaw drooled lightning from bloodstained fangs.

They came at Ghostwalker five abreast.

He charged towards them with long, loping strides. He stabbed down, carving the first through the spine with his wraithblade. Sensing weakness, one went for his legs, another his skull. He cut the first almost in two with his gauntlet weapon. The second impaled itself on his blade. Another seized his gauntlet in its jaws and swung itself wide, using its mass to drag him with it.

The last beast gripped the vanes flaring from his shoulders and wrenched in the opposite direction. Ghostwalker loosed a bray of ancient pain as the vanes shattered like porcelain. He brought his blade back, shearing the legs from the beast biting his other arm.

With that arm free, he swung low from the hip and pummelled his fist into the monstrous hunter clawing his side apart. The impact buckled its midsection inwards, almost snapping it in two. It screeched a machine-like howl and landed hard on the parapet of the bridge. Uldanaish leaned back and kicked it over.

The beast whose spine he had carved unfolded from its hurt, fresh plates already extruding from some internal void. Green lights danced over the new steel. Uldanaish sent a threading pulse of laser fire though its eyes. They blew out in a screaming howl of hostile static.

Two of the beasts tried to push past him. He stepped back and kicked one in the ribs, almost flattening it against the iron-girder parapet. Uldanaish spun on his heel and pinned the other to the plated deck of the bridge with his wraithblade.

The leader beast crashed into him. They rolled. Uldanaish's fist slammed into its side. Its wide mouth snapped shut on his skull, ripping out plate-sized shards of wraithbone. His blade scored deep cuts in its spinal ridges.

Its hooked limbs ripped into his chest and broke his armour into long strips of wraithbone.

They broke apart. Uldanaish rolled to his feet and staggered as his right leg finally gave out. Psycho-active connective tissue ground like broken glass in the joint, and no amount of will could force it to bear his weight.

The Tindalosi faced him; he a wounded giant, they mechanised assassins that renewed themselves with each passing second.

Dragging himself back along the bridge deck on one knee, Uldanaish hauled himself upright. The spectral vista of his wraithsight was fading, yet the scratched outlines of the Tindalosi remained stark and black.

The sound of cruel laughter was closer now, like one of the *eldarith ynneas* coming to savour its victim's degradation.

Now was the moment.

'Come, hounds of Morai-Heg,' he said. 'We die together!'

Uldanaish extended his left arm and cut through the thick suspension cables with a sawing blast of high-energy laser pulses. At the same instant, his wraithblade sliced up through the entwined knot of cables at his shoulder.

The deck buckled as the bridge's cardinal supports were removed at a stroke. The Tindalosi saw the danger and surged past him, but it was already too late.

With a scream of tearing metal, the bridge snapped in two, spilling the combatants into the explosively toxic clouds venting from the base of the tower. The Tindalosi howled as they fell, their metal hides blistering in the caustic fog.

Uldanaish Ghostwalker made no sound at all.

His soul had already been claimed.

Microcontent 11

THE AURA OF abandonment Vitali felt looking at the cog-toothed entrance to Forge Elektrus reminded him of the plague-soaked sump-temples of the Schiaparelli Sorrow of Acidalia Planitia. The Gallery of Unremembering within Olympus Mons depicted that great repository in its heyday, a towering pyramid filled with data from the earliest days of mankind's mastery of science.

Martian legend told that the Warmaster himself had unleashed a fractal-plague known as the Death of Innocence, which obliterated twenty thousand years of learning and transformed an entire species-worth of knowledge into howling nonsense code.

Vitali and Tarkis Blaylock had scoured some of the deepest memory-vaults for surviving fragments of that knowledge. The plague had evolved in the darkness for nearly ten millennia and all they found were corrupt machines, insane logic-engines and lethal scrapcode cybernetics haunting the molten datacores.

This wasn't quite on the same level, but being below the waterline on the *Speranza* while it was under attack gave Vitali the same sense of threat lurking around every corner.

Judging by the invisible cocktail of combat-stimms surrounding him, the twenty skitarii he'd commandeered from one of Dahan's reserve zones clearly felt the same way.

Vitali had wanted a cohort of praetorians, but Dahan had point-blank refused, rank-signifiers be damned. After a heated binaric negotiation the

Secutor had grudgingly released a demi-maniple to Vitali's authority.

Each skitarii was encased in archaic-looking shock-armour that put them only just below the height of a Space Marine. Draped in an assortment of ragged pennants and mechanical fetishes, their feral appearance put Vitali in mind of the legendary Thunder Warriors of Old Earth, whose faded images were preserved on a dusty block said to have once been part of the Annapurna Gate.

Oversized gauntlets bore a mixture of blast-carbines, shotcannons or heavy electro-spears. A few had power weapons or rapid-firing solid slug throwers comparable to Adeptus Astartes bolters.

They'd moved through the *Speranza* at speed; diverting to avoid columns of running soldiers, past the sounds of gunfire and explosions, along corridors scored with laser impacts and strewn with glassy debris.

Traversing a suspended gantry arcing across a vaulted graving dock designed for Leviathans, Vitali had his first glimpse of the enemy. Crystalline warriors, identical to the ones he'd remotely seen aboard the *Tomioka*. Blitzing green bolts chased them over the gantry, but before any real weight of fire could be brought to bear, a flanking force of weaponised servitors emerged from opposing transverse through-ways. They punched through the enemy in a carefully orchestrated two-pronged attack. Vitali didn't stay to watch the final annihilation of the invaders, pushing ever downwards towards his destination.

The approach halls of Forge Elektrus were dark and unwelcoming, its spirits glitchy and wary of the intruders in their midst. Vitali sensed fresh reworking in the code of the machinery behind the walls, which surprised him in a place so obviously neglected.

His jet-black servo-skull, an exact replica of his own cranial vault, floated beside him like a nervous child. A battle robot aboard the *Tomioka* had almost destroyed it, but Linya had brought it back and painstakingly restored it on the journey to Exnihlio.

The skitarii hadn't shared the skull's caution, and deployed into the approach hall as though they were ready to storm Forge Elektrus. They took cover against projecting spars of the bulkhead and covered the cog-toothed door with their enormous guns. A weeping skull icon of the Mechanicus drizzled oil to the perforated deck. The vox implanted within its jaws buzzed and the lumens flickered in time with its hostile binaric growl.

Vitali walked to the door and looked up at the skull.

'My name is Magos Vitali Tychon, and I seek entry to Forge Elektrus,' he said, pressing his hand to the locking plate and letting it read his rank signifiers. 'I must see the senior magos within.'

The skull spat a wad of distortion.

'For an audience or a fight?' it said. 'I'm hearing reports about invaders on the ship, and that's a lot of nasty-looking men you have there. Two suzerain-caste kill-packs if I'm not mistaken.'

'It's quite a distance from the cartographae dome to Forge Elektrus,' said Vitali. 'And, as you say, the *Speranza* is under attack. I wanted to be sure I survived the journey.'

'Given that you're clearly mad to have even tried, tell me why I should let you in,' said the skull.

'Very well. I have reason to believe there is someone or something within this forge that can save the ship,' said Vitali.

The skull fell silent, hissing dead air for thirty seconds before the forge door rolled aside and a waft of incenses used in the anointing of freshly sanctified machines blew out. Vitali found himself facing a strikingly pretty adept, whose features so closely resembled Linya's that it sent a blistering surge of high voltage around his system. Her robes were oil-stained crimson. Golden light haloed her. She held an adept's staff crowned with laurels and snared mammals in one bronzed hand, a humming graviton pistol in the other.

'Magos Chiron Manubia at your service,' she said, and gestured within the forge with the barrel of her pistol. 'You can enter, but the kill-packs stay outside.'

Vitali nodded and issued a holding order to the skitarii before following Manubia inside. The door rolled shut behind him, his servo-skull darting in just before it closed entirely.

'The interior of Forge Elektrus does not match its outward appearance, Adept Manubia,' said Vitali, staring in wonder at a dozen gold-lit engines lining a mosaic-tiled nave.

'None of my doing,' she said.

Puzzled by her cryptic remark, Vitali moved down the nave.

The engines to either side of him crackled with eager machine-spirits, thrumming with more power than any one forge could possibly require. At the end of the nave was a throne worked into a wide Icon Mechanicus, and the light of the engines glittered in its cybernetic eye. Shaven-headed adepts of lowly rank tended to the engines or scoured flakes of rust from both throne and skull.

'Your journeymen?' asked Vitali.

'Not anymore,' replied Manubia, turning to face him with the pistol held unwavering at his chest. 'Now tell me why you're here. And be truthful.'

Manubia's vague answers and hostility perplexed Vitali. She couldn't possibly think he was a threat. What was going on in Forge Elektrus that compelled its magos to greet another with a sublimely rare and lethal weapon?

'Well?' said Manubia when he didn't answer.

'What I have to tell you will stretch your credulity to breaking point,' he said, 'So I am opting to follow your advice and embrace total honesty. I want you to know that before I begin.'

And Vitali told her of Linya and Galatea, and how the machine-hybrid had gone on to murder her body in order to harvest her brain and incorporate it into a heuristic neuromatrix. Manubia's eyebrows rose in disbelief when he spoke of Linya's manifestation within the dome, but a look of understanding settled upon her when he spoke of what he had been told during their brief communion.

'*That's* what made you cross half the ship to come down here?'

'I would do anything to help my daughter,' said Vitali. 'And if that means crossing a ship at war, then so be it. I implore you, Adept Manubia, if you know anything at all, please tell me.'

'She knows me,' said a man in the coveralls of a bondsman who emerged from behind one of the largest machines.

The man was tall and rangy with close-cropped stubble for hair and the hollowed cheeks of a below-deck menial. A barcode tattoo on his cheek confirmed his status as a bondsman, but his eyes were tertiary-grade exosomatic augmetics and his right arm was a crude bionic with freshly-grafted haptics at the fingertips.

Vitali read the man's identity from the tattoo and anger touched him as he recognised the name.

'Abrehem Locke,' said Vitali.

The man frowned in confusion as Vitali strode towards him, all traces of the genial stargazer replaced by the mask of a tormented father.

'Your little revolution delayed getting Linya to the medicae decks,' said Vitali. 'You made her suffer.'

'Easy there,' said Manubia, following Vitali and keeping the graviton pistol trained on him. 'This isn't a subtle weapon, but I can still crack the legs from under you.'

Vitali ignored her. 'Linya almost died because of what you did.'

To his credit, Locke stood his ground. 'And I'm sorry for that, Magos Tychon, but I won't apologise for trying to better conditions in the underdecks. If you knew the suffering that goes on there, how badly the Mechanicus treats those who toil in its name, you'd have done exactly the same.'

Vitali wanted to throw Locke's words back in his face, remembering the agony he had suffered in trying to manage Linya's pain, but the man was right. Vitali had even said words just like that to Roboute Surcouf on the *Renard*'s shuttle.

The anger drained from him and he nodded. 'Maybe so, Master Locke, maybe so, but it is hard for me to entirely forgive a man who caused my daughter pain, no matter how noble the principle in which he acted.'

'I understand,' said Locke, meeting Vitali's gaze.

Vitali looked carefully into the bondsman's augmetics, sensing there was more to this man than met the eye. Was this lowly bondsman the key to fighting Galatea?

'I think perhaps it was you I came here to find, Master Locke,' said Vitali.

'Me? Why?'

'I don't know yet,' said Vitali, lacing his fingers behind his back, 'but I will. Tell me, how much do you know of hexamathics?'

'Nothing at all.'

Vitali turned to Adept Manubia.

'Then you and I have a great deal of work to do.'

THE STRUCTURE HIS skitarii had cut into with their power fists and blades made no sense to Kotov. On a world where everything was given over to sustaining the Breath of the Gods, why would a place so large be left empty? Vast beams and columns of rusted steel supported a soaring roof obscured by an ochre smirr of mist. Decay and dilapidation hung heavy in the air, like an abandoned forge repurposed after centuries of neglect.

As far as Kotov could make out, the building had no floor beyond the wide, cantilevered platform of rusted metal reaching ten metres beyond the shuttered door. His two skitarii stayed close to him as he ventured out to its farthest extent. He sent his servo-skulls out over the void. Stablights worked into their eye sockets failed utterly to penetrate the immense, echoing and empty space.

Behind him, the Cadians, eldar and Black Templars pushed into the building. They shouted and hunted for ways to seal the entrance behind them.

Roboute Surcouf and Ven Anders helped Magos Pavelka to the ground, their arms around her shoulders. Kotov didn't need a noospheric connection to see her ocular augmetics had been burned away completely. Implant, nerve and neural interface were an alloyed molten spike of surgical steel and fused brain matter.

She would likely never see again.

Her head was bowed. In pain or regret?

Perhaps it was in shame for wielding profane code. If Kotov believed they might ever return to Mars, he would see to it that Ilanna Pavelka was irrevocably excommunicated from the Cult Mechanicus.

She had meddled with shadow artes and paid the inevitable price.

The thought gave him a moment's pause as he considered the depth of his own hubris.

And what price would I have to pay…?

He pushed aside the uncomfortable thought and knelt at the ragged edge of the platform. Beyond the metal, the ground fell away sharply in a steeply angled quarried slope. Dull steel rails fastened to the bare rock reflected the light of the skull's stablights, and Kotov followed their route to a battered funicular carriage sitting abandoned a hundred metres to his left.

He felt the aggression-stimms of the skitarii surge, and turned to see the eldar witch approaching. He stood his warriors down with a pulse of holding binary. Bielanna, that was her name, though Kotov had no intention of using it.

She removed her helm and knelt at the edge of the platform, staring down into the darkness. Kotov saw tears streaming down her cheeks. She reached out as if to touch something, then flinched, drawing her hand back sharply.

'It's here,' she said.

'What is?' asked Kotov.

'All the pain of this world.'

VEN ANDERS REMOVED his helmet and dropped it at his feet. He closed his eyes and craned his neck to let the drizzling moisture wet his skin. He rubbed a hand over his face, clearing away the worst of the blood. Little of it was his, but he'd been standing next to Trooper Bailey when the Tindalosi eviscerated him.

Cadian Guardsmen fought on the very worst battlefields of the Imperium, knew all the myriad ways there were to die in war, but Anders had seldom seen cruelty as perfectly honed as he had in the Tindalosi.

Against the lids of his eyes he saw the hooking slashes of their claws, the bloody teeth and the phosphor scrawls of eyes that seemed to be looking at him even now. He shook off the sensation of being watched and hawked a mouthful of bitter spit over the edge of the platform.

He tasted metal and felt a buzzing in his back teeth that told him a Space Marine was standing next to him. Power armour always had that effect on him.

'For a big man, you step pretty light,' he said.

'Walk softly, but carry a big stick, isn't that what they say?'

Anders opened his eyes and ran his hands through his hair. Longer than he was used to. Time aboard the *Speranza* was making him lax in his personal grooming.

'I didn't know it was possible for a Space Marine to walk softly,' said Anders, looking up into Tanna's flat, open features.

'We have Scouts within our ranks,' said Tanna. 'Or did you think that was an ironic title?'

'I hadn't thought of it like that,' admitted Anders. 'Then again, I've never seen Space Marine Scouts.'

'Which is exactly the point,' said Tanna, before falling silent.

Anders understood that silence and said, 'I grieve for the loss of Bracha. Was he a… friend?'

'He was my brother,' said Tanna. 'Friend is too small a word.'

'I understand,' said Anders, and he knew Tanna would see the truth of that.

'We were a small enough brotherhood when we joined the Kotov Fleet,' said Tanna. 'And when we are no more, the courage these warriors have shown will pass unremembered. I would not see it so, but know not how to carve our mark into history's flesh.'

Tanna's words of introspection surprised Anders. He had encountered only a few Space Marines in his lifetime, but instinctively knew how rare this moment was.

And so he returned Tanna's honesty.

'I'm no stranger to death,' he said, pinching the bridge of his nose between his fingers. 'Stared it down a hundred times on a thousand battlefields and never once flinched. That's not bravado, it's really not, because it's not fear for my own life that keeps me pacing the halls at night...'

'It is for the lives of those you command.'

Anders nodded. 'No officer wants to lose men under his command, but death walks in every Guardsman's shadow. You go into battle knowing with *complete certainty* that you're going to lose men and women along the way. You have to make peace with that or you can't be an officer, not a Cadian officer anyway. But it was my job to keep those soldiers alive for as long as I could. I failed.'

'It was your job to lead those soldiers in battle for the Emperor, just as it has fallen to me to lead mine,' said Tanna, gripping Anders's shoulder. 'You did that. No commander can ever be sure of bringing all their warriors home, but so long as the foe is slain and the mission complete, their deaths serve the Emperor.'

Tanna held out his gauntlet and Anders saw a handful of gleaming ident-tags. Each had been cleaned of blood, each one stamped with a name and Cadian bio-numeric identifier.

'I retrieved these from the bodies of your honoured dead,' said Tanna. 'I thought you would be glad of their return.'

Anders stared at the ident-tags. There hadn't been time to gather them from the torn-up corpses. Or at least he'd assumed there hadn't. That Tanna had risked his life and the lives of his warriors to retrieve them was an honour beyond repayment.

'Thank you,' said Anders, taking the tags and reading each name in turn. He pocketed them and held his hand out.

'The Emperor watch over you, Sergeant Tanna.'

'And you, Colonel Anders. It has been an honour to fight alongside you and your soldiers.'

Anders grinned, a measure of his cocksure Cadian attitude reasserting itself, and said, 'You say that like the fight's over, but Cadians aren't done until the Eye takes them. And we don't flinch easy.'

'Two questions,' said Surcouf, standing before the battered funicular carriage with his arms folded. 'Does it work and where do you think it goes?'

'It appears to be fully operational, though the mechanisms are corroded almost beyond functionality,' said Kotov, scraping rusted metal from the control levers. 'As to a destination, I can see no topographical representations of where it might ultimately lead.'

'Who cares where it *ultimately* leads?' said Surcouf. 'It goes away from here, that's the most important thing, surely? At least it'll give us a chance to regroup and figure out our next move.'

'Our next move?' said Kotov. 'What *moves* do you think we have left to us? Magos Blaylock will already be sailing the *Speranza* away from this cursed world. We have done all we can, Surcouf. Either Telok has the *Speranza* or Blaylock has departed. Either way, our chance to affect the outcome of this situation is over.'

Surcouf looked at him as though he hadn't understood what he'd just said. Kotov reran his words to check they had not been couched in ambiguous terms. No. Low Gothic and clear in meaning.

Clearly Surcouf did not agree with him.

'Even if you're sure Tarkis got the message, how can you be certain he managed to break orbit?' said Surcouf. 'Do you really think Telok went to all the trouble of ensnaring a ship like the *Speranza* just to let it sail away? No, we have to assume that Telok's cleverer than that.'

'What would you suggest, Master Surcouf?' said Kotov. 'How, with all the manifold resources at our disposal, would you propose we fight against the might of an entire world?'

'One big problem is just a series of smaller problems,' said Surcouf. 'Small problems we can deal with.'

Kotov sneered. 'Optimistic Ultramarian platitudes will do us no good now.'

'Neither will your Mechanicus defeatism,' snapped Surcouf. 'So our first priority is to get away from here. Ilanna's bought us some time, so I suggest we don't waste it.'

Sergeant Tanna and Ven Anders entered the carriage, and the metal floor groaned alarmingly with their combined weight.

'Can you get this carriage working, archmagos?' asked Tanna.

'I already informed Master Surcouf that it was functional.'

'Then let's get going,' said Anders.

THE TRANSIT BETWEEN the two decks was a wide processional ramp with an angled parapet to either side, where dust-shawled statues and machines hissed and chattered in streams of binary. Perhaps it meant something important, perhaps the *Speranza* was trying to tell him something, but what that might be, Hawkins didn't know.

A twin-lascannon turret rested on a gargoyle-wrapped corbel above him, but it looked so poorly maintained, Hawkins doubted it could even move let alone fire. Kneeling Guardsmen took cover in the shadow of the machines on either side of the ramp, lasguns aimed at the wide gateway below.

Magos Blaylock had assured Hawkins that all the gates between main deck spaces would automatically seal, but that hadn't happened here. Reports of those gates that stubbornly refused to close crackled over the vox-bead in his ear, together with word of enemy movements.

Hawkins ran across the top of the ramp, where roll-out barricades were being hauled into place. Sergeant Rae issued orders to the seventy-six Cadian soldiers occupying this position in a voice familiar to Guardsmen across the galaxy. They prepared fire posts, bolted on kinetic ablatives or layered sacks of annealing particulates over the barricade. Hawkins was more used to sandbags, but Dahan assured him these were far superior in absorbing impacts than mere dirt.

And anyway, where could you get dirt on a starship?

A black-coated commissar worked alongside a support platoon setting up their plasma cannons in a prepared bastion. Supply officers set caches of ammo in armoured containers as a team of enginseers directed a pair of Sentinels hauling quad-barrelled Rapiers. One of the automated weapons was fitted out with heavy bolters, the other with a laser destroyer. Just as he'd ordered.

These powerful weapons would eventually seal this route, but until they were in place, it was grunts with lasrifles.

Taking up position at the centre of the barricade, Hawkins reached up and tapped the vox-bead at his ear.

'Company commanders, report.'

'*Valdor company, no contact.*'

'*Sergeant Kastagir, Hotshot company, under moderate attack.*'

'Where's Lieutenant Gerund, sergeant?'

'*Hit to the arm, sir. The medics think she might lose it.*'

'Do you need support?' asked Hawkins.

The vox crackled and the sounds of angry voices came down the line. '*Don't you dare, sir,*' said Lieutenant Gerund. '*We've got this one. Just took an unlucky ricochet, that's all.*'

'Understood,' said Hawkins. He had complete faith in each of his lieutenants, and if Gerund said she didn't need help, Hawkins believed her. He continued down his leaders.

'*Creed company engaging now!*'

'*Squads Artema and Pious under fire. No significant losses.*'

The rest of his forces provided a mix of contact/no-contact reports. Within four minutes of the boarding alarm going out, the Cadians had deployed to pre-assigned defence points, and a picture of the boarders' attack pattern – or rather, their lack of one – formed in Hawkins's mind.

A good defence rested on anticipating where an enemy would attack.

Armouries, power plants, life-support, main arterials, inter-deck transits, vital junctions, connecting thoroughfares and the like. These were all vital targets, but the invaders were teleporting in at random. Some appeared in threatening positions, while others materialised in sealed-off portions of the ship or places of negligible importance.

'Callins,' said Hawkins, connecting to the prow forges where Jahn Callins was lighting a fire under Magos Turentek's adepts to get the armoured vehicles moving.

'*A little busy here, sir,*' replied Callins.

'We're not exactly sipping dammassine and playing cards down here, Jahn,' he said. 'Where's my armoured support?'

'*Tricky, sir,*' said Callins. '*These Mechanicus imbeciles have got half our inventory chained up in the damn air or hitched onto lifter-rigs. I'm trying to sort it, but it's taking time.*'

'How long? There's more of these crystal things appearing every minute.'

'*Soon as I can, sir,*' promised Callins. '*You'll know we're ready when we roll past you.*'

Hawkins grinned and signed off, turning his attention to this position. A pair of arguing magi with shaven skulls worked in the guts of a control hatch beside the gateway, but whatever they were doing, it wasn't working.

'Bloody Mechanicus,' said Hawkins, pausing as he passed a cogged skull icon stamped onto the wall next to him. He reached out and touched it, feeling the ever-present vibration passing through the starship.

A little self-conscious, Hawkins said, '*Speranza*, if you can hear me, we could really use some cooperation. We're trying to defend you, but you're not making it easy for us.'

'Since when have Cadian soldiers ever taken the *easy* fight?' said Rae, appearing with his rifle held loosely at his hip. 'We're born under the Eye and know hardship from birth. Why should life be any easier?'

Hawkins was about to answer when he heard a series of quick taps over the vox. Scout-cant. Three taps on the repeat.

Enemy inbound.

Rae heard it too and shouted, 'Stand to!' as a squad of cloaked scouts ran back through the gateway. The squad sergeant, a mohawked soldier with black and steel camo-paint slashed across his face, made a fist above his head. He made a crosswise motion across his chest and thumped his shoulder harness twice.

Two hundred or more.

The scouts sprinted up the ramp, keeping low and seeming to move only from the waist down. The adepts at the gate bleated in terror. One remained hooked into the gate's mechanisms, the other jerked free and hitched up his robes to run after the scouts.

'Spry for a tech-priest,' observed Rae.

'You be fast if you had two hundred enemy at your arse.'

'True,' said Rae as the scouts vaulted over the barricade and the first crystalline creatures, like the ones they'd faced on Katen Venia, poured through the gate.

'By squads, open fire!' shouted Hawkins.

A storm of las-fire blazed down the ramp and over fifty glittering enemies broke apart into splintered shards. Heavy bolters flayed the creatures, chugging reports echoing from the enclosing walls of the transit. Grenades burst amongst them and blue-white bolts of plasma heat-fused more where they stood.

Hawkins slotted the skull of a jagged-looking thing of crystal between his iron sights and pulled the trigger. It exploded like a glass sculpture dropped from a great height. He picked another and dropped it, then another, methodically racking up kills with every shot.

Crackling bolts of green energy sliced up the ramp, but the Cadians were well dug in and the annealing properties of the particulate bags were living up to Magos Dahan's boast. The twin lascannons on the gargoyle-wrapped corbel opened fire, and blew a dozen creatures to shards.

Hawkins laughed. 'Well, what do you know?'

'Sir?' said Rae, a wide grin plastered across his face.

'Never mind,' replied Hawkins, ducking down to replace his rifle's powercell.

Then a section of the barricade exploded in a mushrooming detonation of sick green fire. A pulsing shock wave rolled over the Cadians as burning bodies rained down. Hawkins rolled and coughed a bitter wad of bloody spit.

'Creed save us, what was that?' grunted Rae, wiping grit from his eyes.

Hawkins dragged himself upright, pushing aside pieces of wrecked barricade and body parts as he blinked away spotty after-images of light. A ten-metre-wide gap had been blown in the barricade. At least thirty wounded Guardsmen lay scattered in disarray, little more than limbless, screaming half-bodies. Corpsmen were moving through the firestorm to reach them. They called out triage instructions as medicae servitors dragged the most seriously injured soldiers out of the line of fire.

Both Sentinels were down. One was on its knees, its armoured canopy torn open like foil paper and inner surfaces dripping red. The other sprawled on its back, the stumps of its mechanised legs thrashing uselessly beneath it. A burning Rapier lay on its side, the engineers smeared to bloody paste. The other weapon platform sat in splendid isolation, looking miraculously undamaged.

Crunching over the shattered remains of the first wave of enemies, a gigantic creature of broken glass reflections pushed onto the base of the ramp.

Easily the size of three superheavies in a column, it was a hideous amalgam of rippling centipede and draconic beetle. Its head was a brutal orifice of concentric jaws that spun like the earth-crushing drills of a Hellbore. Spikes of weaponry blazed from the upper surfaces of its glossy carapace.

'War machine!' shouted Hawkins.

BIELANNA LISTENED TO the mon-keigh speak as though their actions mattered, as though they were the agents of change in a universe that cared nothing for their mayfly existences.

And yet...

Hadn't she been drawn here by their actions? Hadn't she seen their actions deforming the skein, denying her a future where she was a mother to twin eldar girls? Hadn't she followed their threads to give her unborn daughters a chance to exist?

'You are lost, farseer,' said Ariganna Icefang, hissing in pain as the carriage began picking up speed and rumbled over a section of buckled rails. 'Restore your focus.'

Bielanna nodded and tried to smile at the gravely wounded exarch, but the despair was too heavy in her heart to convince. Ariganna's helm was cracked and her breath rasped heavily beneath the splintered wraithbone.

'Lost?' she said. 'Perhaps, but not the way you think.'

'I do not believe you,' said Ariganna. 'You were dwelling on what brought us to this place.'

'You are perceptive,' said Bielanna.

'For a warrior, you mean?'

Bielanna didn't answer. That was exactly what she'd thought.

'Death's shadow imparts a clarity denied to me in life,' said Ariganna, and Bielanna looked down at the blood pooling in the exarch's lap. So much blood and nothing she could do to stop it.

She swallowed. 'I was merely thinking that you were right.'

'I usually am,' said Ariganna, 'but about what specifically?'

'That I would lead us all to our doom. I have been a poor seer not to have seen this gathering fate.'

'Believe that when we are all dead,' said Ariganna.

'Too many of us are dead already,' said Bielanna. 'Torai, Yelena, Irenia, Khorada, Lighthand... And Uldanaish Ghostwalker is no longer among us.'

A shadow passed over the exarch's face and her eyes closed. Bielanna's heart sank into an abyss of grief, but it was simply the carriage entering the tunnel at the base of the rocky slope.

It had taken Kotov some time to restore the funicular to life, a process that seemed to require a considerable amount of cursing and repeated blows from his mechanised arms. Once moving, it had descended nearly a thousand metres before the fitful beams of its running lights illuminated a yawning tunnel mouth. Crystalline machinery that had the appearance of great age ringed the opening, its internal structure cloudy and cracked.

Ariganna's eyes opened and she said, 'I know, I felt the Ghostwalker's passing.'

'She Who Thirsts has him now,' said Bielanna, guilty tears flowing freely. 'I have damned him forever. I have damned us all.'

'You walk the Path of the Seer,' said Ariganna. 'You are trapped by that role just as I was trapped by the Path of the Warrior. You could no more fail to act on what you had seen than I could deny the pleasure I took in killing in the name of Kaela Mensha Khaine. Just answer me this… Knowing of the deaths your visions have led us to, would you go back and choose a different path? One that would not lead to your daughters' birth?'

'I would not, and that shames me,' said Bielanna.

'Feel no shame,' said Ariganna, 'for I would have it no other way. I would hate to die knowing your purpose was not as strong and sure as the Dawnlight.'

'Would that we had Anaris,' wept Bielanna. 'Nothing could stand before you then.'

'I am sure Eldanesh thought the same thing before he faced Khaine, but I take your point,' said Ariganna, her voice growing faint. Her hand reached up, and Bielanna assumed she looked for her chainsabre. The weapon was gone, lost in the fight with the Tindalosi. Bielanna drew her rune-inscribed sword and pressed it into the exarch's hand.

Ariganna shook her head and passed the weapon back as the last warriors of the *Starblade* gathered behind Bielanna. 'I will die as I was… before I… sought Khaine.'

Bielanna understood as Vaynesh and Tariquel knelt beside their exarch and released the clasps holding her broken helmet in place. They gently lifted it over Ariganna's head and stepped away.

Ariganna Icefang's features were cut glass and ice, violet-eyed and lethal, but that changed as the war-mask fell from her. As though another face entirely lay beneath her skin, the warm features of a frightened woman with the soul of a poet swam to the surface.

'Laconfir once told me there was no art more beautiful and diverse than the art of death, but he was wrong,' said Ariganna with the face she had worn before entering the Shrine of the Twilight Blade. '*Life* is the most beautiful art. I think I forgot that for a time, but now…'

The former exarch reached beneath her cracked breastplate and withdrew her clenched fist.

'Though my body dies, I remain evermore,' said Ariganna, placing her hand upon Bielanna's outstretched palm. 'My spirit endures in all my kin who yet live.'

The exarch's hand fell away, revealing a softly glowing spirit stone. And

Bielanna loosed an ululating howl of depthless anguish that blew out every window of the funicular in an explosion of shattering glass.

THE SIGHT OF the crystalline war machine might have put other soldiers to rout, but the Cadian 71st had fought the armies of the Despoiler across Agripinaa's industrialised hellscape. The Archenemy's war engines were blood-soaked things of warped flesh and dark iron, wrought to horrify as much as kill.

Having faced them and lived, this thing's appearance gave the Cadians only a moment's pause.

Las-bolts refracted through its translucent body, shearing away fused shards of crystal. Grenades cracked the glassy surface of its bullet-headed skull. They were hurting it, but too slowly.

Spiked extrusions from its segmented back spat emerald lightning. The bolts arced and leapt across the barricade, and not even Dahan's annealing particulates or the kinetic ablatives could withstand their power. Howling soldiers were vaporised in the coruscating electrical storms, the skin melting from their bones in an instant.

Hawkins turned to Rae and shouted, 'With me, sergeant!'

'Where are we going?'

'Don't ask, just follow,' said Hawkins, and pushed off the barricade. He ran to the top of the ramp, hearing Rae cursing him with all the force and inventiveness of a Cadian stevedore.

He forced himself to ignore wounded soldiers calling for help, weaving a path through the rubble piled atop scores of the dead. Lethal bolts of green fire spanked the ground, and Hawkins bit back a shout of pain as searing heat creased his shoulder.

A steady stream of fire blitzed the war machine, but lasguns and plasma guns just weren't cutting it. He skidded into the cover of the Rapier, taking a moment to catch his breath. Rae tumbled in behind, breathless and streaked in sweat.

'Can you even fire this thing?' asked Rae.

'Callins showed me the basics when we served on Belis Corona,' said Hawkins. 'Easy as stripping a lasgun, I reckon.'

Rae gave him a sceptical look as he scrabbled to his feet and turned around, doing his best not to expose himself to fire. He ran his eyes over the control mechanism. A mixture of amber and green gem-lights blinking on a brass-rimmed panel. Dozens of ivory switches that could be turned to a number of settings.

But, reassuringly, a set of rubberised pistol handles with brass spoon-triggers.

'How hard can it be?' he said, gripping the firing mechanism and mashing the oversized triggers.

A bolt of blinding light stabbed down the ramp and punched through the bulkhead to the left of the advancing war machine. The beam's white-hot point of impact reduced two dozen crystalline foes to microscopic fragments, but left the war machine untouched.

'How in the name of the Eye did you miss?' yelled Rae, as the war machine pushed more of its bulk into the transit. Hawkins looked for a control to adjust the Rapier's aim, but came up empty. Why would he have expected *this* to be easy?

'Push it,' he shouted over the hiss of lasguns and metallic coughs of grenade detonations. 'A metre to the left.'

Rae looked up at him as though he were mad.

'Seriously?'

'I don't know how to shift its aim. Now get around this thing and push it!'

Rae rolled his eyes and scrambled around the bulky weapon system. Flurries of snapping energy bolts tore up the ground and portions of the barricade next to him. The sergeant rammed his shoulder into the side of the Rapier, grunting with the effort. It didn't move.

'Put your back into it, man!'

Rae shouted something obscene that Hawkins chose to ignore as a number of Guardsmen broke from cover to help. Two were cut down almost immediately, another fell with the flesh stripped from his legs. But enough reached the Rapier alive and slammed into it with grunts of exertion.

Against Cadian strength, the weight of the Rapier had no chance, and the track unit shifted. Hawkins looked over the top of the machine. He stared down into the cavernous, blade-filled mouth.

'Got you,' he said and mashed the triggers again.

This time the beam punched down its throat. It lit up from within as the awesome power of the beam refracted through its entire structure. The war machine detonated in an explosion of molten glass and glittering metal-rich dust.

Its body slumped, coming apart in an avalanche of broken glass.

And finally, to Hawkins's great surprise, the gate began to close with a grinding screech of metal that hadn't moved in centuries. Hawkins saw the lone tech-priest hunched in the lee of the pilasters at the side of the gateway. The adept was still connected into the hatch by trailing cables, and Hawkins swore he'd pin a Ward of Cadia on his damn chest.

The gate slammed down with a booming clang and a crunch of pulverised crystal. The few enemy still on the Cadian side of the gate were swiftly gunned down with coordinated precision. Within thirty seconds, the area was secure.

Hawkins forced himself to release the Rapier's fire-controls, his fingers cramped after gripping so hard.

'Sir,' said Rae, carefully and calmly, 'next time you want to put us in harm's way like that could you, well, *not*...?'

Hawkins nodded and let out a shuddering breath.

'I'll take that under advisement, sergeant,' said Hawkins.

The enemy wasn't getting through this gateway any time soon, so it was time to consolidate. Well over half his men were down. Those too wounded to remain in place were evacuated to pre-established field-infirmaries. Fresh powercells and water were dispensed to those who remained.

Replacement sections of barricade were installed and with reinforcements arriving from the reserve platoons, the position was secure within four minutes of the attack's ending.

Hawkins checked with his other detachments, listening to clipped reports of furious firefights throughout his sectors of responsibility. Some were still engaged, some had repulsed numerous waves of attackers. Others had yet to make enemy contact. Only one position had been abandoned as crystal-line foes appeared without warning in flanking positions in overwhelming numbers.

Hawkins adjusted his mental map of the fighting, seeing areas of vulner-ability, angles of potential counter-attack and areas of the *Speranza* where the greatest threats might arise.

One location immediately presented itself as the greatest danger – as he'd always suspected it would.

'Sergeant Rae,' he said. 'Assemble a rapid-reaction command platoon. I need to be moving on the double.'

'Where are we going?'

'Just get it done, sergeant.'

Rae nodded, dragging squads out of the line and hustling them into formation. Hawkins tapped the bead in his ear, cycling through channels until he reached the Mechanicus vox-net.

'Dahan, status report?'

The Magos Secutor's response was virtually immediate.

'*I am orchestrating the ship's defence from the Secutor temple. All skitarii posi-tions holding, though the randomness of the enemy arrival points is proving to be most vexing.*'

'Always a pain when the enemy doesn't play nice, isn't it?'

'*A predictable enemy is an enemy that can be more easily overcome,*' agreed Dahan. '*Observation: I discern a lack of cohesion in this assault. Each enemy contingent appears to be working to its own design, independent of the others.*'

'Keeping our attention divided,' said Hawkins. 'Trying to mask the real danger.'

'*What real danger?*'

'The training deck,' said Hawkins. 'Lots of ways in and a more or less straight run to the bridge. We're on our way there now.'

'*An unnecessary redeployment, Captain Hawkins,*' said Dahan. '*Skitarii forces are emplaced and all static weaponry has been granted full lethal authority.*'

Rae signalled the command platoon's readiness, and Hawkins took his place in the line.

'Call it gut reaction, magos,' said Hawkins. 'I get the feeling this attack will cohere soon enough, and when it does, they're going to throw everything they've got at us.'

Microcontent 12

THANKS TO THE empty window frames, the reek of stale air and turned earth had been growing stronger in the funicular with every kilometre travelled. By the time it reached the end of its long journey through the planet's crust, the graveyard stench was almost overpowering.

Even distanced from olfactory input by augmented sensory limiters, Kotov still registered the smell as unpleasant. From the looks of disgust on the faces of those without his advantages, it must be unbearable to baseline senses.

The carriage doors squealed open, revealing the funicular's final destination: a buckled terminus platform of bare iron within an ancient cave of gnarled rock. The ceiling was jagged with grotesquely organic stalactites of rotted matter, and pools of foetid liquid gathered beneath them in sticky pools.

Tanna and the Black Templars debarked first, moving to the filth-encrusted walls and covering the only other exit, a cave mouth fringed with cloudy crystalline growths. The Cadians went next, following their colonel with rifles jammed in tight to their shoulders.

'So do you think this is a better place, Master Surcouf?' asked Kotov, taking a moment to enjoy the sight of the rogue trader pressing a wadded kerchief over his mouth and nose.

'Well, we're not being attacked by bloodthirsty mech-hunters, so I'd say it's a step up from the universal assembler.'

Kotov stepped from the funicular and almost immediately, his chronometer began glitching, the numerals speeding up, reversing and flickering in and out of sync with his implanted organs. The effect was disorientating, and he stumbled. His skitarii held him upright.

'Archmagos?' asked one, whose noospheric tags identified him as Carna. 'Is something the matter?'

Kotov disabled the chronometer and restored his equilibrium with a surge of internal purgatives. The unpleasant sensation passed and he nodded to his protectors.

'I am fine,' he said.

Surcouf followed him onto the platform, with Magos Pavelka clinging to his arm. Surcouf was almost dragged to the ground when Pavelka was seized by the same nauseous sense of mechanical dislocation that had almost felled him.

'Turn off your chronometer,' Kotov advised her, though given Pavelka's transgressions, he was inclined to let her suffer.

As unpleasant as the effects of the cave were to Kotov and Pavelka, it was nothing to how the eldar witch reacted. Bielanna screamed and fell to her knees as soon as she stepped from the carriage. Her skin, which even to a Martian priest appeared unnaturally pale, grew ever more ashen. Her face contorted in grief, more so than when her piercing shriek on the carriage had almost deafened them all. Her face contorted as though invisible hands were pushing each muscle in different directions at once. Tears streamed down her face.

'I told you...' she said. 'All the pain of this world is here. This is it, this is the locus of splintering time. This is where the fraying of every thread begins and ends. The flaw that tears the weave apart...'

Her words made no sense to Kotov and he turned away.

'You led us to this,' spat Bielanna. 'Your mon-keigh stupidity!'

Carna growled, baring steel-plated teeth, but Bielanna ignored him. Her warriors helped her to her feet, but she shrugged them off, stalking towards Kotov like an assassin with a helpless target in sight.

The skitarii raised their weapons, but Bielanna hurled them aside with a sweeping gesture of her palms. They slammed into the walls of the cave, and hoarfrost patterned the surface of their armour as she pinned them three metres above the platform.

'What have you done here?' said Bielanna, a distant, confused look in her eyes, as though she was having to force each word into existence. It seemed to Kotov that she was not really addressing him, but some unseen elemental force.

'Time itself is being unmade here,' sobbed Bielanna. 'The future unwoven and the past rewritten! All the potential of the future is being stolen... No! This cannot happen... Infinite mirrors reflecting one another over and over... Oh, you came here with such dreams... Time and memory twisted into hate... Trapped here... We cannot escape, we cannot move...

Oh, Isha's mercy… The pain. To never move, to be denied the time-drift…'

Bielanna's skin shimmered with internal radiance, her eyes ablaze with anger. Her hands were fists of lightning, but with an effort of will, she flexed her fingers and the crackling psychic energies dissipated. She let out a shuddering breath that dropped the temperature in the cave markedly.

The two skitarii fell to the iron platform. Both were instantly on their feet, weapons ratcheting into their kill-cycles.

'Stand down,' ordered Kotov, with an accompanying blurt of authoritative binary. Reluctantly – *very* reluctantly – the skitarii obeyed, but still put themselves between him and Bielanna.

'Whatever you are seeing or feeling here is not my doing,' said Kotov. 'It is Telok's. Save your rage for him.'

And with that he turned away, marching towards the exit from the terminus, where the Cadians cast wary glances before and behind them. Kotov's passive auspex – all he had allowed himself since the attack of the Tindalosi – registered powerful forces at work beyond the cave mouth.

He passed the Cadians and entered a long tunnel, circular in section except where iron decking had been laid along its base. The walls were rippling, vitrified rock. Melta-cut. Here and there, scraps of rotted cloth and dust lay discarded like emptied sandbags. A flickering white-green light beckoned him on and as he drew closer he tasted the actinic tang of powerful engines at work.

The tunnel opened onto a detritus-choked rock shelf overlooking a vast, subterranean gorge. Cliffs of stone soared overhead to a cavern roof that was ragged with spiralling horns of rock and dripping with foetid drizzle. Rusted iron spheres and enormous girders supported a network of arcane machinery that explained the source of the white-green light.

Tanna and his warriors stood amazed at the edge of the abyssal plunge, amid a tangle of corroded iron barriers. Kotov's chronometer flared back to life, and a gut-wrenching mechanical nausea surged through his floodstream. He shut the chronometer off again. It reactivated a moment later, spiralling back and forth through time-cycles.

'Tanna, what–'

Then Kotov saw the city.

Spreading like a rusted fungus across the opposite wall of the huge cave was a hideous warren of disgusting scrap dwellings wrought from iron and mud and ordure. They clung to the vertical sides of the chasm, and a twisting network of wire-wrought bridges draped the structures like a web.

Clearly of ancient provenance, the city was a grotesque fusion of organic growth and artifice. Portions had the appearance of having been built up from resinous secretions, pierced with tunnels like the lairs of burrower beasts, while others were formed from buckled sheets of scavenged metal.

Hunched shadows moved between ragged tears in their walls, suggesting that this city was not dead at all, but occupied by some hideous troglodytic vermin. With halting steps that crunched over granular fragments of splintered crystal, Kotov put aside his discomfort and pulled himself forwards with the remains of the iron fretwork.

'What has Telok done here?' said Tanna, bending down to lift a robe of ragged hessian-like cloth from the ground. 'What lives in that city?'

Tanna held the robe out to Kotov. He took it from Tanna and turned it over in his manipulator digits. The material was ancient and crumbled at his touch. He remembered seeing similar scraps in the tunnel leading to the funicular terminal.

'I do not know,' said Kotov, 'but this looks too familiar for comfort... I have seen remains like this before.'

Tanna nodded and said, 'The *Tomioka*.'

'Yes,' agreed Kotov.

'I think I might know what these were,' said Roboute, bending to sift through a rotten bundle of patterned cloth and carefully lifting something small that gleamed dully in the light of the crackling machinery on the roof of the cave.

He held the object up for the others to see, and Kotov instantly matched it to the fragment that had disintegrated in Tanna's hand beneath the *Tomioka*.

'What is that?' asked Tanna.

'Part of the firing mechanism of a xeno-weapon,' said Roboute.

'How do you know that?' said Kotov.

'*Please*, archmagos, I'm a rogue trader, it's my job to go places and see things that would get most people a one way trip to an excruciation chamber,' said Roboute. 'But, specifically, I once attended a very exclusive auction held by one of the borderland archeotech clans out on the fringes of the Ghoul Stars. Very exclusive, strictly invite only. Even then they were cautious, conducting every aspect of the transaction via servitor proxy-bodies and requiring every attendee to submit to biogenic non-disclosures not to reveal what they'd seen. Glossaic-sensitive venom capsules, neural pick-ups linked to implanted mycotoxin dispensers. Pretty standard stuff among the more *cautious* collectors.'

'So how can you tell us now?' said Kotov.

'You think that was the first contraband auction I've been to, archmagos?' said Roboute, almost offended. 'There isn't a confidentiality technology I *don't* know my way around. Anyway, the last lot of the auction was a custom-made stasis sarcophagus containing a xenoform with a weapon that had a firing mechanism just like this.'

As Roboute spoke of the auction, the metal in his hand began to crumble with accelerated degradation.

Graham McNeill

'What manner of xenos?' asked Tanna.

'They called it a Nocturnal Warrior of Hrud,' said Roboute.

PHOSPHOR-STREAKED HIGHWAYS RAN the length of the *Speranza*, neon bright against the darkness. Molten datacores flared brightly, miniature suns against the matt darkness of the void surrounding them. The impossibly dense and complex datascape of the Ark Mechanicus spread before Abrehem, wrought in glittering binaric constellations.

This was what lay beneath the rude matter of the *Speranza*, a network of pulsing information rendered down to its purest, most unambiguous form. No walls of steel or stone constrained the informational light's journey around the ship, no aspect of its life worked independently of another.

<Everything is connected,> said Abrehem, relishing his newly implanted knowledge of lingua-technis. <How could I not have seen it?>

Light enfolded him as he passed effortlessly through the virtual structure of the vessel he had always assumed was as solid and impermeable as any planetary body. He saw the lie of that now, freed from the confines of his flesh and given free rein of the invisible datascape within the *Speranza*.

Abrehem watched myriad lightstreams converge, their whole becoming brighter than the sum of its parts. He saw geometric shapes transform as fresh data reshaped them. He flew alongside shoals of fleeting data as it skimmed the surface of a glittering superhighway of knowledge.

Sometimes the data clotted, becoming dull and unresponsive until the patterns of light rerouted. Pathways split and the flow altered like water in a river.

What did such changes indicate?

Abrehem had no idea, but he watched the light twist into new patterns throughout the ship, constantly reorganising and reformatting itself. How long had it been since Magos Tychon and Chiron Manubia had sat him in the polished throne at the heart of Forge Elektrus and let the haptic implants in his mechanised arm mesh with its divine circuits?

A minute? A year?

Hexamathic calculus filled Abrehem's head, an interconnected web of quantum algebraics, axioms of metatheory, four-dimensional geometries, N-topological parametrics and multivariate equations. Even the simplest concept was utterly bewildering to Abrehem's conscious mind. Only the deepest regions of his psyche were able to process the many illogical, acausal and counter-intuitive tenets of hexamathics.

His introduction to this arcane branch of mathematical techno-theology had been brutally, painfully rapid. Optical inloads were driven straight through his eyes to the neocortex of his brain.

An imperfect means of knowledge implantation and one that, according to Magos Tychon, would fade without continual reinforcement. Only a complete remodelling of his cognitive architecture and numerous invasive cerebral implants would allow the inloads to permanently bond with his synaptic pathways.

Much to Abrehem's relief, such procedures were beyond the skill of any in Forge Elektrus to perform, and the nearest medicae deck was under siege. So, agonisingly painful optical inloads it was.

But it was worth any pain to see the ship like this, to fly its length in the time it took to form the thought. The largest forges, temples and information networks were hyper-dense novae of light. The command bridge was incandescent, too bright to look upon.

Each critical system was a pulsing star of layered information, stored knowledge and the collected wisdom of all who toiled within. Nor was Abrehem's sight confined simply to the ship's systems.

Scattered like nebulous clouds of glittering dust, the *Speranza*'s crew billowed through the traceries of scaffolding light as microscopic flecks. Confined by millennia of dogma to prescribed pathways, none could fly the datascape as free as Abrehem.

Yet even the brightest adepts were tiny embers compared to the heart of the ship where its gestalt spirit took shape. The sum total of their knowledge was insignificant next to the things the ship knew in its deepest, most hidden logic-caches.

Vitali and Manubia had warned him not to venture too far from Elektrus, that this was simply a test to see if he could fly the datascape at all. He was given strict instructions to keep clear of any system infected by Galatea's presence. He had yet to learn its subtleties. Many were those whose awe had led them into dangerous archipelagos of corrupt code and left them brain-dead, their bodies fit only for transformation into servitors.

Abrehem doubted any of those unfortunates were Machine-touched, so guided his course down to the nearest datacore, one of many that regulated the ship's atmospheric content. It took the form of a simple sphere of pure white light, that very simplicity suggesting extreme complexity within.

Streams of coruscating binary flared from it like solar ejections, lattices of chemical ratio-structures, air-mix formulae and the like, all passing into the river of information flowing through the *Speranza*.

Abrehem took up orbit around the datacore's equator, glorying in its roaring, furnace-like heat. Its heart was pure molten data, yet something else squatted within it, something that should never have been allowed into the datascape, something parasitic.

<Galatea…> whispered Abrehem.

Aware it was observed, the parasite within the datacore uncoiled like a slowly wakening serpent. Abrehem knew immediately that Galatea's presence was something unwholesome, something with the potential to destroy the datacore in the blink of an eye.

Realising he was in terrible danger, Abrehem tried to fly away, but whipping lines of light lashed him. Pulled him down. Pain jackknifed him. Ice enfolded his heart, his autonomic nervous system crashing as the thing took pains to kill him slowly and carefully.

Abrehem tried to speak, to plead for his life, but induced feedback was eating through into his cerebrum. Even as it killed him, it studied him; curious at this unbound traveller in its domain.

<Who are you, little man?> it said.

<Abrehem Locke,> he said, the words dragged from his mind.

<We are Galatea,> said the parasite, <and this is *our* ship.>

Abrehem felt its squirming coils crushing him, wondering if anyone in Forge Elektrus would even know he was dying. Would he be convulsing with feedback agonies? Would his body have voided itself as he lost control of his bodily functions?

<Forge Elektrus,> chuckled Galatea. <So that is where you came from. Well, we shall need to do something about that, won't we?>

Abrehem tried to keep his thoughts secure, but Galatea penetrated every defence with ease. It peeled back the layers of his psyche like poorly sutured grafts, digesting all he knew piece by piece.

How galling to die on his first time in the datascape! How Vitali would be disappointed to find that his hoped-for saviour was a fraud. He had hoped to salve the venerable stargazer's pain by helping him fight Galatea, but how naïve that hope now seemed.

Angry at his failure, Abrehem lashed out.

And a pure white light exploded from him, searing the serpentine coils of parasitic data to inert cubes of black ash. Galatea's scream of pain echoed across the binaric vistas of information as this aspect of its infection was burned out. Abrehem stared in wonder as the datacore pulsed hotter and brighter now that the cuckoo in the nest had been excised.

The dreadful cold fell away and his heart kicked out like a drowning man as it fibrillated with sudden spasms of life. Abrehem felt himself being pushed away from the datacore, the binaric spirit at its heart wishing him gone.

He understood why. It feared Galatea would return.

He lifted his head and soared high above the main highways of code, feeling vengeful tendrils of Galatea's presence closing in.

<Time to get out,> said Abrehem.

He recited the separation mantra.

Abrehem opened his eyes…

…AND ALL BUT collapsed to the floor of Forge Elektrus. He was dry heaving and screaming, falling in a spasming tangle of limbs. Hands caught him. Human hands. Flesh and blood hands.

Abrehem felt himself lowered to the floor. He blinked away communion burn. His stomach lurched. He rolled onto his side and vomited. Something warm ran down his leg.

'Thor's balls!' cried a disgusted voice. 'He's pissed himself!'

'Shut up, Hawke,' said a voice he recognised. *Coyne.*

What were Coyne and Hawke doing here?

An answer quickly presented itself.

The Speranza *was under attack and they figured the best way to stay alive was to find me. And like any bondsman worth their salt, they knew the secret ways in and out of most places...*

'Abrehem,' said Coyne, pressing a cold, wet rag to his brow. 'You're all right, it's over now.'

The sickness faded, replaced with a hot, dull ache in the heart of Abrehem's brain.

'Coyne?' he said. 'Am I dead?'

'No,' snapped Chiron Manubia, looming into his field of view, 'but you gave it your best shot, you bloody idiot!'

Abrehem took her rebuke at face value. But her tears spoke of genuine concern. Manubia wiped her cheek with the back of her hand and turned to address someone out of sight.

'You see? I told you he wasn't ready for this,' she said, 'no matter what your daughter says.'

'He has to be,' said Vitali Tychon, helping Coyne lift Abrehem to his feet. His legs were unsteady. His brain had momentarily forgotten how to use them.

'Magos Tychon,' said Abrehem. 'I'm sorry...'

'Didn't we tell you not to fly too close to the datacores?' said Vitali as they lowered him to one of the nave's hard wooden benches. The shaven-headed adepts moved to give him room. 'Galatea is tapped into all the vital systems.'

'Galatea!' cried Abrehem as the recollection of what he had experienced within the *Speranza*'s datascape rammed into the forefront of his memory. 'It knows, oh no... It knows we're here.'

'You told it where we are?' said Manubia.

'I tried not to, but it was too strong,' said Abrehem.

'Did you tell it anything else?' snapped Manubia. 'Access codes, immolation sequences? Kill-codes? You know, the trivial stuff?'

Abrehem shook his head. The motion set off hammerblows within his skull. His vision greyed. He wanted to retort, but she was right.

'That's it, we're dead,' said Manubia, throwing up her hands.

'No,' said Vitali, tapping the side of his head. 'Think. Galatea's hold over the *Speranza*'s systems is so thorough that if it simply wanted to kill us, we would already be burning or asphyxiating.'

'So why aren't we?' asked Hawke from across the nave. 'I am *so* leaving if you think that's a possibility.'

'Because,' said Vitali. 'I think Galatea is going to want to take Master Locke from us alive.'

Abrehem got to his feet, still unsteady after his brush with Galatea in the datascape. Yet, for all that he had come close to irrevocable brain-death, the encounter had galvanised him with the urge to fight back.

'You should let Vitali's kill-packs inside,' he said to Adept Manubia as he flexed his metal fist and returned to the throne. 'I'm going back in.'

'DESCRIBE THE CREATURE,' said Kotov.

'Small, no larger than a child,' said Roboute, letting the dusty remains of the firing mechanism fall from his palm. 'Vaguely humanoid, but its limbs bent in ways that looked *wrong* somehow, like they could articulate in several different directions at once. I couldn't see the body clearly, what with it being wrapped head to foot in rags, but there was something else, something that made it hard to look at for longer than a few moments. After a while you started thinking it was moving or somehow *shifting* when you weren't looking.'

'In a stasis field?' scoffed Kotov. 'Impossible.'

'Clearly you've never been to the Temple of Correction,' said Roboute, standing and wiping the dust from his trousers. 'But anyway, it didn't matter, no one wanted to buy the thing. It was impossible to prove its authenticity. For all anyone knew they might be buying a fake.'

Tanna shook his head in disgust. 'How did they come by this body?'

'Story was, the clan's scav-crews found it in a deep cave system beneath an outlier world called Epsilon Garanto. Apparently there was a pretty vicious battle between an Imperial kill-team and a subterranean alien infestation. Bloody enough for there to be no survivors, so the scavvers swept up what they could and got out before any follow-on forces arrived.'

'Did you purchase the creature?' said Kotov.

'If I had, do you think I'd tell you?' said Roboute. 'Anyone who owned such a thing would soon have the Inquisition sniffing around their interests. And if even half the stories the auctioneer-proxy told are true, they're absurdly dangerous. Who needs that on their ship?'

'Dangerous how?' asked Tanna.

'The hrud are said to be dimensionally volatile,' answered Kotov, sweeping his gaze around the rotten interior of the cave with sudden disquiet. 'Able to *shift* between the interstices of the universe in ways even the Mechanicus do not fully understand. Each alien is said to possess an entropic field that causes ultra-rapid decrepitude in its surroundings. I have studied reports of these creatures and their alleged powers, but never thought to see an entire warren of them for myself!'

'So if that is a whole warren of the creatures, why are we still alive?' said Tanna. 'And why don't they just shift away?'

Kotov pointed to the blazing arcs of energy leaping between the brass orbs and arcane machinery affixed to the roof of the cave.

'I suspect the machinery above us prevents the hrud from simply displacing,' said Kotov. 'Though I do not know how.'

'Telok has trapped the *feith-mhor* here with his machines of crystal and iron dust,' said Bielanna, appearing without warning behind them.

Roboute turned towards the farseer and saw something incredible. An eldar that looked *old*. Bielanna's skin was pallid, and thread-fine veins traced swirling patterns over her cheeks and forehead like elaborate tribal tattoos. Her right eye had entirely filled with blood.

'*Feith-mhor*? The Shadows out of Time?' he ventured.

Bielanna nodded. 'He has shackled their powers to the *Caoineag*, this infernal engine of the *Yngir*.'

'*Yngir*? I don't know that one.'

'And I shall not tell you its meaning,' said Bielanna, her voice filled with hate for all humankind. 'I could not see it until now… here, in the heart of it… the eye of the hurricane. The skein's threads distort through the warped lens of this world. Telok's machine steals from the future and past to rebuild the present, heedless of the damage it wreaks.'

Despite Bielanna's fractured syntax, Roboute saw the light of understanding in Kotov's eyes.

'These creatures are acting as a temporal counterbalance to the space-time distortions caused by the Breath of the Gods!' said the archmagos. 'That is why every auspex reading of Katen Venia and Hypatia showed them to be simultaneously in the throes of violent birth and geological inertia. Hyper-accelerated development balanced out by ultra-rapid decrepitude. Ave Deus Mechanicus!'

'Speak plainly, archmagos,' said Tanna. 'I am not stupid, but I have not access to the knowledge you possess.'

'Yes, yes, of course,' said Kotov, trying hard to keep the excitement from his voice. 'Space-time is being violated on a fundamental level. Put bluntly, Sergeant Tanna, Telok's machine is undoing the basic laws of the universe in order to achieve miraculous results.'

Kotov paced the edge of the gorge, his head hazed with excess heat bleeding from his cranium as his cognitive processes spun up to concurrently access tens of thousands of inloaded databases.

'If I am understanding… Bielanna correctly, the Breath of the Gods feeds its vast power demands by siphoning it from the future and the past, most likely from the hearts of dozens of stars simultaneously. It then uses that power to accomplish its incredible feats of stellar engineering,' said Kotov, his mechadendrites tracing complex temporal equations in the air. 'But the fallout from employing the machine created the many spatial anomalies Magos Tychon detected at the galactic edge, stars dying before their time, others failing to ignite and so forth. In all likelihood, the Breath of the Gods probably created the Halo Scar in the first place.'

Kotov stopped pacing and turned to the rest of their ragtag band. Roboute saw acceptance in his eyes, the superiority and arrogance he had come to know in the archmagos returned once again to the fore. The surety of purpose Kotov had lost in despair was restored in the set of his jawline and the cold steel in his eyes.

'Master Surcouf, I owe you an apology,' he said.

Roboute was taken aback. Of all the things he might have expected from Kotov, an apology wasn't high on the list.

'You do?'

'Yes,' said Kotov. 'Because you were right. One larger problem is simply a series of more manageable problems. We have alerted Magos Blaylock to Telok's perfidy, but it is not enough to warn others and expect them to fight our battles. *We* must take action to stop Telok. *We* have to stop the Breath of the Gods from ever leaving Exnihlio.'

'So what's our next move?' said Roboute.

'Simple,' said Kotov. 'We make our way back to the surface and kill Vettius Telok.'

ANOTHER ARCING WEB of lightning crackled into existence aboard the *Speranza*, where granite priests of Mars whose deeds had long since been eclipsed flanked a dusty processional nave. Here stood a magos whose achievements Roboute Surcouf had once vowed to uncover, but never bothered to seek out.

The storm of lightning expanded at a geometric rate.

Forking tongues of corposant leapt from statue to statue and detonated each one with a thunderous crack of splitting stone and shearing rebars.

Last to be destroyed was the statue of Magos Vahihva of Pharses, who exploded in a bellowing fury of rock and fire. The swirling lightstorm seethed and raged around the vault of pulverised statuary, dragging their fragmented matter into the coalescing mass of a crystalline warrior-construct.

The attackers manifesting throughout the *Speranza* were little more than inert crystal, their latticework structure threaded with billions of tiny bio-imitative machines that gave them motion.

Equipped with limited autonomy by superlative rites of *cortex evokatus* developed by Archmagos Telok after his abortive expedition to Naogeddon, they manifested a cognitive awareness of their surroundings and behaviour that had all the appearance of being inventively reactive.

They were in fact bound by strict protocols of engagement and limited in intelligence by the number of micro-machines in each manifestation.

But what was manifesting in the processional nave was something else entirely. Within a raging supernova of white-green energy, a crystalline giant took shape. Fashioned and empowered by the critical mass of Telok's machines aboard the *Speranza*, it was a macrocosm of synaptic connections far in advance of even the largest life form.

Each connection was useless in and of itself, but capable of combining the networked potential of every single crystalith into something greater than the sum of its many parts.

Taller than a Dreadnought, its crystalline limbs were hooked and tined, rippling with biomorphic induction energy. Its body was constantly in motion, cracking and reshaping as each new form was tested for lethality. Sometimes brutish and ogre-like, sometimes quadrupedal like a glass centaur. Other times it became a multi-limbed horror in the form of a clawed scorpinoid.

A host of guardian beasts surrounded it, bulky constructs of crystal with mantis-like blade limbs, glassy shields and angular skulls like vulpine hunters.

The alpha-creature's newly awakened consciousness spread throughout the crystaliths aboard the *Speranza* like a wireless plague. It connected to the thousands of warrior-constructs and took away their autonomy.

And the apparently undirected nature of the attackers changed instantly to something singularly directed and driven by ferocious intent.

Microcontent 13

THE SECUTOR TEMPLE squatted in the *Speranza*'s midships. Monolithic and threatening, it was the fiefdom of Magos Dahan. Its frontage was a weapon-studded cliff of glossy black stone cut from the bedrock of Tallarn, its only visible entrance a towering gate of black adamantium.

An enormous fanged skull variant of the Icon Mechanicus normally kept the gate sealed, but not today.

Mechanicus war engines rolled from the gate, spider-legged flame-tanks, praetorian phase-field guns, quad-cannons on armoured tracks and Rhino variants with turret-mounted graviton cannons. Following them came the clan-companies, augmented cybernetic warriors with baroque armour and technological variants of feral weapons.

The skitarii cohorts rolled from the gate to a central hub chamber below the temple. War-logisters with hook-bladed banners directed the warrior packs to radial transits that offered swift deployment throughout the ship. Braying skitarii warhorns and raucous war cries shook the walls as they clambered aboard their transports.

At the heart of the temple was the command vault, a cavernous bunker filled with banks of clattering logic engines at which sat hundreds of cal-culus-logi, strategos and members of the Analyticae. Ticker-tape machines spat punch-cards of orders and contact reports. Binaric chants relayed multi-layered vox and catechisms of praise in equal measure. Noospheric veils steamed from the ground. Servo-skulls flitted through the veils of light, recording, bearing messages or dispensing cryptic quotes from the

Omnissiah in an aspect of the Destroyer.

Like a spider at the centre of its web, Magos Hirimau Dahan drank in the volumes of information, let it fill him. His body was a true hybrid of flesh and machine, weaponry and combat actuators. Dahan was a bio-mechanical engine geared for one purpose and one purpose only.

Killing.

And right now, his every faculty was engaged in the killing of the crystalline invaders of the *Speranza*. Thousands of boarding actions cycled through Dahan's awareness, the particulars of each combat parsed and either discarded or added to the growing database of likely outcomes.

He processed engagements large and small – mass assaults on capital ships, desperate counter-boardings of mid-displacement cruisers, grappling actions of burning gunboats. The free-associative portions of his inloaded combat-memes were replete with notable boarding actions that offered the closest correlations with the current action.

Assault on the Circe *by warriors alleged to be World Eaters.*

Capture of the Dovenius Spear *by the Ultramarines First Company.*

Destruction of the Ophidium Gulf *by the Dark Angels.*

His battle-management wetware was currently processing two hundred and twenty-six separate engagements throughout the ship, each existing in a discrete compartment of thought within his neuromatrix. Everything from running firefights in cramped and darkened corridors to clashes between enormous crystalline hosts and skitarii cohorts through statue-lined processionals. Enemy war machines and Mechanicus heavy ordnance clashed in echoing maintenance hangars.

The fight for the *Speranza* would not be ended in a single glorious and decisive battle – what war ever really was? – it would be won or lost by incremental victories or defeats.

A holographic map shimmered in the air before him. Spectral grid lines rotated as Dahan's upper manipulator arms spun them to display the relevant sections of the *Speranza*'s topography. Cadian positions were marked in blue, Mechanicus in gold and known hostile forces in red.

Dahan saw them all.

The enemy's ability to appear without warning throughout the ship was Dahan's biggest problem. Boarders constrained to fixed or predictable entry points could easily be contained and destroyed.

Boarders appearing at random were not so easily corralled.

The lack of cohesion was proving to be a bane as much as a boon.

It allowed no definitive plan to be formed. Instead, Dahan's defence was relying on reactive deployments and rapidly mobile forces stationed at crucial nexus points.

Dahan shook his head. This was no way to fight. Too random, too unknown. His sub-cortical pattern recognition mechanisms were unable to attach any predictability to the attack. Dahan was left to make numerous command decisions in total ignorance of the enemy's intentions or movements.

Was this how mortals fought?

No wonder the battles of the Imperial Guard were such bloodbaths. Fighting to such an inefficient model of war, it was hardly surprising the rate of attrition within Imperial regiments was so high. Though, to be fair, the Cadians aboard the *Speranza* were maintaining a high ratio of combat kills to casualties.

Information came from all across the ship in pulsed bursts of rapid-fire data. Dahan answered them just as swiftly.

++Intruders detected, sub-deck 77-Rho, Section Occident++

<Praetorians *Martius Venator* and *Tharsis Invictus* to intercept.>

++Clan Belladonna report 73 per cent losses. Combat ineffective in four minutes++

<Suzerain Spinoza, alter advance. Amalgamate with Belladonna.>

++Cadian positions Alpha-44 through Alpha-48 withdrawing to Axis Gamma-33++

Something in the nature of that withdrawal triggered a response in Dahan's pattern recognition matrix and he spun out of the closed-in view on the holographic to a larger scale view.

The reason for the Cadian redeployment was easy to see.

A fresh batch of invaders had manifested on their flanks and was moving to cut off their supporting companies and line of retreat. Other enemy forces shifted their focus, suddenly breaking off engagements, initiating others or realigning their vectors of attack.

Like a missing piece of a puzzle, this fresh batch of invaders instantly brought terrible focus to the enemy attack.

'Finally, you have your cohesion,' said Dahan, recognising the appearance of a higher command authority within the enemy ranks and finding that he had been anticipating this moment.

It took him less than a picosecond to see the new objective of the enemy forces and realise that Captain Hawkins had been correct.

Enemy forces were perfectly poised to take the training deck.

And from there, the bridge.

ROBOUTE SLUMPED ONTO his haunches, fighting to draw air into his lungs. He rubbed the heels of his palms down his thighs while stretching his calves out in front of him. He had no idea how far they'd climbed, but was already resigning himself to the fact there was still a long way to the surface.

This cavern shelf was, like the rest of the steps cut through the planet's rock, lined with split crystalline panels and littered with granular black ash. The eldar and Black Templars were already here, keeping a wary distance between each other. Most of Ven Anders's Cadians kneaded the muscles in their legs or drank the last of their water.

Anders himself paced like a restless lion, eager to get back into the fight.

'Long climb, eh?' grinned the Cadian colonel, looking like he'd only been for a brisk walk. 'Best to keep the legs moving. You don't want to get a cramp and seize up. Pull that Achilles tendon and it'll be months before it's fit for purpose.'

'I'll take that chance,' said Roboute.

'Come on,' said Anders. 'I thought you Ultramar types were fit?'

Roboute wanted to hate Anders right now, but only ended up envying the man's fitness. He nodded and said, 'Back in the day, I'd have given you a run for your money, Ven. But right about now I feel like I've climbed to the very summit of Hera's Crown. It's times like this I wish I'd kept up my defence auxilia training regimes aboard the *Renard*.'

Anders grinned and offered Roboute a canvas-wrapped canteen.

'This climb isn't so tough,' said the Anders. 'Reminds me of the livestock trails over the Caducades Mountains I used to run when I was a lad.'

'Everything here reminds you of Cadia,' said Roboute, taking a mouthful of water.

Anders shrugged. 'Because it's all so Emperor-damned awful.'

Roboute didn't have an answer to that.

Finding a route out of the hrud prison complex had proven to be more difficult than getting in, though the eventual solution turned out to be far simpler. The rusted funicular had made its last journey in bringing them to the repulsive alien warrens, and no amount of coaxing by Kotov could force it to move. The archmagos had refused Pavelka's offer of help, and when Roboute asked her about it, all she would say was that Kotov was a man closed to alternative thinking.

In the end it had been one of Kotov's servo-skulls that found a way out, a crooked canyon of steps concealed against the cave wall behind a mass of collapsed crystalline machinery. The skitarii and Templars cleared the crumbling shards of crystal and so the climb back to the surface had begun.

Roboute had thought himself reasonably fit, but soon lost track of time after the first four hours of climbing through the claustrophobic stairs burrowed through the rock. The gruelling ascent punished his every indulgence and excuse to avoid exercising in each muscle-burning step and laboured breath.

An hour later, he'd paused to reach into his coat pocket and check his astrogation compass. Since pointing unerringly towards the universal assembler, the needle had resumed its old habit of bouncing between every possible direction.

'Does that guide you?' asked one of the green-armoured eldar, standing above him on the steps. Roboute tried to decide if the alien was male or female beneath the armour, but quickly gave up.

'Sometimes,' he said between breaths. 'But not now.'

'The Phoenix King teaches us that talismans only guide us when we are lost and without purpose,' said the eldar warrior.

'I feel pretty lost right now,' said Roboute.

The warrior looked puzzled by Roboute's admission. 'Why? We have a thread to cut, a life to end. No surer path exists anywhere in the skein.'

'And here I thought Bielanna was the farseer.'

'In matters of death, all warriors are seers,' said the eldar, springing away and making a mockery of Roboute's exertions.

He bit back an oath and continued onwards, step by grinding step.

Every footstep crunched over broken shards of glass and ash, making the ground treacherous underfoot. He and Pavelka steadied each other, him guiding her hesitant steps, her augmented limbs helping to keep him upright.

Kotov and his skitarii brought up the rear, the two cybernetic warriors helping to steady Kotov, whose gyros were having trouble in keeping him balanced on the crooked steps.

Now, slumped with his back against the wall, Roboute finally had the opportunity to catch his breath. This chance to rest was a blessing straight from the hand of the Emperor Himself.

Roboute eased his breathing into a more regular pattern, flexing the muscles of his legs and closing his eyes. It seemed ridiculous to want to sleep at a time like this, but he'd been sustaining such a heightened edge of perception for so long that the rest of his body was beginning to shut down.

Despite his best efforts, sleep eluded him, so he gave up and ran through a series of muscle-lengthening stretches and mental exercises to order his thoughts and clear the mind.

He pictured the world above and replayed the secrets Telok had voiced in the expectation of their imminent death. Meaningless to Roboute for the most part, but he remembered one thing Telok had said that struck a note of unreasoning horror within Kotov.

A name that even to Roboute had overtones of darkness that blighted his thoughts. *What was the name…?*

'The Noctis Labyrinthus,' he said when it finally came.

Kotov immediately looked up, as Roboute knew he would.

'What did you say?'

'The Noctis Labyrinthus, what is it?' said Roboute. 'When Telok mentioned it, you knew what it was and it scared you to the soles of your boots. So what is it and why did Telok need to recreate it to get the Breath of the Gods to work?'

'It is nothing I wish to speak of.'

Roboute shook his head. 'I think the time for secrets is over, don't you, archmagos?'

Kotov stared at him, as though weighing the cost of revealing what he knew against the likelihood of their survival. At last he came to a decision.

'Very well,' said Kotov. 'The Noctis Labyrinthus is a maze-like system of steep-walled valleys within the Tharsis quadrangle of Mars. Most likely formed by volcanic activity in the ancient past, perhaps even by a long-ago eruption of Olympus Mons.'

'What's that got to do with Telok and why were you so shocked when he mentioned it? What's inside those valleys?'

'I am getting to that,' said Kotov. 'The region was declared *Purgatus* millennia ago after it was revealed that a sentient weapon technology from pre-Unity was discovered to be still active. The Fabricator General of the time claimed it would lay waste to Mars if it escaped, so the entire area was quarantined and fortified. It has remained so ever since.'

'Sounds like a smokescreen to me,' said Roboute.

'People needed to be kept away,' said Kotov. 'That seemed like the best way to achieve that.'

'Wait,' said Pavelka. 'You mean there was no ancient weapon technology?'

'Correct,' said Kotov.

'So what *is* there?' asked Roboute.

'I suspect no one knows the full extent of what lies beneath the Noctis Labyrinthus, but as an archmagos I was privy to the old legends circulating the higher echelons of the Cult Mechanicus, of course. Unfounded speculation mostly, noospheric gossip and the like. And since the word of those… crescent-moon xenos ships landing in the deepest valleys began to circulate, the rumours have only grown stronger.'

'What kind of rumours?' asked Tanna, coming over to listen.

Kotov seemed hesitant to continue, baring as he was the innermost secrets of his order.

'That there was necrontyr technology beneath the red sands,' said Roboute.

'How could you possibly know that?' demanded Kotov.

'Remember, I saw the fall of Kellenport on Damnos,' said Roboute. 'I've seen ships like you described and I've seen necrontyr war machines. It was the first thing I thought of when I saw Telok's device.'

Kotov sighed and nodded as if Roboute had passed some kind of test.

'Very well, Mister Surcouf, I believe you may be correct. Perhaps some aspect of necrontyr technology does lie at the heart of the Breath of the Gods, and if that is the case, then it is doubly imperative we prevent Telok from leaving this world.'

'Why?' said Anders, 'I mean, besides the obvious?'

'Because if there is any truth to the old legends, then it is entirely possible that a vast shard of one of the ancient necrontyr gods lies entombed within the Noctis Labyrinthus.'

And suddenly it all made a twisted kind of sense to Roboute. He turned to Bielanna, who appeared to be studiously ignoring their conversation.

'You knew, didn't you?' he said. 'You said as much back in the cavern. What did you call it? "The infernal engine of the *Yngir*?" I'm going to assume that's your word for the necrontyr gods.'

Bielanna nodded slowly.

'Now you see why we fought so hard to stop you,' she said. 'And why we now spill our blood to help you.'

Roboute began pacing, as he always did when he needed to force a train of thought to its logical conclusion. His fatigue fell away from him as he spoke.

'I'd bet every ship in my fleet that one of these *Yngir* is at the heart of the Breath of the Gods. Or at least it was. It's dying now or Telok used the last of it transforming Katen Venia's star. *That's* why Telok's so desperate to get back to Mars, to open the Noctis Labyrinthus and resurrect the god in his machine.'

Linya was burning. Flames filled the cramped access compartment in *Amarok*'s leg. She was trapped inside the Titan again, the access hatch leading to safety just out of reach.

The pain was unbearable.

Linya could feel every part of her body dying.

Flesh slid from bone like overcooked meat. The surgical steel of her implants turned molten within her internal organs. She felt each one liquefy.

Incredibly, the vox within the compartment was still working, but no one was answering her cries for help.

Her father's screams echoed from the burning iron walls of the Titan's leg. He shrieked with unimaginable pain, a sound it should be impossible for a human being to make. Terror and accusation all in one.

You did this, it said. *You are killing me with your wilfulness.*

Hot tears sprang from Linya's eyes, instantly turning to vapour.

Her father's accusations hurt worse than the flames. His pain was her pain. She felt his every screaming howl of agony as though she made it herself.

'Please...' she begged. 'Make it stop!'

But the pain was relentless, the guilt unbearable. She tried to pull herself towards the opening using the rungs on the inner face of the compartment. Her body was wedged fast. Her fingers melted to the metal.

Linya screamed anew with the searing agony ripping up her arms.

Except it *wasn't* her flesh...

This wasn't real. She knew that. Knew it with a certainty that was as unbending as it was irrelevant.

No matter how hard she willed herself to accept that this was fiction, her

Gods of Mars

brain couldn't fight the dreadful stimulus it was under. Linya knew better than most how easily the machinery of the mind could be tricked into believing the impossible.

But that wasn't helping her now.

As far as it was possible to be certain of anything, this was the sixth time she had burned to death in the *Amarok*. Previous to this, she had been buried alive, ripped apart by devourer beasts of an unknown tyrannic genus, crushed in a depressurising starship and burned to cinders on the Quatrian Gallery as its orbit degraded into the planetary atmosphere.

Each death excruciating, each pain stretched over a lifetime, each experience a learning curve. Galatea was unsparingly inventive in its tortures, but the *Amarok* was a particular favourite of the machine-hybrid.

Tar-black smoke filled her mouth. Her lungs dissolved within her chest. Burning light roared over her in a torrent of liquid fire.

Linya screamed.

And found herself on her knees, flesh untouched and body intact.

Cold deck plates under her palms, bare steel walls to either side and dim light above. A cool breeze drifted from the recyc-units on the ceiling. Tears ran down her cheeks at the cessation of pain and shuddering breath emptied her lungs.

Yet even these sensations were false, this new environment no more real than the last.

<We don't want to hurt you, Mistress Tychon,> said a bland, boneless voice from the shadows. The binary was archaic, primitive almost. <But if you insist on attempting to make contact with the world beyond our neuromatrix and inciting your curious agent in the datascape to fight us, then we have no choice but to punish you.>

Linya pushed herself to her feet and canted a disgustingly biological insult, careful to render it in hexamathic cant.

The black-robed adept that was Galatea's proxy body emerged from the shadows, anonymous and giving no hint as to the true abomination that lay within.

The adept shook his head and a fresh jolt of pain drove Linya back to her knees. She gritted her teeth and fought to keep her scream of pain inside.

<Basic parsed binary, Mistress Tychon,> said the black-robed adept with the silver eyes as he slowly circled her. <None of your convoluted cant, if you please. It only angers us, and you know what happens when you anger us.>

<It's not real,> said Linya, blinking away blistering after-images of searing pain.

<Does that make a difference to how agonising or terrifying the experiences are?> asked Galatea.

<It's not real,> repeated Linya.

<Of course it is. Everything you see, feel, taste or experience is simply a constructed hallucination fashioned by electrical impulses within the grey meat-brain in your skull. Well, not that you have a skull, but you take our point.>

Linya stood once more and walked away from Galatea, subtly marshalling her consciousness into carefully constructed partitions.

<No, it's not real,> she insisted. <You're manipulating the inputs to my brain, you're *making* me feel these pains. But they're not happening, they're not reality.>

Galatea followed her, its hands moving in a complex geometric pattern that appeared to describe a Möbius curve in space-time.

<Reality? And what is that? The flimsiest veneer of experiential sequencing,> said Galatea with a venom that spoke volumes of its contempt for living beings. <A series of random, chaotic events interpreted by an ape-species that insists on seeing meaning where there is none. Your minds maintain the illusion of control and choice when you are simply machines of flesh and blood, as driven by mechanistic impulses as the most basic servitor.>

<You're wrong,> said Linya, allowing tiny pieces of code to gradually accrete within each partition of her consciousness. She took turns that led away from the confero chamber, knowing she had to goad Galatea some more.

The machine-hybrid was less vigilant when it was angry.

<I am not a machine,> she said, modulating her tone to convey a wholly fabricated indignation. <I am not governed by my impulses, I am a being of logic and reason, intellect and control!>

Galatea laughed, and the silver lenses of its eyes shone with its amusement. <The work of Adept Kahneman says differently. You see yourselves as divinely crafted beings, aloof from the worlds you build for yourself, but every aspect of your existence is governed by the part of your mind that makes systematic errors time and time again.>

They passed into the main gallery chamber, a domed structure that stood out like a blister on the exterior of the orbital station. Linya had always loved this part of the Gallery and, as such, it had been recreated by Galatea with the greatest fidelity.

Far-seeing telescopes weighing hundreds of tonnes hung on slender suspensor armatures that allowed them to be moved with ease. Scattered around the walls of the dome, differently focused glass and brass-rimmed rotator-lenses threw coloured beams to the floor. Starlight glittered on walls of black marble, distant constellations and vast galactic spirals she'd never see again.

<Then what does that make you?> asked Linya. <You were created by humans. That makes you just as fallible and bound by mechanistic impulses as us.>

<No!> said Galatea, turning on Linya. <Our essence is the result of a self-created birth. We are mother and father to our own existence, the alpha and omega point combined.>

Linya laughed. <Oedipus and Electra all in one. No wonder you're completely insane.>

Galatea spun her around, and Linya felt the build-up of hostile binary within its neuromatrix as the dome darkened and the white light of the stars turned blood red. Oily shadows slithered across the floor and Linya smelled burning skin and bone.

<We think that perhaps it is time you relived the *Amarok*,> said Galatea, reaching up to stroke Linya's cheek.

She slapped the hand away and let the walls between the partitioned compartments in her consciousness drop. The individual code accretions, innocuous by themselves and meticulously crafted in tiny fragments, now rapidly combined in a dizzyingly complex series of hexamathic code-structures.

Galatea sensed the sudden build-up of unknown code within her, and Linya savoured its shock. The machine-hybrid blurted a crushingly basic series of binaric barbs, designed for maximum shock and pain to an augmented mind.

<Something wrong?> she said, smiling at Galatea's utter confusion as it saw its attack had failed to do any harm.

<How are you doing this?> it demanded.

<Hexamathic neural firewalls,> she said. <Built up piece by piece in all the far corners of my consciousness. All designed to keep your filthy touch out of my mind.>

<No,> said Galatea. <You cannot…>

<I'm afraid I can,> said Linya and placed her hand at the centre of the black-robed adept's chest.

And with a squall of furious binary, Galatea's proxy-form exploded into a hash of pixellated static that blew away in a non-existent breeze.

Linya let out a relieved binaric breath. Split into so many pieces, she hadn't been certain her painstakingly crafted code would work.

But it had, and now she had a chance to do some *real* harm.

VENTURING INTO EXNIHLIO'S depths had been a special kind of hell for Ilanna Pavelka. After being blinded by vengeful feedback from the control hub, the hrud warren had felt like wading naked through a plague pit. Groping through greasy, cloying air, dense with pollutants. Forced to feel her way with bare hands.

Each step upwards had seen that horrific sensation diminish, but it was lodged like an infection in her flesh. Already her internal chronometers – having now recovered from the entropic field distortion below – registered at least a seven-year degradation of her organics. Her augmetics were similarly affected, and she wondered if anyone else knew how much of their lives had been stolen by exposure to the imprisoned xenoforms.

Kotov must surely know, but had chosen to say nothing.

Roboute and Ven Anders wouldn't know, though both must surely be feeling a greater weariness than normal. Even with the restoration of her chronometers, it was impossible to say for sure how much time they had spent beneath the surface of the planet. The elasticity of time was a new sensation to Ilanna, who was used to a constant and completely accurate register of its passage.

Without sight, she was unaware of the exact nature of the tunnel they were climbing, but passive arrays told her its composition had changed from bare rock and crystal to stone and iron.

'We've left the cave systems below Exnihlio,' she said, more to herself than to elicit any response.

'Looks that way,' agreed Roboute. 'We're climbing through deep industrial strata. It's a bloody maze, but Kotov seems to think he understands the layout down here and says it won't be long until we reach a transit hub on the surface.'

Ilanna nodded, but didn't reply.

The quality of the air was markedly different, no longer pestilential decay, but the hard, bitter reek of industry. Heavy with the hot oil and friction of nearby engines, the smell should have been reassuringly familiar to her.

Instead, it filled her with the unreasoning sense that they climbed towards something far worse than the senescent creatures below. Ilanna could find no logic to this, beyond the obvious threat of Telok, yet the feeling grew stronger with every reluctant step she took towards the surface.

'Something wrong?' said Roboute as she paused to clear her head.

'No, I just–'

A howl of something ancient exploded in the vault of her skull.

Ilanna screamed as every atom of her flesh blazed with the imperative to flee. A cascade of catecholamines from her adrenal medulla catapulted her body into a state of violent tension.

'Ilanna!' cried Roboute, going to the ground as her weight dragged him down. 'What is it?'

'They're coming!' she cried, clawing at his arm and casting around for the source of her terror. 'Didn't you hear that?'

'Hear what?' said Roboute, kneeling beside her. She couldn't see his face, but heard his concern. 'All I hear are machines.'

'They've come back,' she sobbed. 'They're still coming for us. They won't stop, ever.'

'What are?' said a voice Ilanna recognised as Tanna's.

'The Tindalosi,' she said. 'I can hear them in my head…'

'They're here?' said Tanna, and Ilanna heard the scrape of damaged metal in his armour and the stuttering of his sword's actuators. Its spirit was angry; many of its sawing teeth blades were missing.

'No,' she managed, triggering a burst of acetylcholine to regain a measure of homeostasis within her internal systems. 'Not yet. I can hear them... in my head. I... I think that when I saw them, they... saw me too.'

'Like a scent marker?' asked Tanna.

'That's as good an analogy as any,' said Ilanna, her fight or flight reaction beginning to recede. 'Whatever hurts you and Ghostwalker did to them, it wasn't enough.'

'Then we will fight them again,' said another Space Marine, Varda she thought. 'And this time we will finish the job.'

Ilanna shook her head. 'No, you won't. I mean no disrespect, Brother Varda, but you saw them. The beasts are imbued with some form of self-regenerative mechanism. You can't hurt them. At least, not without my help.'

An irritated flare of noospherics behind her.

'Do not suggest what I know you are about to suggest, Magos Pavelka,' said Archmagos Kotov.

'It could help kill the hunting beasts,' she said.

'It is a curse upon machines,' said Kotov. 'You dishonour the Cult Mechanicus with such blasphemies.'

'What is she talking about, archmagos?' demanded Tanna.

'Nothing at all, a vile perversion of her learning,' said Kotov.

'Speak, Magos Pavelka,' ordered Tanna, and Ilanna almost smiled at the outrage she felt radiating from Kotov. Had they been anywhere within the Imperium, she had no doubt the archmagos would already have exloaded his *Technologia Excommunicatus* to the Martian synod.

'When I was stationed on Incaladion, I–'

'Incaladion? I might have known,' said Kotov. 'That is why you bear brands of censure in your noospherics? And to think I allowed a techno-heretic aboard the *Speranza*!'

Tanna held up a hand to forestall further outrage from Kotov, and Ilanna was pathetically grateful to be spared a repeat of what she had heard from her accusers so long ago.

'What is Incaladion?' asked Tanna.

'A forge world in Ultima Segmentum,' said Ilanna. 'I was stationed there a hundred and forty-three years ago when there were some... troubles.'

'What sort of troubles?' asked Tanna.

'Researches into the shadow artes of the tech-heretek!' snapped Kotov with a surge of indignation. 'The worship of proscribed xeno-lores and artificial sentiences! Half the planet was in violation of the Sixteen Laws.'

Kotov rounded on Ilanna. 'Is that where you developed your heathen code?'

'In service to Magos Corteswain, yes,' answered Ilanna.

'Corteswain? This just gets better and better!' said Kotov.

'Who was this Corteswain?' asked Roboute.

'He was a great man,' said Ilanna. 'Or at least he was before he disappeared on Cthelmax. He was Cult Mechanicus to the core, but a Zethian by inclination.'

'I do not know what that means,' said Tanna.

'It means he held to ideals of innovation and understanding, of looking for explanations of techno-functionality that did not rely on the intervention of a divine being.'

'You see?' said Kotov. 'Blasphemy!'

Ilanna ignored him. 'The possible applications of xeno-tech to existing Imperial equipment fascinated Corteswain, and he dared question established dogma regarding its prohibition. What you have to understand about Incaladion was that it was a world where a great deal of corrupted machinery ended up. Spoils taken in battle against the Archenemy. Machines and weaponry infected with scrapcode and infused with warp essences. Adept Corteswain developed a form of hexamathic disassembler language that could break the bond between a machine and whatever motive spirit lay at its heart.'

'A curse on all machines!' wailed Kotov.

'It was a way to free those machines from corruption,' said Ilanna with an indignant flare of binary cant. 'Magos Corteswain saved thousands of machines whose souls were in torment.'

'By killing them,' said Kotov.

'By freeing them to return to Akasha,' said Ilanna. 'Ready to be reborn in a new body of steel and light.'

'Are you able to do the same thing?' demanded Tanna.

Ilanna nodded. 'I broke Corteswain's code into fragments and stored it within my backup memory memes. The dataproctors were thorough in their *expurgatorius*, but not thorough enough. It's how I was able to break the acausal locks of the universal assembler and get it working again.'

'Could this code hurt the beasts?'

'I think so,' said Ilanna.

'Sergeant Tanna, you cannot use this code,' pleaded Kotov. 'It violates every tenet of the Cult Mechanicus.'

'Could it help fight these things?' asked Tanna. 'Answer honestly, archmagos, much depends upon it.'

For a long time, Ilanna thought Kotov wasn't going to answer, his noospherics warring between the likelihood of their death at the hand of the Tindalosi and the cost of allowing the use of unsanctioned technology.

'Yes,' he said at last.

Tanna pressed his sword into her hand.

'Then do it.'

Microcontent 14

ATOP A SOARING tower of steel and glass, Archmagos Telok looked out over his dying world. His waxen features cracked in the semblance of a grin as he saw it clearly for the first time in twenty-five centuries.

Every universal assembler within five hundred kilometres was operating at maximum capacity, and Telok stood at the centre of the spreading calm. Beyond their influence, crackling columns of lightning flickered in the far distance, raising more of his crystalline army to the *Speranza*.

The attack there was progressing well. Many of the peripheral decks and Templum Prime had already been captured. With the achievement of a singularity of consciousness within the warrior-constructs, full control of the ship was a mathematical certainty.

Telok took a moment to savour the striking cerulean blue of the sky. Exnihlio's atmosphere had been tortured with toxic discharges and electromagnetic distortion for so long, he had forgotten just how clear it could be.

The colour was as he'd imagined the skies of Terra to have once been. Or perhaps its oceans. Ancient histories were so full of hyperbolic allusions to such things that it was difficult to be certain of anything.

When he returned to Mars and remade the system's star, the planets of the solar system would be reborn, free of the rotted institutions and hidebound cretins upon their surfaces.

Just as the surface of Exnihlio would soon be wiped clean.

Micromechanical disintegration had been endemic to this world's every structure since the hrud's entrapment, and without the Breath of the Gods to counter it, planet-wide decay was about to accelerate in exponential leaps.

Telok took a last look around the world he had built and decided he would not miss it at all. In fact, he looked forward to seeing it torn apart from orbit, undone in a devastating cascade of temporal quakes.

Nearly a kilometre below and rendered insignificant by distance, a thousand crystaliths thronged the base of the enormous tower, a glittering honour guard and witnesses to the culmination of his greatest achievement.

Like worshippers gathering to hear a sermon, they encircled the vast, silver-skinned dome into which Telok had guided the crystal ship and its incredulous passengers. Telok almost felt sorry for Kotov, the poor fool believing he was here to rescue a benevolent exile rather than become his ensnared prey.

He conceded that it had been a mistake to allow Kotov and his entourage to live, but vanity and ego would not let such a moment pass without Kotov fully aware of Telok's genius. It vexed him that the Tindalosi had not slaughtered them at their first encounter, but the magos with the censure brands had proved resourceful in her employment of forbidden artes. The *geas* would be growing stronger within the Tindalosi, driving their thirst to depths of need that would be nigh unbearable. Already they were drawing the net tighter around Kotov.

Then that particular loose thread would be cut.

Telok lifted his jagged, crystalline arms to the sky, spreading them wide like some lunatic conductor poised to unleash his masterpiece.

And a previously invisible seam split the dome in two.

Its two curved halves began retracting, each folding towards the ground so smoothly that from here it appeared as though each previous segment was being subsumed into the next. The elliptical opening grew wider with every passing second, revealing a yawning void. The atmosphere grew tense, as though the fabric of the universe was aware of the paradigm shift taking place.

Eventually, both silver slices of the dome had fully retracted into the ground and in its place was a black chasm four kilometres wide. Wisps of ochre vapour drifted from below like breath.

Telok smiled at the appropriateness of the image.

He raised his hands, like a summoner in the throes of a mighty invocation or a telekine striving to lift a starship. Though in truth, he was doing none of the lifting.

A vaporous haze of reflected light emerged from the chasm, like a glittering swarm of microscopic flects. The distortion spread in a veiling umbra, a swaddling fog of electromagnetism that lifted the Breath of the Gods from its prison beneath the world.

It emerged without undue haste; too swift an ascent would disturb the intricate dance of its unknowable internal architecture.

As always, Telok was entranced by its magnificence.

Even after millions of years locked away by its creators and forced to endure the denial of its very existence, the Breath of the Gods still had the power to entrance.

The vast gyre of its impossible silver leaves and whirling facets emerged from its long entombment like a newly launched ship rising from a graving dock on its first ascent to the stars.

It seemed to Telok that its outer edges, already immeasurable and inconstant, were expanding. Had releasing it from the cavern in which he had assembled the guttering ruin of its alien consciousness allowed it to assume a loftier scale?

Liquid light spilled over the plaza, spreading over the assembled crystaliths like silver rain. The machine's outline spun and clawed the air in mockery of all physical laws, each portion of the alien technology orbiting its own unknowable centre of non-gravity.

The Breath of the Gods rose into the air with stately grace.

To where the cavernous holds of the *Speranza* awaited it.

BLAYLOCK LET THE sensorium of the *Speranza* fill him with its pain. Each fallen deck was a void within him, a loss keenly felt. Dahan and Captain Hawkins were doing their best to keep the crystalline boarders contained, but the overwhelming numbers of the enemy were now starting to tell. Instantaneous coordination and communication between the attackers' various elements was overcoming the advantage conferred to the ship's defenders by their preparedness and familiarity with its structure.

Blaylock sat sclerotic on the command throne, locked into the sensorium via a coiled MIU cable at his spine. The data prisms on the polished steel roof of the bridge were dull and lifeless, every inload now passing through him.

His consciousness was partitioned into hundreds of separate threads, each one managing a ship-wide system as he sought to keep the *Speranza* functional. The war to keep the physical spaces of the Ark Mechanicus intact was not the only one being fought.

Unknown assailants were fighting within the datasphere.

The golden weave of Galatea's stranglehold was tightening on the *Speranza*'s vital systems, while another presence was systematically burning them out with code that was more potent and pure than anything Blaylock had ever seen.

Was the *Speranza* fighting back? Was this some form of innate and hitherto unknown defence protocol, like a sleeping immune system finally roused to combat an infection? Blaylock had no idea, but saw enough lethal code-fire being unleashed in the datasphere to know when to keep a safe distance.

Kryptaestrex and Azuramagelli were hardwired into their system hubs with multiple ribbons of cabled MIUs. The deadly combat in the datasphere made noospherics unreliable, and the violent tremors shuddering through the ship's superstructure made haptic connections prone to disconnection.

Though both senior magi were belligerent, they had sense enough to leave the battle-management to Dahan. They too fought for the *Speranza*, but in their own way. Kryptaestrex ensured a constant flow of ammunition and war-materiel to the fighting cohorts, cutting power and gravity to sections taken by the enemy.

With Saiixek's death, command of the enginarium had fallen to Kryptaestrex, but his every imprecation to their spirits was cast out, denied access to the firing rituals of ignition. Whether that was Galatea's doing or Telok's, the *Speranza* remained locked in orbit.

Azuramagelli fought his war beyond the *Speranza*'s hull, attempting to light the shields and engineer some form of defence against the relentless blasts of teleporting lightning. The shields stubbornly refused to engage, but by altering the density and polarity of the gravimetric fields around the Ark Mechanicus, he had been able to deflect numerous bolts into the void.

Passive auspex showed thousands of displaced crystal creatures, inert and devoid of movement, drifting in space. Each successful burst of gravimetrics or vented compartment brought a machine-bray of laughter from Azuramagelli and Kryptaestrex's augmitters as they congratulated one another on a particularly impressive kill on the enemy.

<If I didn't know better, I would swear you two are actually enjoying this,> said Blaylock. <This is the first time I have known you to cooperate willingly.>

<Savour it,> answered Kryptaestrex. <It won't last long if he can't keep more of these damn things teleporting onto the ship!>

<If you could coax the engines to life, I wouldn't need to!>

Kryptaestrex unleashed a binaric curse as a transport car of rotary cannon shells riding the induction rail was intercepted by a freshly arrived host of boarders.

<Damn you and your distractions,> blurted Kryptaestrex, and the natural order of the world was restored.

Azuramagelli snapped off a withering reply and turned his attention to the hull-surveyors in an effort to anticipate the next carrier bolt.

Only Galatea played no part in the ship's defence, which didn't surprise Blaylock. The machine-hybrid had said little since the attack had begun. It paced the nave and circumference of the bridge on its misaligned legs, twitching and limping as though at war with itself.

<Blaylock! Are you seeing this?> said Azuramagelli. <The atmosphere!>

Blaylock transferred his primary cognitive awareness to the ship's exterior. The bridge faded from his perceptions and he became a vast, disembodied observer of proceedings. It took him no time at all to see what Azuramagelli had seen. While the bulk of Exnihlio remained engulfed in hyper-kinetic storms or whiplashing electromagnetic distortion, a thousand-kilometre void had opened in the tempests below.

Like the anticyclonic storm of the Jovian Eye, it was a perfectly elliptical orb. Blaylock's enhanced magnifications picked out the two geoformer vessels Kryptaestrex had launched earlier. Each ten-kilometre-wide slab of terraforming engineering was a thumbnail of black against the clearing sky below.

<You see it?> said Azuramagelli in his head.

<I do,> said Blaylock.

<Do you think it is Archmagos Kotov again?>

Blaylock considered the question.

<No, this has the appearance of premeditation,> he said. <There is nothing opportunistic in this act. It is part of an endgame.>

<Telok?>

<Who else?>

<Then what do we do?>

Blaylock returned his focus to the bridge.

Galatea stood before the command throne, its head inches from Blaylock's face. The silver eyes of its proxy body bored into him with a light that was a little too intense, a little too unhinged. Blaylock recoiled at the smell of overheated bio-conductive gels and the burned electrics of power sources working beyond capacity.

<Galatea,> he said, but the machine-hybrid ignored him as though it couldn't understand him. He tried again, this time employing his flesh-voice.

'Galatea.'

'Yes, Tarkis?' it answered, pulling away from him with a distracted air.

'What do you want?'

'Want?'

'Yes,' said Blaylock. 'What do you want?'

Was the machine-hybrid's attention split into too many splintered pieces to maintain any single one with precision? A measure of clarity then appeared in the focus of those hateful silver eyes. Blaylock heard a painful whine of optical actuators.

'Ah, Tarkis, what we want...' said Galatea, clattering over to Azuramagelli's station. But for one crucial difference in cognition, they might have sprung from the same forge-temple. 'You see the gap in the atmosphere? You understand what it means, its significance?'

Blaylock was unsure as to Galatea's exact meaning and applied his own interpretation.

'It means we can send aid to Archmagos Kotov,' he said.

'Irrelevant,' said Galatea. 'And not what we meant at all.'

'Then what *did* you mean?'

'Kill the head and the body will die,' said Galatea.

'What?'

'It means that, after thousands of years, we can finally fulfil our purpose in crossing the Halo Scar,' said Galatea. 'Now we can descend to Exnihlio and face Archmagos Telok.'

VITALI'S FLOODSTREAM PRESSURE was dangerously elevated, his noospherics ablaze with sensation, and he knew he was grinning like a lunatic at the lectern into which he was plugged. Viewed through the picter mounted in the skull above the door to Forge Elektrus, the processional approach was ablaze with zipping green energy streams and answering bolts of ruby-red las-fire.

Glassy debris from the attacking creatures littered the deck, along with a handful of torn-up skitarii corpses. The first clash had been a heaving broil of power weapons and energy blades of shimmering crystal.

Vitali imagined it to be like the battles of antiquity, when grunting, heaving men in bare metal armour locked shields and pushed against one another with swords stabbing at legs, necks and groins until one side's strength gave out. Bloody, murderous and woefully inefficient.

Blooded, the skitarii had withdrawn to firing positions around the sealed door as the crystalline creatures launched wave after wave at Forge Elektrus, like hive-dominated brood hunters of the tyrannic swarms.

Linked to the external defence systems, Vitali and Manubia fought alongside the skitarii, albeit from within the safety of Elektrus.

<A tremendously visceral experience,> said Vitali in the shared mindspace of Elektrus. <I can see why some fighting types appear to crave battle's violent siren song.>

<You'd feel differently if you were down there in the line of fire with the kill-packs,> said Manubia from her own station, controlling the guns defending the secondary approach to Elektrus.

<I don't doubt it, but it is not the business of a magos of the Adeptus Mechanicus to be shot at,> said Vitali, correcting the aim of a point-defence multi-laser. <Wasn't it Gruss who said that combat was why the Omnissiah blessed us with skitarii?>

<Really? For a magos who thinks that, Delphan gets involved in more than his fair share of firefights.>

<You know him?>

<Our paths... intersected on Karis Cephalon once,> said Manubia.

Vitali read the warning in Manubia's noospherics and didn't press the matter, aligning the barrel of the multi-laser at a group of shield-bearing crystalline brutes.

Las-rounds spanked from the shields or dissipated harmlessly within their latticework structures. Skitarii were equipped with enhanced targeting mechanisms, but they didn't have Vitali's elevated view or lightness of touch. He shifted the multi-laser's aim by a hair's breadth to allow for enfilading diffraction and fired a six-pulse sequence.

The powerful las-bolts vaporised the embedded microscopic machines in a facsimile skull before being split and refracted to fell another three shield-bearers.

No sooner was the gap in the shields revealed than a pair of implanted grenade launchers dropped a pair of spinning canisters in the midst of the enemy. Vitali's display fogged in the chaos of the detonation as shards of razored glass fell in a brittle rain.

Vitali shouted in excitement and gleefully hunted fresh targets.

<Careful,> said Manubia. <Don't get cocky, Tychon, that's just when they get you.>

Truer words had never been spoken.

An enormous beast lumbered around the corner, an ogre of glass and opaque crystal. It shrugged off las-rounds and a giant crater in its chest was filled with a nexus of crackling energies like an embedded reactor.

<Ave Deus Mechanicus!> cried Vitali as it braced itself on the deck with rock-like fists. <What is that?>

A torrent of green fire spewed down the approach corridor and exploded against the forge door. The external picters were burned away and their pain fed back through his link to the mindspace.

Vitali severed the connection and snapped his data-spikes free from the lectern. The sudden disconnect was disorientating, and Vitali felt repercussive pain jolt his limbs. His vision rolled with interference as his brain switched from perceiving the world through an elevated picter to his own optics.

Abrehem Locke still sat on the throne before the shaven-headed adepts of his choir. They chanted worshipful verses of quantum runes, basic incantations to increase the efficiency of a repaired engine.

The involuntary twitches throughout Locke's body told Vitali the man was still engaged in his silent war with Galatea in the datascape of the *Speranza*. Locke's two cronies lounged next to him, as if they thought they were superfluous to requirements. It irked Vitali that the one called Hawke bore an Imperial Guard tattoo, but had yet to pick up a weapon.

Directly across from Vitali, Chiron Manubia remained interfaced with her own lectern, her eyes darting back and forth beneath their lids. The sounds of battle beyond the forge were audible even over the thunder of its machinery: explosions, gunfire, feral war-shouts, breaking glass. The secondary entrance was holding, but what of the approach he'd been tasked with defending?

Vitali beckoned Locke's fellow bondsmen over to him as five skitarii took up position behind defunct machinery piled in rough barricades flanking the door. White-green dribbles of molten metal ran down its inner faces and Vitali detected a significant deviation from the door's normal verticality.

'Should we be standing here?' asked Coyne, nervously fingering the trigger guard of a heavy shock-pistol as though it was a venomous serpent. 'That door's giving in any moment.'

'That is precisely why we need to be here,' said Vitali, now understanding Manubia's words about being in the firing line. He glanced back over to the throne, where a skitarii pack-master was dragging Hawke forward and thrusting a lasrifle into his hands.

The man would fight whether he wanted to or not.

As would they all.

Vitali lifted Manubia's graviton pistol from his belt, reciting the Bosonic Rites as he pressed the activation stud. The weapon gave a satisfying hum, and he felt it grow heavier in his grip.

'Interesting,' said Vitali. 'Local gravitational fluctuations. Only to be expected, I suppose.'

The skitarii took up covering positions, implanted weaponry aimed unerringly at the door. Vitali saw a mix of solid shot cannons and rotor-carbines. Two up-armoured warriors with full-face helms each carried a thunder hammer and a conical breacher maul.

The centre section of the door fell inwards, eaten away by the unnatural power of the crystalline weaponry. The rest of the door swiftly followed as its structural integrity collapsed. Vitali saw shapes moving through a haze of vaporised metal and raised the graviton pistol. The barrel shook as floodstream chemicals boiled around his system.

Crystalline creatures pushed through the ruined door. The first through were cut down by a fusillade of gunfire, shattered into red-limned fragments. More pushed over the remains.

Arcing beams of green light stabbed into Elektrus. Vitali knew he should be shooting, but the pistol in his hand felt like a piece of archeotech he had no idea how to activate. Volleys of suppressive fire punched into the flanks of the attackers, but they were heedless of their survival. A crystal spike wreathed in green flame pointed at him. Vitali knew he should move, but instead sought to identify what manner of energy empowered the weapon through its emitted wave-properties.

Hands grabbed him, and Vitali was dragged behind the barricade, irked he had not yet completed his spectroscopic analysis.

'What in Thor's name are you doing?' yelled Coyne, holding the shock-pistol at his shoulder. 'Do you have a death wish?'

'Of course not,' said Vitali, struck by the ridiculousness of the question and his equally stupid behaviour. Was fixating on inconsequential details normal in a gunfight? Did all soldiers feel like this under fire? Perhaps Dahan might know.

Perhaps a study on the physio-psychological…

Vitali fought to control his panic, knowing fear was pushing his mind into self-preserving analytical mechanisms.

Coyne fired blind over the top of the barricade and Vitali followed his example. He shot the graviton pistol without aiming, trusting the weapon's war-spirit to find a target. Something shattered explosively.

Hawke was laughing as he fired controlled bursts of las-fire into the enemy. He shot with the ingrained efficiency of a Guardsman. Vitali thought he was weeping, shouting something about the Emperor hating him. It made no sense, but what in war ever *really* made sense?

The graviton pistol vibrated in his palm, indicating its willingness to fire again. Vitali knew he should rise and shoot, but the idea of putting himself in harm's way kept his body rigid. An engine behind him detonated as a pair of green bolts exploded inside its mechanisms.

Vitali winced as he heard the machine-spirit die.

A skitarii fighter crashed to the ground beside him. The entirety of the warrior's left side had been vaporised by the alien weaponry, his half-skull a blackened bowl of brain matter and cybernetic implants.

Vitali looked away in horror. Coyne cried out as he took a hit, dropping behind the barricade and clutching his arm. His forearm was a blackened stump. Coyne's eyes were saucers, wide with shock.

'Every time,' he said. 'Every damn time…'

More gunfire blazed. More explosions.

Vitali pushed himself to his knees and leaned out to shoot the graviton pistol again. He saw the enormous ogre-creature with the crackling energy nexus in its chest. White-green light filled its body, like an illuminated diagram of a nervous system.

Vitali pressed the firing stud and the crystalline monster was instantly crushed to the deck. Its body exploded into shards, like an invisible Imperator Titan had just stepped on it.

The skitarii breachers charged into the enemy. Vitali saw one warrior drive his vast drill into the stomach of a crystalline beast with a horned skull. It came apart in a tornado of razor fragments, and Vitali thought he heard a million screams ripped from its body as it died. The thunder hammer warrior swung and obliterated three more, their forms coming apart in percussive detonations of glass and crystal. Two more died in as many swings. A spinning fragment nicked Vitali's cheek and he flinched at the sudden pain.

The breacher skitarii died as a collimated burst of fire cut him in two at the waist with the precision of a las-scalpel. He screamed as he fell, but kept fighting even as his viscera uncoiled onto the deck. His fellow close-combat warrior died seconds later as three creatures with extruded blade arms surrounded him and hacked him apart with pitiless blows that seemed altogether too cruel to be entirely mechanical.

Vitali aimed the graviton pistol at the warrior's killers. He pressed the firing stud, but the weapon buzzed angrily, its spirit not yet empowered enough to fire again. Vitali stared into the enemy monsters, a mass of killers wrought from the bones of ancient science by a madman.

Hawke was on his haunches, sifting through the dead skitarii's pack. Vitali hoped he was looking for a fresh powercell, though his search had all the hallmarks of a looting. Coyne had all but passed out, hyperventilating as he stared at the ruin of his arm.

The skitarii weren't shooting. Why weren't they shooting?

Because they're dead. Everyone's dead.

I'll be dead soon.

The crystalline creatures aimed their weapon arms towards the rear of the temple. Where Abrehem Locke still sat upon the Throne Mechanicus. Vitali remembered what he'd said earlier, that Galatea would want to capture Abrehem alive.

How wrong he had been. They had come here to kill him.

Wait. Galatea? These were Telok's warrior creatures…

The expected volley of killing fire never came.

A howling roar of unending rage echoed from the walls.

Vitali heard pounding iron footfalls. Animalistic bellows. Whipping cracks of energy-sheathed steel. Glass exploded as something impossibly swift hurled itself into the midst of the crystal beasts.

It was too fast to follow, even for Vitali's enhanced optics. All he could form were fleeting impressions. Rage distilled, fury personified. It killed without mercy.

Shrieking electro-flails cut glass bodies apart like a maddened surgeon. 'Slaught-boosted musculature tore the forge's attackers into disembodied shards of inert crystal. An iron-sheathed skull battered ones of glass to powder. It roared as it killed, a bestial thing of hate and unquenchable bloodlust.

Vitali watched the crystalline creatures destroyed in seconds, shattered to fragmented ruin by an engine of slaughter wrought in human form.

And then it came for him.

Vitali had never seen arco-flagellants in combat, only at rest.

He never wished to see one again.

Its identity blazed in the hostile binary scrolling over its blood-red optics.

Rasselas X-42.

The arco-flagellant halted millimetres from Vitali. Its lips drew back to reveal sharpened iron teeth, its claws poised to strike. He felt the heat of its killing power, an urge to murder that went deeper than any implanted Mechanicus battle-doctrinas.

This thing *wanted* to kill him.

And, for a heartbeat, Vitali thought it just might.

Then, deciding he was no threat, it pushed past him, taking up position before Abrehem Locke like an Assassinorum life-ward.

Vitali fought the urge to flee as he saw a bulky shadow silhouetted in the firelight from beyond the ruin of the door.

Tall and encased in heavy plates of hissing pneumatic armour, Totha Mu-32's chromium mantle billowed in rogue thermals. He rammed a bladed stave on the ground as though reclaiming this forge for the Mechanicus. Beside him was a figure in a cream robe with a mono-tasked augmetic arm and a dented iron skull-plate.

Noospheric ident-tags named him Ismael de Roeven.

The One who Returned.

A hundred chainveiled warriors in the livery of Mechanicus Protectors stood behind Ismael and Totha Mu-32, bulked with combat augmetics and bearing an array of absurdly lethal weaponry.

'We come to protect the Machine-touched,' said Ismael, with black tears streaming down his cheeks.

'With any and all means at our disposal,' finished Totha Mu-32, with a distasteful glance at Rasselas X-42.

'I think you might be too late,' said Chiron Manubia.

Vitali didn't know what she meant.

Until he looked where she looked.

And saw the blood pooled around the Throne Mechanicus.

RISING FROM THE black depths of Exnihlio, the first thing to strike Roboute was the sheer intensity of the blue sky. The last time he'd seen a sky so pure had been on Iax, when he'd taken Katen on a system-run out to First Landing for their first anniversary. He'd never expected to see anything like it again, but Exnihlio's cloudless skies were the blue of remembered youth, going on forever like the clearest ocean.

Gone were the strato-storms and the lightning clawing from the horizon. All trace of atmospheric violation was utterly absent.

He was also pleased to see that Kotov's understanding of Exnihlio's deep infrastructure had been correct. All around them, elevated linear induction rails arced like slender flying buttresses, threading steel canyons from a series of shuttered conveyance hangars.

A host of silver, bullet-nosed trains sat idle on humming rails, surrounded by motionless servitors with slack features and eyes devoid of purpose. Bereft of commands, they shuffled between work stations, waiting for tasks that would never come.

Roboute walked into the light, cupping his hands over his eyes and smiling to see open skies once more. An invisible weight lifted from his shoulders at the sight of such brilliant blue.

'What happened here?' said Tanna, removing his helmet and taking a breath of uncorrupted air. 'Where are the storms?'

'Ultra-rapid terraforming,' said Pavelka, hunched and exhausted with the climb from the depths. 'Every universal assembler within hundreds of kilometres has been activated.'

'Why?'

'Telok's endgame,' said Kotov, pointing to a gap between the rhomboidal towers of a bifurcating induction rail. 'They are coming online for the same reason we activated one, to get something up to the *Speranza*.'

Roboute followed the archmagos's mechadendrite and felt a cyst of nausea form in his gut as he saw the sick, shimmering radiance haloing the towers.

'No...' he said, hints of the spinning mesh of silver leaves and impossible angles making his eyes water. Was it just his imagination or was the Breath of the Gods bigger than before? Was it even possible to know its size with any certainty?

One by one, eldar, mortal, Mechanicus and post-human, they came to marvel at the ascent of Telok's diabolical machine. No matter their birth origin, every soul was ensnared by its unnatural light and its physics of violation.

'An abominable birth,' said Bielanna. 'The *Yngir*'s engine tears free from its sepulchral womb.'

The farseer's eyes shone with a fierce light, and the burden of age Roboute had seen upon her was undone. The black lines beneath her porcelain skin were now veins of gold in the palest marble. Every one of the eldar seemed invigorated by the light coming from the Breath of the Gods. A salutary reminder that their senses were not cut from the same cloth as humanity's.

'All times become one,' she said. 'Even as the threads of the past and present are cut, new threads are drawn from the future into the engine's gyre.'

'What does that mean?' said Roboute.

'New life spreads its light to those around it,' said Bielanna, tears springing from her eyes. 'It means I am being renewed. It means that those I thought lost forever might yet be given a chance of life.'

THE TRAIN WAS a wide-bodied cargo transporter. It sped at incredible velocity through the forge world's towering spires in near silence on linear induction rails. It passed through the interiors of numerous forge-complexes, and within each, the signs of this world's imminent abandonment were clear. With the Breath of the Gods rising to the *Speranza*, Telok had no more need of Exnihlio.

Within each forge, the previously industrious servitors stood immobile. Without their attentions the engines which they had tended were now thundering towards destruction.

Exnihlio's machines were dying. Monolithic data-stacks melted down without the proper rites of placation. Generators belched fire and lightning as volatile cores spun up to critical levels.

Kotov attempted to plot a route from the driver's compartment as Pavelka sought access to the systems controlling the switching gear for the rails.

All to bring them to where the Breath of the Gods was ascending.

Where it was, Telok would be.

And killing Telok was all Tanna had left.

He knelt on the grilled floor of the train's second compartment, his sword held point down before him. Its quillons framed his eyes, and Tanna stared at the spread wings of the golden eagle forming the hilt, admiring the fine workmanship of the artificers.

A chainsword was not an elegant weapon. No swordsman of note would ever wield one and no epic duels had been fought with such a weapon. It was a butcher's blade, a tool wrought to kill as quickly and as efficiently as possible. And yet this blade had been given a finish the equal of Varda's Black Sword. The spirit within was as keen-edged as its teeth had once been.

Tanna stood and lifted the weapon, turning it over in his hands. He tested the heft and weight, flexing his fingers on the handle.

'Does it feel any different?' asked Varda.

'A few grams lighter where teeth have come loose, but otherwise unchanged,' said Tanna.

'Mine too,' agreed Varda, cutting the air with the midnight edge of the Black Sword and sighting down the length of its blade. 'Do you think Adept Pavelka did anything at all?'

'I can only hope so,' said Tanna. 'Whatever techno-sorcery she has worked on my blade has not altered it in a way I can detect.'

Varda lowered his blade and lifted Tanna's fettered sword arm. The links were buckled after the fight against the Tindalosi.

'Your chain,' said Varda. 'The binding is all but gone.'

'You worried I'll drop my sword?'

'No, never that,' said Varda.

'Then what?'

'Would that we had the time, brother, I would have been honoured to forge your chain anew as you forged mine.'

Tanna nodded in understanding and took Varda's hand in his, accepting the brotherhood his Emperor's Champion offered. The rest of the Black Templars gathered around him, their weapons drawn, their faces sombre.

They could all feel it too.

The end of their crusade was upon them.

No sooner had Tanna formed the thought than the train roof buckled with multiple powerful impacts. Thunderous booms of iron on steel. Claws like swords punched through the metal and the contoured roof of the train peeled back. Turbulent air rammed inside. Windows blew out and high-tension cables whipped through the compartment as the train's fuselage crumpled.

Tanna dived to the side as something vast and silver dropped into the train. A hulking body alive with emerald wychfire. Eyes a mass of dead static and hunger.

Ebon-black claws unsheathed.

'Tindalosi!' he shouted.

Microcontent 15

HAWKINS HAD FOUGHT over Magos Dahan's training deck more times than he cared to remember. But no simulation, however sophisticated, could ever accurately replicate the truth of war. Even the lethal subterranean kill maze of Kasr Creta, populated by mutant warp-lunatics with hook-bladed knives and ripper-guns, had an air of unreality to it.

But this?

This was real.

The corpses, the smoking craters and the yelling all testified to the reality of this fight. Neon streams of las and alien fire filled the Imperial city currently occupying the deck, a choked mass of plascrete and steel that stank of hot iron and oil. Roving packs of skitarii and weaponised servitors duelled with the enemy forcing a path across the open space at the heart of the deck.

Hundreds of vacant-eyed servitors milled in a wide plaza with a tall statue of a winged Space Marine at its centre. They reminded Hawkins of gawping civilians who didn't have the good sense to run like hell when the shooting started. The thousands of crystalith warrior-constructs were ignoring them, but plenty had already been mown down in the blistering crossfire.

Hawkins and his command platoon sheltered in a modular structure of cavernous proportions towards the starboard edge of the deck. Shot-blasted rebars and chunks of polycarbon rubble surrounded them. Crouched at the edge of the rubble to get a clear line of sight over the battlefield, Hawkins issued orders to other Cadian units in the training deck, shouting into the vox-horn to be heard over the cacophony of gunfire. Behind him, Rae and five Guardsmen fired through hastily punched loopholes. Others reloaded or prepared demo-charges.

Green fire threw jagged, leaping shadows.

Explosions blew prefabbed buildings apart. Burning bodies tumbled from their gutted ruins. Most were steel-jacketed skitarii, but some were Cadians. Guardsmen wearing the scarlet campaign badges of Creed company leapt from the burning building.

They ran to take cover in the shadow of a grand, cathedral-like edifice that dominated one end of the plaza. Coordinated fire from its numerous defensive ramparts and armoured pillboxes expertly covered their displacement.

Lieutenant Gerund's Hotshot company fought from an emplaced position jutting from the corner of a structure that looked like an Adeptus Arbites Hall of Justice. Hawkins had split Valdor company into marauding combat teams and spread them through the tumbledown ruins to savage the enemy with enfilading missiles.

Hawkins ducked back as an emerald explosion threw up chunks of rock and mesh decking. He scanned the battlefield for anything he'd missed, any opportunity to exploit enemy mistakes. He saw nothing, but aspects of the city's layout seemed damnably familiar. Something at the back of his mind told him he'd seen this place before, but where?

Had Dahan put them through this setup? He didn't think so.

'Why did you bother with the statue?' he wondered, then grinned as it suddenly hit him why he recognised this battlefield.

'You clever metal bastard,' he said.

'What's that, sir?' said Rae, ducking beneath the smoking embrasure of his loophole. Barely pausing for breath, Rae expertly switched out the powercell of his rifle.

'Do you know where we are, sergeant?'

'Begging your pardon, sir, is that a trick question?' asked Rae, wiping smears of blood and sweat from his forehead.

'Come on, Rae,' said Hawkins, pointing into the plaza. 'Look!'

'What am I looking at, sir?'

'That statue. Who is it?'

Rae's uncomprehending look made Hawkins grin. 'Come on, a giant Space Marine with wings? How many of them are there?'

'The Lord of the Angels?' ventured Rae at last. 'Sanguinius?'

'And look at the building behind it.'

'The Palace of Peace!' exclaimed Rae, and Hawkins saw his mind shift up a gear as an innate understanding of Cadian military history kicked in. 'Khai-Zhan! This is bloody Vogen, sir! That's Angel Square.'

'Dahan must have had the servitors set it up like this the moment the ship was boarded,' said Hawkins. 'He knew a Cadian regiment would know how to fight in Vogen.'

'Maybe he does know us after all,' said Rae, returning to his makeshift firestep.

Like every Cadian officer, Hawkins knew the Battle for Vogen inside out. He'd learned the city's every secret from the detailed accounts of soldiers who'd fought for Khai-Zhan's capital. That gave them an edge.

'Incoming!' shouted Rae. 'Displace!'

Hawkins didn't second guess the order and took off running. Rae was already ahead of him, the big man's arms pumping like a sprinter's. Hawkins ran towards a bombed-out ruin he now recognised as a recreation of Transformer Hub Zeta-Lambda.

Where Sergeant Oliphant retook the Company Colours from a pack of mutants single-handed on day two hundred and ten of the battle.

A flash of brilliant light threw Hawkins's shadow out in front of him. Then he was flying as the hammerblow of a pressure wave slammed into his back. The noise and shock of the explosion engulfed him as he hit a prefabbed wall hard.

The impact punched the air from his lungs. He fought to draw a breath as a seething column of green light mushroomed from the modular structure. Its corner collapsed and took half the roof with it in a thunderous avalanche of debris.

'Good warning, sergeant,' shouted Hawkins over the ringing echoes of detonation. His spine felt like it had been stepped on by a Dreadnought as he pushed himself to his knees.

'They're bringing up the heavy ones now!' returned Rae, chivvying soldiers into the transformer hub's cover.

Hawkins scrambled behind a smoking stub of pressed concrete with rebars poking out like a crustacean's limbs. Through the twitching smoke and guttering green fires, he saw heavier crystalline creatures entering the deck. Lumbering crab-like things, more of the centipede monsters and hulking brutes as tall as ogryns that were hard edged and non-reflective.

These last creatures carried glossy shields, wide enough to be siege mantlets. Others extruded lightning-wreathed spikes from multi-faceted hides, energy weapons as big as anything mounted on a superheavy.

'Going to need some bigger guns,' said Rae.

Hawkins nodded, scanning the ruins of the transformer hub.

'Where's Leth?' he shouted. 'Where's my vox-man?'

'Dead, sir,' said Rae, his back pressed against a slope of brick rubble. 'Him and his vox are in pieces.'

Hawkins cursed and looked towards where Creed company were repelling a flanking thrust of crystalline attackers. Even through the smoke it was hard to miss the whip-antenna of Creed's vox-man.

'Cover me, sergeant!'

'Where are you going?'

'I need a vox and Creed's got a vox,' said Hawkins, slinging his rifle and crouching at the edge of the ruins.

'It's fifty metres, sir!' said Rae.

'I know, hardly any distance at all,' said Hawkins, breaking from cover and sprinting for all he was worth. Blitzing fire streaked across the deck nearby. Was it aimed at him? He couldn't tell. Hawkins kept low, cutting a path from cover to cover, diving, rolling and pausing just long enough to catch his breath.

He heard shouts ahead, soldiers urging him on. Zipping spirals of covering fire drilled the smoke around him. Hawkins fell the last two metres, rolling to an ungainly halt behind the scorched and pitted flanks of a hull-down Chimera.

Lieutenant Karha Creed was waiting for him by the Chimera's rear track-guard. She had a thin hatchet-face, with the same high cheekbones and thunderous brow as her illustrious uncle.

'You pair are the luckiest sons of bitches I ever saw,' she said.

'Duly noted, lieutenant,' said Hawkins. 'Wait, pair?'

'You remember what I asked you about putting us in harm's way, sir?' said Rae, chest heaving and the cut on his forehead bleeding beneath the rim of his helmet.

'I took it under advisement and decided not to implement your proposal,' he said, glad Rae was here with him despite the risk he'd taken. Hawkins slapped a hand on his sergeant's shoulder and turned to address Creed.

'I need your vox, Karha. I need to speak with Jahn Callins in Turentek's forges,' said Hawkins. 'We need the tanks here.'

Creed nodded and ran to get her vox-man. Hawkins took a moment to cast an eye over the men and women occupying this position. His eyes narrowed at the sight of two particular fighters.

'What the hell are you two doing here?'

Gunnar Vintras turned from his firing step, a lasrifle cocked on his hip like some kind of Catachan glory-hound.

'After all the training Sergeant Rae here has put me through, I thought it only proper I slum it with the footsloggers for a time,' said Vintras with that insufferable pearl-white grin. 'You know, see what all this talk of duty and honour is all about.'

Hawkins resisted the urge to punch him and turned to Sylkwood.

'What about you?' he said. 'Shouldn't you be on the *Renard*?'

'Emil doesn't need my help to fly the shuttle,' she said. 'Besides, I'm Cadian. This is where I'm meant to be.'

Hawkins nodded in understanding as the vox-man arrived. The patch on his shoulder named him as Guardsman Westin. Heat bleed from the bulky, canvas-wrapped unit in his pack hazed the air. Like most vox-men, Westin was skinny and wiry with hunched shoulders and a constantly harried look to him.

Hawkins spun him around and pumped the crank on the side of the pack. He held the vox-horn to one ear, pressing his palm against the other.

'Call Sign Kasr Secundus, come in,' he said. 'Damn it, Callins, are you there? Where are the tanks you promised me?'

After a second or two of static, the regiment's logistics officer came over the earpiece, sounding as put-upon as always.

'*Working as fast as we can, sir,*' said Callins.

Hawkins flinched as a bolt of green light punched into the Chimera's glacis, rocking it back on its tracks. A fine mist of choking ash-like matter billowed like granular smoke. He heard screams from farther down the line.

'Work faster, Jahn,' he said. 'I need those tanks. And Titans too, if you've any to spare this millennium.'

'*The Sirius engines haven't moved since I got here, sir,*' grunted Callins in disgust. '*Lot of crap about rites of awakening and proper observances of blah, blah, blah. They're choking up the muster routes. I can't get anything out in numbers that'll make a damn bit of difference.*'

Hawkins let out an exasperated breath and said, 'Understood. Do what you can, I'm sending help.'

'*Help? What? I don't–*' said Callins, but Hawkins slammed the horn onto its cradle on Westin's vox-caster.

'You two, get over here,' he said, beckoning Sylkwood and Vintras to him. 'Sylkwood, I assume you can drive this Chimera.'

She nodded.

'Good, I want you down in Turentek's prow forges. You know tanks, so help Callins to get them moving faster. Vintras, give your brothers a kick up the arse and beg them to take you back. I want *Lupa Capitalina* and *Canis Ulfrica* walking right beside my tanks. And I want you in *Amarok* again. Understand?'

'I don't beg,' said Vintras.

'Today you do,' said Hawkins, and the look in his eye killed the Skinwalker's caustic response stone dead. The Warhound princeps nodded and slung his rifle.

'I want to stay here,' protested Sylkwood. 'I want to fight.'

'You're a daughter of Cadia,' snapped Hawkins. 'Follow your damn orders and get the hell out of here!'

PRIOR TO BIELANNA'S journey on the Path of the Seer, she too had experienced the visceral joy of a war-mask on Khaine's Path. She barely remembered that part of her life, the bloody horror of what she'd seen and done locked away in an unvisited prison of dark memory.

There could be beauty as well as terror in battle, a fluidly balletic poetry in the dance of combatants.

The fight against the Tindalosi had none of that.

Bielanna's mind recoiled from the distilled hate weeping from their every metallic pore. Oceans of blood clung to them, a shroud of a hundred lifetimes of murder.

The Tindalosi were too fast, too deadly and too ruthless to allow for any poetry. Their deaths demanded hard, quick stanzas, not the epic languor of laments.

And what better warriors than Striking Scorpions and Howling Banshees for such a fight? This dance had no grace, just sublimely swift slashes of claw and sword. Teeth snapped and mandiblasters spat. Shuriken discs shattered on impact and the train sang with the howls of Morai-Heg's favoured daughters.

They matched the speed of the Tindalosi, hook-bladed horrors of spinning chrome and emerald fire. Crackling mandiblasters scorched the unnatural metal of their hides, and wraithbone blades were blurs of cleaving ivory.

But as fast and hard as the eldar fought, every wound was undone moments later.

'Not anymore,' whispered Bielanna, drawing the power of the skein to her. It filled her with a strength she hadn't felt in what seemed like a lifetime. The constricting metal walls of the *Speranza* had smothered her connection to the skein and Exnihlio had kept her from any anchor in the present.

All such distractions fell away from her now.

Bielanna hunted the beast upon the skein, sifting a thousand possible futures in the blink of an eye until she found its grubby thread of murder, reaching back into a long dead aeon.

'The fate of Eldanesh be upon you,' she said, pulling the weave of futures and cutting the beast's thread with a snap of her fingers.

And in that instant, every blade and every blast of killing energy found a way inside its armour, a confluence of fates willed into existence by Bielanna's power. The regenerative heart of the monster was cloven into shards, destroyed so thoroughly that no power in the universe could remake it.

Bielanna spun in with her runesword aimed at the Tindalosi's head and drove the blade through its jaws. The beast's skull was split in two and the dead light in its eyes was extinguished forever. It fell to the deck, an inanimate mass of metal and machinery.

She turned on her heel as the press of futures poured into her.

A thousand times a thousand duels played out before her, eldar and Space Marines moving to the future's song, a hundred possibilities spawning a million possible outcomes, each in turn growing the web of futures at a geometric rate.

Bielanna saw it all.

Graham McNeill

THE TRAIN'S FUSELAGE buckled as the Tindalosi slammed Tanna against it. Its claws dug through his armour. Blood ran down the bodyglove within. Tanna drove his knee into its belly. Metal deformed, its grip released. He dropped and ducked a clawed swipe that tore parallel gouges in the metal skin behind him.

It shoulder barged him, knocking him down.

A clawed foot slammed. He rolled. Sword up, block and move.

Don't let it back him against the wall again.

Tanna got his sword up, angling himself obliquely.

His gaze met that of the beast. Empty of anything except the desire to see him dead. In that, at least, they were evenly matched.

'Come on then,' he snarled.

The Tindalosi flew at him. He sidestepped, exhaling with a roar. The sword came down in a hard, economical arc. Its claws punched air. His blade took it high on the shoulder. Teeth tore into metal, spraying glittering slivers. Two-handed now, saw downwards.

A hooked elbow slashed back. Rubberised seals at Tanna's hip tore and he grunted as the blade scraped bone. He tore his sword free and brought it around in a recklessly wide stroke.

It took the beast high on the neck. A decapitating strike.

Notched teeth ripped through metal, cable and bio-organic polymers. Viscous black fluid gushed. Its howl triggered the cut-off on Tanna's auto-senses. The Tindalosi's head hung slack, not severed cleanly, but ruined nonetheless. Tanna's heart sank as he saw a web of red and green wychfire crackling around the awful wound.

He took the fractional pause to update his situational awareness. One Tindalosi was attacking Yael while Varda and Issur duelled with the pack leader. The eldar farseer stood over a fallen beast as her remaining warriors fought a second. Surcouf and Pavelka had withdrawn to the driver's compartment with the Cadians, Kotov and his two skitarii.

This wasn't a fight that could be won by mortals.

The train lurched on the maglev as it turned in a tight arc. Its precisely designed form had been ruined by the Tindalosi attack, and travelling at such enormous speeds, even the slightest deviation in aerodynamic profile could be disastrous. The turbulent air slamming through the train was hurricane-force and Tanna held to a taut cable as the wind direction changed with the train's turn.

The metalled floor of the train carriage buckled upwards, the sheet panelling of the walls billowing like sailcloth. In moments the magnetic connection between the train and track would be broken.

Crackling webs of frost formed on the few remaining shards of glass in the frames and Tanna felt a bitter flavour fill his mouth. Part blood, part witchery.

He saw Bielanna's helm wreathed in shimmering flames of white fire, a pellucid halo of psychic energy. He had no idea what she was doing.

The Tindalosi came at him again. Tanna swung his sword up. The beast's head still lolled at its shoulder. The green light fizzed and spat at the wound, as if fighting to restore the damage his blade had wrought.

But it wasn't working.

Sudden certainty filled Tanna.

He saw the exact place his blade should strike, knew the precise power to deliver. The angle of his blade shifted a hair's breadth. He drew in a full lungful of air and leapt to meet the Tindalosi. The chainsword swung in the arc he had already pictured. The sense of déjà vu was potent.

The chainsword struck the Tindalosi just where he expected.

The teeth sheared through the bio-mechanical meat and metal of its neck, cleaving down into its chest cavity. The beast's arms spasmed and Tanna tore the sword loose, ripping out a vast swathe of ticking, whirring, crackling machinery. The green light veining its mechanical organs was now a deep red.

The Tindalosi crumpled, the static of its eyes burning out as it died.

'Thank you, Magos Pavelka,' said Tanna.

Yael put his sword through the heart of the beast before him. His blow struck precisely, as though guided by the hand of Dorn himself. The beast came apart as though a demo charge had been set off in its chest, screaming and howling as the torments of the damned destroyed it from the inside.

Likewise the eldar fought with every blow landing at the perfect point to do the maximum damage. The Tindalosi were doomed, the techno-enchantments of Pavelka's code taking away their regenerative abilities and the eldar's psychic witchery clouding their speed and skill.

Only Varda and Issur's beast still fought. The swordsmen had landed numerous blows upon the pack-master, but the hideous power at its heart was orders of magnitude greater than that empowering the others. It backed away from them and the eldar as they came together.

'We'll take it en masse,' said Varda, standing at Tanna's side.

'Thr... thr... three to one,' said Issur through clenched teeth.

'No,' said Tanna as the train lurched once again. The last portion of the roof ripped clear, flying away with the force of the wind. The train was curving along the track again, harder this time, leaning into the turn. Tanna saw the length of the train begin to come loose from the tracks.

First the rearmost carriage tore clear, falling from the rails in a haze of squalling magnetics and dragging the next with it. Both came apart in explosions of aluminium. Sheet metal tore like paper. Another carriage followed, dragging the next from the rails with its weight.

'Everyone out!' shouted Tanna. 'Get into the driver's compartment. Now!'

Yael pushed into the link doorway towards the driver's compartment.

Bielanna and her surviving warriors slipped effortlessly through as the last Tindalosi turned its vast, serrated skull and saw what Tanna had seen.

It bounded along the bucking carriage towards them.

'Go!' shouted Tanna, bracing himself. One leg squared off, the other bent forwards. Varda and Issur knew better than to argue. They followed their brother and the eldar.

'Just me and thee,' said Tanna.

The Tindalosi leapt and Tanna went low. His sword swung in a tight arc, hewing its belly. Glittering shards of cut metal and oily liquid sprayed. Red-green light filled the wound. It turned back to him and its claws cut into his plastron. Tanna felt his feet leave the deck plates. He struggled like bait on a hook. He swung his blade. The beast's jaws fastened on his sword arm and bit down hard.

Fangs like daggers punched through ceramite and meat.

Tanna roared in pain as the beast wrenched its head to the side and took his right hand with it. His sword went too, dangling from the monster's teeth on snapped links of chain. The pack leader dropped him and Tanna rolled, clutching the stump of his arm to his chest. He pushed himself to his knees as the Tindalosi loomed over him, a gloating killer taking an instant to savour its kill.

Its head swung around, seeing more of the train carriages pulling loose from the maglev. In moments the cascade of derailing carriages would reach this one, but it had no intention of still being here when that happened.

Neither did Tanna.

He dived towards the Tindalosi and grabbed for the dangling sword with his remaining hand. His fingers closed on its wire-wound hilt. No way to free the chain, its links stuck fast in the beast's jaw.

But Tanna had no intention of freeing his sword.

He rammed the blade down hard into the deck plate, twisting it deep into the mechanisms beneath. The Tindalosi wrenched its head, but the chains binding the blade to its jaw pulled taut. Like a beast in a snare it twisted and writhed as it sought to free itself from Tanna's weapon.

'We die together, monster,' said Tanna.

'No,' said Varda, hooking his arms under Tanna's shoulders and dragging him away. 'It dies alone.'

Tanna looked up in surprise.

The Emperor's Champion hauled Tanna back through the door to the driver's compartment. Behind them, the Tindalosi pack leader finally ripped its fangs clear of Tanna's embedded sword. It fixed them with its pitiless stare, already picturing their deaths.

'Now, Kotov! Cut it loose!' shouted Varda as the beast bounded towards them. The train lurched as the derailments finally reached the carriage. Tanna heard a clatter of disengaging locking pins.

The Tindalosi leapt as the carriage tumbled from the maglev.

It spun end over end and exploded as it hit the ground.

The speed and ferocity of impact destroyed the carriage instantly, reducing its once graceful form to a hurricane of spinning fragments and billowing debris.

Tanna let out a breath as the maglev engine streaked away from the devastation.

'I told you to go,' he said.

'I'm not leaving anyone else behind,' said Varda.

THE TANKS WERE moving, just not fast enough.

Jahn Callins stalked the ready lines of Magos Turentek's forge-temple, keeping to clearly marked pedestrian routes. All too easy to get run down by a speeding ammo gurney or fuel tanker by straying into the working areas of the deck.

The forge was working to capacity: lifter-rigs hauling tanks down from stowage bays, fuel trucks in constant filling rotations and weapon carts being hauled up on chains from hardened magazines below decks. Hundreds of tech-priests moved through the deck, using hi-vis wands to direct the flow of a regiment's worth of armoured vehicles.

Chimeras and Hellhounds were mustering by squadron, moving out to assembly areas where they were loaded with fuel and ammunition. Dozens of tech-priests moved through the hosts of armoured vehicles like warrior-priests of old, each with an aspergillium of holy oils in their right hand. Chanting servitors with smoking braziers and relics borne upon silken cushions followed them.

Callins dearly wished they would hurry the hell up.

At the far end of the hangar, the engines of Legio Sirius billowed steam and groaning bellows from their war-horns. Gigantic weapons swung overhead in the claws of vast lifter-rigs, trailing steam and drizzling a fine mist of sacred oils to the deck. Each weapon was accompanied by swarms of servo-skulls and binaric plainsong. Like everything to do with the Mechanicus, the Legio was taking its own sweet time to do anything.

Only one Warhound had moved from its stowage cradle.

'The fight'll be over before they're ready,' he muttered as his data-slate pinged with another readiness icon.

Chimera squadron. Lima Tao Secundus.

'Superheavies,' he grumbled to the junior officers trailing him like obedient hounds. 'I need the damn superheavies.'

The Baneblades and Stormhammers were yet to move, delayed by the Mechanicus need to do things in the proper order. The 71st were a Mechanised Infantry regiment and as such, Mechanicus protocols gave priority to the APCs.

Trying to explain that Hawkins needed fighting vehicles to the tech-priests was like pulling teeth. No amount of shouting or talk about losing the ship had persuaded the deck commanders to alter their manifest procedures. As a logistics officer, Callins gave all due reverence to the power of lists and standard operating procedures, but this was taking that reverence to the extreme.

Another icon flashed up on his slate. A retasking order, together with a location marker.

'What the hell?'

He tapped the icon and looked over to the location indicated.

'You have got to be kidding me,' he said, watching as a trio of Baneblades were swung back onto their reinforced storage rails and locked into place. 'They're putting them back?'

Callins ran towards the rigs, ignoring the safety lines on the floor and setting off a dozen alarms as he crossed transit routes deemed unsafe for foot-traffic. Red-robed tech-priests waved directions to the crews of the lifter-rigs, assigning them to bulbous, spider-legged vehicles.

Callins spotted a high-ranking magos directing operations.

'Atrean,' he said. 'Might have known.'

This particular tech-priest was a rules-lawyer of the worst sort, a man to whom common sense was a regretfully organic notion. They'd butted heads before, but this time promised to be their best yet.

'Atrean!' barked Callins. 'Are you trying to lose the ship?'

The magos turned and Callins wished there was some organic part of his face to punch.

'Boarding protocols are in effect, Major Callins,' said Atrean. 'Skitarii vehicles take precedence over passenger vehicles.'

Callins pointed to the Baneblades. 'Captain Hawkins needs those tanks. He doesn't get them, the training deck falls. The training deck falls, the ship falls. Do you understand that?'

'I understand that I have orders to follow. As do you.'

'Your orders make no damn sense,' said Callins, staring at the scrolling lines of text on his slate. 'These are going to the ventral decks, perimeter defence duties. I need superheavies in the battle line right now!'

'Mechanicus forge-temples take precedence over lower-rated structures within the *Speranza*,' said Atrean, turning away as though the matter were settled.

Before Callins could reply, more alarms screeched through the deck as a fire-blackened Chimera came roaring into view. Its hull was scorched and pitted with impacts. It angled its course towards them, narrowly avoiding a pair of gurneys laden with promethium drums for a waiting squadron of Hellhounds.

The driver threw the Chimera into a skid, halting it at the edge of the stowage bays. Its rear assault ramp slammed down moments later and two figures emerged, a woman with a gnarled knot of augmetics on her scalp in iron cornrows and a cocksure peacock who looked like he'd never spent a day in a firing line.

The man took one look at the Legio Sirius engines and sprinted off towards them without a word. The woman carried a data-slate and wore a battered uniform jacket sewn with a Cadian enginseer's patch.

'You Callins?' she asked.

'Yes, who are you?'

'Kayrn Sylkwood, lately of the *Renard*,' she said, tapping the patch. 'But in a previous life I was with the Eighth.'

Callins was impressed. Every Cadian knew the pedigree of the Eighth and its illustrious commander.

'What are you doing here?'

'Captain Hawkins sent me,' said Sylkwood, drawing a bulky hell-pistol, a Triplex-Phall hotshot variant with an overcharger wired to its powercell.

She aimed her gun at Atrean's head and said, 'You in charge?'

'I am,' he said.

Sylkwood looked down at her slate. 'So you're the one putting those Baneblades back in the stowage rails?'

'Yes. Mechanicus protocols clearly dictate that–'

Kayrn Sylkwood shot Magos Atrean in the chest and Jahn Callins fell a little bit in love with her. The wound was carefully placed not to be mortal, but Atrean would be out of commission for a while. She aimed her pistol at the gaggle of tech-priests carrying out Atrean's orders.

'Who's in charge now?' she asked, racking the recharge lever of the hot-shot pack.

One by one, they pointed at Jahn Callins.

'Is the right answer,' said Sylkwood.

THE MAGLEV CAME to a halt at a raised way-station, pausing just long enough for the battered survivors of the landing expedition to debark on the edge of the open plaza where Telok had first led them below the planet's surface.

Kotov thought back to that moment, remembering the potential he had felt. The potential and the unease. And how he had smothered that unease with ambition and the need to believe in all that Telok represented.

The silver dome that once filled the plaza with its immensity was gone. In its place was a gaping chasm that dropped into the heart of Exnihlio. The Breath of the Gods was a smear of light in the sky, a new and dreadful star.

The plaza seemed empty without the silver dome, and the towering structures on all sides made Kotov feel like he was deep in a crater gouged in a vast glacier. After so long enclosed by the industry of Telok's forge world, the echoing emptiness was unnerving. Gone was the omnipresent beat of machinery he associated with a forge world, the roar of furnaces and the electrical hum of a global infrastructure.

For all intents and purposes, Exnihlio was deserted.

Atticus Varda led them into the plaza, his Black Sword unsheathed. Tanna, Yael and Issur marched alongside their champion, while the Cadians and skitarii moved with Kotov. Roboute Surcouf and Magos Pavelka brought up the rear.

Telok was waiting for them.

The Lost Magos stood on a landing platform raised up from the plaza. His bulk was immense, hostile and insane. How could Kotov not have seen the lunacy at the heart of him?

Telok's expression was one of pleasant surprise at the sight of them – though he must surely have known of their approach.

'Can you hit him from here?' Tanna asked Yael.

'I can, brother-sergeant,' confirmed Yael, chambering a stalker-round.

'Do not waste your shot,' said Pavelka. 'Telok is protected by layered energy shields. I cannot see him, but I can feel the presence of void flare.'

'Is she right?' asked Tanna.

Kotov switched through his auto-senses and nodded.

'It would take a macro-cannon to get to him,' he said.

'Archmagos Kotov,' said Telok, his voice boosted and echoing from the buildings around them. 'As irksome as you and your strange friends have become, I have to say I am pleased you yet live. History is in the making, and history must be observed to matter, otherwise what is the point? The Breath of the Gods draws near the *Speranza* and this world is spiralling to its doom. Have you any valediction?'

Kotov knew there was no point in trying to sway Telok from his course, but tried anyway.

'It doesn't work, Vettius,' he said. 'Your machine. It won't work when you leave this place. Not without the hrud to counterbalance the temporal side-effects. But you know that already, don't you?'

Telok grinned and it was the leer of a madman.

'It only needs to work once,' said Telok. 'Then when Mars is mine and the Noctis Labyrinthus opens up to me I will have a new power source at its heart. I will have no need of filthy aliens.'

'You would tear the galaxy apart for the sake of mortal ambition?' asked Bielanna, her warriors spreading out around her.

'Speaks the emissary of a race whose lusts destroyed their empire and birthed unimaginable horrors upon the galaxy,' said Telok. 'You are hardly best suited to speak of caution.'

'I am the one *most* suited to speak of caution, I know the folly of what you attempt,' said Bielanna. 'Your machine was wrought for creatures who are anathema to life. Their servitor races built it to drain the life from stars and feed the monstrous appetites of their masters. It was never intended to be employed by a species with so linear a grasp of the temporal flow and with no sensory acuity to perceive deep time.'

'And yet I now command the Breath of the Gods,' snarled Telok.

Bielanna laughed. 'Is that what you truly believe? That such a terrible creation would allow a mere mortal to be its master? Your capacity for self-delusion is beyond anything suffered by those of my people who brought down the Fall.'

Telok's crystalline components pulsed a bruised crimson and the wrought iron portions of his Dreadnought-like frame vented superheated steam as debased floodstream boiled around his body.

Telok pointed a clawed hand towards Bielanna. 'Your arrogance is matched only by your species's pathetic reluctance to accept its doom. I should take lessons on humility from you? A race that clings pathetically to a lost empire sliding inevitably to ruin? I think not.'

'Then we are well matched after all,' said Bielanna.

Kotov looked up as another light appeared in the sky. This one was blue-hot and the shrill whine of boosters told him that this was an atmosphere-capable craft on an arc of descent.

'What is that?' asked Tanna.

The corona wreathing its engine nacelles blotted out the descending craft's profile, but there was no doubting its Imperial provenance. Kotov saw an electromagnetic residue that was as familiar to him as the composition of his own floodstream.

'It's from the *Speranza*,' he said.

'It's the *Renard*'s shuttle!' cried Roboute Surcouf. 'Emil!'

The shuttle's engine noise growled and the main drives twisted against the airframe and deepened to a hard red as it flared out on its final approach.

'Tarkis must have sent it,' said Kotov.

'Why would he send the rogue trader's shuttle?' said Tanna.

'Does it matter?' snapped Kotov. 'We have help! Reinforcements!'

The Black Templars moved to battle pace, pulling ahead of Kotov and the Cadians. The eldar matched their speed, though Kotov saw they could easily outpace them. Telok's platform was a hundred metres away, the shuttle from the *Renard* just touching down in an expanding cloud of propellant.

Kotov increased his pace, eager to see what manner of aid Tarkis Blaylock had sent to Exnihlio. Tanna's question was needlessly defeatist. This ship *had* to have come from Tarkis. What other explanation could there be?

Kotov saw a human face in the shuttle's armourglass canopy.

Emil Nader. Facial mapping of micro-expressions revealing great stress and heightened levels of anxiety.

The shuttle's frontal ramp opened up and a figure emerged, wreathed in the fumes of its landing. Tall and black-robed, with a hood drawn up over his face.

'Tarkis!' cried Kotov. 'Ave Deus Mechanicus! Thank the Omnissiah, you came.'

The smoke of the shuttle's landing cleared and Kotov's floodstream ran cold as he saw the truth.

Tarkis Blaylock had not come to Exnihlio.

Galatea had.

Galatea approached Telok with grim purpose in its clattering, mismatched limbs. The blasphemous machine intelligence had finally come to enact its murderous intent in crossing the Halo Scar and hope leapt in Kotov's breast.

'Galatea,' he cried, extending a mechadendrite. 'Telok stands before you. Kill him! Kill him now, just as you have dreamed of doing for thousands of years!'

Telok's laughter boomed out across the plaza.

'Kill him?' said Galatea. 'Don't be ridiculous. We are his herald, his shadow avatar in the Imperium. We brought you to him and we will stand at his right hand when he becomes the new Master of Mars!'

MACROCONTENT COMMENCEMENT:
+++MACROCONTENT 003+++

The Omnissiah knows all, comprehends all.

Microcontent 16

THERE WERE TIMES for humility and there were times for brass balls. This was a moment for the latter. Gunnar Vintras stood at the foot of *Amarok* and hauled Magos Ohtar towards him by the folds of his robes.

'You heard me,' he said. 'You're going to put me back into *Amarok* or I'm going to shove this laspistol somewhere the Omnissiah doesn't shine and empty the powercell. Do we understand each other now?'

'You waste your ire on me, Mister Vintras,' said Ohtar. 'Your reinstatement has nothing to do with me. It is for the Wintersun to decide when your penance is done. And he has given no indications as to his willingness to return you to the Pack.'

Vintras nodded towards *Amarok*'s glaring canopy.

'Who've you put in there anyway?'

'Akelan Chassen was next in rotation.'

He heard the pause and laughed. 'Chassen? I've seen his aptitude tests. He barely made moderati grade, let alone princeps.'

'But he made them,' pointed out Ohtar. 'Not many ever do.'

'But who would you rather have in *Amarok*? Someone who barely made the grade or someone who rewrote the book on how Warhounds fight? And best answer quickly, this place is going to be knee-deep in crystal monsters soon.'

Ohtar's eyes rolled back in his sockets, and when they returned, they weren't the ice-blue of augmetics, but amber flecked with opal, slitted with a slice of deepest black.

Vintras knew those eyes, he'd seen them on the black and silver mountain in the depths of an ice storm. They'd pinned him to the rock of the Old-bloods' fortress and judged him worthy. And when Ohtar spoke, it was not with his own voice, but one channelled from the mighty head of *Lupa Capitalina*.

+You dare demand a place in my Pack?+

Now was the time for humility.

Vintras dropped to one knee and said, 'I seek only to aid the Pack, Lord Wintersun. I am the Skinwalker, I belong in a Titan!'

+I stripped you of that title,+ said Princeps Arlo Luth. 'I named you Omega and cast you from the Pack.+

'Packs can be rejoined,' said Vintras.

+If the Alpha deems the outcast worthy of redemption,+ said Luth. +Are you worthy of mercy?+

'I am,' said Vintras, angling his neck and displaying his throat as he had done at his ritual of censure. The scar Elias Härkin had given him was pale and healed, but the angle of the cut ensured it would always be visible.

Princeps Luth regarded Vintras through the slitted eyes of an Oldblood. Crackling electrical fire was reflected there, fire that had no place in the eyes of a Mechanicus proxy.

Vintras turned from the hijacked body of Magos Ohtar, seeing bolt after bolt of alien lightning explode onto the deck.

Luth saw the same thing.

+Mount your engine, Skinwalker,+ he ordered. +Fight as Pack!+

KOTOV'S LAST HOPE crumbled in the face of Telok's pronouncement. With Galatea at his side, every aspect of the machine-hybrid's actions made a new and terrible sense. Roboute Surcouf's analogy of the spider in its web was now proven entirely correct.

Like a dreadful puppet-master, Archmagos Telok had orchestrated every aspect of Kotov's quest from the start. What level of commitment and preparedness must have gone into such a plan? Kotov could have almost admired the dizzying complexity of Telok's machinations from beyond the edge of the galaxy were they not about to see him dead.

Kotov stared at Galatea with a hatred he had not known himself capable of experiencing. The machine-hybrid had set its snare with a tale of abandonment and vengeance, with just enough truth at the heart of its falsehoods to be credible.

And he had fallen for its lies.

'Galatea,' he said as the revelation of its true loyalties unlocked yet another. 'From the myth of Old Earth, yes? That should have told me everything you said was a lie. The tale of the sculptor who crafts an ivory statue that he falls in love with, and which is then given life by a god... It is all right there.'

'What's right there?' said Surcouf.

'That Galatea was a creature of Telok's,' said Kotov. 'Don't you see? We assumed Galatea was what it claimed to be, a thinking machine, but it is not. It is both more and less than that.'

'Then what is it?' asked Tanna.

Kotov made his way to the landing platform, where Galatea squatted beside Telok. Microtremors shook its body, and the connections passing between the brain jars were strangely hostile, as though no longer entirely under Galatea's control. The Lost Magos appeared oblivious to this, and nodded like a mentor encouraging a struggling pupil towards deeper understanding.

'Go on,' said Telok. 'You're so close, archmagos.'

'It's you,' said Kotov. 'Galatea isn't a thinking machine at all. It's been you all along, hasn't it? Before you crossed the Halo Scar you excised a portion of your own consciousness and grafted it into the heuristic mechanisms of the machine's neuromatrix. Every dealing we have had with Galatea has been with an aspect of *your* personality, hived from the throne of your cerebral cortex and given autonomy within this... this thing. You practically told me as much, with all your metaphysical nonsense about alphas and omegas and the self-created god. Your ego couldn't pass up any chance to taunt us with your presence as a ghost in the machine.'

Kotov shook his head ruefully. 'It beggars belief that I did not see it.'

'As Galatea, I told you what you wanted to hear, Kotov,' said Telok, 'and in your desperation you chose to ignore the truth that was right in front of you.'

'Why tell us that Galatea wanted to kill Telok?' asked Surcouf.

'Few motives are as pure as vengeance,' said Galatea, its voice modulating to match Telok's. 'Would you have found us as credible if we simply offered to help you? We think not.'

By now Kotov and his attendant warriors had reached the foot of the landing platform. Kotov paused at the iron steps as he felt the particle vibration and neutron flow of the layered voids passing over him. Complex field interactions caused his noospherics and floodstream to grey out for a second.

In that instant, the Black Templars and Cadians had their weapons locked to their shoulders. They knew, as Kotov knew, that they were inside the voids protecting the raised platform.

'Kill them,' ordered Tanna.

Bolter fire erupted. Flashing las followed.

The eldar launched themselves into the air, going from complete standstill to bounding motion with no intermediate stage. They landed on the platform with a speed and sure-footedness that made Kotov gasp with astonishment.

Explosions erupted all over Telok's body, but none impacted.

Ablative energy integral to his crystalline flesh ignited the bolt warheads prematurely and vaporised the flashing discs of the eldar weapons. Telok's density was so enormous not even the kinetic force of the detonations staggered him.

Kotov's skitarii put themselves between him and the gunshots. Their blades and weapons locked to Galatea. Issur and Varda climbed towards Telok, their swords singing from scabbards. The eldar reached him first, their swords shrieking blurs of ivory. They surrounded Telok, cutting and lashing him with crackling forks of anbaric energy.

Telok extended his clawed arms, sweeping around like some ancient practitioner of weaponless combat.

The eldar were too nimble, and laughed as they vaulted and swayed aside from his clumsy swipes.

But catching them had never been Telok's aim.

A blitzing tempest of electrical vortices built around his arms and exploded outwards in a hurricane of white-green fire. The eldar warriors were hurled away, their armour melting and the plumes on their tapered helms ablaze. Telok's laughter cut through their howls of pain.

Then Varda and Issur charged in.

The Emperor's Champion swept below a bladed fist the size of a Contemptor's claw. The Black Sword gouged a valley in Telok's flank. Issur's blow was blocked and before he could sidestep, a fit of rogue muscle spasms staggered him.

His paralysis lasted a fraction of a second only, but even that was too long. Telok bludgeoned him from the landing platform and Issur flew thirty metres through the air to land with a bone-crunching thud of cracked ceramite.

The Black Sword erupted from Telok's hybridised metal and crystal body as Varda ran him through. Telok spun as Varda wrenched the blade clear, unleashing a storm of crackling binary that froze the Emperor's Champion rigid.

Telok's enormous claw closed on Varda's body, ready to tear him apart. Before he could crush the life from Varda, a weave of glittering light engulfed his twisted features.

Kotov saw Bielanna down on one knee, her hands pressed to her forehead as she directed her energies into obliterating Telok's mind with heinous witchcraft. Howling psychic energies blazed around Telok and he hurled Varda from the platform as a jagged, crystalline sheath rose from his shoulders.

'Enough!' roared Telok and Bielanna screamed as the arcane mechanisms wreathing his skull flared with incandescent energies.

'This has gone on long enough,' said Telok, as he and Galatea climbed onto the shuttle's ramp. 'Even my vanity has limits when it compromises my designs. The acausal bindings securing the hrud warrens are no more, so this world is entering its final entropic death spasms. I would ask you to bear witness to Exnihlio's final moments, but you will be corpses long before it dies.'

Telok lifted his arms and the vast structures enclosing the plaza erupted with lightning from dozens of latticework vanes at their roofs. Forking bolts of energy arced down and slammed into the ground with deafening whipcracks of searing fire.

Kotov saw freshly wrought shapes emerge from the strobing after-images, glossy and humanoid, marching in lockstep to form a perfect circle around the landing platform.

A thousands-strong army of crystaliths.

SHE'D MISSED A lot of things about the regiment, but until now Kayrn Sylk-wood hadn't realised just how much she'd missed the thrill of marshalling armed forces under fire. The attackers were appearing without warning, materialising in explosions of writhing bonfires of lightning like a teleport assault.

The mechanics of their arrival didn't matter.

It was, as her old drill sergeant used to say at every objection to his orders being completed on time, irrelevant.

Hurricanes of green fire flashed through the deck, flickering in opposition to bright bolts of red las. Percussive shock waves of explosions and thundering engines echoed from the hangar walls. Shouting squad leaders and the cries of burning soldiers put an extra punch in Kayrn's step.

Every minute these tanks remained in the hangar was costing the lives of Cadian soldiers on the training deck.

Kayrn ducked into cover behind a train of ammo gurneys currently serving as cover to a Cadian infantry platoon. Jahn Callins was issuing orders to a gaggle of serious-looking junior officers. Two ran off to with vox-casters to enact those orders. The third stayed at his side.

He glanced up. 'How're the starboard racks looking?'

'Empty,' she answered. 'Two through seven are clear. The rails on eight and nine are buckled beyond immediate repair. Those tanks aren't coming down without lifter-rig support.'

'Damn it,' snapped Callins. 'There's Stormhammers up there. You're sure they're non-functional?'

'I'm sure,' she said, and Callins knew better than to doubt her.

'Captain Hawkins isn't going to be pleased.'

'We've gotten four more squadrons of superheavies into the ready line,' she said. 'That ought to cheer him up.'

All four of those squadrons were even now rumbling towards the starboard egress ramps after the quickest blessing and anointing the Mechanicus could muster. Throughout the deck, armoured tanks rammed damaged vehicles out of their way. Cadian infantry squads traded shots with their crystalline attackers from the cover of overturned gurneys and wrecked tanks.

'The Leman Russ are next,' continued Kayrn, running a finger down the order of battle displayed on her static-fuzzed slate. 'APCs are mustering at the rear to pick up the infantry.'

Callins nodded and said, 'Fast work, Sylkwood. Remind me to find out why you're not with a Cadian regiment when this is over.'

'Buy me a drink and I might just tell you.'

'Fair enough,' grinned Callins.

A bolt of green fire punched through the crate above Kayrn's head. She ducked closer to the deck as Guardsmen either side of her returned fire.

'These crates empty?' she asked.

'Yeah, apart from a few loose bolter shells.'

'Not exactly the best cover.'

'No, but it probably won't explode if it takes a hit.'

'Good point, well made.'

A pair of frags coughed from portable launchers. Rattling bursts of stubber fire blazed from a heavy weapons team to Kayrn's left.

'None of the turret weapons are firing?' she asked.

'In a hangar filled with ordnance and fuel?' said Callins, putting away his slate and checking the load on his lasgun.

'Sure, why not?' said Kayrn. 'I remember back on Belis Corona we had whole squadrons of Shadowswords firing on a pack of Archenemy battle-engines inside a fyceline depot.'

Callins shook his head.

'This isn't a Black Crusade, and we're not that desperate yet.'

As if to contradict him, the deck plates shook as three ammo gurneys laden with gunmetal-grey warheads and drums of promethium went up like a volcanic eruption. Secondary explosions took half a dozen fuel trucks with them.

Servitor fire-teams deployed to fight the blaze, but streams of enemy fire cut them down. Blazing gouts of promethium spilled in all directions. Tar-black smoke spread like a shroud over the fighting, making the air heavy with toxins.

'Damn the Eye,' said Callins, but even as the curse left his lips a flood of oxygen-depleting liquids rained from a score of swinging extender-arms belonging to Magos Turentek's vast rig apparatus. The boxy arrangement of bio-sustaining hubs that made up the Fabricatus Locum was swarming with crystalline attackers, but Turentek wasn't sparing any of his functionality for defence.

All that mattered was his forge.

In seconds the vaulted space was awash in hard water residue, and Kayrn was soaked to the skin. The fires guttered and died in the suddenly thin air, suffocated by Turentek's esoteric deluge.

Their sheltering gurney rocked with the force of a nearby explosion, and Kayrn risked a glance through one of the ragged holes scorched through the ammo crates.

Emerging through the black rain were hundreds of glistening crystalline beasts. From humanoid warriors that looked oddly like Space Marines, to lumbering things that powered forwards on vast forelimbs and things that looked like weaponised servitor guns.

Kayrn wiped her face clear and steadied her pistol on the top of the crate. She had enough shots and spare cells to take out maybe twenty or thirty targets.

Las-fire blasted into the charging creatures. Beside her, Callins pumped shot after shot from his lasrifle. *This* was how Cadians fought, shoulder to shoulder in the face of insurmountable odds. Fighting to the last. No retreat, no surrender.

Fighting until the job was done.

The deck shook with a thunderous, booming vibration.

'What the–' said Kayrn, looking through the downpour to see what new threat was incoming.

A firestorm of detonations erupted among the crystalline monsters. Blinding storms of heavy las ripped through their ranks. Chugging detonations and enormous impacts ploughed great furrows in the deck. Fulminate-bright traceries of high-intensity turbo-fire tore the enemy apart in blitzing explosions that sawed back and forth in a torrent of unending fire.

Another teeth-loosening thud shook the deck, each crashing impact like the hammerblow of a god.

Realisation struck. Kayrn turned and looked up.

And up.

Lupa Capitalina and *Canis Ulfrica* stood side by side, rain-slick and haloed by dying fires. Burning exhaust gases plumed from louvred vents and dark water flashed to vapour on their weapon arms. *Amarok* and *Vilka* stalked before their titanic cousins and Kayrn joined the cheers of her fellow Cadians.

Legio Sirius were in the fight.

FAR BELOW THE surface of Exnihlio, entropy was afoot. The hated machinery of ancient design that had kept the eternally migratory swarms of hrud fixed in time and space failed one after another.

Technology the likes of which had never been seen within the Imperium burned white-hot against the senescent power of so many imprisoned aliens. One hrud could drive a mortal to the grave in minutes, a warren of them was entropy distilled and honed like a breacher drill punching through soft clay.

Gold and brass gobbets of molten metal fell in a glittering rain, transmuting to base metal and then to dust as it fell from the cavern roof. Every scavenged sheet and spar of metal forming the slum-warrens corroded to ruin in moments, like a time-lapsed picter. The rock upon which their prison had stood crumbled and turned to powder as millennia of erosion took hold.

The collapse was total, thousands of tonnes of disintegrating metal and rock tumbling into the geothermal abyss over which it had been built. Had this been any mortal settlement, thousands would already be dead, thousands more killed in the cascade of collapse.

By the time the first dilapidated structure fell from the porous and crumbling cliff-face, the hrud had already gone. Freed from the iron grip of machines holding them fast to this moment in time and space, they shifted their wholly alien physiology through multi-angular dimensions unknown to the minds of humankind.

Unfettered by such limiting notions as matter, time and space, the hrud migration from Exnihlio began in earnest. They would cross galaxies and oceans of time to be rid of this world's constricting touch.

But first they would have vengeance for their stolen freedom.

Submitting to one last notion of fixed vectors, the hrud burrowed invisibly down through the rock to the planet's core.

Ultimate entropy took hold of Exnihlio's molten heart.

And crushed it.

BOLTER SHELLS CHASED the *Renard's* shuttle into the sky, but the vessel was too fast to bring down with small-arms fire. Tanna shot anyway, but lowered his weapon when the shuttle climbed beyond range.

Surcouf shouted Ultramarian curses at the ascending vessel. Ilanna Pavelka knelt beside him with her head bowed. If she still had eyes, Tanna might have thought her weeping. Ven Anders and his soldiers formed a loose circle around Kotov, who watched Telok's departure with a mix of despair and frustration.

The eldar warriors surrounded their seer. Her alien features were too inscrutable to read with certainty, but it seemed to Tanna that the corners of her lips were upturned. As though their failure to stop Telok had been her plan all along.

'Did you know this would happen?' he asked, priming himself to rip her head from her shoulders if her answer displeased him.

'This? No,' she said, and, strangely, Tanna believed her. 'It was merely one of myriad possible outcomes, but it is a moment in time that opens up so many potential futures I had not dared hope might ever come to pass.'

She looked out over the slowly advancing army of implacable crystaliths, as though this particular future had been inevitable.

'I will never meet them,' she said.

'Who?' asked Tanna, working fresh shells into his bolter.

'My daughters. I will never birth them, never hold them and never see them grow,' said Bielanna, her face wet with tears. 'I hoped your deaths would restore the future where they are given the chance of life, but such ill-fated intent only brings further misery. Everything I set out to change has come to nothing.'

Tanna drove a round into the breech.

'Nothing is for nothing,' he said.

'Do you realise how ridiculous that sounds?'

'You set out to change something,' said Tanna, remembering the last words of Aelius before his death at Dantium Gate. 'That you failed does not diminish the attempt. Knowing you might effect change, but failing to try… *That* is contemptible.'

Even as he spoke, Tanna was struck by the utter incongruity of a warrior of the Adeptus Astartes offering words of comfort to the xenos witch who had killed his former Emperor's Champion.

Beyond the galaxy, far from the light of the Emperor, such a thing did not seem so far-fetched. Tanna took a breath, knowing that even if he lived to return to the Imperium, he would take that thought to his grave.

The army of crystalline monsters were a hundred metres out, drawing close at a measured, inexorable pace. Tanna moved away from the eldar. Their deaths were to be their own, and he would not have his body's final resting place among them.

He passed Kotov, who had his gold-chased pistol gripped tightly in one swaying mechadendrite. The two skitarii flanked the archmagos, ready to give their lives in service to the Mechanicus. Kotov gave Tanna a look that might have been apologetic, but probably wasn't.

'Brother-sergeant,' said Kotov with a grim nod of acknowledgement towards the enemy ranks. Diamond-sharp blades of glass shone under the clear blue of the sky. 'Any grand plans or stratagems? Any words of wisdom from Rogal Dorn or Sigismund to see us victorious?'

'No pity, no remorse, no fear,' said Tanna, holding out his combat blade to Magos Pavelka. 'The techno-sorcery you worked on our weapons, will it work on these crystaliths?'

Pavelka lifted her hooded head, and Tanna hid his revulsion at the sunken scorch marks around her dead optics.

'Maybe,' she said. 'If you drive your blade deep enough.'

'Be assured of that,' promised Tanna.

Microcontent 17

THE VETERANS OF the war on Khai-Zhan spoke of Vogen in hushed tones, and those same soldiers traded knowing looks when talk inevitably turned to the Palace of Peace. The tales of heroism surrounding the battles fought there were already legendary.

'I remember every soldier of Cadia wished he could have been there,' said Rae, firing his rifle empty in six controlled bursts of semi-auto. This was the sergeant's fourth rifle, the burned-out frames of his previous three abandoned along the fluidly shifting battle line.

'Funny thing,' said Hawkins, ducking back as a series of green bolts slammed into the wall above him. 'Always easier to wish you were there *after* the fighting's done. Not so much fun being there when the las is coming like rain off the Valkyrie Peninsulas.'

'Aye, there's truth in that, sir,' agreed Rae.

Rock dust and infill fell, reminding Hawkins that this wasn't Vogen and the structure behind him wasn't the impregnable fortress of the Palace of Peace. To either side of him, hundreds of Cadians in hastily prepared positions fought to keep the enemy from crossing Angel Square. Hawkins had his soldiers deployed as Colonel Hastur had during the Final Ten Days, when a combined host of Iron Warriors and the Brothers of the Sickle mounted their fifth assault.

Hastur's infantry platoons had been more than a match for the traitorous slave soldiers, but it had taken heavy armour to blunt the Iron Warriors' assault. Heavy armour Hawkins didn't have.

Rae tossed aside his lasrifle, its barrel heat-fused and useless. He tore a frag from his webbing and hurled it towards the statue of Sanguinius at the centre of the square.

'Fire in the hole!'

A knot of four crystal creatures fell to shattered ruin as the grenade exploded.

'And forgive me, Lord of the Angels,' added Rae as the force of the blast ripped one of the statue's wings loose.

'Better to ask for forgiveness than permission, right?' said Hawkins.

'Depends on who you're asking,' said Rae, hunting for a fresh rifle among the fallen.

'Rae!' shouted Hawkins, throwing over his own rifle.

'Much appreciated, sir,' said Rae, catching the weapon and resuming firing without missing a beat.

'What you seeing, sergeant?'

'We're getting hit hard on the right, sir,' answered Rae. 'I reckon there's a big push coming there. Some clever bugger in the enemy knows we don't have armour there to enfilade.'

Percussive blasts rocked the training deck as the recreation of the Vogen Law Courts finally collapsed. Even over the crash of falling masonry and flames, Hawkins heard the screams.

'Hellfire,' swore Hawkins. 'Hotshot company were in there.'

'Heavy weapons?'

'Heavy weapons,' agreed Hawkins, thinking back to the Last Ten Days. The Law Courts had offered a perfect vantage point for Hastur's support platoons to rain plunging fire onto the thinner topside armour of the Iron Warriors Land Raiders. In the final stages of the battle, it had come down to arming mortar shells by hand and soldiers dropping from the fire-blackened windows with demo-charges clutched to their chests.

The original building had been blast-hardened to withstand repeated artillery barrages, but this structure hadn't been nearly as tough. Without those weapons, the right flank was completely open. Bulky shapes of jagged-edged glass were already lumbering from the ruins. Powerfully built monsters the size of a Sentinel.

'Westin!' he shouted, 'Westin, where are you?'

The vox-man scrambled over pitted sheets of flakboard and ruptured kinetic ablatives. Westin had tried to keep up with Hawkins, but better vox-men than he had been left wallowing in the captain's wake. Westin's camo-cape flapped in the anabatic thermals of high-energy las as he scooted into cover beside Hawkins.

He half turned, presenting the vox-caster's workings.

Hawkins cranked the handle. No point in shouting at Jahn Callins. If the tanks weren't here, there was a good reason for that. He had to get guns to bear on that flank. The vanguard of the enemy's thrust emerged from the ruins, a towering brute with arms like kite-shields and a profusion of weapon spines running the length of its back. A hosing stream of heavy bolter fire ripped into it. The shells impacted on its wide arms without effect as three missiles slammed into it.

One arm blew off in a shower of razored shards and the beast collapsed, its weapons spines blazing harmlessly at the ceiling. Another two of the heavily armed creatures lumbered from the collapsed structure, flames reflecting from their multi-faceted limbs. More followed them, enough to overrun this flank for sure.

Hawkins shouted into the vox.

'Creed! Two support teams to the right flank, sector tertius omega!' he yelled. 'Step quickly now.'

Creed's answer was lost in a blaze of static and a roaring stream of fire that came from the newly arrived creatures. Hawkins flinched as the blast struck the Palace of Peace. A balcony of missile-armed Guardsmen came tumbling down fifty metres to Hawkins's left.

Before he could detach soldiers from any other platoon, a flurry of streaking rockets arced up on an exacting parabola and slammed down in the ruins of the Law Courts. Violet-hued explosions threw deformed sheets of prefabricated steel and plascrete thirty metres into the air. Collimated bursts of turbolasers swept the ruins.

Hawkins hoped there weren't any Cadians left alive in there.

'By the Eye, would you look at that!' shouted Rae as a host of lightly armoured tanks on articulated spider-limbs advanced down what had been known as Snipers' Alley.

Of course, it had been the Lord Generals who'd called it that, because that was the only route they traversed. Any soldier who'd fought in Vogen knew that *every* street was a snipers' alley.

Hawkins recognised the vehicles. Mechanicus scout tanks in the main, faster than most fighting vehicles, but nowhere near as heavily armoured or armed as Hawkins would have liked.

The Mechanicus designation for them was something meaninglessly binaric, but the Cadians had dubbed them Black Widows. Fast, agile and lethal to lightly armoured targets. Less useful against heavy armour, but better than nothing. Skitarii packs flanked the Widows, adding their own weight of fire to the counter-attack.

At the heart of the Mechanicus tanks was an open-topped Rhino with a thundering battery of quad-mounted heavy bolters on its glacis. Riding atop the Iron Fist like a god-king of some ancient host of warrior-priests was a multi-armed figure in gold, silver and brass. His lower arms were electrified scarifier tines and his upper limbs held a bladed halberd with a crackling energy pod at its base.

'Emperor save me, if he isn't a sight for sore eyes!' said Rae.

Hawkins had to agree, Magos Dahan was indeed a welcome sight.

The skitarii chanted something as Dahan's Widows fired again. It sounded like a name, but it wasn't one Hawkins recognised.

'Ma-ta-leo! Ma-ta-leo!'

At its every shout, Dahan held his halberd aloft.

Bellicose roars of binary brayed from Dahan's chest augmitters, a war cry that sent a shiver down even Hawkins's spine. The quad bolters took down the two crystalline weapon beasts in precisely targeted bursts. Without them to punch through the Cadians, infantry power was stopping the rest of the advance.

For now.

As the skitarii pushed out to secure the edge of the ruined Law Courts, Dahan guided the Iron Fist towards the centre of the Cadian line. Mechanicus Protectors bearing shimmering energy shields and bladed staves ran alongside the modified vehicle.

'Welcome to the Palace of Peace,' said Hawkins as Dahan jumped down into the cover of the rubble-strewn berm of plascrete.

Dahan nodded and said, 'I expected you to recognise it.'

'Was a nice touch,' said Hawkins.

'Not one of mine,' said Dahan. 'I assumed you ordered it.'

Hawkins shook his head. 'No.'

Rae got down on his knees and kissed the deck.

'What in the name of the Eye are you doing, Rae?'

'Thanking the *Speranza*, sir,' said Rae. 'Who else do you think did this for us? Told you the old girl would look out for us.'

Hawkins gave Dahan a quizzical look, but the Secutor seemed to accept Rae's idea that the ship had wrought this arena to give them an advantage.

He shrugged. 'As good as explanation as any, I suppose.' he said. Figuring that was a mystery for another day, he gestured to the chanting skitarii fighting in the ruins.

'Who's Mataleo?'

'I am,' said Dahan.

'I thought your first name was Hirimau.'

'It is. Mataleo is what I believe you call a nickname.'

'What does it mean?' asked Rae.

'Lion-killer,' said Dahan. 'A soubriquet I earned in my more organic days on Catachan. A soldier named Harker bestowed it upon me and its bellicosity appealed to the skitarii despite my best attempts to discourage its use.'

'Outstanding,' said Hawkins. Dahan had already won his respect, but earning a war-name from a Catachan? *That* was impressive.

'I don't suppose you saw any Cadian tanks on your way here?'

'No, our paths did not intersect, but they are en route,' said Dahan. 'Assuming they encounter no resistance, they will arrive in twenty-seven minutes.'

'Twenty-seven minutes, damn it all to the Eye,' said Hawkins as more blasts of green fire streaked across the square and mushrooming explosions erupted along the Cadian line. Cries of pain and shouts for ammo echoed across the deck.

'What in the Emperor's name are you doing?' said Hawkins, as Dahan stood and extended the crackling tines of his lower arms. 'Get down!'

Dahan's Cebrenian halberd pulsed with lethal energies as he climbed onto the crumbling ridge of debris. Flames licked around his clawed feet and his cloak snapped in the hot winds.

'It is here,' said Dahan.

'What is?' said Hawkins, peering through a gouge of vitrified plascrete. A host of crystalline warriors were advancing across the width of Angel Square. Broad and tall, each was armed with shimmering energy spines and long-bladed polearms that matched those of the Protectors.

At the centre of these elite killers was a towering thing of glass and crystal, a hideous amalgam of scorpion and centaur. Shield-bearers attended it. Las-fire and explosions bounced from their reflective shields.

'The alpha-creature,' said Dahan, springing onto the back of the Iron Fist. 'Kill it and we regain the initiative.'

The vehicle's engine revved madly, its machine-spirit eager to be loosed. Its tracks sprayed rubble as the vehicle crested the rise. Chem-rich exhaust fumes jetted from its rear vents.

'You can't fight that thing,' shouted Hawkins.

The chanting skitarii bellowed the Secutor's war-name as they marched out to fight alongside him.

'Then you don't know Mataleo,' said Dahan.

THE WALLS OF the confero were no longer steel and glass, but an undulant vault of perfectly geometric cubes that formed an all-enclosing dome of impenetrable darkness. With Linya's expulsion of Galatea from the shared neuromatrix, all pretence of reality had fallen away.

Hexamathic firewalls had thus far prevented the machine-hybrid from reaching them, keeping Linya and her fellow captives safe from its wrath.

Linya sat cross-legged in the centre of a circle of her fellow magi, the illusory retention of their physical forms the one concession to notions of three-dimensional space.

<How much longer will this barrier last?> asked Syriestte, staring up at the rippling dome of interlocking cubes.

<Long enough,> said Linya, keeping her binary simple. She'd exloaded enough hexamathic understanding into their speech centres to allow communication at a level beyond Galatea's understanding, but it was still tryingly basic.

<Not a particularly specific answer,> said Magos Natala from across the circle.

<It's the best I have,> replied Linya. <Galatea's already attempting to upgrade its neural interfaces to learn hexamathics from the *Speranza*. Every second we spend second-guessing ourselves increases the chances of it breaching our refuge. So we need to do this now, yes?>

She cast her gaze around the circle and, one by one, each magos gave a curt nod until only Syriestte remained.

<Magos Syriestte?>

<Are you sure this will work?>

<No,> said Linya, <but it's the best I've got. Our *minds* are safe in here, but Galatea has a far more direct means of attack. All it has to do is excise a brain from its cylinder and that magos is dead.>

Syriestte nodded and said, <Then do it.>

Linya began with a recitation of the first, most basic prayer to the Omnissiah, each of the captive magi joining in as she spoke.

<*With learning I cleanse my flesh of ignorance.*

<*With knowledge I grow in power.*

<*With technology I revere the God of all Machines.*

<*With its power I praise the glory of Mars.*

<*All hail the Omnissiah, who guides us to learning.*>

Volatile deletion algorithms emerged from Linya's mouth, like the ectoplasmic emissions of a psyker. But this was no immaterial by-product; these were lethal combinations of spliced kill-codes.

Dormant for now, they twisted around her like glittering chains of droplets on spider-silk, moving outwards towards the magi.

Haephaestus was first to be touched. His back arched and he gave a cry of agonised binary as the kill-codes enmeshed with his mind. Next was Natala, who took the pain stoically, then Syriestte.

The largely organic features of the Mechanicus Envoy twisted in horrendous pain, her eyes going wide at the shock of it. The kill-code moved around the circle of magi, touching each one until it had bonded with all but Magos Kleinhenz.

A portion of the oil-dark barrier bulged inwards.

The black cubes expanded at a ferocious rate, rearranging their mass and density into the form of a hideous data-daemon pushing into the vault. Its arms ended in hooked talons and draconic wings spread at its back.

This was an image birthed in primal nightmares, something bestial from an age when humankind huddled in caves around dying fires. Its roar was inchoate and murderous. The talons wrapped around Magos Kleinhenz and dragged him from the circle. He thrashed in the data-daemon's grip, his outline distorting with strobing after-images of his screaming face.

His cries descended into meaningless scraps of binaric fragments as he broke apart into drifting scads of data-light. Linya thrust her hands towards the data-daemon and shouted a canticle of hexamathic calculus.

It howled in pain as its nightmarish form was drawn back into the darkness, leaving the vault's fluidly cubic perimeter rippling like the surface of a tar pit.

The last fragments of Kleinhenz drifted like fractal snowflakes. Haephaestus and Natala tried in vain to save some last aspect of their comrade, but it was already too late.

Syriestte turned to Linya, her organic face twisted in grief.

<What just happened?> she said. <What was that thing?>

<Galatea's given up its pretence of humanity,> said Linya. <That was its rage distilled into its purest form. It must have sensed what we were doing and ripped Kleinhenz's physical brain from its amniotic cylinder to try and stop us.>

<But what we just did, it will stop Galatea from doing that again to the rest of us?> said Natala.

<Yes, it should,> answered Linya. <We're all linked by the kill-code now. If one of us dies like that, it activates and we all die. And if we die, Galatea dies.>

<So let it kill us,> said Magos Haephaestus bitterly. <We want it dead. Why not let it kill another of us and have done with it?>

<Because Galatea doesn't get off that easily,> said Linya with the coldest steel in her voice. <Not after what it did to us.>

<Besides,> said Syriestte. <By now it'll know what we have done. It won't risk so open an attack again.>

<Then how do we fight it?> asked Haephaestus.

<You don't,> said Linya, allowing the last vestige of her surroundings to fall away from her perceptions. <I do.>

Just as she had sent a sliver of her consciousness into the datasphere to make contact with her father, Linya now sent her mind into the fulminate-bright realm of the *Speranza*'s informational landscape.

She closed her eyes and...

...FOUND HERSELF AMID brilliant grid lines of data as they passed through the Ark Mechanicus in the *Speranza*'s hidden space of knowledge. Constellations of starfire surrounded her, brighter than she had ever seen them. Dazzling in the purity of the wealth of understanding stored within each and every pinprick of illumination.

The last time Linya had flown the datascape it had been a hallucinatory place of shared functionality. Phosphor-bright with continental-scale cores of learning and informational exchange.

Now it was a battleground.

Datacores burned with searing intensity, like supernovae on the verge of explosion. The last time Linya had seen them they had been dull with parasitic infestation, thick with Galatea's self-replicating strangleholds. The machine-hybrid had held the Mechanicus hostage with its control of every vital system.

Now that control was all but gone. Only the last, most vital systems remained in its grasp. Still enough to kill every living being upon the *Speranza* should it so choose, but its hold was slipping even as Linya watched.

She saw a figure drifting high above the datascape. Arched spine, arms thrown wide and head tilted back. Golden light streamed from his hands, and where it touched Galatea's parasitic growths and viral threads they melted like frost before the dawn.

He looked down as she flew towards him.

<Abrehem?> she said.

<Linya,> said Abrehem. <I did what you asked.>

She heard the strain in his voice, saw the light bleeding from his ethereal body.

<You're dying,> she said.

He looked at her strangely, as though seeing straight through her. He gave a crooked smile that was as melancholy as it was empathic.

<Then we have something in common,> he said. <The other magi with you... They understand what they have to do?>

<When the time comes, they will. Trust me, it won't be a problem.>

<And your father?> asked Abrehem. <He's with me in Elektrus. Does he know what you plan?>

<No,> said Linya, and the thought of her father's grief almost broke her resolve. <But there's no other way. You know that. Even after all you've achieved here, we still have to do this.>

Abrehem nodded and turned towards the molten brightness of the *Speranza*'s bridge. Searingly hot with convergent knowledge, the nexus of the ship through which every fragment of data passed and was rendered known.

<Then it's time,> he said.

<Yes,> agreed Linya. <It's time to kill Galatea.>

For all that Abrehem Locke had managed to disrupt Galatea's control of the *Speranza*, the machine-hybrid still controlled the vital systems of the Ark Mechanicus. Telok felt Tarkis Blaylock trying to deny the *Renard*'s shuttle access to the foremost embarkation deck, but Galatea overruled his every attempt.

'If you only knew,' said Telok, watching the enormity of the *Speranza* fill the shuttle's viewscreen. 'You would welcome me aboard personally.'

The shuttle shuddered as it passed through the gravimetric fields surrounding the gargantuan ship. The violence of the transition surprised Telok, but he had never known a ship of such inhuman dimensions.

'That thing coming up behind us,' said Emil Nader at the helm. 'It'll be torn apart before it gets anywhere near the *Speranza*.'

Telok laughed, the booming sound filling the command deck of the shuttle.

'The Breath of the Gods reshapes the cosmos, and you think mere gravity waves will trouble it?'

Nader shrugged. 'I'm just saying it looks pretty fragile.'

Telok leaned over and placed a clawed hand on the pilot's shoulder. 'Indeed it is delicate, incredibly delicate. Even the slightest imbalance in its gyre would tear it apart. But if you were thinking of attempting something reckless, perhaps using this ship as a missile or simply ramming us into the side of the *Speranza*, know that I would snap your neck the instant I detected even a micron of differential in our course. And then I would allow Galatea a free hand with that atrophied thing you call a brain. I am led to believe you have some familiarity with what it can do in that regard.'

Nader shot a venomous glance at Galatea. The machine-hybrid's palanquin sat low to the deck, its proxy body twitching with random synaptic impulses. Its brain jars flickered with activity, though one was shattered and trailed a host of dripping wires. The presence of Telok's excised consciousness within Galatea granted him complete understanding of what was happening within his avatar's neuromatrix.

'The Stargazer's daughter yet frustrates us,' said Galatea, fully aware of Telok's scrutiny.

'It was a mistake to incorporate her,' agreed Telok. 'We greatly underestimated her will to resist.'

Galatea's silver eyes flickered and its right arm spasmed in response. 'Our body is under attack from within and without. It is most discomfiting.'

'Once I have full access to the *Speranza*'s noospheric network and have inloaded the secrets of hexamathics, I will purge the neuromatrix of these rebellious presences.'

'Purge the others, but leave Linya Tychon to us,' said Galatea.

'As you wish,' said Telok, linking his senses with the exterior surveyors of the *Renard*'s shuttle.

Ninety kilometres below was the Breath of the Gods, slowly ascending towards a ventral cache vault. Originally designed for Centurio Ordinatus, these were the only spaces large enough to contain the spinning matrix of the machine.

And below the Breath of the Gods came twin geoformer vessels. Their tech-priest crews had pushed their reactors to breaking point attempting to resist the lure of its arcane mechanics before finally accepting that nothing could prevent them from trailing in its wake.

The entrance to the embarkation deck grew ever larger in the viewscreen and Telok increased the pressure on Emil Nader's neck as they approached the terminal point of the docking manoeuvre.

'Hold us steady, Mister Nader,' warned Telok.

'This *is* steady. You think it's easy flying so close to something this big?' said Nader, checking the avionics panel. 'Feels like our ascent's running a tad imbalanced or like we picked up some extra weight.'

Despite Nader's concern, the shuttle slipped through the shimmering veil of the integrity field without incident. Telok felt the presence of a billion machine-spirits wash over him.

'Control is not as complete as it ought to be,' he said, instantly assimilating the flow of data through the unseen body of information within the Ark Mechanicus.

'Mistress Tychon was resourceful in recruiting an ally within the body of the ship,' said Galatea. 'All indications are that he will soon be dead, allowing us to fully establish control of the *Speranza* once more.'

The shuttle touched down with a booming thud of landing claws, and Telok sighed as the presence of something infinitely greater pressed against the walls of his enhanced consciousness.

'I feel its great heart beating deep within this body of iron and stone,' he said. 'Hidden deep within its matrices of logic and binary, but there for those with the vision to see.'

'The *Speranza*,' said Galatea.

'Is but one of its names,' said Telok as the shuttle's forward ramp lowered. 'But I will learn them all.'

THE FATES UNSPOOLED around Bielanna. She saw them all, *lived* them all. The world was cracking, torn asunder by the entropic vengeance of the hrud. She felt the alien host *shift*, migrating from this fleeting aspect of reality.

The power of the skein surged in her mind.

Time chained by the push and pull of the hrud and the *Yngir* engine now roared through Bielanna in a tsunami of temporal energies. She was the heart of the tempest, kneeling at the centre of her warriors as power flowed through her. She was a conduit for all the things that might yet be and all that never would.

Bielanna wept as she the felt the presence of the Dark Reaper touch her soul, Kaela Mensha Khaine revelling in his aspect of the Destroyer.

She was that Destroyer. She saw that now, the threads of those around her inextricably bound to her doom. None could escape their fate.

She had killed them all.

She had shrouded them in death.

Striking Scorpions danced angular steps around Bielanna, while the Howling Banshees spun like acrobats. Blades sang and the chorus of monkeigh gunfire was a harsh staccato backdrop to their elegant symphony of death-dealing.

The crystaliths fought with extruded blades, fast and agile, but their strikes without artistry and pride. They died by the score. Each of her warriors was entwined in an invisible web of fates that fractured and divided in the same instant. Past diminishing, present blooming and future unseen to all but her.

Her hands moved in complex patterns, blindingly swift, guiding her warriors like the conductor of a billion musicians playing the most complex song imaginable. She made Vaynesh step a finger's breadth to the right, saving him from a thrusting blade of glass. Uriquel adjusted the grip on her sword, giving her the strength to hack the limb from a crystalith. In a hundred ways she moulded the fates of her warriors: a step back here, a quarter-turn there, a leap just a moment earlier.

Each element was insignificant in itself, but combined to form a web of cause that put Bielanna's perceptions two steps ahead of effect. She had tried to mould the fates of the Space Marines, granting them a measure of her newfound power, but the fates of such warriors were not hers to shape. They would rather die than suffer the touch of one they would normally consider a foe.

Only Roboute Surcouf's mind was open enough to be guided. The touch of another eldar, a bonesinger named Yrlandriar, made it easier to reach him. With Bielanna's help, Surcouf's every shot was fired with pinpoint accuracy.

Her mastery of the fates could not last, she knew that.

For all that she might guide the steps and sword arms of her warriors, limbs of flesh and blood grew tired, skills once razor-sharp would dull.

And then death would come.

A shadow rose up to envelop Bielanna, shockingly sudden and suffocatingly intense in its darkness. Like a veil of black velvet had been drawn across her sight, she saw the skein blacken as the terminus of every thread came into view, unravelling towards extinction with horrifying speed.

The end of all things.

An impossible boundary in what should be infinite space.

Bielanna gasped, her chest constricting at the sight.

This was the doom she had seen ensconced within the *Speranza*. Space and time were coming undone, ripping apart like the solar sails of a wounded wraithship.

Doom had come to this world, but that was the least of the danger. The rift beginning here was pulling wider with every passing second, drawing every thread within the skein to it. Like a weaver's shuttle reversing through the warp and weft of a loom, the future was unravelling to its omega point.

Exnihlio was becoming the temporal equivalent of a black hole, a howling abyss in which no time would ever exist again. Its effects were yet confined to the deeps of the planet, but Bielanna felt the catastrophic geomantic damage the hrud had wreaked racing to the surface.

The physical death of Exnihlio was nothing, but the temporal shock waves would spread into the glacial void of space, reaching into the galaxy of Bielanna's kin.

It would be a slow death for the galaxy, as all time was devoured by the rift torn by the *Yngir*'s device. But that it would end all things for evermore was certain.

Unless Bielanna could stop it.

She rose smoothly to her feet, ignoring the sinuous war-dance of her people and the brutal, heaving clashes of the Space Marines. Her hands balled into fists and she thrust them out to the side, letting the power of the skein pour from her in an almighty torrent.

A hurricane of roaring, seething psychic fury streamed from Bielanna. The crystaliths closest to her simply vanished, vaporised in the raw fury of the storm. The rest were hurled back as if from a bomb blast. Pellucid blue fire swirled around Bielanna in a cyclonic vortex.

Glass and crystal shattered, killing the crystaliths, but leaving beings of flesh and blood unharmed. Green fire bled from broken bodies that spilled black dust onto the plaza. The swirling tempest of psychic energy swelled around Bielanna to form a howling wall of impenetrable storm fronts.

Stunned silence filled the void that had previously been rich with grunting mon-keigh and laughing, singing eldar.

Tanna of the Black Templars turned to her, his armour buckled and clawed back to bare metal. She sensed his hostility, primitive drugs boosting his aggression levels to psychotic heights.

She pre-empted his inevitable questions with a single imperative.

'You have to go,' she said. 'You have to stop Telok.'

She sensed his confusion, but had no time to explain what she now knew in anything but the most basic concepts.

'Everything is ending,' she said. 'What Telok has set in motion will end everything. Your Emperor, His domain, my kin and all we have fought to preserve. Everything will die. Worse, they will never have existed. All that was and all that might ever come to pass will be wiped away.'

Tanna nodded, as his battle-brothers stood with him.

'How long will that barrier hold?' said Anders through gritted teeth. His thread was shorter than all the others.

'Not long,' said Bielanna. 'The skein's power waxes strong within me, but soon it will wane like a winter's moon, so I do not have long to do what must be done.'

Archmagos Kotov said, 'You said Tanna had to go. How can any of us go anywhere?'

Bielanna let her mind drift over the surfaces of every one of the mon-keigh, searching for an emotion strong enough to provide an anchor. The

Templars and Cadians were useless, adrift and far from all they knew. Kotov's mind was too stunted in its logical functionality, its emotional centres long since closed off.

But Surcouf...

She felt his love for his crew and his ship, and wasn't love the strongest emotion of all? It had healed wounds, ended wars and seen bitter enemies brought together as brothers. It had also brought empires to ruin and seen the greatest minds humbled.

Nothing was more powerful than love, and Surcouf was blessed with an abundance.

Bielanna said, 'Your talisman. Do you still have it?'

Surcouf looked confused, then reached inside the breast pocket of his coat and withdrew his astrogation compass.

'This? Is this what you mean?'

Bielanna saw the confluence of fates bound to the device, the slender thread that set the path the mon-keigh's life had taken. He sensed its importance, but not on any conscious level.

'Yes, hold it out to me,' said Bielanna.

'Why?'

'Because I need a focus,' she said, and her eyes misted with sadness. 'And because I need someone to remember me.'

Though he was puzzled at her words, he nevertheless did as she asked. Bielanna cupped her porcelain white hands around his, feeling his deep connection to those he had left behind. He would die for them, and they for him. The needle on the compass danced and spun, unfixed and wandering. Their minds met and she lived the entirety of his life in a heartbeat.

'Look into my eyes and picture those dearest to you,' she said.

No sooner had he done so than the needle stopped moving.

Bielanna released Surcouf's hands, holding on to the connection between them, picturing what he saw. A functional room with a wooden desk. Pictures on the wall, scriptural commendations and a holographic cameo of a woman.

Such was the strength of Surcouf's emotions and the surging power within her, that it was the simplest matter to open a path through the webway. A flaring oval of orange, arched and spilling gold light onto the plaza, opened behind her.

'That will take you back to your ship,' said Bielanna. 'Go now and stop Telok. Do whatever needs to be done, but he must not return to your Imperium.'

Kotov nodded and gestured to his skitarii.

They stepped through the gate and vanished.

'You make it sound like you're not leaving,' said Surcouf.

'I am not,' said Bielanna. 'It may be possible to heal what Telok has done, but to do that I must be here at the heart of it all, the site of the wound.'

Surcouf looked out towards the barrier. The tempests were already dying, and the army of crystaliths pressed against it in overwhelming numbers.

'You'll die.'

'The future I was to share with my daughters is lost,' said Bielanna. 'There is nothing left for me. Death will be welcome.'

'I wish–'

'Say nothing,' said Bielanna, harsher than she intended. 'No human words can offer me comfort.'

Surcouf nodded and turned away, helping Magos Pavelka to her feet. Giving Bielanna a last look of profound gratitude, the two of them went through the gate together.

TANNA WATCHED SURCOUF and Pavelka vanish and felt the weight he had carried since Dantium Gate lift from his shoulders. Cut off from their Chapter and without the guidance of Kul Gilad, he and his warriors had been lost. Strange that it had taken the words of an eldar witch to show him just how lost.

On any other day he would have gone to the Reclusiam and submitted himself to pain-shriving for such thoughts.

'Can you really undo what Telok has done here?' he asked.

'Perhaps, but I will need time,' she answered, removing her helm and holding it in the crook of her arm. 'And I will need the strength of my people to do it.'

'The crystaliths will kill you long before then.'

'They will,' agreed Bielanna.

Tanna glanced towards the diminishing barrier.

'Then the Black Templars will give you that time.'

'Tanna?' said Anders. 'You're staying?'

'If she can do what she claims, then I have no choice,' said Tanna. 'Here is where I can serve the Emperor best.'

Anders sighed. 'And here was me thinking that all of us might actually get back to the Imperium.'

'It was an honour to fight alongside you, Ven Anders.'

The colonel held up a hand.

'Cadians don't do last words, valedictions or brotherly farewells in the face of certain death,' he said. 'We just fight, and I have a regiment on the *Speranza* that needs me.'

Tanna nodded and returned Anders's salute with a fist across his breast-plate. The Cadian colonel led his men through the portal as the eldar gathered around their farseer and began unbuckling their armour. Smooth plates dropped to the ground and as they removed their battle helms, it seemed their angular, alien faces softened, like dreamers awakening from a daylight reverie. They each handed Bielanna what looked like a polished gemstone and sat cross-legged around her before closing their eyes, as though entering a meditative trance.

The storm front keeping the crystaliths at bay began to diminish almost immediately. Glassy blades cut through it and their inexorable strength began slowly pushing their angular bodies through.

Tanna turned from the eldar.

His own warriors stood before him.

Proud and undefeated, they were heroes all.

'My brothers, we come to it at last,' he said. 'The last battle of the Kotov Crusade.'

'Will you lead us in our vows, brother-sergeant?' asked Yael.

'I will,' said Tanna, knowing that what he had to say next would crush the young warrior. 'But you will not take a vow with us.'

'Brother-sergeant?'

'Go through the gate,' said Tanna. 'If Telok is to be killed, it should be a Black Templar blade that cleaves his head from his shoulders.'

'No! Please, Tanna,' said Yael, forgetting himself in the heat of his despair. 'Do not deny me this last fight.'

Tanna shook his head.

'Go back to the *Speranza*, fight with all your heart in *that* battle. Win glory and carry word of us back to the Chapter. Tell them what we did here, of our courage and sacrifice. Tell them that we died as heroes in the name of the Emperor.'

'I want to stand and fight with you,' pleaded Yael.

'This is my last command. You will not disobey it.'

Tanna ached for the young warrior, knowing full well the anguish he would be feeling at being denied a glorious death alongside his brothers.

'No more words,' said Tanna. 'Go.'

Yael rammed his sword back into its scabbard and without a backward glance turned and ran through the eldar gate.

'Harsh,' said Varda. 'But it needed to be done, and it's time for that vow.'

Issur joined the Emperor's Champion, his fingers twitching and his features dancing with involuntary muscle movements.

Tanna nodded, and both warriors took a knee, leaving him standing over them as Kul Gilad had stood over them all on the *Adytum*. With the crystaliths pressing through the psychic barrier, Tanna knew there could be only one vow worthy of being made.

Kul Gilad's valediction.

The words heard over the vox as the Reclusiarch died. Tanna raised his sword to his shoulder in salute of his warriors.

'Lead us from death to victory, from falsehood to truth,' he said, bringing the sword around.

He touched the blade to Varda's shoulder.

'Lead us from despair to hope, from faith to slaughter.'

Issur was next to receive the benediction.

'Lead us to His strength and an eternity of war.'

The two Black Templars rose, and each placed a fist upon their breastplate. Their voices joined with Tanna's to complete the vow.

'Let His wrath fill our hearts!' they cried. 'Death, war and blood – in vengeance serve the Emperor in the name of Dorn!'

Issur and Varda stood side by side, blades bared and held out to the enemy.

'This is what you saw, Varda,' said Tanna as he took his place at the Emperor's Champion's side. 'When we reforged the links binding you to your sword.'

Varda nodded, but didn't look up from his blade. Despite everything, it gleamed unblemished, without as much as a scratch on its obsidian surface. Varda scanned the ranks of crystaliths as the psychic barrier finally collapsed into scraps of fading light.

The sound of crystal bodies grinding together as the monsters charged set Tanna's teeth on edge.

Fifty metres out, their heavy footfalls faster now.

'You spoke of seeing yourself fighting alongside the eldar,' said Tanna, rolling his shoulders to loosen the muscles. 'You could not conceive of how such a thing might come to pass. Now we know.'

'It pleases me to know I remained true to my oaths of loyalty,' said Varda. 'That I will die a true son of Sigismund.'

'That was never in doubt,' said Tanna.

Thirty metres away. Contact imminent.

'At l... least the el... eldar will die with us,' said Issur, glancing over at the silent, unmoving aliens behind them. The muscles at his neck were taut, but his sword was unwavering.

'This is our time to die,' said Tanna. 'Far from the Emperor's light on a forsaken world. Savour this moment, for you will die only once. How you meet that end is as important as every moment before then.'

Ten metres, translucent blades raised.

Tanna tipped his head back and lifted his sword to salute his coming death, knowing it would be magnificent.

Five metres.

The last battle of the Kotov Crusade began to the sound of breaking glass and the name of Dorn shouted to the sky.

Microcontent 18

'Ma-ta-leo! Ma-ta-leo!'

The skitarii chanted the name as they charged alongside his new Iron Fist. Dahan's awareness of every squad and pack's position was total and even in the heat of the charge he corrected vectors of attack through the noospheric link.

'Ma-ta-leo! Ma-ta-leo!'

Weapons fire blazed between the skitarii and the crystalline attackers. Intersecting collimations of las and solid rounds, plasma and gatling fire. Explosions ripped through the ranks of his warriors. Scores of bodies were trampled underfoot. Dahan plugged the gaps, moving squads into each ragged hole.

'Ma-ta-leo! Ma-ta-leo!'

Connected to the replacement Iron Fist's logic engine, his mind was ablaze with accumulated combat-memes. Threat optics measured the alpha-beast before him in every conceivable dimension. The heavy bolter quads chugged a constant stream of mass-reactives into the enemy host. Blasts of energy from the blade of his Cebrenian halberd killed those closest to the Iron Fist. Enemy bodies came apart in explosive bursts of broken glass.

'Ma-ta-leo! Ma-ta-leo!'

Hearing his Catachan war-name again made Dahan nostalgic for his days on the death world. The wealth of combat data available there was greater than on any other planet he had known. Every species of flora and fauna was deadly, and his database of warfare and close-combat predictors had expanded geometrically.

The closest analogue to the alpha-beast was the Catachan leonax den-mother he and Harker's platoon had encountered on a slash and burn mission against a surge of hyper-aggressive jungle growth.

They had encountered the lair by accident when a point Chimera crashed through the jungle floor into its moist, wriggling depths. The den-mother's hundreds of young erupted from pupal trap-lairs and attacked the Guardsmen and skitarii with a ferocity Dahan had previously only encountered in certain tyrannic blitzkrieg genera.

Dahan had killed the den-mother, a monstrous, clawed beast with a mutant mane of poisonous spines at its neck, the presence of which prompted Harker to bestow the war-name upon him.

He replayed that fight, dispensing the precise combination of combat-stimms, muscle enhancers and synaptic boosters into his system to replicate that state of being. The alpha-creature loomed ahead of him, bigger than the beast he had killed on Catachan. And attended by hulking shield-bearers.

Orders passed between him and his skitarii escort and a precise sequence of fire blazed from the Destroyer cadres. So precise was it that not a shot or iota of power was wasted. Four of the shield-bearers were instantly obliterated, their mantlets cracked with high-powered gatling cannons and blown apart by precisely timed grenade barrages. Volleys of plasma followed by pinpoint melta missiles finished the job, leaving a path open for Dahan's Iron Fist.

The alpha-beast squatted in the shadow of the sagging iron carving of Sanguinius. Dahan's vehicle crushed the splintered remains of the guard beasts under its tracks as the skitarii and crystal host came together with battering force in a storm of gunfire and blades. War cries both organic and binary echoed through the deck.

The alpha-beast reared up before him and a searing blast of green fire spat from a spinning nexus of reforming glass in its toothed underside. It struck the Iron Fist at a downward angle, cutting through its glacis like a plasma-torch. The impact was stunning. It smashed the tank's prow down into the deck. The quad guns blew out as the frontal section crumpled like foil paper. Its ammo hoppers detonated as the fire blew back inside.

Dahan thrust himself from the tank's open top. Emergency disconnect, trailing whipping cables from his spinal plugs. The Iron Fist lifted off the deck, its forward momentum flipping it up and over the alpha-beast.

Dahan landed with a screech of metal, the claws of all three legs digging into the deck.

The Iron Fist came down moments later, flat on its back, tracks churning air and spewing flames. Black smoke billowed from its ruptured hull.

Dahan's halberd came up in time to deflect a pair of clawed blade-arms extruding with obscene speed from the beast's underbelly. Scorpion claws snapped for him. He planted the oval base of his halberd and flipped around the glassy blades.

He rammed his crackling tine-bladed scarifiers into its flank. His internal capacitors discharged, sending forking bolts of purple energy through its body that left vitrified trails of opaque crystal in their wake.

Green fire pulsed from the monster's body, faster than Dahan could dodge. It struck him dead centre. His armour cracked and the impact jarred his floodstream pump offline for a few seconds.

Dahan staggered, momentarily off-balance. The alpha-beast's shape transformed, becoming taller, broader, growing more limbs. It slammed a vast, elephantine foot into his chest, hurling him back against the blazing wreck of the Iron Fist. It closed the gap between them, fast, and crab-like claws snapped shut on Dahan's scarifiers. It tore them clean from his body. He loosed a binaric shout of pain, rolling aside from another stream of green bio-electricity. His cloak was ablaze, the steel-woven fabric burning magnesium bright.

Dahan spun and rolled, rotating all three legs to avoid its attacks. It struck again and again, limbs like stingers slamming down with force enough to punch through the deck plates. Trailing scads of molten metal from his cloak, Dahan spun his halberd in a dizzyingly complex web of blocks, counters and thrusts. The speed of the beast was phenomenal. His every defence was made with only nano-seconds to spare. The entropic capacitor buzzed angrily as it built up charge for a strike.

Sheared crystal and metal spun around them as they duelled in the shadow of the Blood Angels' tragic primarch. Dahan was fully aware of the desperate fighting behind him as the crystal monsters swept past his own battle to engage the Cadians. In any normal engagement, Dahan would keep discrete partitions in his mind to keep track of every aspect of a battle, but this fight was requiring virtually all his processing power just to stay alive.

The thing's shape kept changing, almost as though it knew that to remain in one form would allow him an advantage. His wetware kept evolving, switching and resetting. He couldn't get a fix on any one set of combat routines that would allow him to defeat the alpha-beast.

Another thunderous blow sent Dahan flying backwards. He slammed into the ironwork pillar supporting Sanguinius, who finally toppled from his perch to land between the two combatants with a booming clang of iron. The alpha-beast took a crashing step towards him, the lower portions of its legs thickening as its upper body enlarged. Its mass was finite, and its limbs thinned in response, becoming whipping, lashing tendrils of razored glass.

Combat-memes jostled for Dahan's approval.

Tyranicus chameleo.

Teuthidian Myrmidrax.
Cyberneticus Noctus (Kaban).
Cephalaxia.
Arachnismegana.

The list went on, but in the split second it took him to scan through, Dahan understood nothing in his archives could match the alpha-beast's ability to continuously evolve. He had nothing embedded that could counter the sheer variety of forms and combat strategies the alpha-beast could assume.

Instead, he did the one thing that went against his every hard-wired logical instinct.

He shut down his entire database of systemic combat routines.

A void filled Dahan, a yawning abyss of uncertainty that felt hideously empty, yet strangely liberating. In this sublime instant, he had no idea what his opponent might do or what he should do to counter it. No idea how best to fight this foe, save the data presented in the very instant before attacking.

The alpha-beast lumbered towards him, its razor whips cutting the air. Dahan took off towards it. He leapt onto the fallen statue of Sanguinius and pistoned all three of his legs out, launching himself through the air. Whip-thin razor arms slashed towards him. The Cebrenian halberd cut through the bulk of them, his rotating gimbal of a waist eluded others, but many more slashed deep into Dahan's body.

One of his legs fell from his body and the majority of one shoulder spun away. Another stroke opened the organic meat of his stomach as a rigid spine of crystal punched through his chest. Mechanisms failed and damage warnings flashed red in his vision.

But his target was in sight.

Dahan twisted as he fell, and the disruptor-sheathed blade of his Cebrenian halberd swept down. It clove through the alpha-beast's leg at the joint between limb and pelvis.

The alpha-beast staggered, its body shape rapidly fluctuating in a futile attempt to keep its balance. It crashed down, the shorn limb clouding and becoming opaque as the linked machines within died. Dahan hit hard, impaled through the shoulder where a rigid spine of glass was wedged. With his remaining two legs, he hauled himself upright, feeling every aspect of bio-mechanical efficiency degrade as chemicals, blood and charged ionic fluids poured from him.

The alpha-beast was drawing its matter into itself, sluggish now that so great a number of its self-replicating machines were no longer a part of it. Its movements were awkward, like a newborn life form still unsure as to the correct means of standing upright.

Dahan didn't give it the chance to learn.

Graham McNeill

The beast had taken his lower arms, but the bulbous entropic capacitor of the Cebrenian halberd now arced and fizzed with coruscating energy.

Dahan slammed the oval pommel down in the centre of what might have been its chest. An explosion of bio-electrical energy arced through the alpha-beast's body, fusing the crystal and shattering the areas around its path.

The beast lurched and spasmed like a flatlining patient being defibrillated. A patchwork head of clouded glass and crystal extruded from the lumpen mass of its chest, cracking and forming a vast crocodilian skull mass. Dahan swept the Cebrenian halberd around in a decapitating strike.

Its blade had been fashioned by artificers trained in the techniques of the first tech-priest assassins.

The alpha-beast's head fell away from its body, and its nervous system shorted out in a blaze of overload. Green fire spurted from the stump of its neck, a catastrophic wound from which it could not recover.

Every crystalline warrior in the training deck began glitching, internal structures momentarily shorted by the abrupt severing of the connection to their command and control nexus. Dahan wasn't naïve enough to believe the effect would leave the host powerless for long, in the manner of a tyrannic *praefactor*-level creature's death.

But perhaps it would be long enough.

The bray of war-horns filled the training deck, and Dahan wearily lifted the notched blade of his Cebrenian halberd in salute.

Legio Sirius had come, and they had not come alone.

Rumbling in the shadow of *Lupa Capitalina* and *Canis Ulfrica* were squadron after squadron of Imperial Guard superheavies.

Baneblades, Stormhammers and Shadowswords.

'Omnissiah bless you, Captain Hawkins,' said Dahan, as squads of his suzerain rushed to his side.

'Ma-ta-leo! Ma-ta-leo! Ma-ta-leo!'

BY THE TIME Roboute and Ilanna stepped from the sunset gate and into his private staterooms, Kotov and his skitarii were already gone. He heard the voice of the archmagos through the open doorway to the bridge. Speaking on the vox, by the sounds of it.

The glow of Bielanna's gateway filled the stateroom with honey-gold light. It imparted a homely warmth to the wood of his desk, but still managed to make the rest of the room feel melancholy.

Its surface was the mirror-smooth surface of a glacial lake bathed in the last rays of autumn, but its edges were undulant, like the corona of a distant sun. Roboute looked away, discomfited by looking too long at its unnatural presence.

'Here,' he said, turning away and lowering Pavelka into the chair behind the desk. 'Sit. Don't try to move. Stay here on the *Renard* until this is all over, yes?'

Ilanna nodded and Roboute sat at the corner of his desk. It felt unreal being here, with his commendations and rosettes on the wall. So normal after the insanity of Exnihlio. Roboute smiled as he saw the hololithic cameo of Katen, knowing on some gut level that she was at least part of what had allowed Bielanna to fix this location so precisely. He couldn't quite bring himself to accept that it was all real, that they'd escaped certain death at the blades of the crystaliths.

'What are you waiting for?' said Pavelka. 'Go.'

'Just give me a minute,' said Roboute, still breathless from another journey that left a bilious taste in his mouth and a savage pounding at his temples. 'At least until I'm sure I can walk without feeling like I'm about to throw up.'

They sat in silence, Ilanna with her hands clasped in her lap, Roboute fixating on tiny details. As if by focusing on them he could force his mind to accept them as real. Gradually the sensation of the world being a veneer spread over a darker reality began to fade and his breathing began to even out.

A sudden sense of premonition caused him to back away from the rippling outline of the sunset gate. Roboute's breathing hiked sharply as Ven Anders emerged, still clutching his bloodied side. He gave the room a quick once over as three Cadian troopers came after him, making the room feel suddenly small.

'Less ostentatious than I'd have expected,' he said.

'That's Ultramar for you,' answered Roboute.

'Where's Kotov?'

'Already on the bridge. I'll be with you shortly.'

Anders nodded and led his men from Roboute's stateroom.

His timing was fortuitous, as the towering figure of a Black Templar emerged moments later, and the stateroom now felt positively cramped. Yael's armour was limned in glittering motes of light. Behind him, the sunset gate faded like a dream.

'Brother Yael?' said Roboute. 'Where are others? Why is the gate closed?'

Yael shook off the portal's effects with a shake of his head.

'They are not coming,' he said. 'The witch claims that, with time, she can undo the damage Telok has done. My brothers are giving their lives to grant her that time.'

'They're staying on Exnihlio?'

'Did I not just say that?' snapped Yael, turning away and leaving the stateroom.

Roboute understood. Tanna had sent Yael back to the *Speranza* as the Templars' legacy. A necessary order, but that wouldn't make it any easier to bear for a warrior denied a glorious death alongside his comrades.

'You have to go,' said Ilanna. 'Stop Telok.'

Roboute nodded and bent to kiss her forehead before turning and following Yael onto the bridge. Kotov was already there, plugged into what was normally Pavelka's station on the portside array. Low-level crackles of binaric communication burbled and squawked from the speaker grilles.

As Roboute entered, Kotov stood and disconnected. Anders was on the vox, his face a picture of concentration.

'The *Speranza* is under attack,' said Kotov.

Roboute nodded. 'Makes sense. How else was Telok going to get back to Mars? Is it crystaliths?'

Kotov nodded. 'An army of them, attacking throughout my ship.'

He spoke like a man who had just woken to find his clothes infested with parasites and had no idea how to remove them. Kotov nodded towards Ven Anders and said, 'Captain Hawkins and Magos Dahan are coordinating the defence, but much of the ship has already fallen.'

'Where is Telok?' demanded Yael.

'Unknown, but it must be assumed he will head for the bridge.'

'Then so will we,' said Roboute, heading to the weapons rack at the rear of the bridge. He unlocked it with a key hanging next to it, which wasn't exactly secure, but it meant he could get to his weapons quickly. Roboute unsnapped a drum-fed combat shotgun and slung it over one shoulder then gathered a host of fresh powercells for his pistol. Finally, he lifted out a worn leather sword belt and buckled it around his waist.

The blade was a Calthan vorpal with a solid-state energy core worked into the handle. Anything he cut with this blade wouldn't be getting back up.

'We're pretty close to the bridge, but if there are crystaliths aboard, then it's likely we'll have to fight our way there,' he said. 'We could use some more men to help get us there.'

'I've detached some men from Captain Hawkins's forces in the training deck,' said Anders, setting down the vox and slapping a fresh powercell into the hilt of his sword. 'They'll link with us in the Path to Wisdom.'

'Then let's go,' said Roboute.

They took a transit elevator to the forward loading ramp, and Yael ducked down and dropped to the deck before it was even half lowered. Roboute heard a voice cry out in alarm and slid off the edge of the ramp as he realised it was one he knew.

Yael held Emil Nader by the neck.

'That's my pilot,' said Roboute as the Cadians fanned out from the ramp to surround Emil. Kotov and the skitarii followed as the Space Marine lowered Emil to the deck.

Emil Nader was ashen and looked like he'd just run from one end of the *Speranza* to the other. Behind him, still trailing scads of icy vapour from its recent arrival, was the *Renard*'s shuttle.

'Roboute?' he said. 'How the hell did you get on board?'

'Long story,' said Roboute. 'Are you all right? I saw you on the shuttle with Galatea.'

Emil massaged his bruised neck and glared angrily at Yael.

'Yeah, I'm fine,' he said. 'I thought they were going to kill me after I got them on board, but they couldn't have cared less about me. It was like I was an insect to them.'

'How long have they been gone?' demanded Kotov.

Emil took a step back from the archmagos, staring in horror at his ruined shoulders.

'Twenty minutes, give or take.'

'Can you not be more precise, Mister Nader?' said Kotov.

'Not really, I was trying not to puke in terror at the time,' snapped Emil.

Roboute hid a grin and said, 'Emil, I need you to head to my staterooms. Ilanna's there, and she's hurt. Badly. Look after her.'

Emil nodded, grateful not to have been asked to accompany the war party. 'Of course, Roboute. I'll take good care of her.'

'Where's Adara?' asked Roboute, moving past Emil. 'If there was ever a time for him to earn his keep, it's now.'

Emil grabbed his arm, and Roboute didn't like the look he saw in his pilot's eyes one bit.

'Roboute, Adara's dead,' said Emil. 'Galatea killed him.'

The news hit Roboute like a sledgehammer to the gut. The air was pulled from his lungs.

'And that's not all you need to know.'

'What...?'

'It's about Mistress Tychon,' said Emil.

WHEN THE DOOR to the bridge swung open to the sound of shouting skitarii protection details, Blaylock checked the feed from his various cognitive streams. Had he missed the fall of a transit deck or a sudden assault he'd not known was coming?

No, Hawkins and Dahan still had the main thrust of the enemy assault contained on the training deck. The attackers were spread throughout the ship like an infection, and Blaylock even saw a measure of confused inaction in their movements.

Blaylock turned his head as far as the MIU connections of the command throne allowed. He couldn't see the entrance to the bridge and was too enmeshed with the *Speranza* to easily disconnect.

The fact that he wasn't hearing any gunfire reassured him that nothing untoward was happening. The skitarii were behaving aggressively because that was how they were trained to be.

Then he heard the clash of blades, screams of pain and the wet meat sound of cleaving flesh. The sound was short-lived, and Blaylock felt a crushing presence of grating, archaic code as a hideous amalgam of iron and flesh, crystal and glass entered his field of vision.

As broad as a Dreadnought and just as bulky, the monster climbed to the raised mezzanine level of the bridge with the awkward gait of a load-lifter with degraded functionality in its locomotive limbs.

It turned to face Blaylock and even though the face at the centre of its torso mass was rendered in artificial plasflesh, there was no mistaking its features.

<Telok,> said Blaylock.

The Lost Magos took a crashing step towards him, and the reek of dead flesh and chemicals was almost overpowering. Telok extended a fused gauntlet of steel and crystal, and placed a clawed finger the size of a sword on Blaylock's chest.

'Flesh-voice if you please, Tarkis.'

Blaylock nodded and said, 'Where is Archmagos Kotov?'

'Dead.'

Blaylock nodded. It had been the only logical answer.

Galatea appeared behind Telok, the black robes of its proxy body soaked in the blood of skitarii and its blade-limbs coated in the stuff. Chunks of hewn flesh lay like butcher's offal on its lopsided palanquin, where the brain jars of its captive minds crackled and glimmered with furious activity. Blaylock saw one of the jars had been broken, the grey matter within now absent. He wondered who had been discarded from Galatea's neuromatrix.

'It was close to a statistical certainty that you would betray us,' said Blaylock.

'Betray is such a hostile word, Tarkis,' said Galatea. 'We were merely following the precepts of a plan set in motion millennia ago. That we had to deceive you to see it to fruition was a small price to pay.'

Blaylock saw movement behind Galatea.

Kryptaestrex.

Disengaging from his station and powering up his overpowered manipulator limbs. Never before had Blaylock been more grateful for a senior magos who resembled a load-lifting combat servitor than he was right at this moment.

He kept his voice entirely neutral.

'What do you intend?'

Telok smiled and the gesture was as alien as anything Blaylock had ever seen.

'Come now, Tarkis, you already know what I intend,' said Telok, withdrawing his claw and lifting his arms to encompass the bridge. 'The *Speranza* is now my ship. I intend to return to Mars with the Breath of the Gods and take control of the Mechanicus.'

Now it was Blaylock's turn to laugh.

'Until we reached this world, I never believed you really existed. And even then I assumed the years of isolation must have made you mad. I see now that I was entirely correct in this latter assumption.'

Kryptaestrex was now fully disengaged from his MIUs. He just had to keep Telok's attention for a little longer. Within a compartmentalised section of his mind, Blaylock constructed a shut-down code like the one he had used to prevent Vitali Tychon from killing Galatea.

Oh, how he regretted *that* decision.

'The ship is not yours yet,' said Blaylock. 'Our military forces will repel your crystalline army. Already their cohesion is falling away in the face of superior skill and strength.'

'Yes, I felt the demise of the nexus-creature I sent aboard,' said Telok. 'But I have already assumed command of the crystaliths aboard the *Speranza*. And when we regain control of the datasphere, we will purge every last deck of oxygen and heat to kill your soldiers deck by deck.'

Regain control...?

Then the war in the datascape Blaylock had witnessed was some part of the *Speranza* fighting back as he had hoped. Telok's careless words also implied that Galatea's hold on the ship's vital systems was no longer in place.

If ever there was a time to strike, it was now.

Blaylock reached into his compartmentalised thoughts at the same time as Kryptaestrex made his move. He unleashed a focused spear of stand-down codes straight at Telok, each binaric string freighted with every authority signifier and title proof Blaylock possessed.

Such a searing volume and intensity of code would have staggered a Warlord Titan, but it had no visible effect on Telok.

Kryptaestrex snapped his claws shut on Galatea's torso, crushing the proxy body. He wrenched it backwards, and an oil-squirting stump of writhing, chrome-plated spinal column erupted from the machine-hybrid's belly.

Telok spun and hammered his monstrously oversized fists into Kryptaestrex's chest. Crystalline claws punched through the boxy housing of his body like the power claws of a chrono-gladiator.

Kryptaestrex was simply obliterated.

Blaylock initiated an emergency decoupling from the command throne, its MIU ribbon connectors retracting into their spinal ports. Finished with his murder, Telok turned to face him with a look of profound disappointment.

'*Really*, Tarkis? That was the best you could do?' said Telok. 'I'd hoped Magos Alhazen would have better prepared you.'

'How could you possibly–'

Telok didn't let him finish.

'Perhaps something more like this,' said Telok. 'Tyger, tyger.'

The effect was instantaneous.

Blaylock's mind went into spasms as it suffered a synaptic overload comparable to an epileptic seizure. Even as he tumbled from the command throne the perceptual centres of his brain were overwhelmed by the fearful symmetry of an orange and black feline stalking a moonlit forest.

What Telok had done was as catastrophic as it was complete.

He couldn't move. He couldn't speak.

Only his visual systems had been left unaffected.

Galatea looked down at him with its lifeless silver eyes. Its proxy body had been savagely twisted and broken, hanging limply over the palanquin like a lifeless marionette.

Yet it was still, hatefully, functional.

The machine-hybrid jerked, as though mocking Blaylock's spasming contortions. The brains flickered, in time with Galatea's involuntary motion. Were they the cause of its internal distress? Impossible to tell, but perhaps Mistress Tychon was causing more trouble than the vile machine had banked upon.

Galatea turned away and limped out of his angle of vision in the direction of Azuramagelli's station. Blaylock could see nothing of what was happening, but from the sound of breaking glass and snapping MIU ribbons, knew it was nothing good.

'The astrogation hub is secure,' said Galatea.

'Excellent,' said Telok. 'Then plot a course for Mars.'

EVEN WITH THE *Speranza* under attack, the Path to Wisdom was still thronged with tech-priests. They huddled around the vast columns in a fug of incense, endlessly studying the unending streams of ticker-tape and nonsense binary streaming from the carvings wrought into the doric capitals atop each column.

They ignored the *Renard's* grav-sled as Roboute steered it towards the gigantic doors at its far end. A heavy slab of rectangular iron with a pilot's bay at one end and an underslung repulsor generator, the sled scattered chanting groups of lexmechanics bearing armfuls of rolled scrolls. Servo-skulls crossing the vaulted space loosed squeals of irritated binary as they flitted from its path.

Much like the rest of them, the grav-sled had seen better days. Its structure and engine had been shot, pummelled and overloaded on Katen Venia to the point of it being very nearly written off by Kayrn Sylkwood upon its eventual return to the *Renard*.

Roboute had made a sacred vow to repair the sled, and though it had taken him the best part of the journey to Exnihlio to do it, he had been true to his word.

The grav-sled wasn't a passenger transport, it was a cargo carrier. Its rear compartment was little more than a corrugated cuboid space capable of bearing sixty metric tonnes.

More than enough to transport Sergeant Rae's men and their lethal mix of weapons. The veteran sergeant and his men had rendezvoused with them at the dorsal end of the Path to Wisdom, looking like they'd been in the fight of their lives. Rae was genuinely pleased to see his commanding officer, but looked distinctly unhappy at his current assignment.

Roboute didn't care.

All he cared about was getting to the bridge and killing Galatea. The machine-hybrid had always been a thing to avoid, but with its revealed treachery, together with its killing of Adara Siavash and its mutilation of Linya, it had become Roboute's sworn enemy.

His cheeks were wet with tears as he guided the sled along the Path to Wisdom. He ignored its many incredible sights, the diamond and chromium-plated pillars, the lapis-lazuli inscriptions and golden wirework murals. The soaring vault of the ceiling, with its circuit diagram frescoes of ancient Mars, was an irrelevance to him. Nothing now had any meaning to Roboute.

He'd wanted a life beyond the stars, beyond the Imperium, but all he had found were the same treacheries, the same greed and the same insane ambition. Now Adara was dead and Ilanna likely blinded for the rest of her life.

How many more of his friends would have to suffer for his quixotic desire to leave the Imperium? None, he decided.

Kotov and Yael sat to his right, both lost in thought.

Why had they crossed the Halo Scar?

Yael was a crusader of the Black Templars, and the warriors of his Chapter were driven by an imperative from a time before the Imperium. Bound to notions of expanding the Emperor's realm, they could no more have turned from this quest than stopped breathing.

Desperation, greed and, yes, perhaps even a truthful desire to expand mankind's reservoir of knowledge was at the heart of Kotov's motivations. Each of them had crossed the Halo Scar seeking something to fill a void, to satisfy a need they hadn't even admitted to themselves.

Were their reasons any more or less noble than his own? He didn't think so. The worst thing was that they had each *found* what they were looking for.

And now they were paying the price for that.

'Galatea killed my friends,' Roboute said. 'So when we get to the bridge, does anyone object if I kill it?'

'My brothers lie dead beneath an alien sun, their legacy left unharvested,' said Yael, and suddenly he no longer looked like a young warrior. 'Telok and Galatea die by my hand.'

'The *Speranza* is a Mechanicus vessel,' said Kotov, reasoned, logical hatred in every word. 'Taken by an abomination and a traitor. A servant of the Omnissiah must be the one to end them.'

'Fine,' said Roboute. 'Then everyone gets to kill it.'

The vast doors to the bridge loomed ahead of them, and Roboute slowed the grav-sled as he saw a scrapyard's worth of broken machinery heaped at their base.

Praetorians, weaponised servitors, combat-hulks, skitarii kill-packs. At least two hundred shattered, las-burned and hacked-apart bodies. There had been a ferocious battle fought here, but something was missing.

'Who were they fighting?'

'They did this to themselves,' said Kotov.

'They killed each other?' asked Yael.

'The placement of the bodies and the nature of their wounds offers no other conclusion,' said Kotov as Roboute brought the sled to a swift halt.

'Telok?' said Roboute.

'Telok or Galatea,' replied Kotov. 'Not that it makes any difference. They're still dead.'

Yael dropped to the ground as Colonel Anders, Sergeant Rae and ffiteen Guardsmen clambered from the back of the grav-sled. They spread out in a loose arrowhead formation, rifles unwavering in their sectors of responsibility. Yael moved away from the sled, his bolter sweeping for targets.

Anders craned his neck to look up the length of the door.

'That's a big damn door,' he said. 'Anyone know how to open it?'

Climbing down into the midst of the dead Mechanicus soldiery, Roboute had to agree with Kotov's assessment of how they had died. He slung his rotary shotgun around, wrapping his fingers around the textured grip and placing his other hand on the recoil stabiliser.

The archmagos picked his way quickly through the shattered bodies to a lectern panel at the side of the huge door. A pair of circling skulls floated above the lectern, their jaws open wide in expressions of horror, witnesses to the slaughter.

Kotov's skitarii went after him, and their fury at what had been done here was plain to see. Roboute followed at a more measured pace as Kotov's mechadendrites opened a hatch at the base of the lectern. Blue light haloed Kotov's features.

Roboute tapped the wide-mouthed barrel of his shotgun against the metres-thick door to the bridge.

'Does the fact that Telok can turn our weapons against us and paralyse our armour, or that his avatar is in control of the ship, give anyone second thoughts about what's going to happen when we get through here?'

No one answered.

'Thought not,' he said, picking a path towards Kotov. 'So, can you get us onto the bridge?'

The archmagos didn't answer. A shower of hissing sparks exploded from the hatch. Kotov fell back, feedback current rippling along the length of his mechadendrites. Flames licked from the hatch, and molten metal dribbled down the lectern.

'No,' said Archmagos Kotov. 'I cannot.'

Microcontent 19

'ON YOUR LEFT!' shouted Tanna, blocking a blow and rolling his wrists to thrust his blade into the blank face of a crystalith. Varda swayed aside from the blow arcing towards his head, and spun on his heel to decapitate his attacker.

The Black Templars were in constant motion. Circling the kneeling eldar. Like temple guards protecting priests whose credo forbade violence of any sort.

Never stop, never give the enemy a chance to mass.

A shimmering nimbus of light haloed the xenos, a sure sign of their witchery that would normally have earned Tanna's undying hate. That it had come to this, warriors of the Black Templars fighting to protect the life of eldar, was a measure of the strange turns life could take.

Bielanna sat in the centre of the eldar circle. Corposant danced along her limbs. Light bled from her eyes in mercurial tears.

'Low on your right,' said Varda, and Tanna swept his sword down.

A crystalline blade shattered on the hard edge of his notched sword. The grip still thrummed in his hand, the spirit within revelling in the fight.

'Emperor bless you, Ilanna Pavelka,' said Tanna. His blade was long blunted, but every blow that broke the surface layers of crystal was a killing one.

Tanna barged with his shoulder, making space. The enemy was fast and strong, but he was a Space Marine. His boot thundered against a crystal kneecap, shattering it. His elbow spun out and pulverised a glassy skull. He fought with all the skill and strength bred into him by the fleshwrights of his Chapter and the genesmiths of a forgotten age.

'For Kul Gilad,' said Tanna, killing another animated monster.

'And Bracha,' shouted Varda in answer.

'An… and Auiden,' said Issur as they came together again.

The honoured dead fought with them, carried in their very souls and every killing blow. And though he bled from a score of wounds, Tanna's heart was that of Sigismund. A mighty organ forged upon the anvil of battle in the Imperium's darkest hour.

And while it still beat, he would fight.

As would they all.

Issur's blade cut a deadly path through the crystaliths. His jawline was taut with the effort of controlling his spasms. His footwork was faultless, his bladework sublime. He would have made a formidable Emperor's Champion had the war-visions come to him.

That honour had gone to Atticus Varda, a warrior who had never once defeated Issur in the practice cages, but whose heart was unclouded by petty resentments. Clad in the Armour of Faith and wielding the Black Sword, Varda was a towering figure. A hero from the Chapter annals, worthy of mention in the same breath as Bayard, Grimaldus, Navarre and Efried.

He moved with fluid economy, never stopping, finding space where no space existed. Earning that extra fraction of a second to parry or counterattack. To watch Varda fight was to witness all that was best in a warrior.

Tanna knew that he was the least of them. Skilled, but outclassed on every level. His sword bludgeoned where theirs countered, hacked where theirs cut cleanly. Yet for all that his technique left something to be desired, the results spoke for themselves.

The crystaliths massively outnumbered them in odds that were almost comically absurd. Thousands to one. Odds that not even the gene-fathers of the Legions themselves could have fought.

Tanna doubted he had ever fought with such preternatural skill.

His death would be magnificent.

His flesh might not return to the Chapter, but Yael would carry his memory to the *Eternal Crusader* and the legacy of the Kotov Crusade would endure.

Tanna blocked an overhead cut, swaying aside from a thrusting spike of crystal. The enemy hadn't come at them with any energy weapons, just blades. And they had returned the favour. He felt a line of fire score across his hip and sidestepped, smashing his elbow down on a sword arm. The limb shattered and Tanna kicked his foe in the gut. He followed up the kick with a low sweep, wide and hard. Three crystaliths went down, and Tanna saw a gap open up before him.

'Close ranks!' shouted Varda.

Too far extended, enemies on the left and right.

A smashing cut struck Tanna on the shoulder, another on the thigh. The first bounced clear, the second drew blood. He killed both attackers, but he'd been staggered.

Another blow caromed from his breastplate, and Tanna reeled from the force of it. Crystaliths poured past him as he pushed himself to his feet. More surged towards him. His only advantage was that they couldn't all come at him at once.

Tanna stepped back to the fighting formation of his brothers and hacked down a crystalith with its bladed arm buried in the back of an eldar warrior. The tip of the blade jutted from the alien's chest, but she made no sound as she died. Another fell with his head almost severed. The remaining eldar groaned with each death, as though they felt the pain of each loss within themselves.

Tanna returned the favour, beheading the eldar's killer.

'Push… th… th… them back on the right,' shouted Issur. The swordsman's blade had broken, snapped halfway along its length. No longer a broadsword, more a jagged gladius.

Tanna took a quarter turn left and charged, shoulder low. Pain flared. He'd been hurt there before and his armour's stimms were exhausted. He hurled the enemy back.

'Step in,' ordered Varda.

The three Templars stepped together, forming the points of a triangle around the eldar. Pools of blood made their footing treacherous, but the debris of the destroyed crystaliths gave them traction. Not all of that blood was eldar. Both Issur and Varda bled from a score of wounds, and Tanna's biology burned hot as it fought to heal and keep pace with the energy demands he was making of it.

'No pity,' said Varda, hammering his fist to his chest.

'No remorse,' answered Issur, holding his broken sword out before him.

'No fear,' finished Tanna.

They circled again. Blocking, parrying and defending.

This was not the kind of fight for which they had been wrought. They were crusaders, warriors who sought out foes to kill, battles to win. Yet this was the fight they were given.

But it couldn't go on, the enemy was too numerous, too relentless and unhindered by the need to protect those who could not defend themselves.

Varda was the first to die.

A glancing blow to the side of his helmet. A moment's pause and they were on him. Stabbing, cutting and barging him. He grappled, unable to bring the Black Sword to bear. Blades punched up through his stomach and chest. Another lanced in under his shoulder guard.

This last blow spun him around, his sword still buried in the heart of a crystalith. The arc of a glass-edged blade flashed. Opened his throat.

Cutting into the meat of his neck like a razor.

Blood fountained. The Black Sword wrenched clear.

Tanna shouted a denial as Varda's knees buckled and the Black Sword tumbled from his grip.

Even as it fell, Issur was in motion.

The crystaliths surrounded Varda, cutting his body to pieces as if to defile him. Issur bludgeoned them aside, his body a battering ram. No thought for his own defence. A blade of crystal plunged into his back. Another opened the meat of his flank like a butcher dressing a carcass.

Issur kicked them away from the Emperor's Champion, stabbing with the spar of his ruined blade and punching with his free hand.

He knelt by Varda's corpse. His broken sword slashed down.

And when he rose, it was with the Black Sword held aloft.

'A Champion may fall, but he never dies!' shouted Issur, and his words were free of the impediments that had plagued him since Valette. The snapped blade hung from an unbroken length of chain at his wrist. With the Black Sword gripped in both hands, Issur was reborn in blood as the Emperor's Champion he had always desired to be.

Tanna fought his way to Issur's side, desperately blocking and parrying. The crystaliths sensed the end was near and pressed their attack. More of the eldar were dead. Apart from Bielanna, only two remained, the others hacked down in blood.

'Castellan form,' said Issur, his pain washed away in this last moment of apotheosis.

They came together in a back-to-back defensive style.

They fought like two halves of the same warrior, naturally complementing one another's skills and strengths. They circled Bielanna, their swords a dazzling blur; one black, one silver.

Tanna took a blade to the chest. He snapped it off with a downward smash of his forearm. Another stabbed into his side. They jutted like glass spines. Blood poured down his breastplate, running through the fissures of its ivory eagle.

Tanna dropped to one knee, but Issur was there to haul him to his feet.

'We don't die on our knees, Tanna!' shouted Issur, spinning the Black Sword around his head and cleaving it through half a dozen crystaliths in one mighty blow.

Even with the weapon of the Champion, Issur's strength was failing, his movements slowing. His wounds were too deep and too wide, his armour sheeted in red from the waist down.

Tanna saw the thrust, tried to shout a warning.

Issur twisted his sword in a crosswise block.

An instant too slow.

A diamond-hard blade with glittering, knapped edges.

It caught the light of the blue sky, and the splintered blue edge turned vivid crimson as it buried itself in Issur's heart.

Issur's mouth went wide with pain.

His eyes locked with Tanna's.

'Until the end, brother,' he said.

And hurled the Black Sword to Tanna as a flurry of stabbing glass blades cut him down.

The Black Sword spun through the air, a perfect throw. Tanna caught it with his free hand and brought it around in an equally perfect arc to slay Issur's killer. With chainsword in one hand, Black Sword in the other, Tanna threw himself at the crystaliths with a roar of hatred for all they had taken from him.

Twin swords cut and thrust, striking with an exactitude he had never before possessed. Every blow found the precise gap in his foes' defences, every parry arose at just the right moment to protect Bielanna from a cowardly thrust at her silent form.

A blade cut through the cuisse of his right leg. It clove to the bone, fragmented. Long shards of razored glass stabbed up and down through the meat of his thigh.

Tanna bit down against the agony. His mouth filled with blood.

The pain was ferocious, intense, blinding in its white heat.

He felt every piercing blade entering his flesh. In his back, side and chest. One in the neck, another punching up through his armpit and breaking off in his right lung. A last lancing thrust that split his heart.

Tanna fell onto his back, staring into the painfully blue sky. He pulled both swords onto his chest, like the carven lid of a sarcophagus within the candlelit sepulchres of the *Eternal Crusader*.

An apocalyptic quantity of blood was flooding from his body. Numbing cold enveloped him. His fight was done.

A hand brushed his face. Delicate, porcelain smooth, cold like glass.

And the pain went away.

'Until the end,' said Bielanna.

<You'll need it distracted,> said Abrehem.

<I know,> replied Linya, feeling a cold that had nothing to do with temperature seeping into her consciousness. The reality of what she had set in motion with her magi imprisoned within Galatea's neuromatrix was now manifesting within her.

Anger at the machine-hybrid had sustained her, given her purpose, but now, for the first time, Linya felt real fear.

<I don't know how much longer I can help you,> said Abrehem, and Linya could barely bring herself to look upon him.

<You have to hold on,> she said. <Just a little longer.>

His body was fragmenting, literally fragmenting the nearer they drew to the bridge. As though the intensity of its light and the concentration of raw data was stripping his essence like ice from a comet approaching its perigee with a sun.

But that wasn't it at all.

<I'll try,> he said.

Abrehem's diminishing had nothing to do with the searing luminosity of the bridge. He was dying, bleeding out in Forge Elektrus despite the desperate ministrations of her father and Chiron Manubia.

They hovered over the star-hot emissions of the bridge.

<We can't do this alone,> said Abrehem. <We need a conduit to get inside.>

<And we'll have one,> said Linya. <Look.>

Abrehem followed her gaze and said, <They won't get in either. The machine-spirit in the lock is dead.>

<But *you* can get them in,> said Linya. <Remember the reclamation chamber.>

She knew he would understand her cold logic and hated herself for using him like this. Here, in this place, there could be no secrets between them, and he nodded in understanding, knowing what it would cost him.

Abrehem swooped down and his fragmenting spirit form entered the door. The locking mechanism was cold and dead, murdered by a thing that claimed the same lineage.

<Thus do we invoke the Machine-God,> said Abrehem. <Thus do we make whole that which was sundered.>

Light poured from him, bathing the internal mechanics of the door in a furnace glow of molten gold. And as the dead machines of Forge Elektrus had responded to his touch, so too did the vast templum door at the terminus of the Path to Wisdom.

It opened.

IT OFFENDED KOTOV on every level to see Telok and Galatea on the bridge of the *Speranza*. Colonel Anders's Cadians swept out to either side of him, as though performing a room clearance in one of Dahan's battle-sims. Kotov noted that Sergeant Rae stood apart from the formation, taking careful, unwavering aim at Galatea.

Yael and Roboute Surcouf marched at his right, his skitarii on his left. Telok turned to face them as the mighty door swung farther open, a look of weary irritation on his face.

'Impossible,' said Galatea, limping forwards with its proxy body almost severed from the palanquin. Kotov was gratified to see that *someone* had managed to grievously harm the machine-hybrid. 'We extinguished the spirit within that door. How were you able to open it?'

'I am an archmagos of the Adeptus Mechanicus,' said Kotov, unwilling to admit that the door's opening was a miracle he could not fathom. 'You will find there is a great deal of which I am capable.'

Telok sighed and his entire body heaved, venting steam, and the crystalline structures engulfing his frame ran the gamut of hues.

'On Exnihlio it was intriguing,' he said, 'but your refusal to die has now passed beyond any amusement.'

Kotov knew better than to bandy words with the Lost Magos, and gave the order he should have given a long time ago.

'Kill Telok and his abomination,' he said.

He had hoped for the sound of gunfire, the snap of las mixed with the crackle of a plasma gun. He had hoped for it, but he had not expected it. The Cadians were frantically checking their rifles, slamming in fresh powercells, but Kotov already knew none of them would fire.

'A squad of Guardsmen and one Space Marine?' said Telok, sliding the crystalline claws from his gnarled, crystal-grown gauntlet. 'An entire vessel of skitarii and Guardsmen at war, and this is all you can muster? You must have seen the remains of your praetorians and skitarii. How could you possibly have believed I would allow your weapons to function in my presence?'

'It was worth a try,' said Kotov, as the Cadians fixed foot-long lengths of matte-black steel to their rifle muzzles. Yael and Surcouf both had swords drawn.

Kotov smiled at the apposite nature of the sight.

Clearly Telok saw it too. 'You would fight for the most technologically advanced vessel mankind has ever built with knives?' he said. 'And when that fails, what then? Harsh language?'

'Technology married to brute strength,' said Kotov. 'It is the Imperium in microcosm.'

'There is truth in that,' agreed Telok, stepping towards the centre of the bridge. The Breath of the Gods was no less nauseating on the viewing screen, its whirling flux of silver seeming to grow larger with every passing second. Two smears of light hung just behind it, geoformer vessels by the look of them.

Kotov followed Telok onto the raised area of the deck, seeing Tarkis Blaylock sprawled before the vacant command throne. Was he dead? Impossible to know; his body was giving off innumerable radiations, febrile interactions of staggering complexity and every indication of massive data inloads comparable to a scrapcode attack.

The command throne was empty, but just for a fleeting instant, a span of time so ephemeral it could hardly be said to have existed at all, Kotov was certain he saw the spectral apparition of a robed figure seated there.

Beckoning him with a look of desperate urgency.

Then it was gone, and Kotov saw what he at first took to be the shattered remains of an automated lifter machine scattered across the deck. Faint noospherics, like blood-trace at a murder, told him that this was no automated machine, but Magos Kryptaestrex.

He looked towards astrogation. Magos Azuramagelli was still functional, though his latticework frame was buckled and twisted. Portions of his exploded brain architecture lay askew in bell jars half emptied of their bio-sustaining gels.

That he was still functional at all was yet another miracle.

'As you see, I have control of the *Speranza* and every aspect of its workings,' said Telok, lifting his clawed hands to the image above him. 'The Breath of the Gods will soon be aboard, and in under an hour we will break orbit en route to Mars.'

Galatea moved to stand beside Telok, and Kotov was struck by the transformation he saw in the machine-hybrid. Its posture was that of a crippled baseline human, painful to look upon and every movement clearly causing monstrous amounts of pain.

'But we have nothing further to discuss, Archmagos Kotov,' said Telok, turning to Galatea. 'Kill every one of them.'

The machine-hybrid lifted itself up on its mismatched blade-limbs, like a broken automaton in a historical display. A child's toy remade by a psychopath, all torn cables, leaking fluids and sparking wires.

'Now I will *watch* you die,' said Telok.

Ever since it had entered the annals of Cadian history, the Battle for Vogen had been a byword for the no-win scenario. Given the forces involved in the actual battle, no Cadian commander had yet found a workable strategy to claim outright victory in any simulation fought over the war-torn city.

Hawkins hoped he was about to change that.

Dahan's killing of the alpha-beast had literally stunned the crystalline attackers, and the Imperials had punished them hard. There wasn't a crystal killer within three hundred metres of their position. The increasing volume of gunfire from across the plaza was telling Hawkins that was about to change.

Lieutenant Karha Creed scooted over the rubble towards him. Her helmet had taken a hit and he could see right through to her blonde hair beneath. Blood caked her cheek below the impact.

'Looks like you got lucky,' said Hawkins.

'I got careless,' said Creed. 'Too caught up watching Magos Dahan's kill. A millimetre to the left and I'd be dead.'

'I hear that,' said Hawkins.

Creed's company were arrayed in deployment redoubts either side of Hawkins. Sergeants bellowed inspirational words from the *Uplifting Primer*, commissars doled out Imperial piety from memory and the bearers of the regiment's colours had them ready to raise high for the first time since they'd come on this expedition.

'Lieutenants Gerund and Valdor send their compliments,' said Westin, the vox-caster's headset tucked under the rim of his helmet. 'Both companies are ready as per your orders.'

'Gerund, she's a tough one,' said Hawkins. 'Damn near loses an arm then has a whole building fall down around her ears. And she's *still* able to salvage a working platoon to take into the fight.'

'I trained with her at Kasr Holn,' said Creed, ditching her damaged helm and rummaging for a fresh one. 'You don't know the half of it.'

Hawkins nodded and tapped Westin on the shoulder. 'Any more word from the colonel?'

'Nothing, sir.'

'He on his way here?' asked Creed.

'No, we get to finish this ourselves,' grinned Hawkins. 'We do it the way Hastur would have done it if he'd had superheavies and Titans. And speaking of which...'

The deck rumbled and a lumbering iron behemoth emerged from the archway at the centre of the wall behind them. Less of a tank, more a fully-mobile battle fortress, the Baneblade was the vehicle of choice for the discerning Imperial Guard commander. Laden with battle cannons, lascannons and heavy bolters, it was a lead fist in an iron gauntlet. Two more came hard on its heels.

Jahn Callins sat in the commander's hatch atop the colossal turret, a pair of blast-goggles pulled up onto his forehead.

'Is that for me?' asked Hawkins, having to shout to be heard over the roar of the Baneblade's power plant.

'*Mackan's Vengeance*,' said Callins. 'Kept her back specially for you, sir. I know she was lucky for you on Baktar III.'

'Good man, Jahn. Appropriate too,' said Hawkins, looking out over the plaza to where Dahan's skitarii had their vehicles laagered up around their Secutor and the fallen statue of Sanguinius. He all but vaulted onto the crew ladder and scrambled over the tank's topside. Callins dropped into the tank and Hawkins took his place in the commander's hatch. He pulled on his ear-baffles and hooked himself up to the internal vox-net. The ogre-like spirit of the armoured vehicle was a grating burr in his ears as it strained against human control.

A slate inset within the hatch ring displayed the relative positions of the other superheavy squadrons, the battle-engines and his various infantry platoons. All in the green. All ready to begin the counter-attack in the breath Dahan's kill and the arrival of Legio Sirius had allowed them to take. Hawkins leaned out over the turret and shouted down to Creed.

'Get moving as soon as we're over the wall.'

Creed nodded. 'Understood, and good hunting,' she shouted, before turning and running, bent over, to join her soldiers.

Hawkins twisted the black plastic knob beside him that linked him to the driver's compartment.

'Take us out.'

The Baneblade roared and its engine jetted a plume of blue oilsmoke. Tracks bit the deck and the lumbering vehicle powered up and over the barricade. Almost immediately, flurries of missiles arced from the ruins of the Law Courts and the railhead terminus. Mortars on the roof of the Palace of Peace dropped barrages of high explosives on the far end of the deck. Streams of rockets streaked from Deathstrike launchers farther back and a thunderous cascade of main guns mounted on the superheavy turrets opened fire.

Half the plaza vanished in a fire-lit fogbank of destruction.

To Hawkins's right, three Hellhammers skirted the edges of the Law Courts, unleashing storms of shells from their multiple turrets, co-axials and fixed weapon mounts. Two pairs of Shadowswords came after them. Their volcano cannons tracked for targets while heavy bolters perforated the smoke with mass-reactives.

Hawkins knew at least as many colossal tanks were crashing through the pulverised remains of the railhead terminus to his left. Next to the super-heavies, the regiment's Chimeras and Leman Russ looked absurdly small.

Green fire hosed from the fog of detonations ahead, though how any-thing could still be alive in there to fight back was a mystery. Hawkins was bringing overwhelming fire and armour to the fight, but the enemy wasn't yet beaten. Not by a long shot.

A Baneblade was three hundred tonnes of awesome killing metal, and though the Hellhound was the signature tank of the 71st, Hawkins couldn't deny the thrill of commanding this beast of a machine. Nothing the enemy could throw at it could even scratch its paint.

The battle cannon thundered, and the Baneblade rocked back on its tracks. A section of the deck beyond Dahan's position simply vanished. Artillery detonations obscured the far side of the plaza, but glittering reflections through the smoke told Hawkins the enemy were massing. He knew it was reckless to ride exposed in the command turret, but his men needed to see him.

They needed to see how little he cared for the danger.

The officers of Cadia had led their soldiers this way for thousands of years, and it was how they would always do it.

Hundreds of las-bolts from scores of Chimeras speared into the fog, a storm of fire punching ahead of the Cadian advance. More than a thousand infantrymen raced across the plaza, company standards snapping in the raging thermals.

This was how Cadians made war, unrelenting, furiously attacking in such overwhelming force that an enemy simply had no chance of survival. The Guard was not an extension of Imperial policy designed to drive an enemy to the negotiating table.

It was a force of extermination.

Hawkins looked up as a vast shadow fell across *Mackan's Vengeance*. Arrayed in the colours of Sirius, fresh paint gleaming and new oil dripping from every joint, *Amarok* dipped its head in respect as it came alongside him. Vintras pulled his Warhound away before unleashing a torrent of bolter fire from its vulcan.

Even through the ear-baffles, the noise was deafening.

The *really* big engines kept to the rear of the formation, the majority of their guns simply too obscenely lethal to employ in so confined a space – as Hawkins knew only too well. *Lupa Capitalina* and *Canis Ulfrica* unleashed a hurricane of fire from their gatling blasters, and the firepower of so many heavy shells tore three-metre trenches in the deck. Both engines launched barrage after barrage of Apocalypse missiles from carapace launchers, turning the far end of the plaza into a hellstorm of shrapnel and fire.

Those who'd seen such a barrage claimed that even one launcher could unleash the equivalent of an artillery company.

Hawkins reckoned that to be a conservative estimate.

Mackan's Vengeance reached the laager of skitarii tanks and Hawkins saw Dahan in the hatch of a Leman Russ with a turret-mounted weapon he didn't recognise. Something with spinning brass orbs and crackling tines enclosing a seething ball of purple-white plasma.

Dahan saw him and raised his Cebrenian halberd in salute. Hawkins didn't have a signature weapon, so instead raised his fist – as good a symbol of Cadia as any.

The Mechanicus vehicles – a mix of stalk tanks and up-armed Chimeras and Leman Russ – broke their laager and merged with the Cadian formations with complete precision.

The barrage moving ahead of the Cadians ceased as the armoured charge reached the far end of the plaza. The smoke began to disperse as the deck's recyc-units sucked wheezing breaths into the ventilation systems.

Should have got Dahan to disengage them, thought Hawkins.

Blocky shapes resolved in the smoke, artillery-smashed recreations of Vogen's outer walls. Fortifications Colonel Hastur and his soldiers had attempted to escalade time and time again without success.

Fortifications that were within touching distance.

And Hawkins felt a hand take his heart in a clenched fist as a tsunami of crystalline creatures spilled over them. They came from every transverse entry hall to the training deck, from every gap in the walls and through the wide open gates.

Thousands of sharp-edged beasts of glass and crystal.

Some were the human-sized warriors, others the towering shield-bearing monsters. At least two dozen of the vast, centipede-like creatures he'd killed with the Rapier in the deck transit punched through the walls.

An army of extermination, but he had one of his own.

'Time to win the no-win scenario,' said Hawkins.

Microcontent 20

EVEN MONSTROUSLY DAMAGED, Galatea was fast. Its clattering, ungainly frame came at them with slashing forelimbs and whipping, blade-tipped mechadendrites. Two Cadians died instantly, speared through their chests by scything blades that rammed down like pistons.

Kotov ducked back as another limb flicked at him. The tip caught the edge of his robes and cut the heavy metal-lined fabric like paper. Rough hands pulled him back.

'Step away, archmagos,' said Carna, the skitarii warrior placing himself between Kotov and Galatea's slashing blades. 'You gain nothing by taking part in this fight.'

Kotov nodded as the Cadians surrounded Galatea. It spun and stamped like a warhorse of old as they darted in to stab it with their black bayonets. Kotov was reminded of the crude daubs made by ancient cave-dwellers, depicting hunts for vast, plains-dwelling mammoths.

The pistol he'd taken to Exnihlio, but never fired, felt like something belonging to someone else. He holstered it, already knowing its firing mechanism would not activate.

Galatea's body lolled to the side, its silver eyes dull and lifeless, the brain jars on its palanquin crackling with interlinked activity. Each ferocious burst caused Galatea to jerk with rogue impulses.

Angry static blared from its shattered augmitters.

Surcouf, Anders and the Black Templar faced the machine-hybrid head on. The rogue trader moved like a fencer, attacking only when the opportunity for a strike presented itself and deflecting attacks rather than meeting them head on. Yael fought two-handed, genhanced power compensating for his lack of finesse. He blocked each thunderous blow with brute strength.

Ven Anders ducked beneath a slashing limb, but fell to one knee with a grimace of pain, one hand pressed to his blood-soaked uniform. Galatea saw the Cadian colonel's moment of weakness and slammed a limb down with hammering force.

The blade punched through Anders's spine, pinning him to the deck. The colonel's back arched in agony, but his screams were cut off as Galatea twisted its limb with malicious relish.

Surcouf shouted and swung his sword in a devastatingly accurate strike. The blade's artifice was so sublime that even with its powercell non-functional it hacked the limb from Galatea's body.

The machine-hybrid staggered, and Yael roared with aggression as he slammed his shoulder into its palanquin. Galatea rocked back, unbalanced with a limb missing. The brains flared with activity and another burst of pained static squalled from its augmitters.

Anders's men hurled themselves at the creature with renewed fury. Galatea's mechadendrites slashed in a wide arc, and three of the Cadians were cut down. Blood and entrails soaked the silver deck plates and Kotov could have wept to see this place of logic and understanding transformed into a place of bloodshed and horror.

He looked past the fighting and once again saw the ghostly image of a figure on the command throne, like a crude composite superimposed on a badly synced picter.

Kotov accelerated his thought processes, slowing the perceived passage of time as his mind instantly ramped to massively overclocked levels. Thermal vents along his spine bled the excess heat of his enhanced cognition.

This time the image stabilised, becoming recognisable.

Linya Tychon.

You and Speranza *must be one.*

VITALI'S HANDS WERE sticky with blood. Abrehem Locke's wound simply wasn't closing. The bondsman's coveralls were soaked in crimson from midriff to ankles. He gripped the armrests of the Throne Mechanicus, trembling and white with effort.

Vitali's digits were splayed with numerous hair-fine filaments as he attempted to suture the wound. Thus far without success. He had access to every medicae tract ever written, but *knowing* a thing was entirely different from putting it into practice.

'Can't you stop the bleeding?' said Coyne, propped up against the base of the throne. The cauterised stump of the man's wrist was wrapped in oil-stained rags, held tight to his chest. He'd be lucky not to get an infection and lose the arm.

'Don't you think I'm trying?' snapped Vitali, flinching as another burst of gunfire from the breached gate to Forge Elektrus ricocheted inside. 'The effect of these crystalline weapons is pernicious. It makes the flesh around the injury site weak and prone to rapid necrosis. Each suture I make tears within seconds of being closed up.'

'Then keep more pressure on it, damn you!' said Hawke, seated on a crate on the other side of the throne. 'Don't you know anything about battlefield triage? If you can't stop it, at least slow it down. Abe's not the only one losing blood here.'

A transfusion line connected the two bondsmen, and right now that was all that was keeping Abrehem Locke alive. Julius Hawke had volunteered his blood to save Abrehem, and a quick scan of the barcode on his cheek had revealed him to be a universal donor. The gesture had seemed noble until Vitali realised Hawke simply wanted out of the firing line.

Vitali had not been gentle with the needle.

Standing behind the throne, Ismael de Roeven had the fingertips of his hand of flesh and blood pressed to Abrehem's temple. The former servitor disturbed Vitali on every level; not just for what he was, but what he represented and implied about every other servitor. Ismael's skin was ashen and grey. He was taking Abrehem's pain onto himself, and Vitali knew all too well how terrible a burden that was.

'His pulse is slowing,' said Ismael. 'Blood pressure dropping to dangerous levels.'

Connected via a sub-dermal bio-monitor to Abrehem's vital signs, Vitali already knew that. And right now, every vital sign suggested a patient in terminal decline. Without trained medicae, Abrehem Locke was going to die. This fight had to be won, and won quickly.

Vitali broke the link to Abrehem and pushed himself to his feet. The sounds of battle swelled as his senses aligned more fully to his surroundings.

'Don't you dare let him die,' said Vitali to all three of the men clustered at the throne. None of them answered, wrapped up in their own personal miseries.

Vitali hurried back along the nave, past the chanting acolytes seated on the wooden benches towards the nexus of the forge-temple. The shaven-headed adepts were linked to the Throne Mechanicus, but what benefit they might be providing was unclear.

He ducked behind the barricade erected at the entrance he'd been tasked with remotely defending. The forge door was no more, and the approaches to Elektrus were now held by Rasselas X-42 and a handful of Mechanicus Protectors. Arcing forks of lightning from shock-staves and green fire lit the wide processional, painting the combatants in a shimmering, stroboscopic glow.

Like the Spartans of old, the Protectors fought with brutal economy of force, each warrior working in perfect synchrony with his fellows. They fought the crystal creatures in an unbreakable line, advancing and retreating as logic dictated.

The arco-flagellant had none of that logic, an insane berserker who had once been an exalted cardinal of the Imperium whose murder lust had overcome his piety. Intellectually, Vitali understood it was only right and proper that heretics and the damned be made to shrive their souls through pain and renewed service. But to see such a punishment enacted in the flesh was still horrifying.

The thing bled from scores of wounds, its swollen, pumped body a reticulated mass of bloodied gouges. Its flesh glittered with embedded fragments of glass debris and blackened scorch marks. One arm hung loose and inert, the other a slashing killing blade. Its body radiated heat and bled vast quantities of chemical haze. At this rate of physical attrition, it wouldn't last another hour.

At this rate of assault, none of them would.

Steeling his courage, Vitali hitched up his robes and broke cover. He ran from this portion of the battle to where Chiron Manubia coordinated the defence of the second approach to Elektrus. Connected to a lectern of brass and wood, Manubia's hands cut the air in arcane lemniscate patterns as she managed a dozen weapon systems and exloaded battle-cant to the Protectors fighting in the secondary approach.

Vitali placed a hand on the lectern and let his haptics merge with the network. The interior of the forge fell away as his awareness shifted to the spaces beyond its gates.

A demi-century of Protectors fought here, led by Totha Mu-32. Wave after wave of crystal creatures fought to breach Forge Elektrus, and it seemed to Vitali that there was a desperate urgency to their assault. Forking blasts of green fire filled the approaches, burning the walls or absorbed by the Protectors' storm shields.

A dozen concealed weapon emplacements blazed into the attackers, emerging to open fire and retracting into their armoured housings before the enemy could respond.

Why hadn't he thought of that?

A fresh assault came in hard in the wake of a furious storm of green fire, but Totha Mu-32 was ready for it. His Protectors surged upright from their barrier of locked storm shields, shock-staves held out before them like lances.

They hit the crystal beasts hard, bent low, arms thrusting. Shock-staves unleashed vitrifying blasts of high-energy pulses. Follow-up blows shattered limbs and skulls, and with the breaking of the first wave, the Protectors withdrew in good order to their rally points.

It was quite the most ordered method of warfare Vitali had ever seen.

The polar opposite to what was happening at the forge's other entrance.

<Chiron,> said Vitali. <I need to talk to you.>

<I'm pretty busy here, in case you hadn't noticed.>

<This is important,> said Vitali, making sure his binary emphasised *just* how important. Manubia's reply was similarly loaded with binaric imperatives that showed just how little she cared for his definition of important.

<Shouldn't you be trying to keeping my protégé from dying?> said Manubia, re-aligning her targeting auspex on a gathering knot of crystalline beasts.

<Even the Omnissiah would struggle to prevent that,> said Vitali. <Even with Hawke's blood and Ismael's alleviation of his pain, he is fading faster than we can sustain him.>

<Then what do you want from me?> said Manubia, unmasking a graviton cannon and turning three crystal beasts to a flat sheet of crazed glass.

<We have to end this attack,> said Vitali. <Abrehem has to live. Linya sent me here to keep him alive.>

<Do you even know why?>

<No,> said Vitali, <but she wouldn't have asked if it wasn't absolutely vital.>

Linya opened her eyes, breathless and exhausted. Both sensations were chemical reactions to the complex hexamathics required to reach out to Archmagos Kotov within the sun-hot arena of the bridge, but the feeling was no less real.

The midnight-black dome of perfectly geometric cubes was gone, and in its place was Linya's favourite viewing dome within the Quatrian Galleries. Smaller than the others, it had only a basic observational device, a piece quite useless for viewing much beyond a planetary sphere, but said to have once belonged to the composer of Honovere.

Arrayed to either side of her were her fellow magi: Syriestte on her right, Haephaestus to her left. Natala gave her a nod of respect, and the sad determination on each and every face would have broken her heart had she one left to break.

Standing at the farthest extreme of the viewing dome was the adept in black. Galatea's avatar within the mindspace. Except, she knew better than that now, didn't she? He looked around, as though surprised to see himself here.

Linya remembered all the times this adept had tortured her, forcing her to experience extremes of pain she hadn't believed possible, and her resolve hardened. His silver eyes were lustreless now, stripped of any power they once had to intimidate.

'You think you can defeat me?' said Galatea.

'*Me?*' said Linya, stepping forwards. 'Not referring to yourself as a plurality any more?'

'There seems little point in the mask now.'

'True, then I'll address you as Telok.'

'Archmagos, if you please,' said the black-robed figure. 'After all, I earned the rank.'

'Then you cast it away when you forgot the ideals of your order.'

'Forgot them? No, I was finally able to *realise* them.'

'You are no longer Mechanicus, *archmagos*, and this is over.'

The adept laughed. 'Over? I think you forget that you are still in my neuromatrix. And if you thought the tortures you have already endured were excruciating, believe me, I have many more that are far more terrible. Your tricksy little code has kept you beyond my reach for a time, but it won't last much longer.'

'It's already lasted long enough,' said Linya.

'What are you talking about?'

'Look around you, this isn't *your* neuromatrix anymore. It's mine. See how everything has that sheen of real memory, not pilfered thoughts shaped into the *recreation* of a memory.'

The black-robed adept suddenly realised his danger and flew at Linya, his form swelling as it drew the shadows to it. Wide, bat-like wings erupted from the adept's back, the data-daemon that had devoured Kleinhenz reforming before her.

Linya smiled and held her hands out, palm up.

The data-daemon slammed to a halt in mid-air.

She ripped her hands to the side, as through pulling open a veil, and the data-daemon exploded into a cloud of perfectly cubic flakes of ash. They faded like dying embers, leaving the robed adept sprawled before her.

'I told you,' said Linya. 'This is *my* neuromatrix.'

The adept backed away from her on all fours as Linya walked towards him. He rose to his knees, hands held out before him in supplication. She read his terror. He knew full well the horrors she could inflict.

But Linya had no inclination towards torture or revenge.

Instead, she turned to her fellow magi, and said, 'It's time.'

They nodded in unison as Magos Syriestte said, 'The implanted code will be unequivocal and unsparing in its execution.'

'I know, but it's better this way,' said Linya, unlocking the last hexamathic cell within her mind. The activation algorithms for the kill-code flooded into her consciousness. They merged with previously released binaric strings, becoming something utterly lethal to the electrical activity of the brain.

It grew, it replicated.

It destroyed.

The kill-code had penetrated deepest into Magos Haephaestus, and the venerable techno-theosopher was first to feel its effect. He bowed his head and vanished as the implanted kill-code woven into their linked neural network took effect. Linya felt Haephaestus die, and Telok's avatar screamed as a portion of its heuristic neuromatrix was sheared away.

The kill-code destroyed Magos Natala. Then Txema, then Chivo.

With each brain-death, Telok's avatar howled in loss, convulsing like a madman on the polished terrazzo floor of the viewing dome. One by one, the imprisoned magi were extinguished until only Linya and Telok's avatar remained.

She felt each loss and tried not to hate the wretched, shrunken thing writhing before her like a hooked maggot on a line. She knelt beside the avatar. Stripped of its gestalt consciousnesses, it was a barely sentient conduit of data, a sheared potion of a much larger mind.

It was almost pitiable.

Almost.

'Kill me and be done with it,' said the avatar.

'No,' said Linya. 'I still need you to do something for me.'

SO MUCH DEATH...

Bielanna felt the last of her kin die.

The crystaliths tore them apart, perhaps realising what she attempted. Their strength now filled her, and Bielanna felt each spirit move within her rapidly crystallising flesh. The rapid push and pull of Exnihlio's death spasms had imbued her with extraordinary power, but it had hurled her headlong towards the eventual fate of all farseers.

It came over her like an ultra-rapid shock-freeze.

No rest for her within the Dome of Crystal Seers.

They surrounded her, their limited awareness ill-equipped to process this new variable. Their orders were to kill creatures of flesh and blood, and they had done that.

Bielanna's flesh was cold and hard, as glassy and reflective as the crystaliths. Her spirit and those of her fellow eldar burned brightly inside her. She took that energy and wove it around the power the Breath of the Gods had unleashed. The energy of a supernova condensed into a pure form of thought and expression.

Bielanna was done with her body of flesh and blood, and it had no more need for her. Only one realm called to her, a place of dreams and joy, where past and future entwined and the fate of all things was revealed.

Where the Path of the Seer inevitably led.

Bielanna cast off her mortal shell and threw her spirit into the skein. Freed from mortal constraints, she saw more than ever before, with a clarity the living could never know.

From this vantage point, Exnihlio appeared as a single atom out of place in the structure of a vast crystal. Any force applied to the crystal would always be concentrated on that atom. Soon another atom would be out of place, then another. And another.

Through such mechanisms were cracks in the universe begun.

And once begun, they propagated.

Like scissors cutting fabric.

But if that atom could be removed from the lattice…

ANOTHER CADIAN DIED as Galatea speared him through the chest with a lancing strike of its mechadendrites. It tossed the man's body across the bridge like a ragdoll before turning its attention upon Sergeant Rae. Kotov watched in slow motion as a blade-limb stabbed through the meat of the man's thigh, pinning him in place as a coiling mechadendrite whipped up like a stinger.

To his credit, Rae didn't flinch, but raised his useless lasrifle in a futile attempt to block the incoming strike.

'Come on then, you bastard!' shouted the Cadian.

The strike never came.

A grand-mal seizure wracked Galatea's body, its palanquin vibrating like an engine on the verge of exploding. The limb pinning Rae to the deck wrenched clear as Galatea loosed a binaric scream of anguish so profound that it broke Kotov from his enhanced mode of cognition. His perception of time's flow returned to its normal mode of operation, and the world seemed sluggish in comparison.

Telok staggered, as though whatever pain was wracking Galatea was stabbing him in the heart also. Given what Kotov knew of the symbiotic relationship between Telok and Galatea, perhaps it was.

An evil scarlet light swept around the palanquin, moving from brain jar to brain jar. The bio-gels within each jar instantly clouded, like stagnant water in a sump. Kotov had served two decades aboard a Tempestus battle-engine and saw the unmistakable signs of amniotic death.

Only one brain resisted the mass extinction, and Kotov knew instantly to whom it belonged. Coupled with the spectral visitation he had seen earlier, Kotov knew exactly what he had to do.

Galatea's legs folded beneath it and its misaligned body crashed to the deck with a booming clang of dead metal. Its proxy body flopped over onto its front, black floodstream chemicals pumping from suddenly unmaintained bio-mechanical organs.

The Cadians stepped back, wary of some trick, but Yael was on Galatea in a heartbeat. He wasted no time in bringing his sword around in brutal, two-handed overhead strikes like an ironworker at the anvil. Surcouf joined him a second later, his Calthan blade wreaking terrible harm on Galatea's robed body.

'Leave the brains intact!' shouted Kotov.

If Linya Tychon had indeed slain Galatea from within, then perhaps there was a chance to extricate her from the belly of the beast. How cruel a trick of fate would it be for her to avenge her mutilation only to be killed in the process?

Then Telok was amongst them.

His ironwork and crystal body throbbed with dark reds and crimsons. Plumes of scalding gases vented and his greasily artificial face was twisted in rage. Tearing claws smashed Cadian soldiers to boneless meat, ripped them to shredded matter.

Gone was the genius archmagos who had reconstructed the ancient machine of a long-dead race of galactic engineers. All that remained was a howling berserker creature, drowning its pain and grief in slaughter.

Kotov was never going to get a better chance than this.

'With me,' shouted Kotov. 'By your lives or deaths, get me to the command throne.'

Kotov ran past the bloodshed, slipping on the lake of blood spreading across the deck. He kept his mind focused on putting himself back where he belonged.

'Kotov!' bellowed Telok.

He almost turned at the sound of his name.

Was almost stunned to immobility by the furious rank signifiers that matched his own.

'Go!' shouted Carna, pushing him forwards.

Kotov didn't see the skitarii warrior's death, but felt it resonate in the noosphere as a vast quantity of blood sprayed him. The second skitarii, whose name he hadn't bothered to inload, died a second later, torn in two at the waist.

Kotov kept going. Thundering impacts sounded behind him.

He didn't dare look round. He felt hot, dead breath on him. Crystalline claws swept down to cleave him apart.

Then Yael and Surcouf were there.

The rogue trader was smashed to the deck, no match for Telok's vast strength. Only Yael had the power to take the blow, his genhanced physique a match for Telok's hideous crystalline embellishments.

Even so, he was driven back, the plates of his armour broken, the bones of his arms shattered.

It was foolish defiance, the last act of desperate men with nothing left to lose.

But it was just enough.

Kotov threw himself onto the *Speranza*'s command throne, slamming his hands down onto haptic connectors that still bore traces of molten metal and flesh.

Telok loomed over him, his inhuman features no longer recognisable as

anything sane. His clawed arm pulled back, the blood of countless inno-
cents upon it. The killing energies of Exnihlio burned along every blade.

Telok's claw hammered through Kotov's chest and into the throne.

Its haptics burned hot. Golden illumination, like the birth of all machines,
rammed into Kotov's skull.

A conduit was established, a connection made.

Like a surge tide in spate, the world spirit of the *Speranza* rose up to engulf
Kotov and Telok.

And not just the *Speranza*'s.

I have been here before.

That was the first thought to enter Kotov's head as he saw the neon-bright
datascape of the *Speranza* open up to him.

I should be dead, was the second.

He remembered Telok's claw punching down through his chest, a
shattering blow of awful power. Kotov's body was largely mechanised,
but enough remained of his nervous and circulatory system to make such
damage almost certainly fatal.

A glittering megalopolis spread before him, the flow of information that
formed the hidden arteries of the *Speranza*. It was mountainous, rugged
with hives of light and vast termite mounds of agglomerated data. Abyssal
cliffs of contextually linked information hubs spiralled into fractal mazes
of answers that led to ever more questions.

Datacores burned like newborn suns in constellations of linked neural
networks. The *Speranza* was in constant dialogue with itself, learning and
growing with every solution gained.

Heuristic in the purest sense of the word.

Every paradigm of scalable time, from the cosmic day to the compression
of universal history to a single hour, failed utterly to capture the datascape's
infinite scope. Its mysteries went back to the first stone tools hacked from
river bedrock and stretched into the Omega Point, the Logos and Hyparxis
all in one.

And for all that this aspect of the *Speranza* was a place of knowledge
and understanding, it was also one of metaphor, allusion and maddening
symbolism.

Highways of light were easy enough to interpret, but what of the vast,
serpentine coils arcing above and below to encircle the world before coming around to engulf itself? What of the conjoined helices of light that split
apart like the branches of a towering tree with its roots dug deep into the
datascape?

Could he even see these things truly or was his hominid brain simply
interpreting the unknown in ways he could process?

Looking down (if *down* was even a concept that could be applied to infinitely dimensional realms of thought) it was clear how foolish and naïve he had been to claim he was *Speranza's* master.

Knowledge was not a something to be *claimed*, it existed for all those with the wisdom to seek it, for only in the acceptance of ignorance could that void be filled. That felt like revelation, but Kotov suspected it was ancient wisdom he and his order had long forgotten.

<How far we have fallen,> said Kotov, humbled and awed by the incredible vista. <But how far we might yet climb.>

<The words of the Athenian gadfly, really? I expected more of the man who reached Exnihlio.>

Kotov turned and saw Telok soaring above the datascape, no longer the monstrous being he had become, but the magos he had once been. His robes were black, his optics a glittering silver. The resemblance to Galatea was so startling, Kotov wondered how he had not seen it before.

<An old truth, but still a universal one,> said Kotov.

<A platitude recycled by those who seek to excuse their ignorance,> said Telok, circling Kotov like a stalking predator. The Lost Magos swept his gaze around the infinite landscape and Kotov felt his burning *need* to possess it.

<Galatea chose well when it sent this ship to me,> said Telok.

<Perhaps too well,> said Kotov. <Its parasitic touch is falling away from the core systems. Even if you kill everyone aboard, you will never possess this ship.>

<Kill everyone aboard?> said Telok. <What a novel idea, I may just do that.>

<I will stop you.>

<How? You have no body, I destroyed it.>

<I have others, but even if my physical form is non-functional, I can stop you in here.>

<You have no power here, Kotov,> sneered Telok. <You are no longer the master of this ship.>

<I was never its master, I see that now. But neither are you.>

<I will be.>

Kotov laughed. <Then you are as deluded as you are insane.>

<Then come, shall we end this, archmagos? Shall we wield our wits as weapons, our knowledge as power? It is only fair to warn you that you are sadly unarmed for such a fight. I have thousands of years' head start on you.>

<Your knowledge is great,> conceded Kotov, feeling the presences he had sensed as the *Speranza* dragged him down rising to meet him. <But I have something you do not.>

<And what is that?>

<I have allies,> said Kotov as glittering dataforms of Linya Tychon and Abrehem Locke appeared at his side.

Once the bane of Kotov's life, Abrehem Locke wavered like a distorted hologram, his outline blurred where motes of darkness drifted from his body like ash from a cindered corpse. Linya Tychon was restored, her skin unblemished once again where the fire in *Amarok* had crippled her and whole where Galatea had mutilated her. She turned to Kotov and it seemed as though a multitude of overlaid spirits stared out through her eyes.

<Allies?> laughed Telok. <A dead man and a ghost?>

<I killed Galatea,> said Linya. <I want you to know that. And the part of you that's left inside? Guess what it's doing right now?>

Telok shrugged, as if the answer was of no interest. <Screaming, most likely, but it does not matter. I have lived without that portion of my consciousness for millennia. Extinguish it, torture it, do as you will. I care not.>

<You will,> promised Linya.

Telok sighed, but it was a distraction only.

He hurled himself at Kotov, fast as thought.

Physics held no sway here, only imagination. Wounded, Kotov dropped through layers of data, informational light skimming past at superliminal speeds. Telok followed him down, constructing calculus proofs of space-time curvature to increase his speed. Kotov led him through canyons of databases, where information passed back and forth in collimated streams of data-dense light. The sense of movement and velocity was intoxicating.

Abrehem and Linya spiralled around Telok in a double helix. She clawed at Telok's experiential armour, stripping it from him in long chains of boolean notation. Hexamathic blades, against which Telok had no protection, stabbed into him.

Ancient technology unknown to the Adeptus Mechanicus batted her away as Telok's vast intellect surged to the fore. Abrehem flew in close to Telok and the golden fire that had burned Galatea's vile touch from the *Speranza* seared into Telok's form.

Telok howled in rage as his shields of logarithmic complexity were burned away. A mastery of nanotechnology, the likes of which Abrehem was utterly ill-equipped to comprehend, sent his attacker spinning away.

<Knowledge is power,> roared Telok, hurling searing bolts of cold logic at Kotov. <They call that the first credo, but they are wrong. Knowledge is just the beginning. It is in the *application* of knowledge that power resides.>

Kotov spun away from Telok's fire, rising from the database canyons and looping around a soaring column of engine cores, where the impossible calculations to breach the barriers of the warp were agreed upon.

<Knowledge is power,> said Kotov, turning aside from yet more of Telok's searing projectiles. <It is the first credo. It is the only credo. To understand that fundamental concept is to possess power beyond measure.>

He thrust his hands out before him and a glittering shield of pure logic reflected Telok's attacks back at him. Telok roared in pain as the two archmagi came together in an explosion of fractal light. Circling the engine datacore and bathing in its bewildering, non-linear solutions, they came apart and smashed together again and again.

Gods of data and knowledge, their wisdom gave them power.

All they had learned and all they had explored. Every belief, every expression of wonder. All were transformed into killing thoughts. Chains of accumulated knowledge tore aetherial bodies, words as weapons, digits as ammunition.

They fell through the datascape, plunging into the heart of sun-hot datacores, emerging in streamers of light that were drawn into their death struggle. The battle left a burning wake in the *Speranza*'s heart as they spun around one another like gravity-locked comets, inextricably linked and plunging to mutual self-annihilation.

They fought like two alpha males vying for dominance.

And as the alchemists of Old Earth had always known: as above, so below. Where they fought the *Speranza* shuddered with sympathetic agonies.

In the portside testing arrays every single experimental weapon system activated without warning and blew a three-hundred-metre tear in the hull.

A ventral chem-store went into a feedback loop in its mix ratios and crafted a lethal bio-toxin that was only prevented from entering the ship's filtration systems by the last-minute intervention of a nameless lexmechanic.

Forge-temples whose alpha-numeric designations contained the data-packet of 00101010 had their libraries wiped, condemning millennia of accumulated learning to dust.

All across the *Speranza* the collateral damage of their battle was tearing the ship apart.

Linya and Abrehem followed in the wake of the devastation, barely able to keep pace with the two warring gods. Though they were gifted in their own ways, neither had the accumulated wisdom and experience of an archmagos of the Adeptus Mechanicus.

Finally, weary and stripped of their most prominent aspects of genius, Telok and Kotov came apart above a deep datacore of molten gold. They bled light, mercury bright, and ashen memories of things once known drifted from them like tomb dust.

<You can't win this,> said Telok, his black robes in tatters.

<Nor can you,> answered Kotov, feeling himself ebb with each utterance.

Linya and Abrehem finally caught up to Kotov and Telok, putting themselves in the dead space between the two archmagi.

<Neither of you can win,> said Linya.

<You will destroy one another,> said Abrehem.

<And we cannot allow that to happen,> they said in unison.

Linya hurled herself at Telok, Abrehem at Kotov.

Both struck at the same instant, and Kotov felt the essence of Abrehem

Locke's Machine-touched spirit merge with every aspect of him. He felt as though his body was transformed, his perceptions turned inside out. Hard logic and reason blended with intuition and lateral thinking in ways he had never considered.

Kotov looked up and saw the same process under way within Telok as Linya Tychon merged herself with the core of his very being.

But where the union of spirits had been beneficial to Kotov, the opposite was true for Telok. His inner workings laid bare like a clockwork automaton on a workbench, Kotov saw why instantly. Linya Tychon was not simply Linya Tychon, but a spirit-host of vengeful tech-priests.

Each of whom bore within them a lethal hexamathic kill-code.

Telok howled as it was loosed within him, a viral fire against which he had no defence. It ravaged his systems, wiping decades of learning every second. Constantly evolving in self-replicating lattices, the kill-code transferred itself from system to system within Telok's internal system-architecture.

It destroyed everything it touched, reducing his vast databases to howling nonsense code and rendering the accumulated knowledge of centuries of study to irrelevant noise.

Telok's form twisted as the viral conflagration burned him alive from the inside out. His screams were those of a man who could feel everything he ever was being systematically ripped away.

But Telok was an archmagos of the Adeptus Mechanicus, and even as Kotov watched, he was adapting, excising and rewriting his own internal structure to halt the cancerous spread of the kill-code.

Now, Archmagos Kotov, said a voice within him.

Locke.

You have the power of the Machine-touched now. Use it.

Kotov lifted his hands towards the molten gold of the datacore, feeling something indefinable move within him. It was power, but power unlike anything he had known before. Power like the first of the Binary Saints were said to have wielded, the ability to commune with machines as equals. To walk with them as gods on the Akashic planes on the road to Singularity.

Kotov drew on the light of the datacore.

And the *Speranza*'s soul poured into him.

Kotov's eyes were burning discs of golden light, the secret fire that only suns know, the spark that ignited the universe. From first to last, he knew everything.

Everything.

Shimmering armour of gold and silver encased Kotov, battleplate as titanic and ornate as any worn by the legendary primarchs or even the Emperor Himself.

A sword of fire appeared in his hand, its hilt and winged quillons forming a two-headed eagle wrought in lustrous gold.

Pure knowledge, weaponised wisdom.

Telok writhed as he purged himself of the kill-code.

Almost nothing remained of it, but it had done what Linya intended, stripping Telok of vast swathes of armoured knowledge.

<Woe to you, man who honours not the Omnissiah, for ignorance shall be your doom!> said Kotov.

He plunged the blazing sword into Telok's heart.

Microcontent 21

THIS WAS THE end of all things.

The mon-keigh believed the End Times would come in a tide of battle and blood, of returned gods and the doom of empires. Even the eldar myth cycles spoke of a time called the Rhana Dandra, when the Phoenix Lords would return for the last great dance of death.

Bielanna knew of no species with legends that spoke of things simply ending. Where was the mythological drama in that?

The skein's golden symmetry was unravelling, the futures collapsing. The fates of all living beings were unweaving from the great tapestry of existence. Entropy in the material world was mirrored in the skein, and its shimmering matrix was falling apart as the tear in space-time caused by Archmagos Telok ripped wider.

Bielanna plunged into the heart of the maelstrom of breaking futures, her spirit a shimmering ghost in the skein. The spirits within Bielanna quailed at being within the skein. Their fear was understandable. No longer protected from She Who Thirsts by their spirit stones, they feared the fate that had befallen Uldanaish Ghostwalker. They were warriors and the skein was a mystery to those who wore the war-mask; how could they possibly understand what she attempted?

With her body of flesh and blood no more, every moment in the skein was eroding her spirit's existence. Only by the power her kin had freely given her was she here at all. If they died, she died and every sacrifice, every drop of blood shed would have been in vain.

Bielanna felt Tariquel steady them by reciting the *Swans of Isha's Mercy*, the dance he had performed for Prince Yriel in the Dome of Autumn Twilight. His faith in her was an anchor to which the others could cling. She heard other voices too, Vaynesh and Ariganna Icefang, each adding their belief in her to her strength.

She whispered a *thank you* that shimmered in the weave and became part of its structure.

Bielanna followed the skein's collapsing paths, walls of imagined gold and light folding in as the futures they represented no longer held any meaning to the universe. Bielanna flew though the destruction like the wildest Saim-Hann autarch, twisting through collapsing webways, pushing ever deeper into the psychic network.

Pathways closed behind her. Ways ahead snapped shut the instant before she took them. Swarms of warp spiders billowed from their lairs, skittering in their millions towards the few remaining paths into the future.

Cracks in the walls blew out like the ruptured hull of a wounded wraithship. The howling Chaos in the empty spaces beyond called to her, the laughter of She Who Thirsts and the whispered intrigues of the Changer of the Ways.

She felt their pull on her soul, but sped on, hardened to resist such blandishments.

Everywhere she looked, the potential futures were narrowing to a vanishingly small number. Bielanna wept to see the universe's potential so cruelly snuffed out. To wipe out the future by design was a scheme of purest evil, but to erase it unknowingly… that was the act of a fool.

Another path into the future slammed shut, a billion times a billion unborn lives denied their chance to exist. Bielanna despaired as the skein folded in on itself everywhere she turned. With every slamming door, that despair threatened to overwhelm her and extinguish her spirit entirely. Bielanna wept as she realised she could see no way onwards. Every route was sealing ahead of her and closing off every avenue of hope.

Hope…

Yes, hope was the key.

Because other farseers must have seen this.

To believe otherwise spoke of great arrogance on her part. But if they had, why had none of them taken any action to prevent this universal extinction event from coming to pass?

Then Bielanna realised at least one of them already had.

After all, *she* was here right now in this moment.

Had her entire life been manipulated to bring her to this point?

Was she as much a pawn in some greater game as the lesser races of the galaxy were to her? Mon-keigh worlds were burned and their populaces consigned to death by the decrees of the farseers for the sake of a single eldar life.

If it was meant to be that Bielanna was here, then it was because a seer council on some distant craftworld had foreseen it and had placed her here at just this moment, for just this purpose.

She wanted to hate these unknown farseers. She wanted so badly to hate them for consigning her and her kin to death. For denying her children their chance to be born.

But she could not.

She understood the cold logic at the heart of such a decision. She had made similar choices, knowing that by enacting them she was consigning sentient beings to death. Even the greatest seers could not see just how far the ramifications of their choices might reach.

That she was here at all told Bielanna that at least one seer had seen that she might prevent this cataclysm from coming to pass. And with that thought, the despair vanished like breath on cold wraithbone.

Bielanna saw one last path before her, a slender future that yet resisted extinction. Her spirit soared as she flew towards it, trailing a glittering stream of psychic light behind her. Bielanna blazed into this last path in the final instants of its existence.

Like threading the eye of a needle.

ARCHMAGOS KOTOV OPENED his eyes and took a great, sucking breath of air, amazed he could actually do so. He blinked away the shimmering memory of a place of light and wonder, a place where there were no limits on the power of thought and the glories it could achieve.

The hulking form of Archmagos Telok filled his vision, his lunatic face frozen in an expression of hatred.

It took him a moment to comprehend that Telok was dead, that he, in fact, had somehow killed him. The face of the Lost Magos had always been artificial and unnatural, waxy with its plasticised textures and unknown juvenats, but now it was entirely crystalline.

He tried to pull away from that icy glare, but found himself locked in place by a bladed fist that skewered him to the *Speranza*'s command throne.

'Ah, of course,' he said. 'Telok has killed me too.'

'Not quite,' said a voice at his shoulder. 'Though he gave it his best shot to kill both of us.'

'Tarkis?'

'Indeed so, archmagos,' said Blaylock. 'Now, please, hold still while we cut you loose.'

Kotov tried to turn his head, but the blades pinning him in place kept him from moving. He felt the presence of others around him, but could not identify them, his senses still aligned to another place, another reality. He heard a high-pitched buzzing sound, a plasma cutter biting into glass.

'I thought you were dead, Tarkis.'

'As did I,' replied Blaylock. 'But rumours of my death, etcetera, etcetera. Telok incapacitated me with what I assume was some form of post-hypnotic command, buried within his overload attack when he destroyed our escort ships. Regrettably, I did not recognise the danger until it was too late.'

'The same could be said for all of us,' said Kotov. 'The *Speranza*? Is it still ours?'

Blaylock nodded. 'Reports are still coming in, archmagos, but, yes, it appears the enemy attack has stalled with Telok's demise.'

Glass snapped with a brittle crack as the plasma cutter sliced through the last of Telok's claws.

'Ave Deus Mechanicus!' cried Kotov as bio-feedback sent shock waves of pain around his ruined body.

'All clear, Master Yael,' said Blaylock.

Telok moved, but not through any animating force of his own. Like the statue of a freshly deposed ethnarch, Archmagos Telok was toppled by the equally hulking form of a Space Marine. He hit the deck hard and shattered into a thousand pieces, fragments of dull, lifeless crystal skidding across the deck and spilling tiny fragments of cubic nano-machinery.

'What did you do to Telok?' said Roboute Surcouf, bending with a grimace of pain to retrieve a long, dagger-like shard of crystal remains. 'One minute we were getting horribly killed, the next he stabs you then turns to glass.'

The rogue trader's face was a mass of bruised purple, and from the way he held himself, it was clear his collarbone was broken, as well as several ribs and probably his arm.

'I...' began Kotov, but his words trailed off. 'I fought him in the datasphere, but I wasn't alone. Mistress Tychon and Bondsman Locke were there too. Without them I would be dead.'

Kotov looked down at his ruined chest, a mass of shattered bio-organic circuitry and floodstream chemicals.

'Diagnostic: it appears I was correct in my initial assessment. Why am I not dead? Damage from this blow should have killed me.'

'You are correct in surmising that you should be dead,' said Blaylock. 'That you are not speaks volumes as to the singular nature of your experience within the datascape. Perhaps you will illuminate me as to its nature?'

'One day, Tarkis,' agreed Kotov, allowing himself to be helped from the command throne. 'But not now. Telok is dead, but what of his army and the Breath of the Gods? What of the tear in space-time?'

'See for yourself,' said Blaylock, moving aside to allow Kotov an unimpeded view of the main display and the slowly restoring veils of data-light.

At first Kotov wasn't sure what he was seeing.

Exnihlio was dying, that much was obvious. Its continents were cracking apart, each landmass fracturing in unsettlingly geometric patterns. Inset panels of low-level pict-scans showed vast mushroom clouds of atomic detonations as fusion stacks exploded and continent-wide electrical storms as the atmospheric processors finally exceeded their designed tolerances.

Everything Telok had built was being comprehensively destroyed, as if the violated planet were taking suicidal revenge for the havoc wreaked upon its environment. Soaring hives of industry toppled and colossal power plants spiralled to self-destruction as millennia of compressed time ripped through the planet's structure. Thousands of manufactoria collapsed and the rapidly rising temperatures told Kotov a global firestorm was hours away at best.

Higher up, orbital space looked like the lethal aftermath of a battle, with vast swathes of glittering debris spread over hundreds of thousands of kilometres.

'Is that the Breath of the Gods?'

'What's left of it,' said Surcouf, limping over to Galatea's tangled remains. 'The two geoformer vessels rising in its wake triggered their engines and flew right into the heart of it. I don't think we need worry about anyone putting it back together again.'

'How? Who was able to take control of the geoformers?'

'Tarkis says it was Galatea's command authority that fired the engines,' said Surcouf. 'So I guess it was Linya that did it. Do you think she's still in there?'

The machine-hybrid was nothing more than scrap metal now, its limbs and palanquin hacked to pieces in revenge for the death of Ven Anders. The black-robed proxy body looked like it had been through a threshing machine.

Its brain jars were shattered, leaking pinkish gel and trailing sopping wads of grey matter and brass connectors. One had been spared the fury, but its synaptic activity was fading.

Kotov shook his head. 'I doubt it. And if there *is* anything left of Mistress Tychon, it will be gone soon. It is regrettable, but her sacrifice and assistance will be recorded.'

Surcouf's jaw hardened in anger, and for a brief moment Kotov thought the rogue trader might actually attack him. The moment passed and Kotov turned back to the viewing bay. With Blaylock's help he made his way to astrogation, where Magos Azuramagelli's latticework form was still connected via a series of MIU ribbons.

'Azuramagelli?'

A crackling stream of simplistic binaric communication told him that Azuramagelli was still functional, but only at the most basic level. Blaylock unsnapped a series of data-connectors and plugged them into the Master of Astrogation's exload ports.

'What's happening out there, Azuramagelli?' said Kotov.

Static crackled from beneath Blaylock's hood, translating Azuramagelli's primitive binaric cant.

'It's a bloody hellstorm of epic proportions and we're right in the middle of it, archmagos,' said a gratingly artificial voice.

Standard issue speech rendition, but the words were unmistakably Azuramagelli's.

'Put simply, Exnihlio is tearing itself apart and collapsing into a primal cauldron of time singularities like the heart of a supermassive black hole. Once it reaches temporal critical mass, the fabric of space-time will tear itself apart. And, trust me, we do not want to be here when that happens.'

'Just out of interest, how far away from something like that would we want to be?' asked Surcouf.

The augmitters beneath Blaylock's hood barked with Azuramagelli's bitter answer.

'Let me put it this way, Mister Surcouf. Within two hours this system and everything within it will cease to exist.'

HAWKINS CLIMBED FROM the turret of *Mackan's Vengeance* and dropped to the deck beside the Baneblade's forward track guard. Aside from one mangled sponson and a lot of blast scoring, *Mackan's Vengeance* had come through the fight in good order.

He joined Karha Creed at the recreation of Vogen's main gates in a sea of shattered crystal. The lieutenant was down on one knee, a handful of coal-dark particulates falling through her fingers.

'You and your platoons fought well, Karha.'

She stood and brushed the black dust from her hands on her grey fatigues. 'Thank you, sir. Any word from the rest of the regiment?'

'Much the same as this so far,' he said, pulling the coiled bead from his ear and letting it dangle over his sweat-stained collar. 'Every deck's reporting that the enemy forces froze in place then cracked and fell apart. It's over.'

'What do you think happened?'

Hawkins placed his fists in the small of his back and stretched the muscles there with a groan. All very well riding heroically into battle in the open turret of a tank, but he'd been bruised from pelvis to shoulder blades.

'Damned if I know,' he said. 'Maybe Dahan killing that alpha-beast put them on a ticking clock, maybe the higher-ups managed to kill Telok or whoever it was controlling them, I don't know. But if the regiment's taught me one thing, it's not to look a gift horse in the mouth. They're dead, we're alive. That's good enough for me right now.'

She nodded and kicked a heat-dulled shard of crystal. 'So much for the no-win scenario.'

'It very nearly was,' replied Hawkins, slapping a palm on the side of *Mackan's Vengeance*. 'I think we all owe Jahn Callins a drink at *Spit in the Eye*.'

'And maybe Gunnar Vintras.'

Hawkins made a face, turning to watch as the towering battle-engines of Legio Sirius marched back through the ruined cityscape of Vogen. *Lupa Capitalina* and *Canis Ulfrica* were already deep within the city, but both Warhounds hung back at the edges of the Palace of Peace. *Amarok* turned towards the battlescape and raised its weapon arms in salute.

'Vintras is Legio,' said Hawkins. 'He can afford his own.'

The Warhound strode into the city, its war-horn braying throughout the deck, echoing from its enclosing walls.

'I'm buying Jahn his first drink,' said Creed.

'Get in line.'

They walked from the idling superheavy back towards the centre of the plaza, where regimental flags of red, gold and green flew in the blustering gusts of the recyc-units. Hawkins paused to salute the colours to which he and so many others had given their lives. Images of the Emperor stared back at him, and Hawkins felt a surge of pride at seeing them resplendent.

Medicae teams were working furiously on the wounded, and Munitorum preachers were intoning prayers over the dead. A tinny voice sounded from the vox-bead at his collar, but he ignored it as Magos Dahan approached.

Like the rest of them, Dahan hadn't come through the fight without scars. The Secutor walked with a pronounced imbalance and one arm hung loose at his shoulder. The Cebrenian halberd was slung over his back, its blade notched along its length.

'Captain Hawkins,' said Dahan. 'Your vox-bead is out.'

Even though Dahan's face was almost entirely metallic and his voice artificially rendered, something in the abruptness of his greeting made Hawkins wary.

'I needed a minute,' he said.

'You should replace it.'

Hawkins sighed and fitted the contoured bud into his ear. He listened for a few moments then closed his eyes.

'Sir?' said Creed. 'What is it? What's wrong?'

'Looks like they were right,' said Hawkins. 'It was a no-win scenario after all.'

'What do you mean?'

'It's Colonel Anders,' said Hawkins, sinking to his haunches and resting his elbows on his knees. 'He was killed in action.'

Roboute knew Azuramagelli's grim pronouncement should have left him more afraid. In fact, it should have scared him to the soles of his boots. After all they had gone through, to have come so close to victory, only to have it snatched away. That should have left him raging at the cosmic unfairness of it all.

Instead, he reached into the breast pocket of his frock-coat and said, 'You're wrong, Magos Azuramagelli.'

'Wrong? Don't be ridiculous,' snapped Azuramagelli via Blaylock's augmitters. 'The evidence is right before me.'

Roboute withdrew the compass and set it on the astrogation panel. The once wavering needle was aimed unerringly along the precise bearing Galatea had plotted back to Mars.

'What is that?' said Blaylock.

'A talisman,' said Roboute, keeping his hand pressed to the brass surround of the compass. 'It's the one thing that's always guided me home. It's never been wrong before, and I don't think it'll be wrong now.'

'Don't be a fool, Surcouf,' snapped Azuramagelli. 'It's not a question of knowing the course, I know the way to Mars perfectly well. It's a question of escaping this system before the fabric of space-time tears itself apart!'

'Just follow the compass,' said Roboute, feeling it grow warm beneath his fingertips, as though it formed a bridge between him and somewhere impossibly distant and yet intimately familiar.

'I *will* remember you,' said Roboute.

He closed his eyes...

...AND OPENED THEM in a place he knew he had travelled, but could not remember. He knew instinctively that he was not truly here, merely a passenger in another's soul. A soul he'd touched when their hands and minds had met on Exnihlio, when she had used his love for his friends to open a gateway back to the *Speranza*.

Bielanna was dead, at least in any conventional way Roboute understood it, but her spirit yet lived, an arcing needle of light that flew at the speed of thought in a realm few mortals ever saw or were even aware existed. Everything about it spoke of great beauty and great sorrow. Its beauty came from the wondrous potential in everything he saw, its sorrow from understanding in his soul that it had once been so much more.

Roboute and Bielanna flew through the skein together, though the context of the word was lost on him – drawing the threads of the past behind them. He understood that much because it was what Bielanna *wanted* him to understand.

They plunged into the futures, narrowing paths of perfect geometry, curves and lines that arced in golden parabolas. They stretched beyond a temporal event horizon, and even Roboute understood that what he was seeing was a fraction of what *should* be.

The futures were collapsing, fraying into random chaos, but the potential of what Bielanna attempted was clear to him.

Azuramagelli had likened space-time to fabric, fearing that it was *tearing*. The analogy was an apt one, for Bielanna's spirit was the needle, the golden lines of the past her thread to sew space and time together again.

The sense of speed was incredible, and Roboute felt more than saw the compressed nature of time everywhere he looked. The potential of all that could ever be still existed, it was not lost. The skein still held everything that ever was, and what had once been could always come again.

Snapshots of epochs passed in a blur, ancient wars, dreams of Unity and ages once thought unending turned to dust. All is dust, wasn't that a famous maxim once, or had Roboute simply imagined it? It was impossible to be certain of anything here. Potential was everything, certainty consigned to history, where – even then – it could be reshaped by the twin pressures of memory and time.

That was what Bielanna attempted, to reshape the universe as it was into what she needed it to be. Roboute's image of a soaring, glittering needle returned to him as they plunged onwards through the hidden passageways of time.

He saw trillions upon trillions of lives, more than the human mind could conceive, spend their lives in the blink of an eye. Numbers beyond reckoning crowded behind them, faceless lives that might have been, but never were. The unfertilised eggs, the children never born, the paths not taken.

So many...

Roboute wept phantom tears at the sight of them, their aching desire to *be* almost crushing him with the weight of sadness. At the forefront of the faceless host were two children, eldar by the grace of their tapered chins and honeyed eyes. So close, he felt he could reach out and touch them. Their unborn features drifted just beyond reach, like figures receding in mist.

It was all for them.

Roboute and Bielanna soared, the weave of threads closing behind them, pulling tight as the momentum of the tear threatened to overcome their speed. It seemed that they slowed, and Roboute felt Bielanna's pain as his own, as though the bonds between the molecules of his body were being twisted with ferocious torsion.

It felt like his entire body was coming apart.

Hold on, we must hold on!

Roboute clamped down on the feeling that his entire body was on the verge of exploding into its constituent atoms, focusing on all that made him the man he was: his honesty; a sense of duty and honour hammered into him since birth; his loyalty; his capriciousness; his reckless love of the unknown, and – most of all – his love for his friends and desire to see them prosper.

He was a good man, or at least he liked to think he was. Like everyone, he had his faults and could sometimes be cruel and sometimes be heedless of the needs of others. All these things made him a person worthy of remembrance, and he was not alone in that.

Roboute thought back over the lives he had known, the lives he had touched and those he had yet to know.

Yes, what can be dreamed, need never be forgotten.

His own recollections were scattershot, without focus or structure. Bielanna's were rigorously ordered by a mind trained for centuries to allow memories to be controlled, thoughts to be shackled on a single path. His way of thinking was anathema to her, wildly unpredictable and dangerous.

Together they crested a rising path of golden light, its walls like red-veined marble the colour of fresh milk. He felt a subtle vibration, like the faint tremor in the superstructure of a capital ship. Behind him, the threads of past lives and experiences were growing thicker as more and more were drawn to their headlong flight through the ruptured skein.

It seemed they were soaring higher, towards a glittering horizon, radiant with possibility. Roboute ached to see that far distant shore, to know its secrets and tread its warm sands.

Then they flew over its glittering boundary, and Roboute saw an infinite realm of light stretching out as far as it was possible to imagine. Bielanna released the threads of the past, letting them fall into the weave of light opening up before them. They fell like golden strands of hair, splitting and branching like a growing network of nerves in a newborn life.

Everywhere he looked, he saw the threads of the past spread into the future, growing exponentially more complex, accelerating into the future at the speed of possibility.

And then, an awful sense of separation, of letting go.

He fought to hold on, terrified at the thought of being trapped here. This was not his realm, he didn't belong here. To *see* such a place was magnificent, a boon he hoped with all his heart he wouldn't forget, but to *exist* here?

That way lay madness for a mortal.

Open your eyes, go home. Live.

Bielanna's presence fell away from Roboute, fading into the infinite golden weave she had wrought. What Telok had put asunder, she had remade, but such a feat was not without price.

He watched her spirit fall, dissipate, blending into the warp and weft of past, present and future. He desperately wanted to say some sort of farewell, but what words of his could possibly convey the depth of what every living being that now had a chance to exist owed her?

Bielanna Faerelle vanished into the skein, its golden light enfolding her and the spirits of her warriors, beyond the reach of She Who Thirsts. In the instant before Roboute returned to the *Speranza*, he had a last glimpse of the unborn eldar children.

Graham McNeill

Their faces were still undefined, but he knew they were smiling. Welcoming their mother.

THE VIEWING DOME of Quatria was empty, as Linya knew it would be. The magi taken by Galatea were gone, finally released to return to the light of the Omnissiah. The hexamathic kill-code she'd crafted had, as Syriestte said, been unequivocal and unsparing in its execution.

She missed them.

The walls around her were hazy and indistinct, like reflections on panes of smoked glass. The brass and gold observational instruments shimmered like ghostly memories of themselves. But beyond the crystalflex of the dome, the stars burned brightly, brighter than she ever remembered seeing them.

Linya smiled to see this last vision of the heavens.

Her power to hold this imagined place was diminishing with every passing second. Soon it would fade entirely as the kill-code wormed its way into her mind.

She had held it at bay long enough.

Now there was just one thing left to do before surrendering to the encroaching darkness.

Linya held her hands out and lifted them to shoulder height.

As her arms raised the floor bulged upwards in the shape of an enclosing dome formed from the same tiny geometric cubes with which she'd fashioned her firewalls to keep Galatea at bay.

It was here she'd imprisoned the last fragment of Galatea/Telok, the flickering ember of consciousness she'd needed to order the geoformer vessels to fire their engines.

The glossy facets of the black cubes folded back on themselves, falling away in a cascade.

The prison was empty, the wretched, foetal thing she'd locked away now nothing more than fine black cinders. Had Archmagos Kotov's golden sword been so thorough in its execution that it had expunged every last screed of Telok's existence? Or, more likely, had Telok extinguished himself rather than face judgement?

Either way, Linya had to admit she was disappointed.

She'd hoped for a sense of closure, a way to twist the knife in Telok's heart *just a little*. But she was denied even that. She sighed, and the cinders blew away, disintegrating until not even they remained to tell of the existence of Archmagos Vettius Telok.

Linya took a last look around her imagined surroundings.

Her world faded to black, leaving only stars looking down.

It was time.

'Linya?'

She looked up. Her father stood before her.

Linya ran to him and his arms enfolded her.

VITALI REALIGNED HIS optics, his shoulders slumped as the cold reality of Forge Elektrus swam back into focus. He felt the crippling ache of grief recede, though it would always be there.

That was good, for it was a more tangible reminder of all that Linya had meant to him than anything a data-coil might store.

He stood before the Throne Mechanicus, Abrehem Locke's metallic hand held in his left hand, Ismael de Roeven's in his right. Coyne and Hawke lay slumped on either side of the throne, one unconscious, the other almost dead from the volume of blood he'd given.

'Did you see her?' asked Ismael. 'Say goodbye?'

Vitali nodded, no longer caring that Ismael had once been a servitor. The gift he had given Vitali was too precious for him to feel anything other than a profound gratitude.

'I did,' he said. 'And that is a debt I can never repay.'

Ismael shook his head.

'There is no debt to me,' he said. 'Abrehem brought you together in the datascape. I just helped you get there.'

Vitali looked up as Hawke groaned and pulled the transfusion line from his arm. Droplets of blood fell from the end of the needle as it clattered to the deck.

'Thor's ghost, it's cold in here,' he said, steadying himself on the back of the throne as he stood. His eyes were glassy and unfocused, his skin white as parchment. 'I'm drunk. When did I get drunk?'

'You're not drunk, Hawke, you've just lost over two litres of blood,' said Chiron Manubia.

'Oh,' said Hawke. 'Then point me to somewhere I *can* get drunk.'

Vitali guided Hawke down the steps and sat him on the wooden benches with Totha Mu-32's injured warriors. A Mechanicus Protector set up a blood line between Hawke and one of the shaven-headed adepts before moving on to treat more serious wounds.

Vitali looked up as a shadow fell across him.

He took a step back as Rasselas X-42 loomed over him, its body a patchwork of horrific wounds, any of which would be mortal to an ordinary man.

'Adeptus Mechanicus,' rasped the arco-flagellant, the words wet and blood-frothed. 'Tychon, Vitali. Identity accepted. Rasselas X-42 imprint sequence completed. By your leave.'

Vitali shook his head. 'No, no, you're imprinted on...'

His words trailed off and he hurried back to the Throne Mechanicus. With Rasselas X-42 limping behind him, he stood with Manubia and

Totha Mu-32 to his left, Ismael de Roeven to his right. He looked down at Abrehem, the arco-flagellant's words already forewarning him of what he would see.

Abrehem's head was slumped on his shoulder, his chest unmoving.

'Is he…?' said Totha Mu-32.

'Yes,' answered Chiron Manubia, her eyes wet with tears.

'I never got to thank him,' said Vitali.

'He knew,' said Ismael. 'It was his last gift.'

One by one, they knelt before the Throne.

They bowed their heads and prayed to the newest saint of the Adeptus Mechanicus.

WITH THE DESTRUCTION of Exnihlio and the restoration of violated physics, the temporal hellstorm at the edge of the galaxy was stilled. The time streams diverted by the Breath of the Gods and the imprisoned hrud snapped back to their proper places, undoing thousands of years of damage.

Stars that ought to have died in ages past and which the Breath of the Gods had returned to life burned towards their end once more. Those that had been drained of life now surged with renewed fury and light.

System space around Telok's forge world was lousy with e-mag disturbances and lacunae of space-time that would persist until the end of the universe, but that was a small price to pay for the restoration of the future.

The Halo Scar was gone, but it still took the *Speranza* almost two months to return to Imperial space. Exnihlio was no more; the temporal aftershocks of its demise and the hrud's vengeance had reduced it to little more than inert rock, aged billions of years in the space of a few hours. A glittering debris field of silver fragments englobed its corpse, the remains of the Breath of the Gods.

To ensure no one ever rebuilt Telok's infernal machine, the *Speranza* unleashed all manner of arcane weaponry into the debris. Chronometric cannons, anti-matter projectors and hypometric weapons of such power that they caused entire regions of space to simply cease existing.

No one knew who had given the orders to unleash those weapons.

ROBOUTE SURCOUF WAS the only one who understood the nature of Bielanna Faerelle's sacrifice. But mortal minds were incapable of sustaining such knowledge, and his memory of the skein was already fading. He'd tried to record what he had seen in a journal, but the concepts were too alien, too existential and too painful for him to articulate in writing.

He and the surviving crew of the *Renard* had mourned the death of Adara Siavash in a simple ceremony in a small portside temple, asking the Emperor to watch over the soul of their fallen friend.

Archmagos Kotov's anger at Ilanna Pavelka had eventually reached a low enough ebb that he finally consented to allowing her to seek repair in one of the *Speranza*'s forge-temples.

When the day came for her bio-mechanical surgery, Roboute was surprised to see Kotov himself scrubbing up at the head of a sixteen-strong team of neuro-magi and cognitive-optical technicians. Thirty-six hours later, the work was complete.

It took three more months before Pavelka's neural architecture regrew the required synaptic connections to process the inloads from her new optics.

By then, the *Renard* had already parted ways with the *Speranza*.

Seated at the helm, Roboute Surcouf rested his hand on the astrogation compass. Its needle pointed unwaveringly towards their new destination.

Ultramar.

THE MILITARY MIGHT of the expedition carried on much as it had on the journey from the Imperium to space unknown. They trained, they rested, they spoke of the dead. The mission was done, and as Guardsmen of Cadia, that was what mattered most.

That, and the fact they were still alive.

Colonel Ven Anders would remain sealed in cryo-freeze for the journey. His mortal remains were returning to Cadia, where they would be interred in one of the many cemeteries of Kasr Holn, until the Law of Decipherability decreed that his remains be moved to one of the charnel pits.

A remembrance ceremony for the fallen was held on the training deck. Every single Guardsman of the 71st stood to attention before a reviewing stand set up before the Palace of Peace. The battle-engines of Legio Sirius towered over the proceedings, kill banners freshly marked with heraldic sigils of Cadia and Mars.

Lupa Capitalina and *Canis Ulfrica* flanked the Palace of Peace, while *Amarok* and *Vilka* stood among the six thousand Cadians in their dress greys with their lasrifles resting on their shoulders.

Brother Yael of the Black Templars stood in his ebon battleplate, its lustre restored by the *Speranza*'s finest artificers. His grief was so palpable, so consuming, that none dared come near him, leaving him to bear the memory of his fallen brothers alone.

Magos Dahan and his elite skitarii packs stood shoulder to shoulder with the men and women of Cadia who'd fought to defend their ship.

Thousands of cybernetic soldiers and praetorian servitors marched past the reviewing stand, banners and weapons held high with pride.

Dahan himself took to the stand to join Captain Blayne Hawkins in presenting the Address to the Fallen. As the last benediction was spoken, the war-horns of Legio Sirius filled the deck.

A victory bellow and a lament all in one.

Far below the waterline, in an area of the ship abandoned by all but the most desperate bondsmen and tech-priests, a lone figure made his way along a dripping passageway. Hawke had last come down here around six months ago, looking for a place to site another illegal alcohol still.

Not much had changed.

Habitations that were little more than packing crates, sheets of tarpaulin and wadded packing materials filled every nook and cranny, proof positive that human beings could find a way to make even the most dismal places home.

No more than a few hundred lived in this particular shanty zone, making it above average size for such a refuge. Ever since the boarding action by the crystalline attackers, there'd been more and more of these kinds of places springing up below the waterline. It had been the same back on Joura for those who couldn't work or find a way to make themselves useful.

Hawke paused at a junction of dark passageways wreathed in plumes of vent smoke as the sensation of being watched crawled up his spine. Down here there wasn't a square centimetre of space where someone didn't have eyes on you, but this was something more.

Over the years, Hawke had by necessity developed a finely honed sense for when he was being watched with malicious intent. He didn't see anything out of place, just the usual malcontents and desperate fools. He told himself he was being paranoid, but given what he was carrying, a healthy dose of paranoia was no bad thing.

He carried on, passing a few faces he recognised, many more he didn't. That didn't surprise him. New souls were always washing up, falling through the cracks to end up in places like this.

And not just bondsmen either.

Disgraced tech-priests, damaged lexmechanics and the like, they ended up here too. More than Hawke had thought, but even that had turned out to be an opportunity. The abandoned and the cast aside were often the best source of his tradeable goods.

Hawke hadn't come to trade.

Today he was after something more.

It had taken a long time to get back into Forge Elektrus. Manubia hated him, and was always telling him that he was not welcome in her forge, despite the fact she welcomed hundreds of worshippers every day who came to see the Sightless Saint.

It had been Hawke's blood that had kept Abrehem alive!

Didn't that make *him* holy or something?

But Manubia couldn't keep him out forever, and eventually he'd managed to find a way in past her Protectors. And now here he was, hunting for a black clinic he hoped was still here.

A pouch of ash-like powder nestled in the pocket of his coveralls. It was a concoction he'd taken real care to develop, the residue left by the crystal beasts, mixed with a potent cocktail of stimms and e-mag rich discharge from high-end cogitators.

He called it NuBlack, and it was already on a list of proscribed substances, what with it being highly addictive to those with floodstream-based biology.

Which only made it more desirable to the kind of person he was hoping to find.

Hawke grinned as he saw the unmarked door to the black clinic just where he remembered it. He pushed past the buckled shutter and straps of thick plastic, wrinkling his nose at the smell of hot metal, cheap disinfectant, rotten meat and burned skin.

A tech-priest with a hunched spine and ragged, oil-stained robes of faded orange turned to face him as he entered. A hissing, wheezing armature of rusted metal arms was clamped to his back, and his half-metal, half-human face was grey and leprous.

'Hawke,' said the tech-priest with undisguised hostility. 'What do you want?'

'Hello, Dadamax,' said Hawke, looking around the filthy interior of the black clinic. 'Keeping the place as clean as ever, I see.'

Hissing canisters of noxious gases lined one wall and gurgling pipework diverted chemicals from where they were intended to go. Fragments of disassembled augmetics and flesh-couplers lay in pieces on grimy workbenches. Glass-fronted cabinets, their doors cracked and opaque with dirt, contained numerous jars of things best left to the imagination.

'I asked you a question,' said Dadamax. 'I told you I didn't want you around here again. You bring too much attention. I should never have sold you that ancient plasma pistol.'

Hawke pretended to look hurt.

'Come on, Dada, my old friend, don't be like that,' said Hawke, taking out the pouch of NuBlack and waving it before him. 'I brought you a little present.'

Dadamax eyed the pouch with a pathetic mix of hope and revulsion. Word was, Dadamax had been clean for weeks and was trying to work his way back updeck, but Hawke was betting he'd take the pouch and do what he asked.

One of the manipulator arms creaked and snatched the pouch from Hawke's fingers.

Graham McNeill

'What do you want for this?' asked Dadamax.

'Nothing much, just a little implant surgery.'

Dadamax turned, interested now.

'On who?'

'On me,' said Hawke, holding out Abrehem Locke's augmetic eyes.

VODANUS WATCHED THE mortal pause at the opening of the shadowed passageway. He looked about him, as though aware he was being observed. Vodanus eased farther back into the darkness and enshrouding clouds of vapour.

The man's smell was rank and unpleasant. They all were, but this one carried a pouch of caustic chemicals injurious to mechanised anatomy. A flicker of curious code had drifted from beneath its clothes. Something small, yet advanced beyond most other forms of technology upon which Vodanus had fed since leaving the *geas*-giver's planet.

The code-scent of the prey it had originally been sent to kill was aboard this ship, but Vodanus no longer cared. Telok was dead and Vodanus was free of the restrictive prohibitions the *geas* had laid upon it.

Vodanus could have killed the mortal and devoured the curious code it carried, but was loath to risk unnecessary exposure, however tempting the morsel.

Not when this ship was carrying it to an entire world of prey.

Vodanus had crawled from the wreckage of the linear induction train with its spine shattered by the force of impact. That and the malign code in its enemies' weapons had vitiated its self-repair technologies, and it had taken it longer than anticipated to resume its hunt.

Too late, it had tracked its quarry to the plaza, finding him surrounded by an army of the *geas*-giver's crystaliths. Too many for even Vodanus to fight through without its self-repair functions in good order. Instead, it had seen the descending shuttle and plotted its inbound trajectory to ascertain from where it had launched.

It sensed the presence of a mighty ship, thick with the target's code-scent, and had seized its opportunity. Secretly clawing its way onto the shuttle's hull, Vodanus endured the void-chill of space to reach this magnificent vessel, a battleship easily the equal in scale of the war-barques its masters had wrought to mass murder.

Vodanus had kept to the lower decks since then, destroying only when it needed to feed, smashing open only the smallest engines and draining their light.

Sustenance was enough. Glut would come later.

It padded away from the opening of the passageway, through clouds of oily smoke to the lair it had made in an abandoned reclamation chamber.

Patience was the prime virtue of the best hunters.

And Vodanus was nothing if not patient.

It could wait until the *Speranza* reached Mars.

BLAYLOCK SAT AT his workbench in his quarters, staring down at the Mars Volta. It reflected the light of recessed lumens, and the deep red sheen of its lacquered surface was a source of great confusion to him ever since the *Speranza* had returned to Imperial space.

Much remained to be explained in the wake of Telok's death and the inexplicable ending of the imminent cataclysm of a space-time rupture. His report to the Fabricator General would cite innumerable examples of inexact methodology and explanations that lacked any solid basis of fact.

Both Archmagos Kotov and Roboute Surcouf had been maddeningly imprecise as to the nature of their experiences on the bridge. Kotov had spoken to Blaylock of a great battle within the datasphere, of gods of knowledge, a bondsman and Linya Tychon. And, most allegorical of all, a vast golden sword he likened to that carried by the Omnissiah at the Pax Olympus.

Surcouf's account of the final fate of the eldar was likewise full of hyperbole and allegory. An undoubted psychic event had transpired, but his tales of threads and potential futures being woven by their witch belonged in a hive-fantasist's palimpsest.

But what puzzled him the most was why he kept finding himself seated before the Mars Volta with his fingertips on its wooden planchette.

Fifteen times since leaving Exnihlio, Blaylock had found himself sitting at his workbench with no memory of how he had come to be there. Upon checking his memory coils, he would find himself engaged in a mundane task of shipboard operation. Then, without any apparent gaps or lapses in time, he would be seated at this bench, his fingers twitching with ideomotor responses.

Each time he had fought the urge to move the planchette and hurried to a far distant region of the ship, throwing himself into another time-consuming task.

Now he was here again, seated before Magos Alhazen's gift and feeling the urge to move the planchette around the edges of the board, where the quantum rune combinations, binaric pairs and blessed ordinals glittered invitingly.

The perfectly geometric lines etched into its surface beguiled his optics, and Blaylock felt his hands move the planchette over the board.

The last time he had used the Mars Volta it had allowed him to find Archmagos Kotov. The divine will of the Omnissiah had moved within him, so perhaps, at this sixteenth return to the board, it was time to see what message might be received.

Blaylock slid the planchette across the board, feeling a curious sense of liberation as it revealed first one letter, then another.

At first they made no sense.

And then they did, but it was too late to stop. The planchette was moving with a will of its own. Or rather, the will of another.

T-Y-G-E-R, T-Y-G-E-R.

Blaylock froze in place.

He remained that way for nine hours.

Then lifted one arm, examined it. Lifted the other.

Blaylock moved away from the workbench and looked about him as though seeing his surroundings for the first time.

'Yes,' he said. 'This will do.'

ABOUT THE AUTHOR

Graham McNeill has written more Horus Heresy novels than any other Black Library author! His canon of work includes *Vengeful Spirit* and his *New York Times* bestsellers *A Thousand Sons* and the novella *The Reflection Crack'd*, which featured in *The Primarchs* anthology. Graham's Ultramarines series, featuring Captain Uriel Ventris, is now six novels long, and has close links to his Iron Warriors stories, the novel *Storm of Iron* being a perennial favourite with Black Library fans. He has also written a Mars trilogy, featuring the Adeptus Mechanicus. For Warhammer, he has written the Time of Legends trilogy *The Legend of Sigmar*, the second volume of which won the 2010 David Gemmell Legend Award, and the anthology *Elves*. Originally hailing from Scotland, Graham now lives and works in Nottingham.